"Pull on your comfies, climb into your favorite chair, and enter Oddertown, a place you might recognize or wish you could know, inhabited by a host of characters, both charming and challenged, who together find a way to hold on to what truly matters in life—not fortune or fame but authentic congregation and fellowship. What makes this book so engaging is the author's deep appreciation of rural life, an understanding he came to by immersing himself in small-town Vermont and finding there the kind of human interaction we all need in a time of growing anonymity and disengagement."

—Yvonne Daley, author of six books, including *A Mighty Storm, Octavia Boulevard* and *Going Up the Country: When the Hippies, Dreamers, Freaks, and Radicals Moved to Vermont*

The Wizard
of Odd

*A Vermont Tale of
Community Devotion*

The Wizard of Odd

*A Vermont Tale of
Community Devotion*

Gary K. Meffe

GREEN PLACE BOOKS | *Brattleboro, Vermont*

Printed in the United States

10 9 8 7 6 5 4 3 2 1

The Wizard of Odd is a work of fiction. Apart from the actual historic figures, events, and locales that provide background for the narrative, all names, characters, places, and incidents are products of the author's imagination or are used fictitiously.

Green Writers Press is a Vermont-based publisher whose mission is to spread a message of hope and renewal through the words and images we publish. Throughout we will adhere to our commitment to preserving and protecting the natural resources of the earth. To that end, a percentage of our proceeds will be donated to environmental activist groups and The Southern Poverty Law Foundation. Green Writers Press gratefully acknowledges support from individual donors, friends, and readers to help support the environment and our publishing initiative. Green Place Books curates books that tell literary and compelling stories with a focus on writing about place—these books are more personal stories/ memoir and biographies.

GREEN PLACE BOOKS   GReen writers press

Giving Voice to Writers & Artists Who Will Make the World a Better Place
Green Writers Press | Brattleboro, Vermont
www.greenwriterspress.com

ISBN: 978-1-7327434-8-9

Designed by Rachael Peretic.
Drawing of antique nail by the author.

To the good and decent people of Vermont, especially the town of Brandon, who make living in and writing about this state endlessly compelling, fascinating, and rewarding.

Prologue

Saturday Morning, Five Years Ago

S IMON ODDERTON CAREFULLY MANEUVERED down the old wooden stairs into the dank basement, wisely holding on to the hand rail which, like the steps, was original equipment. He wasn't sure which creaked more, the stairs or his achy joints. *This trip used to be so much easier,* he thought to himself. But it should be a simple and quick one today; just grab a #10 can of baked beans and head back up to his customers.

Shuffling over to the wooden storage shelves full of cans and jars, Simon couldn't help but notice what he had been trying to ignore. It was becoming more evident that his mostly bald head was getting closer to the ceiling joists at the north end than it used to be, and he was pretty sure he wasn't still growing. Yet one more sign that this old building had seen better days and was in a slow but sure state of decline.

Having spent all of his 92 years here it was difficult to accept the steady, incremental decay of something he so dearly loved. Today looked pretty much like yesterday, so how could he be sure that real decline was taking place? Just like with his own body, time—that subtle and covert devil—took its imperceptible toll each day, surely not noticeable as it occurs, but callously apparent in full hindsight. His hip did seem to be more painful than, what, five years ago? He did seem to recall that his eyesight used to be clearer and he had better night vision. It indeed used to be easier to turn his neck while parallel parking. When had he decayed so much? When had the building fallen into disrepair? Was this just his imagination or did he have a real problem? Could he deny the natural aging process much longer?

As Simon made his way further toward the north wall he pulled up short. Even in the dim light and heavy shadow cast by the one bare ceiling bulb, he could not ignore a new development. Two more foundation stones had fallen out of place and were now lying on the hard-packed dirt floor. This brought the total to, what, seven now? No wonder he seemed to be getting closer to the ceiling joists. The building was sinking and this could no longer be dismissed as simply his imagination.

Simon could feel the weight of previous generations pressing on him: his father Clive, grandfather Andrew, and especially his great-grandfather Peter, the legendary man who built all this. And then there was his son John who, tragically, was no longer here to carry on the tradition. They all depended on him to keep this thing alive and well. And let's not forget the townspeople, who would be lost and adrift without the place.

And of course there was Simon himself. He loved this old building—every creaky, worn, and aging piece of it—and all it had held and done over more than thirteen decades, including his own nine and counting. It was part of his essence and he was part of it. If it died, surely he would die with it. So might the town. This store was its lifeblood and its loss could be like a fatal coronary to village life.

As Simon slowly ascended the stairs he knew what he had to do. He would make some calls on Monday morning and start to deal with something he had dreaded and tried to ignore for far too long. He had absolutely no idea how he would pay for it, but if he wanted the Odderton Country Store to remain standing, he had to do something soon.

As he reached the upper landing and opened the door, Simon looked down at his empty hands, and in frustration snapped his red suspenders. "Jeezum Crow, I forgot the damned beans!" Back down he went.

Tuesday Afternoon, Seven Months Ago

Kate Langford felt stunned as she opened the door to her fifteen-year-old Subaru. She leaned over to drop the file of paperwork onto the passenger seat, sat down, and gripped the steering wheel like it was the last life jacket on a stormy sea. As she stared blankly into the bright October colors behind the small parking lot of the old Victorian that housed Schmidt and Nielsen, Esq., she reflected on the last 45 minutes and the bomb that her grandfather's lawyer—Knut Nielsen—had dropped on her out of the blue. If she had been hit from behind with a two-by-four she could not have been more surprised.

Yes, she knew she would inherit the family store. She realized that Grandfather Simon loved and trusted her like no other, and that nobody else would be a logical benefactor and caretaker of the building and business that had passed through five generations before her. She had the experience to run the place, to serve Oddertown's residents, to make a decent living and perhaps even a rewarding life under those old timbers. All of that was fully expected and, though she missed him terribly this last month after his death at 96, she knew she could carry on the traditions and responsibilities that the inheritance entailed.

But she had not been prepared for the bonus surprise package attached to the deal: a $116,000 debt. And the debt needed to be paid off in less than 16 months, or the bank would own the store. It was nearly an eighth of a million dollars, for Chrissake! Kate had all of $4000 in her life savings.

"Gramps, what the hell were you *thinking*?" she shouted to the empty space, slamming her hands on the steering wheel. "And why didn't you tell me about this? Did you think it would just go away? That nobody would notice?"

After a long and deep exhalation, and some staring out the side window at an adjacent cow pasture, some of the pressure abated. Kate knew he had done the best he could under the circumstances, and now realized that what she thought was a little forgetfulness and slight dementia had actually been far more serious. Simon had had little choice but to incur the debt over four years ago or risk the place falling down, but why hadn't he told her about it? Why hadn't he asked for her help? He missed so many payments, he struggled so mightily, and she could have been there for him had he only confided in her. Between what now appeared to be serious dementia, and perhaps his fierce and deep sense of Yankee independence and pride, he never mentioned a word to her about the loan.

Another deep breath and she loosened her grip on the steering wheel; pink soon replaced the white that had shrouded her knuckles. Now finally seeing the colorful maples, oaks, beeches, and ashes behind the building, she began to focus and breathe normally.

"I forgive you, Grandpa Simon, but I sure wish you hadn't waited for your death to share this little tidbit with me. It would have really helped knowing about this, oh, maybe a couple of years ago don't you think?"

Realizing that this bemoaning would get her nowhere and that she needed to start the drive south from Newport to face her newfound challenge, Kate inserted the key and turned over the reliable old Subaru engine. *OK, old girl, you can do this,* she thought to herself. *You're smart and energetic and tough, and you'll figure a way out of this little mess. You survived that asshole of a husband, you can survive this. You've got it in you.*

As she backed out of the space and headed down the driveway and through the stunning and calendar-worthy pastoral landscapes that would take her home, Kate hoped she really was as confident as she had just told herself. She would need all of that and more if she was to clear up this mess and make a life here.

The Wizard
of Odd

*A Vermont Tale of
Community Devotion*

Chapter 1

Wednesday, May 1, 4:45 AM

———

THE ALARM PIERCED THE QUIET MORNING air like an ice pick shattering glass, and startled Kate Langford out of a sound sleep and a pleasant dream. *Damn,* she thought as she slapped the sinister device into silence, *quarter to five already. Seems like I just laid down.* She immediately tried to remember the dream but all she could recall were birds flying free and unencumbered. Though disoriented and a bit woozy from the abrupt shift of deep sleep to waking consciousness, she knew from experience that if she didn't get up immediately she would only make things worse for herself. So Kate took a deep breath, swung her long, athletic legs out from under the warm, cozy mound of bedding, and settled her bare feet onto the cold wooden floor. Her whole body shivered in the cool darkness.

It was early May and the morning chill still had a bite to it. But it was a significant improvement over some of those icy winter mornings she had

3

just been through, even though this winter had been warmer than usual with little snow and, as a result, an even more depressed economy in the Kingdom than usual. Slipping out of her flannel nightshirt and into her regular uniform—a T-shirt, flannel shirt, blue jeans, woolen socks, L.L. Bean rubber moc boots, black fleece vest—she thought, as she did so many mornings, *there's got to be a better way to almost make a living.* Shuffling to the bathroom, Kate flicked on the light—another shock to the system—relieved her bladder, splashed water on her face, brushed her teeth, and began to feel awake. Selecting from her near-infinite collection of dangling earrings—the only bit of jewelry she usually wore and her familiar trademark look—she inserted into her earlobes a pair of oblong green and gold ones made by a local artist. Looking at the dazed face staring back from the mirror she muttered, "OK, bring it on world; I'm ready for another day in Odd."

Kate flipped on the second light switch of the morning and started down the creaky, deeply worn stairs that she knew all too well. *These sure have seen some action,* she thought, holding the old wooden railing, smoothed to a glossy finish by well more than a century of wear. Reaching the first floor she opened the door to the right of the landing and walked through. Turning on her third switch, the banks of fluorescent lights flickered on, and brightly illuminated the four rows of shelves with their wide variety of canned and dry goods, the wine rack with over 40 selections, the corner nook that held the small bank of ancient brass post office boxes, the glass-doored coolers of drinks and dairy products, the dining area with its five tables, the small kitchen to her left where she spent so much of her life of late, the entire black hole that was threatening to suck that life right out of her.

Now in its 137th year, "Odd Country" was preparing to open yet again. It had witnessed and participated in so much history—so much *life*—both good and bad: horses to automobiles, the Wright brothers to moon landings, two world wars and a depression, Korea, Vietnam, the '60s counter-culture, pencil and paper to the internet, September 11, Iraq, globalization. And all the generations that grew up and died here, each certain that theirs was the last decent bunch, and convinced that the good old days were gone. If these old walls could talk, oh, the stories they could tell! But now, after so many recent days in the red, all of that history was at risk, and Kate desperately hoped for some positive cash flow with the arrival of spring. If things did not turn around soon, and in a big way, she didn't know if the store would be open for its 138th year.

Kate entered the kitchen and used a long fireplace match to light the pilot, which then fired the burner of the vintage Heartland gas oven her Great Grandfather Clive had acquired nearly 100 years before and had been so proud of. This initiated the familiar routine that began most of her days: making her trademark cinnamon and walnut buns, always in high demand by her faithful regulars and the few lucky visitors fortunate enough to stumble upon them. By expert memory made perfect by repetition, she mixed the flour, sugar, salt, and wet ingredients, rolled out the dough, felt its cool stickiness, shaped it into long sheets, spread the rich cinnamon/nut/butter mixture on top, rolled them up, cut them into buns, laid them onto greased baking sheets, and put them into the now-hot oven. Four dozen, like clockwork.

Kate never failed to appreciate the rich smell of the cinnamon-nut mixture, and it often took her back, just for a moment, to a carefree time as a little girl with no worries or responsibilities, when her mother made those same buns each morning. She could imagine being the 8-year-old Tomboy again, tucked in her warm bed upstairs, the rich smell of cinnamon buns drifting up through the ancient floorboards to her room, making her feel safe, secure, and well-loved, and enticing her to get out of bed and embrace a new day with its endless mysteries and wondrous possibilities. She would run down the stairs, pigtails flying, into the welcoming arms of her mother, and they would split one of the fresh buns hot out of the oven. She had thought her mother was the most beautiful woman in the world and always hoped that she would take after her. She did.

Brought swiftly back to the present by the realities of her current life, Kate next started two pots of coffee brewing; the rich and familiar smell that filled the cool air always helped to perk up and comfort her. Needlessly glancing at the clock, she could have predicted the time, plus or minus a minute: 5:28. Her fastest time ever was 5:25; slowest, on a morning with a bad cold, 5:41. Today, thirty-two minutes until opening, when old Phil and Jubal would be lumbering up the front steps, coffee mugs in hand. And so it went, just like yesterday, just like tomorrow.

Kate took a short break to gaze out from the kitchen through the serving counter and into the store to appreciate what she had—and what she could lose. It was a gorgeous old building with a deep and fascinating history, and she would do anything to keep it. Its loss would be a personal and public tragedy, and as the sixth-generation owner she felt the strong pull of ancestral gravity to keep it going. She *must* keep it going! Her community— the place where she grew up and which she loved and whose people she felt a close kinship with— depended on her and the store for so much of its core identity, as well as everyday shopping needs. It was an honor to continue the family tradition and to serve Oddertown, and she did *not* want to be the one responsible for its demise, even if that awful possibility was inherited along with the building and through no fault of her own. She was paying the price for someone else's mistake, but pay she must.

When she let the challenges of life in Oddertown get to her, Kate sometimes wished she was back in Boston with Jason, where the store and town were physically and emotionally distant. But after sober reflection, she always concluded that, no, she would much rather be here and away from him, even with the heavy financial burden. This situation had to be better than her experience with Jason; at least this was an honest and true problem, well worth the effort. She might lose the store but it would never betray her trust.

And then, out of the blue, it hit her, that now-familiar surge of realization and emotion that occasionally overwhelmed Kate, a flood of understanding that placed her life in a fuller context. This moment of intense lucidity reminded Kate of how vastly fortunate she was, despite any day-to-day struggles and challenges she might have. This tsunami of awareness had become a personal and welcome friend and even had a name: *The Wave of Clarity*. The Wave reminded Kate that she was a privileged individual living in a modern civilization—safe, well fed, capable, empowered, loved, respected—and not a medieval peasant farmer trying to survive to the next day, or a Saudi Arabian woman owned by a man and prohibited from voting or having an opinion. She was neither a black slave on a cotton plantation in the early 19th century, nor a child laborer in some forgotten corner of an oppressive dictatorship. Of the countless times and places and ways she could have spent this one life, this one precious existence, she had hit the jackpot: she was a healthy, free, independent, 21st Century Vermont woman doing what she wanted. Whenever The Wave struck it overtook her with a comprehension that flooded her body and washed away any feelings of doubt, self-pity, or fear of the future. When all was said and done, and despite any tests or trials that might come her way, she was fortunate beyond measure. Once again *The Wave of Clarity* re-focused Kate and then gently deposited her on a solid shore where she stood up, dripped dry, thanked the powers that be, and got back to work, refreshed and grateful for the challenges ahead.

As The Wave receded and she came back to reality, and to break the stony silence that filled the room, Kate turned on VPR for some company, and with a renewed energy directed her attention to getting the other breakfast items in order. Pancake batter mixed, check. Oatmeal started, check. Bacon, sausage links, sliced ham, eggs—out of the fridge and all lined up—check. Potatoes cut for home fries, check. Onions, mushrooms, peppers, and olives, chopped, check, check, check, check. Orange slices and parsley sprigs for garnish, check. She tried to keep things simple while giving her customers what they wanted, within reason.

By this time her cinnamon and walnut masterpieces were finished and Kate felt a comforting blanket of warmth envelop her when she opened the oven door. She removed the buns and admired how nicely they had puffed up and browned; they filled the kitchen with a rich and reassuring aroma that infused any empty spaces. Having completed the morning prep, Kate finally had time to pour herself a cup of steaming fresh coffee, pop a bagel in the toaster, and have a relaxing five minutes to herself.

Before she could finish her bagel spread with creamy butter from the Carson's dairy, Jodi Simpson arrived through the front door to wait tables from 6:00 until 7:30, when she would catch the bus to finish her junior year at North Country Union High in Newport. Jodi was a good kid, dependable, respectful, and well spoken, unusual for a 17-year-old these days. She was both athletic and artsy, and participated in field hockey, basketball, and school plays as much as her busy schedule permitted. Her long and straight brown hair—pulled into a pony tail for work—framed a plain but pretty face with big brown eyes, a long nose, and thin but confident lips, and her positive and outgoing personality quickly won over all who crossed her path.

"Morning, Ms. Kate," said Jodi in a voice far too cheery for this time of day and for her age.

"Morning back at ya, Jodi," said Kate, in as cheery a tone as she could muster this early. She always appreciated Jodi's upbeat, if naïve, attitude, which never failed to lift her spirits.

"Mr. Keller and Mr. Haderlie are coming up the steps. Are we open yet?"

"Sure, Jodi, let 'em in. Let's go ahead and start the day." Jubal Keller always swung by Phil Haderlie's house and picked him up for their thrice-weekly breakfast at the store. Phil was getting on in years (who wasn't?) and appreciated the ride. His shrapnel souvenir from Korea gave him a nasty limp, his eyesight was shot, and he no longer drove, wisely giving up his license two years earlier.

Jodi opened the front door, turned the "closed" sign to "open," and welcomed the old gents, who each carried their own "Odd Country" mugs with their names on them.

"Good morning, kind sirs," greeted Jodi with an exaggerated curtsy. "And how are you on this fine day?"

"You bucking for a big tip already, young lady?" joked Jubal Keller while wiping his shoes on the entry rug. "Lemme get some coffee in me before you go flirting with me," he said with his trademark crooked grin.

Following close behind, Phil Haderlie barely managed "Hey kid." He was a man of few words until his second cup, whereupon he would happily launch into full action, usually complaining about the government and promoting his latest conspiracy theory.

Keller and Haderlie took their usual seats at the big corner table, the largest one in the place and the only one that would hold three or four or maybe even five more of the "Odd Balls," as they called themselves. The Odd Balls were Oddertown's version of the ever-present group of old guys that gathered early mornings at every country store, café, and diner in New England to get away from their wives if they still had them, seek the company of contemporaries, talk about the town, start arguments, "ping" each other—as they called their mock mockery—and solve all the world's problems, all within an hour or two. The Odd Balls met here reliably every Monday, Wednesday, and Friday, skipping the other four days of the week only for financial reasons: it would just be too expensive to do it every day.

Jubal and Phil were always the first two on hand, as neither slept well, so they had a good 15 minutes to themselves until the others showed up, by which time they would be on their second mugs. Jodi poured their steaming coffees without asking and backed away to prep the other four tables, while the boys sat drinking to the new day while waiting for their compatriots to shuffle in.

Phil Haderlie was a physically imposing man—which he used to his advantage when arguing politics, about which he was passionate. An unwavering conservative, Phil was a verbal bully if given half a chance. Well over six feet tall and well over a healthy weight, he sported a full head of gray hair—rarely seen under his various and ubiquitous baseball-style caps—and a leathery, weathered skin from a lifetime of hard and honest work outdoors. Jubal Keller was a smaller man, kindly and well-liked by all. Politically moderate, he had a ready smile and was more accepting and less judgmental than Phil. They made for an unlikely duo, yet had retained their tight friendship for decades.

Predictably, at 6:18 (set your watch), in came Only Oswalt, whose unlikely name demanded frequent explanation, which he had been giving his whole life. The story goes that his mother, Mae-Lynn Oswalt, had heard nothing but horror stories about childbirth from *her* mother and several aunts. Their family line was rather narrow-hipped, you see, with pelvic structures not well-suited to the rigorous demands of childbirth, and as a result they tended to have difficult and painful deliveries. Consequently, 19-year-old Mae-Lynn was frightened to death going into her first delivery ten months after her marriage to Henry Oswalt, a fear that was well-justified after a 31-hour labor, 29 of which were pure agony, given that it was a time and place without epidurals or much effective pain relief. An hour after giving birth, when her husband finally entered the room to see his wife and newborn son, the exhausted, sweaty, and angry Mae-Lynn declared, "Henry, take a good long look at this here newborn, because that's the onliest child you will ever get out of me. I'm never doing this again."

To enforce that promise in writing, she named her boy "Only," with no middle name that could distract from her intention of "never doing this again". And to ensure that this would, in fact, be her "onliest" child, she refused to have any marital relations with Henry from that day on, fearing that if she did she would end up right back in the same place. That denial lasted two months before Henry took off for greener pastures, which was just as well given that he had become a useless alcoholic. Six months later she heard that Henry had died in a car crash while silly drunk and chasing skirts over in New Hampshire. She felt little grief or remorse, as it was not much of a loss for her or the world, and she went on to raise Only Oswalt in the best way she could.

Like Johnny Cash's *Boy Named Sue*, Only had spent much of his early life defending his honor and his name, and had consequently developed a tough exterior and learned to take grief from nobody. For his first several decades he used the second syllable of his name and went by "Lee." But that habit was quickly abandoned in late November of 1963, when "Lee Oswalt" bore far too great a resemblance to "Lee Oswald." Nowadays he sometimes used a nickname taken from the first syllable of his unfortunate name, "Own."

Less than a minute after Only's entrance, in shuffled Silas Miller, guardedly making his way to the table. Silas was slight of build and in good shape despite his physically inactive career in banking. However, his failing eyesight from macular degeneration slowed down his actions the last few years, and he was necessarily cautious and deliberate in finding his way around.

Bringing up the rear, two minutes later, always the last one, moseyed Steven S. Benson. Steven's middle name, oddly enough, was Stephen. He was named for his two grandfathers who were Steven and Stephen. Upon his birth, his parents argued for three days about which spelling would be adopted for their new son, as both wanted to honor their father and neither would back down; the impasse finally ended when they decided to simply use both names. They flipped a coin to see which would be first, his maternal grandfather won, and he became Steven Stephen Benson. His friends just called him Steve.

Unfortunately, Steve's parents had a life-long habit of constant bickering over any old thing, offspring names being among the least of their battle grounds. The relentless tension in the Benson household that resulted from their persistent combativeness took its toll on young Steven Stephen's nerves, and he developed an unfortunate stutter that stayed with him his entire life. To this day, he paid the price for his parents' inability to simply get along.

All five men now had their coffee mugs in hand, and all made snappy and good-hearted derogatory remarks about each other while settling into their regular positions. The core group was now in place, the pinging was well underway, and the day in Oddertown could truly begin. One or two others might make cameo appearances, and would be most welcome, but you could not predict for sure. Life, after all, did need *some* uncertainty to spice it up.

Jodi came by to take their orders because, curiously enough, despite their clockwork-like behaviors, they did vary their breakfast diets. Not much, mind you, but vary they did. All except one. Silas Miller had the same breakfast every day: one waffle, a scoop of butter, and one ounce of maple syrup from neighbor Dave Johnson's sugar bush. He never considered anything different, and Silas was—by his own admission—a waffle junky.

As Jodi took the last order, in tromped Willard Bennett, an occasional member and oddest duck of the group, who noisily and gracelessly plopped down at one end of the table. Willard was a bachelor pig farmer, never married—probably never even dated—and one could easily see why. Willard was crude, both physically and socially. He bathed far too infrequently, even were he *not* steeped in pig manure each day, which he was. His feeding habits were not unlike those of his livestock—with whom he spent far too much time—and he sported a rather active digestive system that frequently expelled interesting sounds and pungent gasses from both ends; he rarely seemed to notice. His dozen or so remaining teeth were hideous from lack of care and a steady habit of guzzling Mountain Dew, and his breath could pretty much knock a buzzard off a three-day-old carcass. To complete the package, Willard changed his clothes only weekly, if that, and he rarely controlled a foul mouth. All in all, Willard Bennett was quite the specimen. Still, he was part of the group, part of the town, and was grudgingly accepted by his buddies, if not physically embraced.

"Heya boys, ya old fart bastards, how the hell are ya?" expelled Willard with a big smile as he settled in, fully comfortable in his noxious role and oblivious to the heads turning to avoid his acrid breath. The boys all muttered their return greetings, trying not to encourage further verbal exchange, lest it burn their nostrils and upper GI tracts and ruin their breakfasts.

Just when they needed a distraction, like a gift from God, here came Paul Johnson, the youngest and most-formally educated member of the group, a 40-something organic farmer with an agriculture degree from UVM, whom they sometimes called "Hippie Boy." Paul enjoyed hanging out with these older fellows when he could, and he tried to pick through their nonsense and verbal detritus to find the hidden pearls of wisdom that inevitably come with age. Unfortunately, Paul's smarts did not help him avoid having to sit right next to Willard, as this was the last available chair. He took a deep breath while still standing and tried to limit his subsequent inhalation to shallow efforts. Jodi took his order and one from Willard, while keeping back an extra two feet from the latter.

"So, P-Paul," queried Steve Benson, quickly trying to steer conversation away from Willard and his corpse-like breath, "how's the fly f-fishing doin' ya? Been out m-m-much?"

"Nah, none at all yet this year, Steve. After all that winter rain and runoff I wanna let the streams calm down and warm up a bit. Would just be thrashing around mostly, and trying not to fall in. Maybe another week or two, if I can get away from early planting. I'm not like you retired types who can do whatever they want whenever they please. I've still got a farm to run and it doesn't run itself. I need to work first and fly fish second."

"Hey, Hippie Boy, I still work plenty," responded Phil Haderlie, his beefy, cracked, and weathered hands caressing his coffee mug like a well-loved pet. "I work at gettin up in the morning, I work at peein past my old prostate, I work at puttin my pants on without fallin over, I work at chewin my food with bad dentures. Never worked so damned hard in all my life!" The boys chuckled knowingly; getting old wasn't pretty for any of them, and at any given time one or another faced significant health challenges.

"So, Phil, whaddya think of this drive for universal gun registration down in Washington?" asked Only Owens with a sly grin, knowing he had pushed a major button of the extremely conservative Haderlie. Phil shoved back the NRA cap from his brow and started in, immediately getting red in the face, while the others grinned, knowing full well what was coming.

"Cripes, you know them sons a bitch liberals can come right on up here and make me register any time they want. If they can get past the barrel of my 12 gauge, that is. And my Colt 45. And my Ruger semi. I don't know what the hell is happening in this once-great country when they wanna disarm the honest people, all the real Americans, and give the place over to all them Mexicans and Muslims and terrorists and homosexuals. I didn't take shrapnel in Korea for this crap. And hell, that ain't even my biggest concern. It's all them shit-fer-brains do gooders down in Washington I'm more worried about! There's no room for us real Americans anymore. Did you hear about. . ."

"OK, OK, Phillip, I didn't mean to get you all worked up again," interrupted Only, holding his hands up in mock surrender. "We've heard the speech before. Stop before you stroke out on us, eh?"

They all laughed, even Phil. Oswalt, along with Keller, had also served in Korea, though Only was fortunate to not have taken any metal, and was more laid back about the issues that had a hair trigger for Phil. But he couldn't resist getting his buddy's blood pressure pushed up a couple of notches whenever he could. It added a sporting element to his life.

At that point, Jodi came by with the first round of breakfast orders and the boys calmed down and minded their manners as she set the plates in front of the hungry crew. The rich and comforting smells of eggs, bacon, sausages, home fries, and those cinnamon-walnut buns not only soothed their minds, but helped to cover up the various stenches emanating from Willard's end of the table.

Back in the kitchen, Kate was keeping up with steady breakfast orders coming in from the several other customers that were starting to fill up the small eatery, happy that early morning cash flow looked good. *Might be a decent day*, she thought to herself. *About time; maybe things are turning around.* She hadn't had too many decent days of late. In fact, she hadn't been much in the black since holiday sales in December. And her debts were piling up fast, while her cash reserves were rapidly depleting. Kate wrestled each day with ways to bring the Odderton Country Store—the "Odd Country"—back to some degree of solvency, of sustainability, of long-term viability. So far, she had few answers, and right now she couldn't see a way out to save her soul. Or the store.

Chapter 2

Wednesday, May 1, late morning

LARRY CARSON SHOWED UP RIGHT ON TIME AT 10:30 and began to prepare the lunch lineup. Kate was happy to have found Larry. Two years out of North Country Union High, he had yet to find his path in life and was happy to live at home while working part time for Kate, taking on the job of line cook for lunch. When not cooking, he stocked shelves, took inventory, placed orders, and generally did whatever needed doing.

Larry was a strong kid, 6 foot 2 and solidly built, and helped Kate with the heavy lifting. He had been a star running back at North Country, and the state scoring leader his Senior year with 35 touchdowns, so he was no stranger to dedication, strenuous work, and hard knocks. During that extraordinary Senior year some folks had started calling Larry "Leary," a nod of respect to Carson Leary, a great running quarterback from Otter Valley Union High in Brandon, who a few years earlier attracted much attention with his remarkable skills on the field, led his team to a state championship, and was widely celebrated as the best player in Vermont. The names "Larry Carson" and "Carson Leary" were too similar to leave alone, so Larry went through much of his Senior year, and even beyond, being called "Leary." He took it well, and felt honored by the comparison.

On top of all his great attributes, Leary... rather... Larry was a nice kid, polite and respectful, an outgrowth, no doubt, of his upbringing on a dairy farm, growing up with all the chores and responsibilities, the need to understand nature's annual cycles, and the realization that there were things on this earth far bigger and more important than himself. He learned early on that the world did not revolve around him, and consequently he was unusually humble, considering all his abilities and successes. He started out at the store handling general duties, but had recently shown an interest in cooking, so Kate brought him into the kitchen. Larry quickly demonstrated an aptitude for and even command of that domain, so Kate made him her line cook at lunch, which freed up a couple hours of her time so she could focus on other aspects of the store. Larry even started talking about going to cooking school and pursuing a career in the restaurant business. Nobody in Oddertown could have predicted that.

About 11:35, Victor S. Kemper, sober for now but not for long, maneuvered his creaky bones through the front door. Victor was a withered old barber working out of an even older barber shop up the road that largely hadn't changed since the Reagan administration. Magazines dating back to the 1980s were strewn about, as was his mail, including unpaid bills. His two barber chairs would be better placed in a museum, and even his prices were stuck in an earlier decade. His sterilizing equipment was archaic and no doubt ineffective. His hair was scruffy and a poor endorsement of his skills, and he usually wore a scraggly, several-day growth of beard, making him look more like a homeless vagrant than the town stylist. For all of that, Victor was quite a good barber and the men in town all used his services, but you'd better get your hair done in the morning. Victor, you see, had a long-term love affair with Old Crow, a cheap and abundant Kentucky bourbon whiskey. He usually started shortly after lunch, slowly at first, building momentum throughout the afternoon, and reaching a grand crescendo around 7 PM, when he would go to sleep or simply pass out. The local rule of thumb was that any haircut after 2 PM fell into the "buyer beware" category.

The bulk of Victor's daily nutritional intake was lunch at Odd Country, so Kate and Larry made sure he got bigger helpings than normal to try and keep some meat on his stiff old bones. He was a nice enough man, and completely harmless even when soused, but between his drinking and excessive smoking of filterless Camels, people wondered how he was not long ago in the ground.

"Hey, Mr. Kemper" greeted Larry with a warm smile. "What'll it be today? Our specials are a tuna melt with fries, or maple-glazed pulled pork on a bun, also with fries. Soup is beef barley."

"Ahhh, I don't know, Larry," said Kemper as he pondered the colorful menu on the chalk board to the right of the counter. "Lemme see. . .got any a that good cheddah from down Grafton way?"

"Sure do, a big chunk."

"Can you make me a grilled cheddah with a slice a ham? Some fries too?"

"You got it, Mr. Kemper."

As Larry went to work on his first lunch order of the day, the bell above the front door announced another entry, this time Dr. Anthony Delfasio. Tony, as he was known to everyone, was a large-animal Vet in town and spent much of his time on, or driving to or from, farms within about a 30-mile radius of Oddertown. He took good care of all the critters in the area, from Willard's pigs, to milk cows, horses, sheep, alpacas, and even a herd of yaks that a young couple was raising for their high-quality meat three miles north of town. Sometimes his clients could not afford to pay for his services, at least not when rendered, and that was fine with Tony. Without a formal agreement or bill for services, he knew they would eventually settle their debts. During the occasional fat times they might deliver to his house a side of beef or half a pig, a bushel of garden produce, or a cord or two of wood. Or they might trade their skills for his when an electrical or plumbing problem arose, or when his truck needed work. Like so many in this part of the world, a mutual dependence had developed between Tony and his clients, a symbiotic relationship that benefitted all parties. Nobody kept an accounting, but all accounts were eventually and honorably paid in full.

Tony was well regarded by everyone and knew his craft well; even the animals seemed to trust him. He did have one of Victor's unfortunate habits, however, and smoked Marlboros. If he had to smoke, Marlboro was a good choice, as he uncannily, and seemingly without effort or awareness, resembled the Marlboro man. Tony was tall, ruggedly handsome, knew his way around horses, and always wore his trademark tan cowboy hat—now well-worn and replete with many reminders of his profession.

"Hi, Victor, what's good today?" he said as he sat on a counter stool next to the old barber. "Oh, I don't know, Tony. I'm gettin' a grilled cheese and ham. I don't get too fancy with food; just something to keep me going."

Yeah, to the next glass of Old Crow, thought Delfasio.

Larry came over and repeated the specials to Dr. Delfasio. Tony ordered the tuna melt. "Haven't had tuna in quite a while and probably getting low on mercury, so gimme a full dose," he said with a smile, reaching for a copy of the *Newport Daily Express* laying on the counter.

The bell chimed over the front door once again announcing another entry, and in came Dr. James D. Watson. Watson's improbable name hung around his neck like the proverbial albatross, and haunted him through most of his adult life, the source of several points of awkwardness and humility over the last 40 years. You see, Jim Watson was immediately measured—by those in the know—against several famous Dr. Watsons. First, there was Dr. James *Dewey* Watson, co-discoverer, along with Francis Crick, of the structure of DNA back in 1953, one of the greatest scientific discoveries of the century, earning them and Maurice Wilkins the Nobel Prize in Physiology or Medicine. Also having a Ph.D. in biology, our Dr. James *Daniel* Watson never lived down the monikered comparison with the famed and fabled other Dr. Watson. He lost count of the number of times smart alecs asked him where he kept his Nobel Prize.

If that wasn't enough—and for those not especially knowledgeable about molecular genetics or the history of biology—there was "Doc Watson," the famous and blind multi-Grammy award winning guitarist, songwriter, blues, folk, and gospel singer. Oddertown's Doc Watson could plunk out a few tunes on his guitar and sing a few songs nearly on key, but that's as close as he got to the legendary Doc Watson.

And if that didn't cover all the bases, there was also Sherlock Holmes's renowned sidekick, "Doctor Watson," after whom Doc Watson (the Grammy Award winning singer), curiously enough, was nicknamed early on by a fan. Got all that? It was often more than James Daniel Watson cared to handle and he sometimes wished his parents had just named him Bubba! But then there would be the professional golfer, Bubba Watson, to deal with. He couldn't win.

Jim Watson had had an interesting, rewarding, and exceedingly happy life until about five years ago. Growing up in Middlebury as a second-generation Vermonter, he had good parents, a loving home, and excelled in school. Between involvement in every summer-through-winter outdoor activity he could think of—including the Boy Scouts, where he achieved the top rank of Eagle—and having an innate aptitude for science and math, he naturally majored in biology when he entered the University of Vermont in 1968. Along the way, he secured a student deferment that kept him out of the insanity that was Vietnam. After graduating with high honors in 1972, he went to the University of Maine for his Ph.D. in evolutionary ecology, finishing in 1977. Jim's particular field of interest was plant chemical defenses against insects, and he published four highly regarded papers from his dissertation on how birches and maples use different chemical strategies to defend themselves against insect galls. While in graduate school, Jim met, courted, and married the true love of his life, Margaret Swenson, a Mainer two years his elder and a middle school teacher. They were two halves of a whole and dove into a rich and rewarding life fully devoted to each other.

You can take the boy out of Vermont, as they say, but you couldn't take the Vermont out of this boy. Wanting more than anything else to live again in the state he loved, Jim Watson was willing to forego a promising research career to move back to Vermont where he accepted an Assistant Professorship with a heavy teaching load at Green Mountain College in Poultney. He and Margaret settled in and Jim spent most of his career teaching biology, ecology, and botany to bright undergrads with a strong interest in the natural world. He managed to do some research along the way with his students, and saw many of them go on to outstanding careers in science and service to nature.

All in all, Jim Watson was awfully satisfied with his life. He was quite proud of his two beautiful daughters, Melissa and Laura, who each made their own careers and found their own loves. Unfortunately, they were now building their lives in Oregon and Virginia, further away than he would like. But otherwise he and Margaret, his "Maggie," had it all, and after 39 years of marriage they were still deeply in love when they both retired early to pursue some of their lifelong dreams. Plans included lots of travel, new hobbies, and time with the grandkids that were on the way.

They say if you want to make God laugh, just tell Him your plans. Barely six months into retirement, Maggie began to experience abdominal bloating and pelvic pain, and it didn't take long for a dreaded diagnosis of ovarian cancer to emerge. Surgery removed the original tumor but revealed that the cancer had spread into her mesentery, bladder, and large intestine. Chemotherapy and radiation were largely ineffective and Maggie succumbed after seven grueling months. Jim felt his life was over at 63.

Jim and Maggie had done everything together. They were two parts of one soul and were never happier than when together. Maggie's loss was beyond devastating and Jim experienced pain and loneliness that he hadn't realized were even possible within the realm of human experience. Tears were the least of it; there were times when he almost could not breathe through his grief, when it felt like he was encased in plastic wrap, claustrophobic, grasping for something to pierce the bubble. Nights were especially bad, and sometimes even terrifying. On several of the worst nights, rather than uselessly try to sleep, he sat in the living room with all the lights on, just waiting for sunrise to ease the feeling of dark panic.

He found temporary relief in a bourbon bottle, which lasted about a month, whereupon Jim Watson woke up one afternoon, filthy and unshaven, became thoroughly disgusted with himself, and realized how disappointed Maggie would be in him. He could hear her tell him to get on with it, that he was better than this, that life was too precious and too short, that he shouldn't waste the time he had left, and other assorted pieces of wisdom she had always lovingly offered.

He did manage to clean up and dry out but soon realized he could never heal in the house that they had shared for so long; too many memories oozed out of every corner. He literally could do nothing in that house—not so much as make a cup of tea or take out the trash—that didn't put Maggie squarely in front of him. She was everywhere, and the house was becoming a shrine and mausoleum to her; he knew he had to either immerse himself in pain every day or go cold turkey and get away. After two weeks sober he chose the latter.

Jim looked for a house he could buy in a remote and friendly part of Vermont, some place that he and Maggie had not visited and which therefore held no memories of her. That excluded so much of the state where they had traveled so widely, and the pickings were slim. But after scanning maps and taking some drives, he wandered into Oddertown in the Northeast Kingdom. The Kingdom was known for its remoteness, its independent streak, its colorful characters, and its live-and-let-live attitude; it seemed just what he needed.

Jim liked the feel of Oddertown from the outset. It was set in a hollow, about one-half mile wide and two miles long, between two north-south running low-mountain ridges. Several streams flowed down thickly forested mountainsides and into Odder

Creek, which ran through the eastern edge of town, along the base of Copperhead Mountain, a curious name given that copperhead snakes do not now and never did occur there. A covered bridge built in 1868 spanned the creek and still accommodated one-lane traffic flow. Three men were killed during its construction when a support timber snapped, and some old-timers believed the bridge to be haunted by their restless spirits to this day. Parents mostly used that tale to keep their younger children from playing on or around the old structure.

Oddertown had about 700 residents scattered in and around the little village, which consisted of a main street running north-south, eight side streets, and several country roads running off into farms and then up the ridges to disappear into who-knows-where. The town had most of the essentials and basics, but nothing fancy. At the south end was a combination town office and small upstairs public library, an adjacent town garage with two mainte-nance trucks that doubled as snow plows in winter, and a volunteer fire department with a single fire truck and a rescue vehicle. At the north end of town sat an elementary school with a small kindergarten room and three larger classrooms that handled the combined first and second, third and fourth, and fifth and sixth grades. There was a small playground out back that provided the only recreation for chil-dren in the area.

In-between the two ends of town, where the road split and widened barely enough to grudgingly accommodate it, laid a modest town green, barely 40 feet wide and 110 feet long, the Oddertown "Town Square." This was in fact a rectangle, but square was so much easier to say—and so in keeping with the tradition of New England town squares—that nobody seemed to notice or mind the geometric inaccuracy.

A small and quaint white gazebo anchored the middle of the green, while the southern end held a small granite monument honoring the town's founder, Francis S. Odderton, and the five subsequent generations to date that had inhabited the village. The northern end was graced by the town clock, an old-fashioned time piece standing on a beautiful black metal pedestal nine feet tall supporting the nearly three-foot-diameter clock face. The clock pleasantly chimed out every hour from 8 AM through 8 PM but was respectfully silent through the night. Surrounding the clock base of colorful flowers— present from mid-May until the first freeze—was a circular brick walkway, and beyond that, at the four cardinal directions, sat four wooden benches, shaded by nearby stately maple trees. The town green was affectionately known by locals as "Time Square."

The business district around Time Square— such as it was—included Victor Kemper's barber shop, a small bar (Duke's); a gas station and fix-it garage (Lou's); a small branch of the Passumpsic Savings Bank of Newport, complete with a Branch Manager and a teller; and a second-hand store/ junk shop called "Odds n' Ends." A few other small shops and businesses, as well as a Methodist and an Episcopalian church, were scattered through as well, but the center of it all, the most important structure in town, the glue that held everything together, was the Odderton Country Store. Odd Country. Kate Langford's place.

Jim found an old farmhouse a half mile north of Time Square, about a quarter mile off the main road to the east, up on a little rise at the edge of the hollow and bordering Odder Creek; it came with 35 acres, most of it second-growth forest after farming became marginal many decades before. He bought it, quickly moved in, and at 64 was the newest resident of Oddertown, Vermont. Now, four years later, he felt at home and part of the community. He was accepted.

At 68, Jim Watson was still a reasonable male specimen. Standing nearly six foot two and sporting a reasonable 190 pounds, he was in good shape for a man his age, at least well above the average for his cohort. His peppery hair had added some salt over the last decade, but his mane remained full, if rather unruly. Despite his and Maggie's best efforts, Jim's hair seemed to enjoy a life of its own, with different sectors going their own way and acting as though they disliked all other sectors. He eventually gave up any attempt at control, and his rowdy and wild mop had become a trademark.

Jim sported no facial hair. He had tried growing a beard in his early thirties, perhaps to look more like an academic, but it was so patchy and multi-colored that Maggie gently suggested it resembled the back end of a mangy dog. He shaved it, and had remained clean-shaven ever since. Jim's facial features were otherwise average, though not unpleasant. His brown eyes were alert, friendly, and youthful, and they tended to draw people to him. His was an open and welcoming demeanor, reinforced by an easy smile.

As Jim sidled up to the counter to order lunch,

Tony Delfasio fondly greeted him with a "Hey, look, it's the Wiz!"

Oh no, here we go again, thought Jim; it was like fingernails on the blackboard. The one thing Jim Watson did not like about life here—other than Maggie not being a part of it—was the latest nickname the locals had bestowed upon him. All the "Dr. Watson" issues had mostly resolved themselves here, because not many Oddertown residents were aware of Dr. James Dewey Watson the molecular geneticist, Doc Watson the musician, or Sherlock Holmes's sidekick, Doctor Watson. They were in fact blissfully ignorant of or did not care about these other Watsons for the most part, and Jim got by for more than a year without his name causing embarrassment, explanation, or consternation.

Then the townsfolk began to learn about him: professor, teacher, smart guy, knows a lot, has the answers. Oddertown. Oddtown. Odd. A smart guy, a real wizard. . .living in Odd. Within a year, Dr. James Daniel Watson had unwittingly become "The Wizard of Odd." In retrospect, it was inevitable.

Jim responded to Tony good naturedly. He long ago realized that the best way to sidestep his wizardly title was to ignore it and not throw any fuel on the fire. Folks usually did not pursue it beyond one or two tries. "Hi, Tony, how goes it in the big critter world? Any fun cases lately?"

"Nah, not really. Had to put down Lauren McCallum's old horse the other day though. Poor thing; Lauren, I mean, not the horse. Horse was 31 and had a good life but Lauren had him for the last 17 years and bonded deeply. She was pretty broken up, though she knew it was inevitable. Gosh, Doc, she's a sweet woman! Very attractive too. You know, she's been widowed about five years now and might be open to seeing someone. School teacher, kind and gentle soul, still got some good years ahead of her, Jim. You should look in on her. Hell, I would if I wasn't happily married."

"No thanks, Tony. I'm not interested in anyone after Maggie. Besides, Lauren's what, 50, 52? What would she want with a 68-year-old geezer like me?"

"Jim you look 10 years younger, and I suspect you still have one or two good years left in you. Why not take a risk?"

"Well, I do admit to getting lonely sometimes," said Watson, pondering, "but nah, I'm too old to start over with someone. Besides, I'd feel like I was cheating on Maggie. Couldn't do it."

"Suit yourself, Wiz. Lauren's a helluva nice woman. I'm just saying."

Jim was happy when Kate came by and changed the subject. "Hey, Doc, how's tricks today?"

Before he could respond, there was a loud commotion and scuffle out on the front porch. Jim turned around and immediately knew what the problem was. Darwin was at it again, dammit! Darwin was Jim's four-year-old golden retriever, a beautiful specimen and great company who helped him heal after losing Maggie. Named after one of Jim's scientific heroes, Charles Darwin, *his* Darwin happened to be of the female persuasion. Undaunted, he named her Darwin anyway figuring that a) there were in fact female Darwins, even if lesser known than their famous husband or father, and b) his Darwin would little realize the gender inappropriateness of her name. So Darwin she became and Darwin she remained.

She was a delightful dog in every respect, with one significant imperfection: in her zeal to assist Jim with his recycling chores, Darwin had developed an irrational and generally unhelpful passion for aluminum cans. She simply could not resist grabbing any aluminum can within her purview and collect it for recycling. Strangely, she displayed no such fervor for tin cans, plastic, styrofoam, or any other recyclables, just aluminum, and with a singular and steadfast devotion perhaps unmatched in the long annals of dogdom. No soft drink or beer can was safe once Darwin laid her eyes on or sniffed it out, despite Jim's continued efforts to discourage the practice and change her ways. And that included cans still very much in use by their temporary human caretakers.

In this case, Jim saw that Darwin had snatched a can of Coke from an unsuspecting young boy's grip as he and his father walked out the front door, where the dog was tied to the railing. The father was attempting to retrieve said Coke can from Darwin's jaws, when a stream of pressurized sweet brown foam shot out from where Darwin's upper right canine had punctured it, hitting the boy squarely in the face. The youngster thought it was all pretty funny and giggled hilariously as the cold and sticky liquid oozed down his face, but the father was somewhat less amused, especially as he had just handed over $0.99 to the Odderton Country Store for the now-perforated can of Coke.

At that point, Jim burst out the front door, scolded Darwin (not that that would do any good), grabbed the can from his jaws, and apologized to the man for this unwelcome behavior. He immediately offered to buy another Coke, which the man graciously accepted, after which they all had a good laugh while cleaning up the child's gooey face with wet paper towels from the Odd Country restroom.

The victims of Darwin's escapades nearly always were understanding, and often even amused, as the dog's singular enthusiasm, beautiful and emotive face, and goofy demeanor quickly overcame her failings as an incessant recycler. There was, however, one significant and memorable exception to that rule. Last summer, a man whose just-opened can of Budweiser was snatched away after one sip became rather unhinged when the beer suddenly changed ownerships, spilling half a can on the porch in the process. When Jim appeared outside to apologize and make amends, the man promptly lit into him, suggesting several unpleasant and painful fates that ought to befall the animal and its owner, all expressed at greatly elevated decibel levels and with wretchedly foul language rarely heard in the Oddertown public arena. Rather than answer any of the charges and modify the man's perspective on the situation, Jim looked him over, pulled out his wallet, extracted a $5 bill and gave it to the man, untied Darwin from the railing, and walked away without saying a word.

One look at the visitor had told Jim that further discussion would be fruitless. This dyspeptic and ugly man, you see, was obviously beyond redemption. For starters he wore a pair of black polyester slacks complimented by flamboyant and hideously overpriced fluorescent lime green Nike athletic shoes, though he bore no resemblance whatsoever to anyone even remotely athletic. His flabby and expansive pink torso was covered by a black T-shirt proudly sporting a picture of a fisted hand, middle finger dexterously pointed skyward, with the short but pithy inquiry 'Any questions?' written in a most forceful and unmistakable font. As if that weren't enough, partly covering his balding crown was a gaudy red hat displaying the quaint little phrase 'Bite Me.' Furthermore, from among the more than 20 varieties of delightful and compelling craft beers available in Odd Country's cooler, many made in Vermont, he emerged with, of all things, a six-pack of Budweiser. To complete the picture, his black Lincoln Continental proudly displayed a New Jersey license plate that read BIG-SHT, leaving it to the reader to decide which vowel would most appropriately be inserted between the H and the T. Obviously, common sense, good taste, and decorum were not within this gentleman's circle of life experiences.

Being a person of quick intellect, Jim rapidly concluded that the specimen before him was an unfortunate nincompoop of the first order, well out of his element here in Oddertown. He was, clearly, a primitive evolutionary throwback, a dead end that had—we could only hope—left no offspring. There was no point in further pursuing any reasoned discussion with the gentleman, prompting Jim to pay up and walk away. With this one memorable exception, all the other Darwin victims had responded much more understandably and with some level of humor, as had the one just now.

Returning to the lunch counter, Jim sheepishly re-engaged in conversation with Kate.

"Landed yourself another one, huh Doc?" asked Kate with a devilish smile.

"I gotta stop bringing her into town, I guess," he replied, shaking his head. "I can't seem to break her of that habit. But she sure loves coming in with me, and howls if I leave her home alone. I swear, she knows if I'm coming to the store as opposed to anywhere else. What a crazy animal! Well, anyway, you asked how I'm doing and I'd say pretty decent, other than having a thieving dog. And you?"

"Getting along, I suppose. Another day older and deeper in debt, as the song goes. Not sure where it will end," Kate said after a deep sigh and with some real despair in her voice.

"Seriously, that bad?" returned the Doc.

"Yeah, 'fraid so. I keep hoping for something to break, but so far it hasn't. Maybe if we get a nice spring and summer we'll get more folks coming through here recreating, and boost my sales. But I need a pretty major boost, tell you the truth. Hey, maybe all my extra sales of sodas and beer that Darwin destroyed will do it, huh? Ah well, never mind all that, what'll you have today, Doc?"

Jim Watson thoughtfully pondered the colorful menu board and then replied, with a smile, "I'll take whatever gives you the highest profit margin, my dear."

"You're the best, my friend."

Chapter 3

Monday, June 3, 12:55 PM

I T WAS INDEED A BEAUTIFUL SPRING SO FAR, WITH above-normal temperatures and frequent blue skies, but the good weather had not yet translated into the increased business Kate had hoped for. She was holding her own and meeting her bills, but was nowhere near digging out of the hole she had inherited. Most folks in town were vaguely aware there were problems at Odd Country, but they did not know the magnitude or fully realize that their community core, their center of gravity, the thing that defined their town more than any other, was in serious jeopardy. Even had they known, there wasn't much they could have done about it.

It was now past the burst of lunch activity, if you could call nine customers a burst, and the action was dying down. Larry had things in the kitchen under control as usual, and Kate sat down with a sandwich and an iced tea near the corner of the front serving counter. Two men walked in, their expensive, many-pocketed vests with various accoutrements hanging from them clearly indicating they were fishermen on a lunch break. They smiled and nodded to Kate as they moved to the chalkboard menu, and she immediately noted they were not hard on the eyes. Rugged, outdoorsy types, mid-40s, well-conditioned. No middle-age guts on them. God how she hated beer bellies in men! Why did they let themselves go to hell like that just when they were coming into their most-attractive years? At least to her. It showed a lack of self-respect and control. These two obviously respected themselves a great deal.

"Well, what's good here?" one of them said to Kate, not lifting his eyes from the menu.

"Everything," she replied.

"C'mon, really," as he turned to her. "Can't all be good."

"It sure is. I own the place. And I know good when I see it," she replied with a slightly flirty grin.

"Well, I guess we'll just have to test that theory." Turning to Larry he ordered the grilled chicken breast sandwich with Vermont cheddar and lettuce, tomato, and onions, with a side salad instead of fries.

"Nice, healthy choice," noted Kate. "And you?" she said, turning to the other fellow. "You healthy too?"

"You know, I am darned healthy, which means I can break loose once in a while. I'm gonna have the Italian hoagie with chips, young man," he said to Larry.

"Ooooh, living dangerously," oozed Kate through exaggerated, pouty lips. They all laughed.

"So, I'm Paul, Paul Simon," said the first one, turning to Kate and extending his hand. "And before you ask, no, I'm not the *Sounds of Silence* guy and I can't carry a tune in a bucket with two hands." Kate laughed, extending her hand to his. "Good to meet you Paul Simon who can't carry a tune."

The second guy came around with an extended hand: "Bruce Bivens. I can sing better than Paul, but that's not saying much."

Kate likewise greeted Bruce and said to them, "I'm Kate Langford, latest owner of this here storied establishment. Nice to meet you both. Looks like you've been fishing. Any luck?"

"Kate, we are *fly* fisherman," replied Paul, with prolonged emphasis on *flyyyy*, "and luck has nothing to do with it; milady, it is *all* skill."

"Really?" replied Kate. "Well, did you have any *skill* today, Paul Simon?"

"You bet we did," interjected Bruce. "We hit the Trifecta on Odder Creek about three miles south of town, while landing a couple dozen between us."

"The Trifecta?" queried Kate.

"Yeah, that's what we call it when you land brookies, browns, and rainbows all in the same outing," returned Bruce. "And if you get all three species in your first three fish, it's a Perfecta. Get 'em in alphabetical order—brookie, brown, and rainbow—and it's a Super Perfecta!" he laughed.

"Sounds like you fellas should be spending some time at the race track instead of on our streams. So where are all these Trifecta fish you claim to have caught?" Kate said, looking around behind them, palms up, eyebrows raised. "Why aren't you eating a trout lunch?"

"Well, because we're mostly catch and release. It's pretty much the ethic among fly fishermen these days. Strictly sport, maintain the resource, respect the fish, and all that," replied Paul. "We take a few occasionally, especially if a stream has too many stunted fish. We never take trophies though; we respect those big monsters too much."

"Interesting," nodded Kate, mulling over their philosophy, which had not, to her knowledge, widely taken hold in this neck of the woods, where fish, as far as she knew, were for eating or bragging, but not returning. "I'm thinking you two aren't from around here."

"It shows that badly, huh?" returned Paul. "We're up from New Jersey for a couple of days, working streams throughout the Northeast Kingdom. We have a few decent trout streams in New Jersey, believe it or not, but nothing like here and nowhere near the beauty. God, this place is incredible! I really don't care if I catch anything, or even fish, to tell you the truth. I just love being out on these streams in these mountains. I hope folks here appreciate what they have."

"Some do, I think, and I'm sure some take it for granted," responded Kate, "just like anywhere else, I suppose. But deep down, people here love this land and this little oddball town, and most wouldn't leave for much of anything."

"Oddball, huh? So you admit it! What a weird name, 'Oddertown.' We even heard the gal at the gas station call it 'Odd'," said Paul.

"Yeah, what's up with that?" added Bruce. "How'd this place get a name like that?"

Before Kate could respond, the lunches for the two visitors arrived. After an awkward moment when nobody quite knew what to do, she realized she wouldn't mind spending some time with these two good-looking gents, and volunteered, "You *really* want to know about this place? Well, it'll take a lunchtime to explain it. If you don't mind some uninvited company we can grab a table and I can finish my lunch and talk while you two eat. Unless you want some privacy to discuss your rainbows and brookies, that is."

"No, hey, that would be great," replied Paul.

"You bet," added Bruce. "We're tired of each other's company and ready for anyone else."

"Wow, what a heartfelt endorsement," grinned Kate. "I'll do in a pinch, huh?"

"Sorry, no, I didn't mean it that way," apologized Bruce. "Let me try this again. Ahem…Paul and I would be *delighted* to have you join us, Ms. Kate, if you would so care to honor us," said Bruce, bowing slowly.

"Well, when you put it *that* way, how can a lady resist?" she smiled while grabbing her lunch. "OK, let's settle in over here."

After grabbing some napkins and cold drinks, and paying up at the register, they all sat comfortably at a round table and Kate began.

"Well, here it is, ready or not. A fellow by the name of Frances S. Odderton came over from Gloucestershire, England, back in the early 1800s, actual date unknown. He was a young man at the time, early 20s, strong and kind of wild, looking for adventure. He started out in Nova Scotia, then wandered down into Maine for a couple of years, roamed across New Hampshire and, God only knows why, didn't stop 'til he hit this area of Vermont around 1815. Some think he kept causing trouble and was moved on; others think he just had wanderlust.

Anyway, apparently he liked the lay of the land here, and I guess he'd gotten tired of wandering and was ready to settle down, and for whatever reason he built himself a little farm here."

Paul and Bruce paid close attention as they began to dip into their lunches. Even if they weren't interested in the history of the place—and they were—Kate's big green eyes, long auburn hair, and satin-smooth and slightly olive complexion were compelling enough to reel them in. Those eyes were not only attractive but intelligent, energetic, and honest. She was quite beautiful in a strong and wholesome sort of way. For someone who apparently spent most of her life indoors, she still had a fresh, outdoorsy quality about her.

"So he soon meets a young woman, about 10 years his junior, on a supply run to St. Johnsbury, the story goes. She is actually on her own, her parents having died when she was a teen from some unknown disease that came through, probably TB or whatever. A quick courtship and pretty soon Frances had himself a wife. Molly. Long story short, they had several kids and started to settle the area. As other folks moved into the valley they deferred to the seniority of Frances and crew, and started calling the place 'Odderton.' After some time it changed to 'Oddertown,' and that became the official name in the town charter, adopted in 1857."

"And that's how the town got its name? Just named it after the first guy who settled here?" queried Paul.

"That's it, but there's a lot more to the story of how we got from there to here, if you want to hear it," replied Kate.

"Sure, you bet," they both nodded, tucking further into their lunches. "By the way," added Paul, "you were right. This sandwich is delicious."

"Yeah, mine too, Kate," added Bruce, while munching. "Very good."

"Well, thank you, gentlemen. Nice to hear." Kate brushed some stray hairs away from her eyes, jangling her hanging earrings—today bright red and black—and continued.

"So anyway, Francis and Molly's oldest boy was Francis Jr. and he carried on the family farming tradition, building himself a farm house not far from the original one. He also started a lumber mill, harvesting trees in the forests around here and supplying milled lumber to folks who were settling in. As the original forests with their huge trees were cleared for farms he would buy the lumber cheap, mill it, and sell it back to the farmers for construction. Francis Jr. did quite well for himself, but his main contribution to the world was his second son, Peter. Peter is the real focus of Oddertown's story and he started what you see here today." Kate paused for a bite and a sip of tea; the fellows waited patiently.

"Peter was born around 1842, making him quite eligible twenty years later for the Union Army when the Civil War rolled around. Like so many Vermonters, he enlisted and headed for points south. It seems he saw quite a bit of action, but his most important role was at Gettysburg, believe it or not. Peter Odderton was part of the 2nd Vermont Brigade, which did none other than help turn back Pickett's Charge at a critical point of that battle and the whole war. But what he did the day *before* the charge was his biggest contribution to U.S. history."

"And what was that?" inquired an engrossed Bruce, locked onto those compelling eyes.

"Well, on the afternoon of July 2, 1863, the day *before* Pickett's Charge, Peter and two other Vermont boys got separated from their regiment and found they had wandered into the Maine 20th at Little Round Top, which they joined up with just as it was entering a skirmish with an Alabama contingent. As you may know, that was a critical juncture at Gettysburg when Confederate forces tried to flank the Union army on their left. If successful in that maneuver, they would have controlled that geography and might have won Gettysburg and maybe even the war." Paul and Bruce had stopped eating, and now were hanging on every word.

"Anyway, by getting lost it turns out that Peter Odderton saved the life of the Maine's Lieutenant Colonel, Joshua Chamberlain. The story goes that, while Chamberlain's attention was elsewhere in the confusion of his counterattack down the hill from Little Roundtop, an Alabama boy charging up the hill raised his rifle and was about to fire a slug into the Colonel. Peter Odderton saw this, shot the Confederate first, and saved Chamberlain, whose troops then turned back the Rebs. Colonel Chamberlain eventually went on to become the Governor of Maine and then the President of Bowdoin College. So, no Peter Odderton, no Joshua Chamberlain, and who knows how history would have been changed!"

"Holy cow," said a bedazzled Paul, "that's pretty amazing! Did Peter survive the war?"

"Remarkably enough, the worst things that happened to him were some nasty cases of the trots and a gash on his hand from food prep gone astray. He pretty much came out of the war unscathed, and quite a local hero."

"So wait," interjected Bruce. "How do you know all these details about the Oddertons?"

"Patience, my new friend. All will be revealed in due course. There's more story to tell."

Before Kate could continue, the bell on the door chimed and an old, scowling fellow came shuffling in. "Oh good, there's old Charlie," muttered Kate under her breath. "How nice. Come to complain about something, no doubt."

"Troublemaker?" asked Paul.

"No, he's harmless, just the town pain-in-the-neck. Charlie Harbrough. People call him 'Charlie Horrible.' He always finds something to complain about: taxes, Select Board decisions, the way our fries are cooked; you name it, he'll find something wrong. Just constantly grumpy and grouchy. Never saw him smile, never heard him speak a kind word to anyone."

"Hi, Charlie," said Kate cheerfully, waving.

"Hrrrmmm," responded Charlie with a reluctant nod in her direction. Her assessment confirmed, Kate knowingly smiled at her two companions, and they returned the same.

"So back to our story. Peter comes home from the war and settles back in, marries, and continues on at the saw mill with his father. By the early 1880s there's enough of a population here that he determines they need some local services. Folks are getting tired of going to St. J. or other towns for supplies and Peter gets the idea that he will build a general store here. And he does, in 1882, and you're sitting in it."

"Really? This place goes back to 1882?" asked Paul as he and Bruce started looking around, noticing, for the first time, details like the huge, random-width floorboards that obviously had seen over a century of wear, the square-headed nails in the floor and walls, and the 12-foot-tall, stamped tin ceiling that was elegant in any century.

"Yep, it sure does. Peter built this large building as both a store on the first floor, and a house above for his family—which by now included three kids. He also put in a pounded dirt basement with a rock wall foundation. Did a good job, too. The place is still standing, a hundred and thirty-seven years later, though it has gone through some major structural fixes."

"That's quite a story," said Bruce. "How does it get from 1882 to now, and to you?"

"Well, more patience, please. Two more generations follow Peter, through son Andrew and then his son Clive, who both ran the store. The mill died out in the 1890s when the forests had all been stripped bare, and the father-and-son duo of Andrew and Clive began a sometime lucrative and sometime losing whiskey distilling operation up in the hills. With a recipe brought from the old country they made cheap Scotch whiskey to sell in backroom deals throughout the Kingdom. Their whiskey-running adventures are legendary and they had some really close calls, until Clive was finally caught during prohibition, fined, jailed, and the operation shut down for good."

"So there's some criminal activity in the lineage, huh?" observed a smiling Paul.

"You betcha. Folks did whatever they needed to do to make a go of it up here. If they needed to bend the law a bit to feed their families, they'd do it. But I really want to get to the other important figure in this whole thing, Clive's son Simon, who was born upstairs in 1922. Actually, all of them were born upstairs, come to think of it," realized Kate.

"Simon Odderton came of age just in time for World War II and continued the Odderton tradition of military service. Incredibly enough, like his Great Grandfather Peter, who was at Gettysburg, Simon was in another famous and critical battle; he was in the second wave of marines storming Omaha Beach on D-Day. He was wounded, but not too badly, some shrapnel in the meaty part of his thigh. But before he was tended to he managed to crawl through enemy fire and drop a grenade into a German machine gun nest that had been cutting down our troops badly. He received the Silver Star for bravery. Simon returned here after the war, married Beth Peterson, and proceeded to have a family while running the Odderton Country store. They kept the family name for the store, by the way, never changing it to Odder*town*."

"So again, you know an awful lot of detail about these people and this store," observed Paul. "Why the interest?"

"Well you two are just too impatient! OK, here's the punch line. Simon's son, John Odderton, was born in 1947. John and his wife, Lynette, a gal from Cape Breton, had their only child, a baby girl, in 1980 and named her Kathryn, who went by Kate." She paused, waiting for the realization.

"Kate....well that's you!" exclaimed Paul. "This is all *your* family and you're an Odderton! Is that right?"

"You got it, pal. I'm Kate Odderton Langford, 8th generation Vermonter, at your service," she said, saluting her two new acquaintances.

"Well I'll be darned," observed Bruce. "So how did you come to run the place?"

"Well, now that's the sad part of the story, Bruce. My folks ran it right along with my grandfather since before I was born. I grew up in the store, played with dolls in the back, lived upstairs, went to school here. Things were great, I loved my childhood, we were all happy. Then in 1991, nine days before Christmas, my parents were driving home in a snow storm, hit a downhill icy patch, and ran off the road in the hills about two miles north of here. They rolled down a steep embankment toward Odder Creek, flipped twice, and then hit some trees. My dad died right away. Mom lasted two days but her injuries were too severe." Kate paused at this point, tearing up at the memories. Paul reached over and touched her shoulder with a sympathetic hand.

She sniffed, dried her eyes, and then continued after a moment. "Sorry, that part of the story is never easy to tell. So…once everything was settled, funerals and all, my grandparents took over raising me. Poor folks, they were in their early 70s at that point and sure didn't need an 11-year-old girl to raise, but there I was. And I loved them dearly and they couldn't have been nicer to me. Grampa Simon had been about ready to retire but he found himself back at the helm of the store. Not only was it the family business, but folks here really depended on the place and he couldn't let them down. So on he went, working more years than was good for him."

"So sorry to hear that, Kate," said Paul, with Bruce nodding in sympathy. "It must have been tough."

"We did OK," Kate pondered. "There was a lot of love among us and we clung to each other pretty tightly. And the town really supported us too. Grandma died in 2000 and Gramps lasted until last year. Was 96, bless his heart. One of the kindest, gentlest men you'd ever hope to meet. I miss him dearly."

"So your name is, what did you say, Langdon? Obviously you're married," observed Bruce.

"Actually, it is Langford, and I was, for eight years. To Jason Langford. I went to UVM after high school, where I got a degree in interior and landscape design. I got a job with a design firm in Boston, and eventually met Jason there. Got married when I was 28 and it ended eight years later. Turned out he had a desire for more female companionship than one woman could offer, and couldn't control it. God, I can't believe I'm telling you two all this. What am I *doing?*"

"Hey, you must feel comfortable with us, and sometimes it's easier to talk to a stranger," replied Paul. "But I gotta say, he must have been a total jerk to cheat on you!"

"Well thanks, and yes, he was. Glad I got rid of him. Anyway, that's my story and I'm sticking to it."

"Wait a minute, though," interjected Bruce. "How'd you get back here from Boston?"

"Oh yeah. Well, I really didn't like Boston anyway, I missed Vermont, and I wanted out, so Jason kind of did me a favor and moved the process along. A year after we divorced I came back here to help

Gramps with the store—he was already well into his 90s. It was only supposed to last until I found something here in my field. Then he died last year and willed the store to me, lock, stock, and barrel of debt. No other family alive. It's been in my family for six generations now and I feel a strong sense of obligation to keep it going, so here I am. I can't just walk away. Assuming, of course, I don't lose it. Business has been slow and I inherited some pretty heavy debt with the store."

"Really?" said Paul. "It'd be a shame to lose this place. I can see this is an iconic, historic building you have, and I feel really comfortable here. What would happen to it?"

"Probably get shut down and go back to the bank unless someone with deep pockets and a masochistic tendency came in and bought it. You know what they say about these things: wanna make a million bucks running a country store? Easy—start with two million! Well, enough of that, we'll see what happens. Hey, geez, look at the time! I gotta get back to work; I've taken too much time already, and my boss is a real hardass," joked Kate as she stood up and extended her hand. "It was really nice meeting you guys and spilling my family history right in your laps. Thanks for listening to my trials and tribulations. If I didn't bore you too much maybe you'll come back for another sandwich tomorrow and put me into the black."

"Fraid not, Kate," answered Bruce. "As much as we hate to leave this place, we're heading back down to Jersey tonight after a few more hours on a stream. Duty calls. But we sure enjoyed your place and your story. Thanks much for sharing."

"Yeah, same for me," added Paul, shaking her hand and getting a last look at those green eyes. "Good luck to you Kate. I hope you make it. And here's my card. If there's ever any way we can help, give me a call. Seriously, I mean that."

"Thanks, guys," she said, backing away toward the counter. "Travel well. Send your friends up here." She looked at the business card and it said "Paul G. Simon, Attorney-at-Law," with contact information. She put it in a corner with her business papers.

As her two new friends got ready to leave she glanced over and saw them reaching into their pockets, looking for something, and deep in quiet discussion. After they left she wandered over to clean the table and saw a folded piece of paper. Opening it up, five $20 bills spilled out. The note read "It's not much, but a little something to give a boost from two admirers. Hang in there, Kate."

She clutched the note to her heart, smiled, and wiped away a tear. Sometimes people truly were wonderful.

Chapter 4

Monday, June 10, 9:50 AM

"HEY, KID, THIS AIN'T A LIBRARY; BUY THE comic or get out!" said Lou, berating the young boy for sneaking a peak at her holdings. He put the comic back on the rack, walked toward the front door, and at the last minute stuck his tongue out at Lou and gave her a resounding 'ppptttttt' for emphasis. She gave him a false chase and a "damn you!" as he scooted out.

Louanne Quentin—Lou—waged an ongoing and never-ending battle with the Oddertown youngsters, and even some of the oldsters. In addition to running the gas station and garage, Lou sold cigarettes—which Kate refused to do—along with magazines, comic books, and candy in a small adjacent office/sales room.

She had been in love with comics since she was a kid—the way they looked, felt to her hands, even smelled—and still enjoyed buying, trading, and selling them. But she hated freeloaders who would come in and browse through her goods and then not buy them. She felt it was like taking a bite out of a sandwich or a spoonful of soup in a restaurant and then not buying the meal. Why would people think they could get a free sample of *her* merchandise when they couldn't do it elsewhere? You don't get to try out a towel or a bar of soap before you buy it; why should you try out a comic or magazine? No, you got no freebies with Lou Quentin and she was happy to staunchly defend her territory each day with her admonition that *this wasn't a damned library!*

For many of the townsfolk, it had become a challenging game to see what they could get away with before she caught them. One of the rights of passage for every kid in town was to go in and get a good peak at her comics. You were not admitted into adulthood in Oddertown without having had at least one good confrontation with Lou Quentin.

Lou was an interesting specimen. Mid-40s, she stood all of five feet tall but was solidly built with a 155-pound frame and looked like she could wrestle testosterone-enraged bulls and come out the winner. With short-cropped dark hair, numerous tattoos on her neck and arms, and a cigarillo usually dangling out of her mouth, Lou's name wasn't the only thing that was gender- vague. More than one customer passing through "from away" had mistakenly referred to her as "sir." They only did that once, and then usually did not remain in town for long.

Born and bred in Oddertown, Lou wandered into Burlington several years after high school and got a job at Girlington Garage, a female-owned and operated car-repair shop, where she spent nearly six years learning the auto repair trade. Knowing that there was no garage back home, but a real need, she saw the opportunity to start a business in Oddertown. It had done well ever since and she settled in and found her niche in life.

"Hey, Lou" called Billy Wilson from the garage. "We got a serpentine belt for an '08 Subaru in there?" Subaru's were, of course, the unofficial state car of Vermont, and outnumbered the next four most-popular models combined. Billy knew them backwards and forwards and could make most repairs in his sleep.

"When did you break your damned leg, Billy? Or did you maybe mistake me for your mother? Look for it your *own* damned self!"

Billy replied, "I just thought you were closer and. . ."

"You didn't think, and that's your problem, Billy. I ain't here to be your handmaiden, and I pay you a good salary. Go find it yourself!"

Despite outward appearances, Lou had made a great find in Billy Wilson, and they really appreciated each other in a grating, horn-locking, faux-fighting sort of way. Billy had been a car nut since he was nine when, without permission, he disassembled and reassembled the carburetor of his Dad's prize '68 Mustang. His backside was sore for three days after Johnny Wilson found out, but it began a burning passion for cars that could not be doused. Billy loved cars, all cars, and spent his life working on, thinking about, buying, and selling them. And he was a complete NASCAR devotee. Billy never missed a televised race and also did some racing of his own, when and where he could, though tracks and competitors were in limited supply in this neck of the woods. In short, Billy Wilson was happy as a pig in the mud working for Lou at the garage, and always sported his greasy NASCAR hat over his shaggy and unkempt light brown hair.

With Billy looking for the serpentine belt, the shop door opened and a "Hullo, Miss Loo" came from Raymond Pulan as he shuffled his way in. "How ahh you too-day?"

"Raymond, my dear," exclaimed Lou as she came around from behind the counter to hug her friend. "I'm fine now that you're here. And how are *you* doing?"

"I'm Ayy Ohh Kay," replied Raymond, exhibiting the OK sign with his thick index finger and thumb in a circle, and a big smile on his face.

Raymond Pulan was special to Lou. A 25-year-old man with Down Syndrome, Raymond was anything but a victim. He was high functioning, tried to be as independent as he could, and was one of the few people in town who could find and bring out Lou's soft spot, deeply hidden though it was. Raymond gave his bottomless well of love to everyone, easily and unconditionally. In return, Lou adored him and felt that the world would be a much better place if more people were like Raymond: gentle, innocent, giving, full of wonder. She sometimes felt that Down Syndrome was a gift rather than a burden.

Lou allowed Raymond privileges that nobody else in town could dream of. He had full access to all the comics, a chair in which to enjoy them, and always got a piece of candy of his choosing, on the house. Lou and Raymond were good friends and he brought out sides of her that she otherwise would not know she had. Raymond was a precious gift from the world, and the best teacher Lou ever had.

"Raymond, I have a new Spider Man just in. You want to see it?"

"You bet!" replied Raymond enthusiastically, his smile getting even bigger, if that was possible. He loved looking at Spider Man, and sometimes pictured himself scaling buildings, constructing webs, and fighting bad guys, a tall order for someone who found it a challenge to just make it up the cracked cement steps with his heavy and awkward gait.

As Raymond got settled in with Spider Man, Lou saw Larry Carson headed into the garage rolling a tire in front of him, trying not to get too dirty in the process, and was curious what was up. "Hey, Billy," Larry called. "Can you fix a flat for me real quick? I need to get this back in the car in a wicked big hurry!" he said, puffing from the exertion and haste of it all.

"Sure, but what's the rush?"

"I took my Dad's Forrester out last night to visit Becky Lefante over in Johnsville. He and Mom went out in her car and I'm not supposed to touch his precious Subaru after I dinged it last time out, but I wanted to see Becky real bad. I'll be darned, I got a flat on the way home. Think I might have picked up a nail. I changed it out but now need the flat fixed before he finds out I took the car. I was working at the store this morning when I look up and see his car parked right out front! So I quick grabbed the tire and ran it over here. I need to get it back real soon before he finishes up whatever he's doing in town."

"OK, gotcha, Lar. Gimme 15 minutes, 20 tops," replied Billy, happily joining the conspiracy.

"Awesome. Thanks, pal. I gotta get back to work

but I'll be back in 20. I owe you one," said Larry as he turned and hoofed it back to the store.

Billy lifted the tire into the water tank to locate the leak. He rolled the tire completely through the water but saw no air bubbles emerging anywhere. *Hmmm... thought Billy. I guess the pressure is too low to see a leak. Better add some air.*

Billy grabbed the compressor hose, set at 35 psi, and connected it to the tire valve. A little air pumped into the tire and then it stopped.

"What the hell?"said Billy. He grabbed a tire gauge, applied it to the valve, and it read 35 psi. "This tire ain't flat at all!" concluded Billy, looking back toward Odd Country. He walked to the grease-covered phone on the garage wall to call Larry.

Back at the store, Larry came through the front door and was greeted by Kate. "Hey, where you been?" she asked.

"Sorry, Kate, I had to run to the garage real quick." He proceeded to relate his tale of woe, sure that she would hold his confidence and not betray him to his father. He finished by saying how he saw his Dad's Subaru out front and took the opportunity to grab the flat out of the back and get it fixed before his Dad could find out.

"You mean that green Subaru there?" she pointed.

"Yeah, that's it."

"That green Forrester, parked right there?"

"Yep, that's the one."

"You mean the Forrester sitting there with the *Ohio* plates?" she added.

"Huh?" replied Larry, eyes flying open, head craning to look out the window. The sudden realization hit him. "Oh no, that's not my Dad's car!"

Chapter 5

Friday, June 14, 7:15 AM

—————————

"IT'S A BUNCH OF ENVIROTERRORIST CRAP!" expelled Phil Haderlie, summarizing his feelings on the matter. "They want to take over and scare everybody and have us living in caves. Hell, you can't have a big car, you can't burn coal, oil is evil, even cow farts are bad for the climate. Bunch of nonsense. World's been changing forever and that's all there is to it. Global warming's nothing but a bunch a hippie horse shit!"

"C'mon, Phil," replied Jubal Keller, "there's got to be some truth to it. You gotta admit, things here have been strange the last couple of years. Last winter was warm, we've been having more storms than we used to, more rain, sugaring season's been starting a couple weeks sooner. Things just seem different around here."

"Things have always been different around here, Jubal!" returned Phil. "The difference ain't no different than it ever was."

Paul Johnson chimed in. "Phil, thousands of scientists around the world have been studying this stuff for decades, measuring carbon dioxide, temperature, sea levels, glaciers, and a hundred other things, and can clearly show that the climate is changing, humans are mostly to blame, and the world is changing as a result. You can't deny all that."

"I sure as hell can deny them, Hippie Boy!" replied Phil. "You're listening to all the wrong people, Paul. *'Oh no, the ocean's rising, oh no, the birds are dying, oh no, its hot in Timbuktu, oh gosh, what are we gonna do?'*" Phil continued in a mocking, effeminate voice. "You should listen to people who don't just buy into what all these so-called 'experts' say, and who can think for themselves."

Jodi—who was out of school for the summer and could now work longer hours—came by with another refill of coffees and smiled at this latest installment of the argument of the day. She received a pretty good education on the human condition each morning from the Odd Balls, and payed attention to them more than they realized.

"Listen to who, Rush Limbaugh?" asked Silas Miller. "Glenn Beck? Sean Hannity?"

"Exactly!" answered Phil, beefy index finger pointed strongly at Silas. "They keep on top of this stuff and aren't bought and sold by the liberal media who are in cahoots on the whole sham. It's just a damn hoax to strip away our freedoms and have the liberals control us. And I'm not buying it, and if you had half a brain you wouldn't either, Silas."

As if punctuating Phil's last sentence, the door to Odd Country popped open and the bell dinged, announcing another early-morning customer. In walked Jim Watson, hardcover book in hand—his second reading of Howard Frank Mosher's classic "Northern Borders" set right there in the Northeast Kingdom—innocently looking for a quiet breakfast and a little quality reading time. Jim soon learned he was not in control of his morning.

"Hey, Doc," called Silas. "C'mon over here and settle something for us, would you?"

Jim naively and obediently ambled over to the corner table and scanned the Odd Balls, all looking up expectantly at him, their dirty breakfast plates piled up, refilled coffee mugs in hand: Phil Haderlie, Jubal Keller, Silas Miller, Steve Benson, Only Owens, Paul Johnson. All the usual suspects.

"Hey, fellas," Jim offered. "What's up?"

"You're the Wiz," Silas said, Jim subtly wincing at his unwanted title. "We want you to settle something for us. Is this global warming stuff for real or not? Phil says it's enviro-liberal crap, Paul says it's all real, and the rest of us are stuck somewhere in the middle. What's the deal with it? You study all this stuff, right? We'll believe what you say, won't we Phil?"

"I'll listen to 'em, that's all I can promise," replied Haderlie, sunburnt ham hock arms folded defiantly across his chest. "But I'll believe what I want to believe."

"C'mon, Phil," replied Silas. "This is the Wiz. He knows what he's talking about and we know him and trust him. He's practically one of us now. Let's see what he has to say on the matter. Give him a chance."

"I don't know, guys," said Jim. "I just came in for a little breakfast, not a lecture, and I don't want to get in the middle of your argument. This isn't a simple 'yes-no' thing. Well, it is, really, but it's more complicated than you might think."

"T-tell ya what, Doc," replied Steve Benson, pulling out an empty chair, "you sit down r-right here and we'll buy you b-b-breakfast, anything you want, w-won't we boys, and you can t-tell us all about it."

"Yeah, sure, great idea!" they all agreed enthusiastically. The group's momentum gave Jim little choice but to sit with them. This was the price he paid to society for his experience and reputation for knowing things, well-deserved or not. He was resigned to his early-morning fate, and Mosher would just have to wait.

Jodi came by and took his order—pancakes and sausages, OJ, and coffee—and left him to his fate with the Odd Balls.

"So go ahead, Doc, tell us about global warming," prompted Silas.

"You really want to go through this, guys?" replied Jim. "I gotta tell you, it's a long story without a happy ending."

"Sure, Doc, we've got p-p-plenty of time," replied Steve. "Give it to us s-straight."

"Alright, but don't say I didn't warn you," said the Doc, leaning forward and entering professional mode. "Well, first of all, let's get some terminology right. I've always felt that 'global warming' is not the best name for it. Sounds too nice and benign. Like, 'ahhh, a nice warm feeling, what's wrong with that?' No, not at all. It's proper name really is 'climate change' or, better yet, 'global climate disruption,' because that's what it is."

"Yeah, OK, we don't care about the names," Phil said. "I just don't believe anything is happening. I look out the window, it looks like it always did."

"Phil, you can't just look out your window, or consider the last year or two. This is a *global* event that is taking a long time to play out," explained Jim. "You have to consider the entire planet and decades and even centuries."

"Well I don't care about centuries, Doc. I don't likely have but a few years left, so I care about here and now," answered Haderlie.

"And there's the problem, Phil. Too many people are focused on the here and now. You have to look further and longer when thinking about a global climate disruption," answered Jim.

"I agree, Jim, but let's not get bogged down in terminology," interrupted Paul. "Tell Phil about some of the science and evidence."

"Yeah, sure, OK. So it starts with gasses in the atmosphere. Mostly carbon dioxide, or CO_2, but also methane and other gasses. When the sun beats down on the earth and bounces off back into space, these gasses trap heat and keep it here. That's why life is able to exist here at all; otherwise the earth would be cold and lifeless, like Mars. It's the greenhouse effect, basically the same thing that makes a greenhouse warmer inside than outside. Heat is trapped by various gasses in the atmosphere."

"Yep, so these gasses are good and keep us warm," replied Phil. "I'm all for that. What's the big deal then?"

Before he could reply, Jodi arrived with Jim's breakfast and set it down before him. He deftly spread butter on his pancakes and smothered them with maple syrup made not a ¼ mile away by Dave Johnson, Paul's older brother.

"The big deal, Phil," continued Jim, "is that the amount of CO_2 in the atmosphere has been going up steadily for several hundred years, due to our burning of fossil fuels. First coal, and then oil, mostly. It was about 280 parts per million in the mid-1700s, to over 400 ppm now, and continuing to rise each year. All this carbon that used to be locked away and stored in the ground is now in our atmosphere, trapping more heat. Two eighty to 400 is a *huge* increase, and the numbers are solid and indisputable."

"Now hold it right there, Doc," replied Phil just as Jim began stuffing some pancakes and sausages into his mouth. "I got two quibbles with you right off. First, I heard that carbon dioxide has been way higher in the past, much more than we have now. So what's the big deal? And two, how in the hell do they even know what it was in the past? We weren't able to take measurements back in the 1700s or before that, and nobody cared then anyway. Am I right or am I right?"

"Well, first question first, Phil. Yes, CO_2 definitely has fluctuated a great deal over time. But never as fast as we're seeing now, and never after humans had built major civilizations around the world, civilizations that have depended on a particular climate regime. In other words, these changes wouldn't have bothered people in the past because people either weren't around yet, or could easily adapt to the changes by moving. Sure, at times in the past the earth was a steamy place, when CO_2 was higher. And that just supports the idea that increased CO_2 causes climates to change." Jim downed a swallow of coffee.

"OK, so what about measuring? How do you supposedly know what happened in the past?" asked Phil.

"Sure. As far as measuring, we have really sensitive techniques to measure past CO_2 levels, largely through ice cores in glaciers. They pull out long cores of ice; they have air bubbles trapped in them, and that's the air that was present at the time the bubbles were made, hundreds of thousands of years ago right up to the present. So you can extract those bubbles and measure the amounts of any gasses from any period. We can go back over half a million years and get extremely accurate measurements of ancient atmospheres."

About this time Kate wandered nearby, leaned her butt on an adjacent table, arms folded in front, and watched the proceedings, quite interested in Doc's explanations. Jodi Simpson had also been listening intently from a distance.

"OK, so I give you this CO_2 stuff. They can measure it. So what?" said Phil. "I can still breathe just fine. I don't smell any carbon."

"You *can't* breathe just fine, Phil," interjected Jubal, "but it has nothing to do with carbon dioxide. You're an old fart who sucks air just walking across the room!"

They all laughed at their common experience that none were as vigorous as they once were, and their systems were failing one by one.

Bringing back the focus, Jim continued. "The 'so what,' Phil, is that all this extra CO_2, along with other gasses like methane, increases temperatures around the world. We know that for an absolute fact; both air and ocean temperatures have been rising over the last century or so. Not steadily, but definitely upward." Jim paused to sample more breakfast and wash it down with OJ. "Again, you can't argue with it. The numbers are there. Nobody's making them up."

"OK, fine, Doc, I accept that. I believe you know the numbers. Again, so what if it's a little warmer? Isn't that good? I mean who doesn't want it a little warmer? I can burn less wood in the winter and save money. That's great! These hippies and liberals make it sound like the damn world is gonna end next week if we don't do something. I don't buy it, even if your numbers are right."

"Phil, it isn't just that we'll get a little warmer. The whole climate is becoming disrupted. That means the global patterns that existed for centuries during which our civilizations were built up are changing, and quickly. It means more and bigger storms. It means more Irenes for Vermont and Sandys for New York. And other hurricanes in many places. It means changes in rainfall patterns—some places getting more rain, including flooding, and other places less, including droughts. It means changes in agriculture. If the Midwest gets consistently less rain it could reduce or even eliminate corn and soybean production in some places. The Southwest is in a long-term drought right now, and if that continues, it could literally dry up. Places like Phoenix, Tucson, L.A., Las Vegas, could lose their water supplies, which are questionable even going into this."

"Well I wouldn't mind that one bit," interjected Phil, with a laugh. "Them places just have a bunch of wackos anyway!" The others shook their heads and rolled their eyes at Phil's easy dismissal of millions of people.

"And if they dry up, Phil, where will they go?" asked Jim. "They will migrate to places with more water, places like Vermont. How would you like a half million refugees from the Southwest wanting to move into Vermont because we have water and they don't?"

"Hell no, and that's where my arsenal that you all laugh at will come in real handy!" responded Phil.

"C'mon, Phil, you know that's no answer," chimed in Paul. "Jim's being serious here; you need to hear him."

"I hear him fine, Hippie Boy," said Phil. "I just don't believe all this is gonna happen. Now it's an invasion of Vermont by millions of thirsty people! Jeezum Crow, what next? Martians? They're just trying to scare us to get their liberal way."

"Phil, it'll be this and a whole lot more," continued Jim, undaunted. "Glaciers are already melting around the world—we know that, we can measure it—and the sea level is rising. We can measure that too. Coastal cities around the world are likely to be anywhere from soggy to actually under water in the next half century. We're talking about places like Boston, New York, Baltimore, Washington, Miami, Tampa, New Orleans, and I could keep going right around the US and into Asia and Europe; London, Cairo, Calcutta, on and on. We're talking hundreds of millions of people, over a billion, displaced, forced to come inland and upland. I hope you have lots of ammunition for those guns of yours, 'cause you'll need it."

"I won't be here then so I'm not worried," replied Phil with confidence.

"Do you have kids, Phil, grandkids?"

"Yeah, Doc, you know I do."

"And I know you love them. They'll be dealing with all this and more. I hope they won't count on maple syrup or the ski industry for a living, because both may be gone from Vermont in 50 years or less," added Jim. "What happens when maple trees start dying because it's too warm? What happens to the ski industry when we get more rain than snow each winter? What happens to your friends around here who cut and sell firewood or plow roads and driveways as a good part of their income? What happens when that all declines?"

"Doc, I just don't believe this will all happen. I keep hearing the other sides of this, people who say this is wrong, the patterns aren't there, it's actually getting cooler. I hear of scientists who disagree with all this, who say there's no evidence for this. What about them?" asked Haderlie.

"There are a few scientists out there who disagree, Phil. They are in a tiny minority, and they usually aren't in a field that actually has expertise in this area. And we know for an absolute fact that the fossil fuel industry has funded a huge disinformation campaign for years to cast doubt on the science. But Phil, there are literally thousands of scientists around the world who have done tens of thousands of studies, and they've concluded, with something like 97% certainty, that this is all happening."

"So they don't all agree? Or they aren't completely sure, you admit that then, Doc?" asked Phil.

"Phil, nothing in science is 100% certain. We work with probabilities all the time, and we never say we are absolutely certain about anything. We are always open to further evidence, further testing, refinement of theories and perspectives. So yes, there is not complete, 100% certainty on this. That's how science works."

"So you're really not sure about this climate change then?" challenged Phil.

"No, Phil, we can't be 100% sure. But let me ask you this. Suppose you were getting on a plane in Burlington, flying to Chicago. You learn that 100 aeronautical engineers inspected the plane, and 97 of them said it is not flight worthy and is likely to crash. Three of them say they think the plane is safe and will do just fine. Would you get on the plane because there is not 100% certainty it will crash?"

"Hell no, I'd get off and wait for the next plane," laughed Phil, with the others joining in.

"Of course, and that's the obvious smart decision. Nobody would fly if the experts were 97% sure it was going to crash. But the experts in climate change are 97% sure that this is occurring and it is mostly caused by humans and that there will be extremely bad consequences for the planet, yet many people are skeptical and don't want to believe them. The problem is, Phil, if the scientists are right, there is no 'next plane' to wait for. There's no other planet to go to; we don't have that option. This is it, this is our only plane, it is in flight, and there is that 97% figure hanging over us. We can't wait for the next one to come along. That's why we need to fix this one, Phil! That's why we desperately need to address climate change in a big way, right now." Jim was gaining momentum and getting caught up in an emotional reply, his voice gaining in volume and intensity.

"And that's why this generation of political leaders—going back to the 1990s—will be known as the worst and most ineffectual group of leaders the world has ever known," he continued, "because they were repeatedly told about this, they mostly ignored or disputed the warnings, and did way too little, way too late. They stuck to the status quo, they ignored all the warnings, they fiddled while Rome burned. Through their inaction, stalling, and outright denial, they are condemning the world to misery for the next thousand years or more. And I'm sorry to say, Phil, it is almost entirely your conservative friends who are to blame. *They* are the ones who are denying this. *They* are the ones who have long blocked effective solutions. I even heard one idiot Republican Congressman recently suggest that the oceans were rising because rocks were falling in! If that's the level and quality of national discussion we're having on the subject, we are doomed."

Jim stopped his mini-lecture, took a deep breath, calmed down, and returned to his breakfast. The boys sat and looked at one another, some eyebrows raised. Even Phil was quiet, and seemed to be pondering.

"Well, I warned you," concluded Jim. "You asked for it and you got it. Told you it wasn't a happy ending."

A few minutes later, on his way out of the store, Jodi stopped Dr. Watson and asked him several questions she had about climate change and other environmental issues. They huddled in a corner and he patiently answered all her queries for a good 10 minutes before he walked out, Mosher book under his arm.

As Kate went back to work she marveled at Jim's solid grasp of reality and ability to see the big picture. For a moment his take on climate change made her financial problems at Odd Country seem pretty insignificant and put them in a whole different perspective. But only for a moment.

Chapter 6

Wednesday, June 19, 7:05 PM

"OK, EVERYONE, QUIET DOWN PLEASE," instructed Board Chair Caleb Smith. "It's a little after 7 and I'd like to call this special meeting of the Oddertown Select Board to order. Please find a seat if you can. David, are there any more seats available back there?"

"One or two," replied David Johnson. "Still lots more folks trying to come in."

"OK, let's see if we can get everyone in. Please scoot your chairs together, folks. Make room please." Caleb waited a minute for everyone to settle down.

The weather was unusually warm for a June evening and the room was stifling hot, even with the windows open. Caleb wasn't sure how this would work. Normally a Select Board meeting drew a half dozen people at most, but this emergency meeting was really packing them in. There were already 35 or 40 squeezing into the Oddertown Library, above the Town Office, in a room meant for half that number.

"Caleb, there's still eight or ten more outside trying to get in. We're never gonna fit 'em all," reported David.

Caleb thought for a second and turned to Kate, seated to his left; they had a brief discussion and she nodded her head in agreement.

"Folks, there's too many of us to fit in to our library so Kate has kindly agreed to open up the store for us. We will temporarily adjourn the meeting and re-convene across the street in 10 minutes. There should be plenty of room for everyone over there."

The grateful crowd began to shuffle out, relieved they would have a little more elbow room in the store, where it would also be cooler; they filed down the stairs and moved across Time Square and up the street to Odd Country.

When Kate arrived with the key there were already more than 50 people crowding the large porch and steps, and they parted like the Red Sea for Moses, letting her through. She unlocked the door, found the light switch, and illuminated the store. Townsfolk began piling through and arranged themselves at the tables in the eating area, soon filling all the chairs. The others stood in the back, lined the walls, and filled the aisles; fortunately, the shelves were low enough for an average-height person to see over them. The three Select Board members—Caleb, Kate, and Gregory Mitchell—stood behind the serving counter, facing everyone.

Caleb Smith was the much-beloved Chair who had served on the Board for more than 20 years now and counting. Despite his job as the Oddertown Postmaster—where he worked in the tiny mailbox cubicle within Odd Country when not out delivering mail—and a small flower business he ran on the side out of his garage, he devoted countless hours to the town he loved, and volunteered wherever help was needed. Standing six foot four and weighing a scant 178 pounds, with a mostly bald head and a large, hooked nose, Caleb called to mind an undernourished scarecrow. Anything but scary, he was the nicest man you'd ever hope to meet and you could always count on Caleb for whatever help was needed. Everyone in town thought highly of him and trusted him completely.

Gregory Mitchell was a 48-year-old teacher at the elementary school who was in his second term on the Board. If there was an award for the most boring person in the Northeast Kingdom, Gregory (never "Greg") would have been strong in the running, if not the outright winner. Physically average in every conceivable way, and as socially bland and uninteresting as white milk, he also was smart, stable, impeccably honest, and wholly dedicated to whatever task he was given. You may not want to play poker with him on Friday nights, but Gregory Mitchell was the perfect Select Board member.

Kate Langford rounded out the Board; elected last year, she was still learning the ropes. Kate really did not have time for this job, with all her financial challenges at Odd Country, but everyone in town knew and liked her and she was well regarded. With her family's deep history in the town, her growing up here, and her excelling academically and athletically at North Country Union High—home town girl done good—she could hardly turn down their demands that she serve.

"Alright, everyone, please settle down," began

Caleb. "I'm re-convening this special meeting of the Oddertown Select Board. I know it's warm and crowded in here, but please make yourselves as comfortable as you can. As you know, we are here to discuss the situation with our police cruiser. This is a potentially costly item for us and we'd like to minimize the impact on everyone. I'd like to start out by having Chief Johnsgaard explain to everyone what has happened. Carl?"

Carl Johnsgaard was the Oddertown Chief of Police and the sole police officer in town. Now in his eighth year on the job, with a wife and six-year-old son, he was settled into the job for the long haul. Standing six feet tall and solidly built, with a friendly and approachable face, but with a no-nonsense demeanor when he needed it, Carl Johnsgaard was a good choice for this job. People liked, respected, and trusted him.

"Thanks, Caleb. As some of you know, four nights ago the engine on the cruiser pretty much blew out. Without going into all the details of the damage, Billy Wilson estimates it will cost about $3200 to fix. He also reminded me that the transmission is on its last leg and likely won't make it past the end of the year. That would be another three grand or so. The car is a 2001 model and has over 180,000 miles on it, some hard miles too. Rather than throw good money after bad fixing it up, it might be a good idea for the town to consider replacing the cruiser altogether."

"And how much will *that* cost us?" came a voice from the back.

Carl turned toward Caleb with a questioning look. Caleb told him to go ahead and respond.

"Well, as much as I'd like a new cruiser, I'm actually recommending a used one," explained Carl, "which is much more affordable. Traditionally, the standard police cruiser was the Ford Crown Victoria, but they stopped making them a few years back. A real shame, they really did the job. Other vehicles have been used including a Ford Interceptor, several Jeep models, various Chevies, and so on. The one I'm recommending is a real nice used Chevrolet Suburban, available at the state excess property lot in Waterbury. It has the advantage of being a little larger and could carry bigger items in the back when needed."

"Carl, give us some numbers, would ya?" said Caleb.

"Sure." Chief Johnsgaard pulled out and consulted a small notepad. "A typical new cruiser—not a Suburban but a sedan—would go in the $32,000 range, plus another $6,000 to outfit it, so we're pushing 40 grand. This Suburban is a 2015 model with about 55,000 miles on it. New and fully outfitted we're talking $45,000. This used one, also fully outfitted for police work, is available to us for $16,900. It was used by the Newport Police Department."

"What kind of shape is it in, Carl?" asked Gregory Mitchell. "We don't want to buy someone else's problems, you know."

"Billy and I went over yesterday to have him check it out," responded Carl. "Billy, what did you think?"

Billy Wilson stood nervously, not used to speaking in public before so many people, and hesitated while he looked over the crowd, over a hundred anxious eyes fixed on him, waiting expectantly for his report. "Well, Chief, umm… I, uhh, I think it's a pretty good deal. The. . . uhh, the basic mechanics are good. Body's in good shape. . . uhh, engine, trannie, differential are good. Frame is sound." Billy paused and took a deep breath before continuing. "Could use a new set a tires, battery, some belts, a few other things. Would cost maybe another $800 or so to get 'er up to speed, but I think you'd have a good car there." Billy sat down self-consciously, glad that his major oratory was over. He had been nervous for the last two hours, knowing he'd be called upon.

"OK, so we're talking 18 grand in round numbers," concluded Caleb. "That about right?"

"Yeah, that should more than cover it, Caleb," replied Carl.

"Carl, is this all that's available to us through the state?" asked Caleb.

"Yeah, that's it for now; there's no indication the state expects any others coming along soon. I should add we do need to move quickly if we want this one. We're first in line, but need to commit this week, after which they'll release it to another party."

"Gregory and Kate, how do you feel about going for a used vehicle versus a new one versus trying to fix the one we have?" asked Caleb.

Kate thought for a few seconds and replied, "I don't see that we have much of a choice, Caleb. We surely can't afford a new one, and I'm not even sure how we'd pay for the used one, but it's a much smaller hill to climb. And I agree we shouldn't throw money into the old one; we'd just have to replace it soon anyway. And we can't do without a police car. So I say let's try and get this vehicle."

"I concur," added Mitchell. "I don't see any other options."

"As do I," added Caleb Smith. "So the Board is unanimous in pursuing a used, rather than new, vehicle. I now open it up to the floor for comment. Anyone wish to speak for or against a used vehicle? Or for trying to fix the old one?"

"Yeah, I'll speak," called Charlie Harbrough from the back wall as the crowd girded themselves for his typical attack on whatever was being debated. "I don't think we need a cop at all. There's no real crime in Oddertown and we put a lot of tax money into having Barney Fife here on our payroll."

"Charlie," interrupted Caleb, "I'll remind you that we speak respectfully of others in our meetings. No name calling, please. Regardless of your personal opinions, Carl is a town employee, he works hard for us, and he deserves your respect."

Carl maintained a look of quiet demeanor and showed no emotion in response to Charlie or Caleb; he well knew the truth about his work and his worth to the town. Carl grew up in Oddertown and got into law enforcement in an unusual and brutally unfortunate manner. When he was 18, a week before his high-school graduation, his 16-year-old sister was raped by a drifter passing through. Such a crime was unheard of in these parts and shocked Oddertown, and villages throughout the Kingdom, to the core. Local law enforcement was sparse and ineffective back then so Carl took the matter into his own hands. He found the rapist at the edge of town, and in a fit of blind rage and with the full power of vigilante justice, beat him to a bloody and unrecognizable pulp in the deep woods near Odder Creek. The man was never seen in the area again,

and nobody questioned Carl's wounds or the where-
abouts of the rapist, though they were quietly grateful for his actions.

It was while walking home with bruised and
bloody knuckles, two broken fingers, a broken toe,
and crying like a baby, that young Carl Johnsgaard
decided to go into police work; he swore an oath to
himself and to God that nothing like that would
ever again darken their town or affect his family,
and he had kept that promise to this day. Given
his arduous journey, Charlie Harbrough's ignorant
comments meant nothing to Carl.

"Yeah, fine, alright. I still don't think we need to
spend money on a cop," replied Charlie. "I think
when that big nasty crime spree hits—like, oh, I
don't know, a speeder coming through town—we
can call the state police. Our taxes are too damned
high already and he's a big chunk of them. Get rid
of 'em and problem solved. You can even refund
some of our taxes!" Charlie's voice got louder and
more emphatic as he went.

"Now hold on, Charlie," came a voice from along
the wall. It was Tony Delfasio. "I disagree completely. We need a cop in town, and he does lots
more than deal with crime, which I agree is low.
He's there whenever anyone gets in trouble and
needs assistance. When we had that flood two years
ago Carl was out there leading rescue operations
and getting folks to safety. He makes sure our kids
get to and from school safely. He deals with animal
control, he's a communication pipeline to the State
Police, and on and on. I think he does a lot for us."

"And did you ever think, Mr. Harbrough, that
we have so little crime *because* of the Chief?" came a
soft voice from the front row. It was Emily McIntyre,

young teacher at the school. "I think he's a deterrent to crime and well worth the cost. I feel much safer knowing he's here on the job, and I'd like to thank him for his dedication."

"Ahh, I think you're all nuts. We don't need a cop any more'n a cow needs a hat," replied old Charlie.

"Charlie, you're a damned old fool, so why don't you just shut the hell up!" expelled Willard Bennett, the only person in the place with a little elbow room.

"Now, Willard, I'll remind you as well to be respectful. Charlie has as much right to an opinion here as anyone else," reminded Caleb.

"Stupid though it may be," came a wry, anonymous voice from an aisle behind one of the shelves, followed by a chorus of chuckles.

"Alright, enough of the name calling," said Caleb, trying to regain control of the meeting. "Does anyone else have a specific and constructive comment on the proposal at hand, to purchase this used police vehicle?"

"I think it's fine," offered Phil Haderlie.

"Me too," added Lou Quentin.

Several other affirmatives were heard around the room. An obvious consensus was being reached, with 'Charlie Horrible' the only one vocally opposed, his sour-faced and hand-waving disgust expressing his typical displeasure with anything the town ever did.

"OK, if there's no further discussion, let's take a formal vote of the Board," directed Caleb. "All in favor of purchasing the vehicle in question say 'aye.'" Three "ayes" were heard. "None opposed, the proposal passes. Now for the tricky part: how to pay for it. Obviously we have not budgeted for this item, and $18,000 is a significant addition to an annual town budget of $382,000. That's nearly a 5% unplanned hit. Our new fiscal year starts in just over a week and that budget and the tax rate is already set. Next year's budget won't be decided until Town Meeting next March. The soonest we could have this budgeted is next July, over a year from now. So we're in a bit of a pickle and need to discuss options."

Some murmurs went through the room as reality began to replace optimism.

"Yeah, you're all so gung ho about your cop, how ya gonna pay for it? Not so positive *now*, huh?" Charlie again, on cue.

"How about reserve funds," came a query from Lauren McCallum. "Don't we have reserve or emergency funds?"

"We do, Lauren," answered Caleb, "but they are very low. Between trying to keep taxes low and then covering road damages from our storm two years ago, we are down to about $1500 in reserve funds, which is a really dangerous position to be in. We tried to raise taxes last budget cycle to build the fund back up, but you'll recall that no one was willing to entertain a tax increase over 2%. In fact, the first two budgets were voted down, as you remember. So we haven't been able to rebuild the fund, and now we see the down side of that."

"Well if you didn't spend so goddamn much on useless stuff around town you'd have money for your reserve fund," pitched in Charlie.

"Charlie, please watch your language, and we are not here to discuss the town budget or spending. Tonight we need to find a way to replace our police vehicle. Let's please focus on that," said Caleb. "So let's look at our options. There are four I can think of: one, cut back all spending by nearly 5% across the board and redirect to the police car; two, make one or more targeted cuts—that is, a specific area or areas would be cut back and redirected, library, road crew, administration, maintenance, and so forth—targeted cuts would incur well more than 5% hits, probably 10-20%; three, approve an emergency supplementary assessment on all property taxes, raising the money, again, close to 5%; and four, borrow the money in a municipal loan and pay it back over time. Each has down sides, obviously. I'll open the floor to discussion."

Numerous comments flew around the floor, for or against various options. Some favored an across-the-board spending cut, while others wanted to target specific programs. All were quite predictable, such as those who didn't use the library wanting to cut it deeply, while others would staunchly defend it, nearly to the death. Retirees were happy to zero out the tiny Fourth of July celebration with fireworks—saving all of $800—while parents with small children who looked forward to the show all year shot them daggers. It soon became apparent that cutting anything was not an option, as somebody's ox would be gored. With the nearly lone exception of Charlie Horrible, the crowd came to the realization that raising more money—either through a supplementary tax assessment or a loan—was the only palatable option.

"So let's get a loan for $18,000," concluded Lou Quentin. "Then we can pay it back over time and it won't be so painful. We get the car and have no tax increase right now."

"Sounds good to me," responded Only Owens.

"M-me too," added Steve Benson.

"And me," added Silas Miller. The Odd Balls were all climbing on board, and the collective wisdom in the room seemed to coalesce around this option. Quick, easy, painless.

"So I'm getting the sense that borrowing the money is the way most of you want to go," concluded Caleb. "Am I hearing that correctly?"

The crowd mostly nodded and confirmed his impression. They liked the idea that their taxes would not be affected, at least not this year. Then Jim Watson's hand went up.

"Yeah, Jim, go ahead," nodded Caleb.

Jim stood up to address the crowd. "Well, folks, I'm not so sure this is the best way to move ahead. Sure, it's painless now but think about a year or two down the road. You still have to raise taxes to pay off the loan, plus interest, and you will still have a nearly empty reserve fund. What about other emergencies? What if we get another storm, or the fire truck breaks down, or there's some other unforeseen event? Then we're in the same place, with no reserves. I believe we need to bite the bullet and think about the future. If we impose a one-time supplemental tax assessment now, we carry no debt. Then next year we can begin to build up the reserve fund gradually, with small tax increases, and protect ourselves against future surprises. Nobody likes higher taxes—I sure don't—but the fact is it costs money to run a decent town and have the services we all want. None of this comes free. We can put ourselves on a better financial footing if we admit that we've been unrealistic in our budgeting and start to build up reserves for the future. So I urge you to consider taxing ourselves now for the car. Let's get it behind us and move on. I don't think it would be all that huge a tax bill."

"Yeah, that's easy for you to say, you don't work two jobs to make ends meet," replied Steve Hudson, electrician and part-time landscaper. Others confirmed that any tax increase would be a burden.

"Well, I think Dr. Watson makes a good point," observed Kate Langford. "Why don't we at least estimate what an average tax increase would look like so we know what we're talking about? Then we're in a better position to decide."

"Good idea, Kate," replied Caleb. "Gregory, you're our resident number cruncher and I see you have your calculator with you. Can you run some numbers?"

"Yeah, sure, Caleb," replied Gregory obediently. He ran some figures based on the number of property holders in Oddertown and the amount they needed to raise and came up with an average supplementary assessment of $90, or a 4.7% rate.

"So the $90 figure per household is simply an average for the town," concluded Caleb. "For those who can least afford it, your increase would actually be less, maybe $60 or even $50. For those with higher property values, it might be as much as $150 or so. That's the ballpark we're looking at. Remember, folks, this is for police protection for everyone, not some luxury that we could live without. We're not talking new playground equipment or a welcome sign at the edge of town. I think this is a wise investment. Jim, I like your perspective that we bite the bullet, no pun intended, and get this done, rather than have it hang over us as a loan for five years. Then we could really focus on building the reserve fund against such emergencies in the future."

General discussion ensued, with the usual suspects, such as Charlie Horrible and a few others, opposing any immediate tax, but with the majority starting to see the wisdom, if grudgingly so, of an emergency tax assessment. The crowd gradually reached the consensus that they would be better off as a community in the long run if they agreed to it.

"Folks, I'm not clear about the law here, and whether the Select Board can vote for this tax," informed Caleb. "But even if we could, I am not comfortable with three of us making that decision for the citizens of Oddertown. I think taxation should always be *your* decision, just like approving a budget each March. Because this was a legally warned meeting, with possible tax implications clearly stated, I would like us to vote now, as a community, on whether or not to impose a one-time emergency tax on ourselves, at the level of 4.7% of your present tax rate. All funds raised would go toward buying the police vehicle as discussed. Any extra funds would be placed exclusively into our reserve fund. Are the terms clear to you?"

They all nodded their heads that they understood.

"Alright, we will take a hand vote and see how that goes. Gregory, please count hands on the left; Kate, count on the right. All in favor of this assessment, please raise your hand, high, and keep it up."

Gregory and Kate counted their respective sides of the room and reported in. They counted 33 and 29 "yes" votes, respectively.

"Alright, now all opposed, please raise your hands." Three hands went up, including Charlie's.

"The vote clearly passes, 62 to 3. Thank you all. Sue Granger, as town Clerk you are hereby instructed by the Select Board to mail out an emergency tax assessment notification to all taxpayers. Can this be done within one week?"

"I'll do my best, Caleb. I'll have to set some other work aside, but nothing too time critical right now," replied Sue. She was an efficient and experienced Town Clerk and the Select Board had every confidence in her abilities.

"That would be fine, Sue, and we will try to leave you alone to get that done. Thanks. To wrap this up," continued Caleb, "I'd like to thank Chief Johnsgaard and Billy Wilson for finding this vehicle and bringing us the information we needed to make an informed decision. Chief, please inform the folks at the state that we want the car, and do whatever it takes to get that ball rolling." Carl nodded in understanding. "And much appreciation goes to Dr. Watson for having us see the wisdom of going ahead with this action. It is never pleasant to impose a new tax, but I do believe in the long haul we will be glad we did. This way we can focus on our reserve fund and budget stability. Thank you so much, Jim, for your typically wise assessment of things."

"My pleasure, Caleb," Jim replied with a modest wave of his hand. He really didn't like attention drawn to him, or to have himself set apart intellectually from his neighbors, but it was becoming his lot in life here in Oddertown. He was, after all, the Wizard of Odd, like it or not.

"And I would especially like to thank the good people of Oddertown for participating tonight, and for the reasoned and productive discussion, regardless of your views. It takes many people with varied opinions to make up a community worth living in, and I am personally happy and proud to call all of you my friends and neighbors. Thank you so much for seeing the importance of civic participation and supporting the town even when it hurts your pocketbook. This meeting is adjourned."

As the crowd began to shuffle out and the Select Board members closed up their notebooks, Kate made her way over to Jim Watson. "Hey, Doc, I want to thank you for showing us the way forward tonight. You seem to have a knack for seeing through problems and analyzing them clearly. We really appreciate having you here in town."

"My pleasure, Kate. Sometimes it just takes a little thinking outside the box, or stepping back from the problem and seeing it a little more clearly," replied Jim in his typical humble manner.

"Jim, speaking of outside the box, I wonder if I could pick your brain on another financial matter? You'd get a free dinner in return, home-cooked, of course. Can I invite you over one night soon? We can have a nice dinner and you can solve my problems all in one shot."

"Kate, I'd be happy to, though I can't promise I can help you. Can you give me a clue what you're talking about?"

"It's the store. I'm in a real financial mess. Deep hole. I don't want to discuss it now, but maybe if I lay it out there for you, you might see something I don't. Wanna give it a try?"

"Uh, sure. When?"

"I can't do it tomorrow," said Kate, "but what about Friday, say seven o'clock?"

Jim smiled. "I think my normally crowded social calendar might just be open that night," he said, then laughed. "I can probably squeeze you in. How's about I bring a bottle of wine?"

"Not necessary, but wouldn't be turned down either." said Kate. "I'll look forward to it. And thanks."

"Don't thank me yet, I haven't done anything. I can only promise I'll keep up my end of the eating!"

Chapter 7

Friday, June 21, 7:01 PM

———

A S HE ASCENDED THE WORN, WOODEN outside stairs to the back door of Kate Langford's house up above Odd Country, Jim Watson admired the ancient and gnarled elm tree shading the back half of the structure, its huge branches spreading widely in a quiet and dignified manner. He understood the tree was already a modest presence when the store was constructed in 1882 and it had made many a warm summer afternoon comfortable for six generations of Oddertons. Unfortunately, it was not working so well for Jim today.

For some reason that he could not fathom, Dr. James D. Watson felt unsettled going to Kate's for dinner, and the small beads of perspiration appearing on his forehead seemed out of proportion to the mild temperature. Although it had hit the mid-80s by early afternoon, it was now a comfortable 73 and falling quickly, and Jim had showered no more than an hour ago; the sweat was a result, he believed, of the anxious feeling in his stomach. Could he be nervous because he was having dinner with an attractive, single woman? Cripes, he had lectured in front of big classes, given scientific talks to hundreds, and never got nervous. Yet here he was, going to Kate's, Dr. Butterfly Stomach. He told himself that surely she had nothing more in mind than picking his brain, as she had so clearly stated. Still, his imagination had gotten the better of him and he was on edge. You just never knew with women. At least Jim Watson didn't, having had precious little experience with them before Maggie, and none at all since.

A knock quickly brought a smiling Kate to the wooden screen door. "Hi Jim," she said, swinging it open. "Welcome and thanks for coming."

"Well thank you for the invite, Kate. I've been looking forward to this home-cooked meal. I understand you're a pretty darned good cook."

"I don't know that I'd say that, but I do love to cook when I have the time. My grandmother taught me so much in the kitchen. But usually by the end of the day I'm pretty beat, and with just me here I'm never motivated to cook a big meal. It's nice to have someone special to cook for tonight."

Jim didn't quite know how to take that 'someone special' comment, and it didn't help the situation on his glistening forehead one bit. There followed a moment of awkwardness until he remembered the bottle of wine he was carrying. "Oh, here's some wine to help grease the wheels a bit."

"Jim!" said Kate, smiling. "And here I was thinking you're a gentleman!"

"What?" Jim blushed. "Oh no, I didn't mean anything....uh, I what I meant was, you know, the thought process. Grease the wheels of the thought process."

Kate laughed at his flustered response and said "Relax, my friend, I know just what you meant, and thank you for the wine."

A relieved Jim quickly added, with an embarrassed smile, "Got it from downstairs, of course." As with most general stores in Vermont, and even many gas stations, Kate's wine shelves were diverse and well stocked. She had many selections, ranging from inexpensive box and jug wines through a rich supply of mid-range wines, and on up to a few selections in the $30-$40 range, usually bought only by tourists passing through. Even in remote outposts in Vermont, you were never far from a good selection of wines. Beers too. Vermonters were nothing if not picky and demanding when it came to adult beverages.

"19 Crimes," said Kate, cradling the bottle. "Yeah, I saw that our supplier added that one a couple weeks ago. I'm not familiar with it. What a funny name!"

"I've had 19 Crimes before," responded Jim, "and I think it's really good. It's Australian, a red blend. The name comes from when Australia was a penal colony for England. There were 19 different stated crimes that could get you sent there. Each cork is labeled with one of the crimes. I've started a collection and want to get all 19. I'm anxious to see which one this is."

"Well then you better open up that puppy right now," suggested Kate. "Here's a corkscrew."

Jim applied the instrument to the cork, popped it out, and read the crime printed on the side:

"Number 12. Bigamy," he announced. Even the darned cork reinforced his nervousness, as in a strange way he felt like he was cheating on Maggie just by being here.

"Bigamy? Good thing you're not married," responded Kate with a broad smile and a cocked eyebrow, misinterpreted by Jim as flirtatious; he could feel a blush coming to his face. Seeing that, and immediately regretting a comment that would have reminded Jim of his loss of Maggie, she quickly added "I guess Mormons would not have done well over there." Another awkward moment hung between them.

Jim immediately re-directed the subject. "I have two other corks so far. Number 10 is 'stealing fish from a pond or river' and 5 is 'impersonating an Egyptian.' I can't imagine why someone would have wanted to impersonate an Egyptian or why that would be dealt with by shipping them off to Australia."

"Wow, that's bizarre! I wonder if they had a big problem with people impersonating Egyptians back then?" responded Kate. "And stealing fish? Now was that *any* fish or only certain types? Or was there a minimal number that would get you in trouble? How strange. Sure glad we're not living in England back then. We'd probably be in all sorts of trouble!"

Again, Jim didn't know how to take that. Was that a general 'we,' meaning modern society, or a specific 'we,' the two of them tonight, in this situation? Jim tried to stifle his imagination, while wishing he knew women a whole lot better.

"Well, give me a couple of glasses and let's try this out," he said, mostly to divert his crazy thoughts to something more concrete. He poured the wine, they swirled it in their glasses, and each sniffed the bouquet.

"Well, cheers and salud," said Kate, clinking glasses with Jim.

"Cheers," he replied, now back out of his head and into reality. They both sampled while inhaling some air to get the fullness of the flavors, which soon exploded on their tongues.

"Wow, that *is* good," concluded Kate. "Nice full, rich flavors, lots of depth to it. Thanks for introducing me to this criminal world of yours."

"My pleasure," replied Jim, glad to have the wine tasting behind them. "So what's for dinner? I brought a pretty good appetite."

"Well here's some Vermont cheddar from Jasper Hill, with Castleton crackers to get us started. Let's see, I have 'Rutland Multi-seed Rye' and 'Middlebury Maple.'"

"Two of my favorites," replied Jim. He quickly recognized that, as with many Vermonters, the origins of food were important to Kate. She was a localvore, and tried to get her food from as close to home as possible, while avoiding the corporate garbage that so much of America feasted upon and was being poisoned by, with the double-dagger result of making corporations rich and Americans obese. She also tried to go organic whenever she could and avoid the rich chemical mix that came with industrial food.

"Great!" she said. "Me too. Then I thought we'd start out with a garden salad; I just picked some lettuce, spinach, and arugula from my garden."

"I didn't know you had a garden," responded a surprised Jim. "Where is it?"

"It's kind of hidden back in the far corner of the lot. There's a small spot in the northeast corner where sunlight actually gets through. That six-foot wooden fence behind the yard makes it nice and private back there. I have a small garden and a little sitting area, complete with a soothing fountain. I love to go back there with a good book when I can. It's my escape from reality, which I need a lot more of these days."

"Don't we all," chuckled Jim.

"So then the main course is a chicken harvested by Paul Johnson last night, slow roasted with my garden herbs. And a side of my snow peas and baby onions simmered in a vegetable broth, with a hint of mint, unintentionally poetic though that may be."

"Sounds good enough to eat," said Jim, while munching down on a cracker with a hunk of cheddar. "Doesn't get any fresher than that."

They soon proceeded with dinner, which was nothing short of exquisite to Jim. The salad was crisp and fresh, with a tangy garlic-and-herb dressing of Kate's own design. The chicken was moist and tender inside, with a crisp and savory skin, just as he liked it. The hearty aroma alone was worth the price of admission. The snow peas and onions were cooked to perfection, with a hint of crispness and some life left to them, and a burst of flavor that could not be approached by supermarket veggies. Kate indeed knew her way around a kitchen; her grandmother had taught her well. Jim was pleased that the small talk now was easy and unforced; he soon relaxed and the butterflies in his stomach were replaced with comforting food and wine. He could get used to this.

"Kate, that was an extraordinary meal!" said Jim, pushing his plate away and leaning back while rubbing his belly. "You are some incredible cook. Thanks so much."

"Oh, my pleasure, Doc. It really is nice to cook for someone who appreciates it, and it was all pretty simple fare. If you really want to be impressed, some-day I'll have to treat you to my beef bourguignon, which is an all-day process, but well worth it in the end. Shoot, if the store keeps going the way it is, I may have lots of time on my hands for things like that."

"So I guess that's our cue to begin talking about your financial problems," observed Jim.

"Do you mind? Maybe we could chat for a while and then when you figure everything out we'll dive into my homemade carrot cake. How's that sound?"

"Great, but if I can't solve your problems can I still have some cake?" replied Jim.

"I suppose so, but it might be soggy with my tears."

"Gosh, I hope it's not that bad. Do tell."

"Let's go over to the sofa and settle in. This could take a little bit and we may as well be comfortable. How about a wine refill?"

"Sure, you bet. Might make us smarter," said Jim, holding out his glass.

Glasses refilled, they settled into opposite ends of the worn and comfortable sofa, angled toward each other, one leg each up on the sofa, one hand holding the wine glass, the free arm slung over the back in a mirror image of each other.

Kate took a deep breath and proceeded. "Well, as you probably know, I came back to Oddertown three years ago. I guess right after the time you moved here, come to think of it. I was freshly divorced and moved here to get back on my feet and help Gramps with the store. I had nowhere else to go, and intended to only stay a short time in this safe haven until I figured out my next steps in life. But he was struggling and badly needed me, and I started to really enjoy it here after Boston, so I stayed. And then Gramps died last fall, as you know, and I inherited everything."

Jim nodded as she spoke, intent on all she said, and also drawn in magnetically by those bright and compelling green eyes. Kate was one of those people who was at once strong, commanding, and in control, yet subtly vulnerable. He very much wanted to help her if he could.

"So now I have the store all on my own, passed in full ownership from Grampa Simon to me. I was actually quite happy to take it on and decided I would like to make a real go of it. I've made some changes for the better, and I have plans for bigger improvements. I think I can make this a local and even regional destination if given half a chance. The problem is that, along with the store, I inherited a big debt, and it could take me down."

"You want to get specific on that?" asked Jim.

"Yes, I'd like you to know the details, as that may be the only way you can help me." She took a long, slow sip from her glass of wine, kicked off her shoes, and tucked her legs under her, side saddle. "Over four years ago, before I returned, the stone foundation of the building was really failing. It had been getting bad for years, of course, and finally Gramps had no choice but to have it rebuilt. The whole building was starting to tilt, and the north end was a good four inches lower than the south. You could drop a marble on the floor near the lunch counter and it would roll straight to the far wall, with a hard bounce at the end! The building wouldn't have stood much longer without a huge fix."

"I heard that it had just finished a big reconstruction, right about the time I moved here," added Jim.

"Big is an understatement. The whole building was jacked up, the old rock foundation removed, and a completely new foundation of reinforced poured concrete was built in its place, complete with spray foam insulation. Since they had to disconnect the plumbing and electric, and they were old anyway, they also installed and insulated new pipes and wiring under the building. The good news is that the structure is now solid as granite and should stand for another 100 years. And the insulation has really helped with the heating costs. The bad news is the price. The job cost over $175,000, and Gramps borrowed $150,000 of that. It was a five-year business construction loan and is due in full early next year, February 1 to be precise. Bless his heart, Gramps missed many payments along the way, partly because he couldn't afford them and partly because sometimes he simply forgot. He was getting really forgetful the last couple of years and with 20/20 hindsight I now realize he must have had pretty bad dementia. He never even mentioned the loan to me and I assumed all was well. Anyway, I've tried to catch up since Gramps died and keep up the payments, but I still owe $110,000. And it's due in less than eight months." Kate shifted uncomfortably in her seat as she laid out these gruesome details, and then took a large sip of wine. "I don't have the resources to pay it off, Jim. Not even close."

"Wow, that's quite a debt," said Jim "It's times like this I wish I had pockets deep enough I could just write out a check. But I'm sorry to say I don't."

"No, gosh, that's not why I asked you here!" replied Kate as she sat up straight. "I'm not asking for, nor would I ever accept, charity. But I *am* hoping for a brainstorming session; maybe your analytical skills could help identify something I hadn't thought of."

"Nothing comes immediately to mind, but let's dig deeper so I can understand the numbers better. You mind talking about cash flow in the store? That might be a good place to start."

"Yeah, no problem. I've run the numbers over and over and I can't find a solution there." She stood up to grab a pad of paper with numbers on it from a nearby shelf. "But anyway, in round numbers we gross about $500 a day—of course with a lot of variation around that, some days higher, some lower. But that's the average. More than half of that comes from the kitchen. On an annual basis, the gross take is about $180,000, give or take. Roughly 50% of that goes into buying the goods we sell, so that's around $90,000 just to stock the shelves and kitchen, another $90-something thousand left. Electric bill, taxes, building and liability insurance, water, and so forth take about $18,000, so we're down to around $72,000. Salaries for my two part-timers run to $28,000 and I draw a small salary of $35,000, which barely covers my living expenses. That leaves about $9,000 for everything else, including paying off the loan, emergencies, repairs, replacement of old equipment, and whatever else comes up. Forget about investing in retirement or ever getting a new car."

"Hmmm. Some tough numbers there," responded Doc. He pondered for a few seconds, with silence hanging over them. "I guess you can't get blood from a turnip. Even if you could boost sales or cut costs, the changes would be no more than tweaks. You might see a few thousand dollars extra, but it wouldn't help much, certainly not in the time frame you're looking at."

"Agreed," responded Kate.

"Have you tried to extend the loan payback date?" asked Jim.

"I have spoken with the bank and explained my circumstances. They will extend the loan three years, with proportionally lower payments stretched over that time. However, they want a 20% payment on the balance up front, which is $22,000. I have a few thousand I could cobble together but nothing like that."

"I wonder if anyone around here has the kind of cash to loan you 20 grand?"

"I really don't want to be in debt to anyone else, though if that was my only option I suppose I'd have to consider it," replied Kate. "But I don't know anyone with that kind of money around here. Let's remember where we are Jim: a little village in the Northeast Kingdom of Vermont. This place doesn't exactly draw the rich and famous."

"I gotcha on that. What about fundraising? Your store is quite important to the townsfolk, and if they knew you were in trouble they might just come through."

"You mean one of those online fundraising things?" asked Kate. "Like a Kickstarter campaign?"

"No, I mean some kind of fundraiser where you sell or raffle or auction stuff. You know, find something that people want and sell it with proceeds going to the 'Save the Odderton Country Store' fund."

"You think we could raise much money that way? Raffles or auctions?"

"I honestly don't know," answered Jim. "But I guess there's one way to find out. I know we wouldn't be able to address the big debt but maybe we could get a ways toward extending your loan. Might be worth a try. Of course this only postpones the big day of reckoning, but at least that's something. You never know what could happen in the next three years. Maybe you'll hit the lottery or a rich uncle you don't know existed will die and leave you his fortune."

"Well, I don't ever play the lottery and I'm pretty sure there's no rich uncles lurking out there. Not even poor ones. I think I'm on my own here."

"OK, Kate, let's think about options for the big picture," said Jim, trying to reset their discussion. "Let's brainstorm on how we can address that. Number one, do you have any hidden assets? Investments, another house or property anywhere, an IRA, stocks or bonds, anything out there of value that could be sold?"

"Nothing, nada, zilch," answered Kate. "What you see is what you get," spreading her hands and gesturing to her house. "I've got a house, a store, an old car, and a big debt. I brought a small chunk with me from the divorce but poured most of that into store improvements."

"OK," said Jim. "Number two, any relatives that can help you? Aunts, uncles, cousins?"

"Nothing there either. All my aunts and uncles are dead. I have one or two cousins out there, but

I've never met them and have no idea where they are. I'm pretty much alone in this thing."

"Alright, that's out," concluded Doc, starting to run out of options. "Hmmm. What else? How about door number three, inviting in a partner and sharing ownership?"

"I suppose I could try that but who in their right mind would want to buy into a general store in the middle of nowhere with so much debt, only to work your butt off each day to make ends meet? This is not the sort of business that attracts investors. It's a labor of love, and you have to know and love the community to get up each morning and do it. Besides, I don't know that I want someone else in a family business that goes back six generations, though I guess if it's a choice between doing that or losing the store, I'd do it. But where would I find someone crazy enough to take this on?"

"I see what you mean," replied Jim, who was starting to better understood her situation. "A buy-in is a huge long shot at best, and even if it worked you'd no longer fully control the store. Tough situation. You really need a rich sugar daddy to give you the money and let you go on your way!"

"Know any of those? I'm listening."

"Geez, this is tough," Jim replied. He took another full sip of wine and stared at the floor.

"Hey, you know, I've heard of some failing—OH CHRIST!!" shouted Jim involuntarily; his whole body jerked as he half jumped up on the sofa, spilling some of his wine in the process.

"Oh my God, what is it?" asked a shocked Kate. "Are you OK?"

Jim immediately regained control, set down his glass, took a deep breath, put his head in his hands, and got a sheepish grin across his face. "This is really embarrassing, but I guess I have no choice but to tell you," he admitted as he slid his fingers from his forehead slowly down across his face, distorting his features in the process. He then wiped up the spilled wine with his napkin, and, with a funny look on his face, continued.

"This is especially embarrassing because of my profession, the great biologist, professor, outdoor teacher, but the fact of the matter is. . ." he paused, not wanting to go on but having little choice, "the fact is, I have a horrible phobia about mice, and I just saw one scamper along your baseboard."

"You did?" she replied, looking at the far wall. "Gosh, I really try to keep them under control. I have traps out all the time. But you know how it is here in Vermont, they're all over. Sorry about that. You OK?"

"Well, my ego just got badly bruised but otherwise I'm fine. It just surprised me, I wasn't expecting it. God how embarrassing. It's a recognized condition called musophobia, after the Greek for 'mouse', and also after the genus of the house mouse, *Mus*. Turns out this is one of the most common phobias out there. It's so bizarre and totally irrational and I hate it, but there it is. I don't know how I got it but it's been with me since I was a kid. I thought I'd grow out of it but I never did. As an ecologist and teacher I've handled snakes, frogs, salamanders, birds, other small mammals, every plant in the northeast, insects of every type, but for some reason mice freak me out. I've even seen a therapist to try and kick it, and made a little progress, but if I'm not expecting it I still jump uncontrollably. It's so embarrassing and makes me feel like a total weenie.

I have to keep those traps in my house where you never see the animal, it gets caught inside and you just throw the whole thing away. I've spent a fortune on the damned things over the years!"

"Well, everybody has their hang-ups Jim, and your secret is safe with me, I promise. But it's kinda fun to see a chink in your armor," she said with a twinkly smile. "On second thought, maybe now I have something to Lord over you if I ever need leverage! Hmmm. . . this could come in real handy, actually," she said with a devilish grin. "I'll have to file this one away carefully in the memory banks for ready availability."

"I guess I am at your complete mercy," he admitted, and returned the smile.

"I suppose then you were never a Mouseketeer?"

"No way, and I never was able to watch most of the Disney cartoons for fear that Mickey Mouse would show up. Even that cartoon figure would kind of spook me. I tell you, it's been terrible!"

"Well, there are worse afflictions, Dr. Watson, so if that's the hand you've been dealt then I think you got off easy."

"I suppose. But can we now move on past my musophobia? Talk about anything else maybe? War, pestilence, famine, anything more fun than my nuttiness?"

"OK, you got it, Mouse Man. . . sorry, I couldn't resist. But seriously, now, where were we? I think you were about to say something, umm. . . oh yeah, you were saying you had heard of some failed . . . and then you jumped like you saw the Devil."

After a thoughtful pause he said "Oh yeah, right. I've heard of some failing country stores in Vermont being re-formed as co-ops. But I guess making it a co-op has the same problems. I can't imagine a bunch of people around here would have the cash or interest to buy into it, and even if they did you'd lose even *more* control."

"I did think about that and I think it's a long-shot at best," replied Kate. "I just don't see something like that working around here, but, still, I'm planning on making some phone calls to see if I can stir up some interest. I'll do that on Monday. There's a pretty tight network of general stores in this part of the world and we're all friends. Maybe one or more of them might want to join forces, or buy in a share of Odd Country, or know some crazy people that might be interested in forming a co-op. I'll try but I won't hold my breath."

"Well, it's a shot anyway," said Jim. "But I feel like I've hit a dead end."

"Welcome to my world, Doc. I was hoping you might see something I didn't, but I guess this one is even beyond what the Wizard can do."

"The Wizard. God, how I hate that name!"

"Oh really? Sorry, I didn't realize that. I thought it was complimentary, showed how people around here look up to and respect you."

"I see it as setting me apart from everyone, and I don't want to feel that way. I'm just another Oddertowner and don't like any special attention. I'm just me, just Jim."

"I'll remember that and promise not to 'Wiz' you again. But I can't make any guarantees about 'Mouse Man'."

"I guess I'll take what I can get. And now to the problem at hand, Kate, the only thing I can think to do is come up with that $22,000 and try to push this thing down the road. Maybe something would break in the next three years, or at least that would give you time to think about other approaches."

"That may be my only way forward—just buy some time," concluded Kate.

Jim paused to gaze around the modest living room in quiet thought. Pictures of Kate's parents and grandparents dominated one wall, while the others were mostly populated by bookshelves loaded with classic literature from her college days when she minored in English Lit. There were also a few historical objects from the store: an old sign advertising hair tonic, a box for ladies' gloves, several yellowed doilies, a large apothecary jar that had once held penny candy. He noted there was no television in the room.

"Oh, hey, wait a minute!" interjected Doc, his face brightening. "This is a historic building. What about a grant from the state's historic preservation grant program? I bet they would love to keep this old place going, and they're really focused on small communities."

"I actually investigated that one, Jim, and the problem is they award grants only to properties owned by non-profits or municipalities. This is a private structure and the business is for profit, though it may as well not be for all the money I'm not making. But they don't cover my situation. Plus, you need to match what they give you. So if they gave me $10,000 I'd need to come up with a $10,000 match. And grants only go to $20,000 so at best this would only cover the loan-stretching idea. And they only cover actual repair and restoration work. Mine is a loan payback for repair. I'm screwed at every turn. And the same problems exist with the Preservation Trust of Vermont. I checked, doesn't apply to me, but good thinking."

Doc sat there looking a bit dejected. He was out of ideas. "Well, you've thought of everything so I guess this leaves us with trying to come up with $22,000 to buy some time. Have you asked around town?"

"No. Nobody other than you really knows the details yet. There're some rumors out there that I'm having some problems but I doubt anyone knows the scope of it. I guess I can't and shouldn't hide it much longer. They'd all know eventually when the store closes down."

"And that's exactly what we need to avoid, Kate. Let me get out there, talk with some people, and see if anything will shake out."

"Please don't ask people for charity, Jim. This is my problem and I need to figure it out."

"I know, Kate, but an awful lot of people depend on this place. They get goods here they'd otherwise have to drive 20 or 30 miles round trip for. Lots of folks eat here. Hell, Victor Kemper would probably starve to death if it wasn't for you! And for many it's the center of their social universe. This is where people come to visit and catch up. What would the Odd Balls do if they couldn't come here? No, I think lots of people would like to help, and for selfish reasons; they need this place as much as you do. It wouldn't be charity. Let me poke around and see what I can learn out there."

"That'd be great, Doc. I kinda like the idea of an auction, get the whole town involved without asking any single person to do too much. And if we could find something valuable to raffle off that might really help as well. Let me think about what I might have, though it is mostly dusty old junk in the basement."

"Alright, sounds like the start of a plan," concluded Jim.

"Jim, thanks very much. If nothing else I feel better just sharing this with someone," she said, reaching over to pat his arm in a genuine gesture of appreciation. He didn't interpret it the wrong way, and patted her hand in return. It was a nice statement of growing friendship between them.

"So how about some of that carrot cake," he inquired. "Have I earned a piece?"

"Doc, you've earned more than a piece, especially after your little phobic mouse shock. Have all you want."

"Well, one piece should do for starters. And no tears on it, please."

"No tears at all, Doc. I do feel better after talking with you, even if we didn't solve the problem tonight. Thanks so much; you are a great sounding board and I may need to call on you again. And I even had a little comic relief with your mouse dance!"

Chapter 8

Saturday, June 22, 7:35 PM

———

A S JIM PULLED OPEN THE HEAVY WOODEN DOOR
to the bar, a visual and aural wall of humanity greeted him, while the sharp and tangy
smell of hops in the air simultaneously aroused his
olfactory sense. Duke's was already crowded, which
was not surprising, given this was a Saturday night.
Most of the semi-circular bar was already full—the
regulars all positioned in their familiar seats—as
were most of the booths and tables. And more folks
were standing around in small groups, beers and
wines in hand, catching up on the week's activities.
Between the loud conversations, bursts of laughter,
the Red Sox-Orioles game showing on three TVs,
and background music—at the moment Elton
John's "Saturday Night's Alright for Fighting"—
Jim knew he would have a tough time fulfilling his
goal in venturing out tonight. But determined and
undaunted, he pushed forward.

Duke's was Oddertown's single watering hole where much of the community gathered at one time or another, especially on Friday and Saturday evenings. It was a family-friendly place, with decent bar food to go along with seven different draft beers from Vermont craft breweries, and a good selection of wines and cocktails. In decades past, however, it had a reputation as a far rougher establishment. Duke's got its start in 1955, when Jamie "Duke" MacDougal opened its doors as a place where loggers, farmers, and other rugged types could blow off some steam with hard liquor after harder days working the land. Fights were not uncommon and Duke had to replace the front window every couple of months when someone was inevitably thrown through it after a neighborly dispute that was usually forgiven in the sober light of the next day. Over the decades the reputation of Duke's had softened, and today—now run by Duke's grandson, "Mac" MacDougal—it was simply a fun and safe place to hoist a few and get a bite to eat with friends and family.

Jim looked around and soon spotted some familiar faces at a booth on the far left wall, with an empty chair sitting at the end. At that precise time, Tony Delfasio saw him and motioned him over to the empty seat. "Hey, Doc, c'mon and join us!" said Tony enthusiastically, pulling back the chair; Jim accepted with equal enthusiasm. Greetings then went out around the table. Besides Tony and his beautiful, raven-haired and olive-complexioned wife Marie, there was Lauren McCallum and Emily McIntyre, two of the three teachers—along with Gregory Mitchell—at the Oddertown Grade

School. Lauren was the older, attractive widow that Tony had tried to get Jim interested in last month. She had a very pleasing face and a wonderful personality that complimented her smart brunette hair with wisps of grey, and Jim did give her a second glance as he sat down. Emily was a new teacher added this last year, slim, fresh-faced, innocent, idealistic, and full of energy and ideas. She had recently completed her teaching degree at Amherst College in Massachusetts and was gung-ho in her new job. Together McCallum and McIntyre were already pegged as "Big Mac and Little Mac."

Rounding out the table was Malcom S. Hinges, who went by the nickname "Rusty." Yes, Rusty Hinges. As if to prove that God had a sense of humor, not only was Rusty appropriately red haired and freckle faced, thus looking like oxidation had begun to wear him away from the outside in, but he had an unusually hoarse, high-pitched, and borderline squeaky voice that sometimes sounded like, well, a rusty hinge! It was so unlikely a convergence of name and physical characteristics that, if Rusty Hinges had been invented for a novel, he would be dismissed as being too absurd. Yet here he was, flesh and blood. Rusty was a massive man, over six foot five and pushing 255 pounds, almost all of it muscle earned from his profession as a logger, and his bulk took up most of two full seats on one side of the booth. Despite being in his mid-40s with three kids, because of his baby-faced features, Rusty retained the youthful appearance of a 25-year old. He also was one of the kindest and gentlest men you could hope to find in the whole Northeast Kingdom. Jim felt comfortable with this group and was happy to settle in with them.

Within a minute, Dora Stevenson, the no-nonsense middle-aged waitress, came by to see what Doc needed. He asked for a bottle of Fair Maiden from Foley Brothers Brewery. The last year or so, Jim had enjoyed sampling the avalanche of local craft beers from all over Vermont, and this was his latest favorite. Dora also took orders for several other refills and left to fill them.

"So, Doc, what brings you out to Duke's on a Saturday night?" asked Rusty in his high-pitched voice. "I didn't think you were much of a barfly."

"No, I'm not, Rusty," replied Jim, "but I'm on a bit of a mission tonight. I was hoping to catch some good folks like yourselves and start spreading the word on a pretty serious problem we could be looking at for the town."

"What's that?" squeaked Rusty, eyebrows raised. Everyone else suddenly became attentive, trying to listen carefully over the high noise level in the bar.

"Well, it's the Odderton Country Store. Kate inherited a helluva debt from her grandfather when she got the store, to the tune of over $100,000. It's due in full next February and she doesn't have a prayer of coming up with money like that."

"Pfffeeeeew," replied Tony. "That's a helluva debt indeed. How did *that* happen?"

"It's from the reconstruction work on the place four or five years ago. They had to raise the whole building and construct a new foundation, as you know. Kept it from collapsing, but also saddled her with this debt. Her grandfather didn't plan too well for paying it back, plus he was facing dementia there toward the end and didn't take care of things, and now she's stuck with it. I don't think he fully understood what he was getting into. If it doesn't get paid off, she could lose the store to the bank."

"That'd be awful for the town!" exclaimed Emily. "I've only been here a short time but I can already see how everyone uses it all the time. It's the center of life here. Oddertown would seem like a ghost town without that store!"

"You just went to the heart of the matter, Emily," concluded Jim. "It's not just another business: it's the heart and soul of Oddertown, and the thought of losing it is. . .I don't know. . . unthinkable!"

Dora brought Jim's beer and the refills, expertly setting them down with minimal disruption.

"Well what could *we* possibly do?" asked Lauren. "I'm just a schoolteacher and don't have any kind of money to help her. Most people in town are in the same boat."

"I know," replied Jim, with a nod of his head. "But there is one possible way forward. The bank will extend her loan another three years if she can give them 20% of the remaining balance up front. That's $22,000. A lot of money, but more do-able than the alternative. She has a couple thousand, so if the town could somehow raise about 20 grand, it could at least buy some time for her, and us."

"Do you have any ideas how we might do that?" asked Emily.

"Well, I do, but was also hoping that others might come up with something as well. First, we need to encourage people to spend as much as they can at Odd Country. Shop there more, eat there more. If you spend money elsewhere, try and spend it there instead. If we can boost her sales for six months, it could add up. And she doesn't want charity, so this way people are getting something for their money and her cash flow improves."

"Sounds reasonable," concluded Marie. "But it means we need to get the word out."

"For sure," replied Jim. "I think word of mouth could help a lot, but I also think we need an organized effort. I was thinking, what if we worked up a 'Save Our Store' campaign? It can be a community effort with an eye-catching 'SOS' slogan that would get some attention. Maybe we could print up some flyers, even get an article in some newspapers in the Kingdom, try and get people to come over here. Use the long history of the place as a hook to get people interested."

"Sounds good, Doc, but we'll need more than that," concluded Rusty. "I can't see raising 20 grand that way."

"Absolutely," agreed Jim. "And that's where we need to be creative, Rusty. Kate and I thought of a couple of things that could serve as fundraisers: a raffle for one or more items, and maybe a town-wide auction. If we could find one or two good items that somebody wants to donate, we could raffle them off. Or even a 50:50 cash raffle. You sell a bunch of tickets and then pick a winner who gets half of the haul, the other half goes to Odd Country. With any luck, the winner might donate their share to the store."

"Those both sound fine, Jim," observed Tony, "but we might get, what, a couple thousand at best? It doesn't take a big chunk out of the problem."

"No, Tony, it doesn't, but I think we have to look at a bunch of small steps rather than one big one. I don't see many options in a town or area like this for one big step. Nobody's wealthy here—that I know of anyway—and I think we need to chip away at it."

"I see your point Jim, and I can't argue with it," replied Tony. "So what else are you thinking?"

"Well, there's the town auction idea," said Jim. "There are some towns in Vermont that have these and raise some pretty good money. I understand the Chamber of Commerce in Brandon, over by Middlebury, does one each summer and they raise 10 or 12 grand. They're bigger than us, but it shows it can be done. You just need three things: people willing to donate reasonably decent items or services, someone to serve as auctioneer, and people willing to buy. I'm thinking we could come up with all of those."

About that time, Layla Liederman wandered over to the table and greeted the group from her shaky standing position. "And how are all you fine-looking ladies and gentlemen doing tonight?" she inquired, her words slightly slurred, though it would likely get worse this evening before it got better. Layla was a wild and colorful character. Now pushing 60, she was the hard-drinking, man-chasing, fun-loving owner of Odds 'n Ends, the second-hand store and junk shop two doors up the road. Layla had gone through three husbands so far and would not be averse to breaking in a fourth, though her options in Oddertown were limited, to say the least. Between the small population, her three ex-husbands spreading tales of woe throughout the Kingdom, and everyone in town on high alert, the most she could hope for was a brief and fleeting encounter. That did not, however, stop Layla from flirting with anybody in pants, and even an occasional skirt. Though still somewhat attractive in a "rode hard and put up wet" sort of way, she had her amorous work cut out for her. But you had to give her points for staying in the game and trying.

The table greeted her in a polite and guardedly accepting way. "What are ya'll talking about so intensely over here? Been watchin' ya puttin' your heads together like yer plottin somethin' serious," Layla said in a conspiratorial way. "Wanna let me in on the secret?" Though ostensibly addressing the whole group, she clearly was focused on Jim, the highest-quality target, just ripe for her cross-hairs. Jim recoiled ever so slightly.

Lauren jumped in and explained the problem they were discussing, along with the possibility of a town auction and a raffle for a big item. Layla was no dummy; she quickly grasped the implications for the town, and immediately got serious. She pulled over an empty chair and sat down at the booth to join forces.

As they resumed discussing a possible town auction, Layla suddenly interrupted. "You know," she said, thinking out loud in her gravelly smoker's voice, "I've got that old cedar strip canoe in the shop my dad left me. He built it back in the late 40s and it's a beaut. It's been in the shop forever, taking up room. Lots of folks would like it but I have $2800 on it; nobody's gonna bite at that price and I don't want to let it go for much less, given it was Dad's, and that's what it's worth. But I *would* donate it for a raffle. Dad woulda liked that. It's for the town and the store, and he loved it here and that's more important to me than hangin' on and tryin' to get big bucks. Plus, it would open up some room for me." After a pause to convince herself she was doing the right thing, she added "So, ya want it?"

The others looked at each other with surprised and delighted expressions before Jim responded with "Sure, Layla, if you really want to donate it. That's very generous. Thank you! I think we could have a *great* raffle with that canoe." The others quickly concurred, they all thanked her profusely, and Jim bought her another beer. After brief discussion they decided on $5 raffle tickets. They would have liked to go with $10 but felt that would cut out too many people. They would announce the raffle next week, sell tickets aggressively, and select the winner in late July or August. They set a sales target of at least 400 tickets, which would net them $2000, though they all hoped for more.

Before they knew it, their little group became a self-appointed, de facto SOS committee: "Save Our Store." Given the level of noise and confusion in Duke's, and the liquor they were all imbibing, they agreed to not plan anything else right now but to meet again Monday night, 7 PM, at Jim's house to discuss other plans and options. Jim would act as informal chair/organizer. Finishing business, they called for another round, happily picked up by Tony. The group began to feel empowered and had positive hopes that they might be able to help Kate—and their town—out of this predicament. And their optimism came from such an unlikely source. Who could have guessed that the town's most eligible bachelorette and fun-loving loose lady would be the source of their new-found hope and energy? Life never ceased to surprise. They happily raised their glasses and clinked to "SOS," the newest civic organization in Odd, and what they hoped would be the savior of their beloved store.

Chapter 9

T HE INAUGURAL MEETING OF "SOS" AT Jim's house two nights earlier went well. Surprisingly, the group's half-life of enthusiasm for the effort lasted much more than the typical six hours for these sorts of things. Everyone from the bar discussion attended, as well as Kate, who could not thank the group enough for their help and concern, while stressing repeatedly that she did not want charity. But the group countered that Odd Country was just as important to them as to her and was the focus of life here. If it took some charity to save it, so be it. She offered a resigned smile in return. Everyone was quite energized and felt they were doing good, honest work, pledging to give it their all over the next couple of months. "SOS" was on its way.

Kate reported that, as she had feared, nothing in the Odd Country basement was appropriate for a raffle, so the group went ahead and formalized the raffle for the canoe. She also reported, with great disappointment, that four phone calls to friends in other general stores in the Kingdom turned up nothing more than sympathy and encouragement. Everyone was operating close to the bone and none were interested in buying into Odd Country or pursuing any sort of co-op arrangement or profit-sharing deal. Nor were any of them aware of anyone who might be vaguely interested in getting in on something like that, but they all wished her well, and really meant it.

Jim agreed to design and print up signs to hang around town, as well as the raffle tickets to be sold. Everyone would take at least two dozen tickets to begin with, and would try to sell them to friends and neighbors. They also made preliminary plans for the auction, including getting out the word with more signs, an article for local papers announcing the threat to the store and formation of "SOS," and email and Facebook campaigns. They would call for auction donors as well as buyers, constantly stressing the importance of saving their store, arguably the most important single element of their community.

Jim started this sunny spring morning by going door-to-door to the various businesses and offices in town to hang raffle and auction signs that introduced the "SOS" campaign. Having hung at least a dozen signs he then walked over to Lou's Garage. "Hey, Lou, how you doing today?"

"Not too bad for a grease monkey with a bad comic habit, I suppose," she replied, cigarillo dangling from the corner of her mouth. "What can I do you for, Doc?"

"I wondered if you'd mind if I spoke with Billy for a couple of minutes. I promise I won't take much of his time."

"Sure, no problem, Doc. Speak away."

Jim found Billy deeply immersed in a brake job but he was happy to surface and chat.

"So what's up, Doc? Oh, sorry, that sounded kinda like a cartoon, didn't it?"

"No problem, Billy, and yeah, I've gotten that line before. I just wanted to come by and see if I could enlist your help with something." Jim briefly explained the situation with the store and the "SOS" group that had just come together. He then told him about the auction they were planning, probably for early August.

"Billy, we could use your logistical help. We'll probably need to transport a bunch of auction goods to Time Square and you and your big old truck are just what we need. Whaddaya think, could you spare a few hours for us and drive around and make some pickups of goods and deliver them to the park? One or two of us—probably big Rusty—could go along and help load things."

"I sure could, Doc, and would be happy to. I like the store and I eat there sometimes and will do whatever it takes. And I can even do you one better," he added, emphasizing with an extended greasy index finger. "I'll get my buddy Gizmo to help. He's from over in Johnsville and has a big pickup, too. He can help us."

"Gizmo?" inquired Jim.

"Yeah, that's what we call him. His real name is Wendell but he's always fooling with cars and any mechanical stuff so we call him 'Gizmo.' That's better 'n Wendell anyway, don't you think?"

"Yeah, I suppose so," chuckled Jim. "That would be great if the two of you could help. That would be huge, actually. I'll get with you on details, date and so forth, as we get closer, Billy. But for now, thanks a million. Big load off my mind."

"No problem. I'm seeing Giz tonight so I'll ask him. Scratch that, I'll *tell* him. He owes me a couple favors."

"Fantastic, and thanks a bunch." Jim went to shake hands but Billy showed his greasy palms and shrugged. So Jim gave him a pat on the shoulder instead, thanked him again, and made his way out to the street, but not before selling him and Lou two tickets each.

Having settled that critical element, Jim Watson headed toward Odd Country, the focus of their efforts, both to get some lunch and to try and sell some raffle tickets to anyone who might wander in, locals and visitors alike. Jim would leave nobody unscathed and no stone unturned in his mission.

In front of Odds 'n Ends—ironically enough where the raffle canoe quietly sat—Jim saw Faith Golightly walking toward him and he jumped at the chance for another ticket sale. Though well outside of the mainstream, Faith and her family were good-hearted, community-minded souls who no doubt would support this worthy cause.

"Hi, Faith" called Jim cheerfully.

Faith returned his greeting with her classic, ethereal smile that could melt the heart of an angel, but then offered a mild rebuke. "*Feather*, please, Dr. Watson. You know I now go by *Feather*. As in 'light as'?"

"Ah, yes," replied a corrected Jim. "Sorry, Feather, I forgot. And how are you and your family on this beautiful day?"

Ahhh, the Golightly family; quite the story there. Long and involved, yes, but well worth the telling, if for nothing more than to better understand a piece of quirky American history in this little corner of Vermont.

It all started back in August 1969, when Stanley Schwartz and his girlfriend Barbara Kozlowski—both native to Brooklyn, N.Y.—found themselves headed north on the New York State Thruway toward a music and art fair to be held on a farm near a little-known town called Woodstock. Two years back from Vietnam and shaken to the core by his experiences there—including the horror of killing two fellow human beings in self-defense—Stanley was now long haired and shaggy and as anti-establishment, anti-war, and peace-loving as is possible to be. He and Barbara were prototypical hippies, flower children, peaceniks, out for music, drugs, free love, and an escape from the clashing social realities that defined an era in dark turmoil.

Driving in massive traffic through the town of Woodstock and into the rolling countryside, Stanley tootled his VW bus out onto a freshly-mowed hay field that would soon become a giant mud puddle, where he and Barbara set up their camp in an old canvas tent—ironically, Army surplus. Later that day, during Joe Cocker's rendition of "With a Little Help from My Friends," Stanley and Barbara's first child was conceived, a boy they would name Joe, after Mr. Cocker himself, of whom they were devoted fans and who was a significant presence at the time. Of course, they knew nothing of the conception until some six weeks later.

Through addled, fuzzy, and barely remembered conversations with several other concert goers over the next two days, Stanley and Barbara decided not to return to Brooklyn after the festival but instead join the others and continue north and east into the hinterlands of Vermont, getting as far away from establishment life as they could. Six couples would thus wander a semi-random and tortuous path that, after several dead ends, false starts, and two mechanical breakdowns, ended at the outskirts of an insignificant and unknown speck on the map called Oddertown. They would soon buy a forgotten and discounted 110-acre worn-out farm, mostly using the funds from one individual with a wealthy daddy who was all-too-happy to be rid of his problem child and have her settle in a backwater boondock and out of his short-cropped hair. Thus began the commune known as EarthPeace.

After some sobering up and drying out—which took a good two months and the harsh realities of the first hard freezes—the six couples began a serious quest to live off the land and be self-sufficient. Unwittingly becoming vanguards of the back-to-the earth-movement, they staggered and stumbled their way—with periodic support from their sugar daddy—toward a communal existence and ideology that was taking hold throughout much of the country. Armed with the newly published book that would become the bible for this movement—Helen and Scott Nearing's *Living the Good Life,* and the new *Foxfire* series soon to follow—the group learned to live off the land and on the margins of society. They grew most of their own food, boiled maple syrup, did odd jobs, raised livestock, sold excess goods, hired themselves out for construction work, harvested wood, made love, and populated EarthPeace.

One of the first things they all did was shed their previous cultural identities and don new ones. Rejecting all that went before, they began with their names, representative of the core of their previous, military-industrial-complex lives. Stanley and Barbara decided that, in wanting to live lightly upon the earth, they would "go lightly" which they adopted as their last name. Further identifying with Mother Earth, Barbara would be known as "Gaia," and Stanley as "Rock." Thus, in a communal ceremony involving a huge bonfire, copious quantities of Mary Jane and psychedelic mushrooms, and lots of chanting, nudity, percussion, and ceremonial cleansing, everyone in the commune adopted their new identities, including Rock and Gaia Golightly. When they all awoke 30-some hours later, they gingerly and shakily went back to work on their new lives with their new identities.

Joe Golightly was born in May of 1970, three days after the Kent State shootings, and his Cocker-esque name was soon supplemented with the more-earthy nickname of Clay. Fourteen months later, his little sister was born shortly before midnight during a full moon and was appropriately named Moonbeam. It was not long after Moonbeam's birth that Gaia and Rock decided that condoms were far cheaper than children, whereupon they welcomed that part of the modern world into their lives. They had no more children, and no more mouths to feed or burden the world with; Clay and Moonbeam would be their generational legacies.

Life continued apace in the commune and the kids grew, as kids are wont to do. EarthPeace avoided contamination from larger society by setting up a communal home-school system, complete with a log school house. In this way they met legal mandates from the outside world but managed to insulate their children from its evils, indoctrinating them with their own ways of being. Their one compromise was to conduct enough commerce with outsiders to buy the necessary goods they could not make or grow themselves. In 1971, one of their own was instrumental in starting NOFA—the Northeast Organic Farming Association—the keystone that helped ignite the organic food movement that flourishes in the state to this day.

Some 20 years down the road, in a pagan ceremony officiated by his father, Clay Golightly married fellow commune member Amber Rivers, with whom he had grown up. And they wasted no time in begetting children, a boy followed by three girls, all within a span of six years, after which they too discovered modern birth control. The boy, named Rock after his paternal Grandfather, inexplicably rejected the whole communal way of life when he came of age and took off for more traditional pastures. He legally changed his name from Rock to Robert and eventually became a hedge fund manager on Wall Street. He rarely had further contact with his family, who, on the few occasions they recalled him, referred to him as "Bob, Bob, Black Sheep."

The three girls of Clay and Amber were named, in order, Faith, Hope, and Charity. Faith, as you just witnessed, preferred to be known as "Feather," reflecting her pledge to live lightly upon the land. Hope favored the epithet "Harmony," as that is how she tried to live her life with all other beings and non-beings. And Charity, oh sweet Charity. At 14 she became known as "Chastity," which is how, she proclaimed and swore, she would live her life henceforth and forevermore, in a pure, virginal state that would bring clarity and purpose to all that she did. That pristine condition changed abruptly two years ago on July 4 after the town's modest fireworks display when, at age 19, she took off with Billy Wilson in his pickup truck, whereupon they made some fireworks of their own. Soon after discovering the sensual pleasures of the flesh, Chastity reverted to her given name of Charity, perhaps, some suggested, because she gave so freely of herself. To anyone. At any time.

And that is where the Golightly family presently stood. Miraculously and enigmatically, while everyone else from that era had moved on from their earthy, communal phase to more-conventional lifestyles, they alone stood firm in their 1970s convictions and way of life. They were Oddertown's own living time capsule.

Feather answered Jim's polite inquiry about her family with her usual response, that they were lovely, at peace, and in touch with Mother Earth and all Her energies. After assuring her that he was happy to hear that, Jim explained the situation with the store and the "SOS" campaign, and asked if she would be interested in supporting them by buying a raffle ticket or two. "Dr. Watson, you know that I do not like to be weighed down with the burdens of money. I leave that to others in my family, who reluctantly take on that task. Though in my heart I would love to help your pure and worthy cause, you will need to ask one of my parents or sisters or maybe my Aunt Moonbeam to purchase your raffle tickets, which I am certain they will. Have a blessed day." And with that, she shimmered away to wherever such people go on a beautiful June day.

Jim walked away muttering to himself, "Whew. I sure hope it gets easier than that!"

And indeed it did. On the front steps of Odd Country he ran into Victor Kemper coming out from an early lunch and hit him up for two tickets. Inside he sold six more to some construction workers from St. Johnsbury working on a house nearby when he promised to personally deliver the canoe if any of them won. He struck pay dirt with a couple visiting from New Haven, Connecticut, who so loved the cause that they bought five tickets and said they would drive back up if they won.

While Jim was occupied with his sales, Kate was delivering lunch to the table of a middle-aged couple visiting from New Hampshire when the man looked up past her and suddenly blurted out, "Good God, what in the world is *that?*" Kate followed his gaze and landed on a portly, late-middle-aged man at the serving counter wearing a sleeveless dress and high heels. His pale, hairy arms and legs stood in stark contrast to the soft chenille aquamarine dress that covered his pear-shaped torso. A lovely, wide-brimmed hat with a small and tasteful egret feather complimented the string of pearls that adorned his hairy chest, exposed by the daring, plunging neckline. The entire outfit was tied together with 3-inch heels of a deep turquoise color studded with a few well-placed turquoise stones. The heels nicely accentuated his hairy calf muscles. He essentially looked like Klinger from *M*A*S*H*, only more stout.

"Oh, that's just Pernell Basington-Smythe,"

chuckled Kate in a matter-of-fact way. "Pernell's harmless. He's our local eccentric artist and author, transplanted from the Mother Country—as he calls it—England. When he's writing a novel or working on a painting or sculpture, he often dresses as one of his characters. He says it helps immerse him completely in the role and makes it more real; the characters come alive for him, and it inspires his creativity. He'll do that for a week or two and then move on to the next character." The couple watched Kate with rapt attention, wide-eyed, slack jawed, and somewhat disbelieving.

"Let's see, so far I've seen Pernell dressed as Teddy Roosevelt, a Samurai warrior, Queen Victoria, and, oh yeah, a Civil War rebel soldier," said Kate, counting them off on her fingers. "Oh, but the worst time," added Kate, leaning in and becoming much more animated, "was last summer when he was a California beach babe. He wore a skimpy, fluorescent pink bikini and pink flip flops for the better part of a week. My God, that was awful! I was nearly nauseous," she finished with a chuckle. "Yeah, we have some pretty strange characters here in old Oddertown. Pernell's not the only one."

"I'm almost afraid to ask," inquired the woman, with a worried look. "But do go on."

"Oh nothing too crazy," replied Kate, "just some eccentric folks. Like, let's see, we have a fellow, Gussie, who collects and keeps hundreds of salamanders as pets. He knows everything there is to know about salamanders and loves them to death. Can you imagine, salamanders as pets? Gussie can talk salamanders with you for hours if you'll let him. Then there's the strange old gal Janet, who collects paper clips. Every kind of paper clip you can imagine: plastic, metal, novelty clips, whatever. She has over 800 individual, unique, paper clips, and she's so proud of them! I never knew there were so many. Oh, and then there's Ranger Rick, as we call him, also known as 'Scat Man.' He collects animal scat, poop, if you will. Yes, you heard right," clarified Kate at their askance looks. "He's really into nature and wildlife and has made detailed studies of poop. Rick can tell you who visited a place, when they were there, and what they ate, all by their scat. I've made sure to never shake hands with him!" she laughed.

The couple seemed rather dumbstruck by this cast of eccentric characters, but was reassured by Kate that they were all good and decent people who had merely acquired strange habits and interests along their way in life. She explained that they all contributed to the rich and colorful tapestry of this strange little experiment called Oddertown, all had their roles to play and niches to fill, and were appreciated and accepted for who they were, with relatively little judgment from others. The couple initially seemed reluctant to accept that positive spin but finally agreed that the world might be a better place if people were more accepting and less judgmental. And after all that talk, Kate sold them each a raffle ticket.

The most touching sale of the day, however, occurred when Raymond Pulan barreled into the store, arms pumping, looking for Jim. Apparently he saw the tickets Lou had just bought and asked her about them, whereupon she explained the whole situation to him and the possibility of the store closing.

"Doctor Watson, I want to buy a ticket," said Raymond in his halting manner and out of breath as he came through the front door.

"You do, Raymond?" replied Jim.

"Yes, I want to buy a ticket and I have five dollars right here for you. I want a ticket. I want to save my store," explained Raymond as he handed over a crumpled wad of dollar bills. Raymond's humble and honest love for the town was so palpable that Jim fought back a tear as he filled out a ticket and handed it to Raymond.

"Good luck, Raymond. I hope you win. Be sure you keep that ticket in a safe place where you can find it later."

With his simple and pure wisdom Raymond replied, "I want you to keep my store. Please keep my store."

By the end of the day Jim Watson had sold 44 tickets, a very good start. He even, surprisingly, sold one to Charlie Horrible. But none was more satisfying, and gave him more hope, than the one sold to Raymond Pulin.

Chapter 10

Sunday, June 30, 8:45 AM

———

PAUL JOHNSON WAS NEARLY GIDDY WITH excitement as he steered his old blue Chevy pickup truck up the narrow, rutted, winding dirt road that paralleled Trout Brook, a tributary of Odder Creek. Joining Odder from the west side a half mile north of town, the aptly named Trout Brook was a haven for native brook trout. Unspoiled by any significant development or agriculture along its steady, nearly 2-mile descent from Francis Peak, the brook ran gin-clear and icy cold all year long, perfect habitat for native brookies. Its abundant and diverse insect life—dominated by mayfly, stonefly, and caddis fly larvae, classic indicator species of a healthy and intact stream—not only kept the trout fat and sassy, but spoke to the near-pristine nature of the place. To further enhance its value, it had never been stocked with hatchery trout, a rare occurrence in Vermont. It thus had no flabby and stupid hatchery fish placed here with the best of intentions, but in an endless and senseless cycle of put-and-take. And a fortuitous geological feature—a limestone ridge that formed a vertical, 11-foot, waterfall just before its confluence with Odder Creek—ensured that no downstream fish ever invaded upstream. So it did not have rainbow or brown trout—non-native species that typically out-competed the native brook trout. As a result the natives thrived here as in few other places in New England, and Trout Brook was a local treasure, jealously and fiercely protected by generations of local trout bums and meat fishermen.

Finally, *finally*, Paul had found some time away from the farm to dust off his gear and spend a few hours of quiet and glorious contemplation of nature in his favorite habitat. If Paul had not gotten into farming he would have been an ichthyologist or maybe a fisheries manager, just so he could spend time in these places he so deeply loved. But farming also called to him strongly, as did the good agricultural land that had been in his family for five generations now, and he felt a sense of duty to stay on that land and work it, as did his forebears. So fly fishing took a back seat to farming, to be pursued whenever he could, which was not nearly often enough.

This was Sunday morning, a time Paul tried to take advantage of as much as possible to avoid crowds and maybe have the stream all to himself. By nature a generous and sharing person, Paul was admittedly selfish when it came to fly fishing. This was the one time in life when he did not feel compelled to share with or to be nice to others. He fly fished *his* way—with blissful solitude unsullied by another soul, even close friends.

Being a committed atheist, Paul figured that he owned Sunday mornings, when all good Christians would predictably flock to their various churches for a couple of hours. This was the one time of the week he could count on to have few people out and about. Although he did not believe in a personal God or Creator, Paul was nevertheless a deeply spiritual person. He was in complete and indescribable awe of the Creation, regardless of whether it arose through a creator—which he did not for a minute believe—or through millions of years of Darwinian evolution—a view that he fully embraced.

From the universe down to atoms, and at every level of organization in between, Paul Johnson found Nature to be mind-boggling, endlessly fascinating, and far more worthy of respect and awe than any deity man could conjure. His reverence for Nature was as profound and sincere as that of the most pious religious zealot for their God. To Paul, *this* was his cathedral, and *here* was where his spiritual needs were met. In Trout Brook he could *see* nature, touch it, revel in it, and especially respect it and wonder at it, and he could feel profound pain for its possible destruction and loss. He did not require a church or a God to be spiritual; his spirituality was all around him each and every day in the grand and wondrous diversity of life, and he practiced it faithfully.

Paul was thankful that he lived in a place and time where such beliefs would not only be tolerated, but even respected. In Oddertown, and throughout much of Vermont, people generally believed what they believed and did not interfere with or try to change the beliefs of others. It was a refreshingly "live and let live" attitude, in contrast with so many places in the country or in many parts of the world where religious beliefs were the basis for so much strife and conflict, even war and death. He was aghast at how supposedly God-fearing people could persecute others whose belief systems were at odds with their own, and how they tried to force their beliefs into school systems or governance. He was baffled at what was so hard to understand about the principle of complete separation of church and state. No, atheism was just fine with him, and he relished his open Sundays.

As he slowly bounced up the road alongside Trout Brook, Paul was deep in thought about his approach to fishing today. It was now well enough into summer's warmth that trout should be looking to feed on the surface, and dry flies could be effective. If not, he could always choose to bounce nymphs along the bottom where trout usually feed, but dries were so much more fun. He loved the grace and elegance of casting tiny dry flies to imitate emerging or egg-laying mayflies, trying to land them delicately and perfectly on the surface with no indication they were connected to a hair-thin line. Then he would drift them downstream with no drag, perfectly naturally, until, he hoped, a hungry brookie would rise to the surface and be fooled by his stealth and skill. The strikes could range from a calm and gentle "sip"—barely breaking the surface tension—to a violent attack with the fish coming completely out of the water in its eagerness to feed on a floating insect. The excitement and satisfaction he felt at that moment of connection to a wild trout was something he could not convey to someone who had never done this. It was magical every time.

Paul's daydreaming was disrupted when he saw a pickup truck parked along the right side of the road, about a half mile up from the confluence with

Odder Creek. "*Oh crap,*" thought Paul, "*someone else is here.*" Then he recognized the truck from its jacked-up and pimped-out appearance. The big, black, Dodge Ram on stilts had to belong to Billy Wilson, the mechanic and NASCAR fan who worked at Lou's garage. Paul thought Billy was an OK guy, though he was strictly a worm fisherman— something that Paul found distasteful, as he felt that fly fishing was so much more sporting and challenging. Still, just like religious tolerance in these parts, Paul had a "to each his own" attitude and did not try to convert anyone to his way of fishing. If Billy wanted to dunk worms in pursuit of trout, then that was his prerogative, and more power to him.

Paul quickly decided he would move further upstream and try to get ahead of Billy. Then he remembered Peter's Falls about a half mile further up. It was a beautiful waterfall named after Peter Odderton, the fellow who started the Odderton Country Store way back in the 1880s. The falls dropped a good 10 feet over three levels of cascading limestone rocks and formed a gorgeous swirling pool at the base, usually frothing with the powerful signature of water mixed with gravity. That pool, over six feet deep and spreading out 30 feet in diameter, was the gathering place of many a fine brook trout moving upstream in spring. They held up here and found abundant food coming over the falls, along with cold, deep water in later summer when temperatures went up and flows went down, a situation that could stress this cold-water species. The biggest fish in the brook would be found here in the best habitat, displacing (or eating) smaller individuals. So Paul quickly decided he would drive about a quarter mile ahead of Billy, park, and work his way up to the falls, fishing all the way.

Two minutes and many bounces later, Paul found a pull off on the right and nestled his truck into the tight space. Getting out, he sucked in a deep breath and took in the beauty all around him. It was a picture-perfect day. With a hint of overnight coolness remaining in the air, temperatures were headed to the mid-70s, and a few puffy white clouds harmonized with and gave a third dimension to a cerulean blue sky. The vegetation was lush and well-watered, and the leaves of the trees retained a hint of the lime-green brilliance of newness that appeared miraculously each spring. It was past black fly season and the air was blissfully lacking in mosquitoes.

The melodic rush of the brook 30 feet away, down a steep incline through a dark and moist hemlock grove, sang a song whose beauty could not be matched by Rogers and Hammerstein or the angels themselves. Paul couldn't have asked for a better day and reminded himself that, if there was indeed a God, this would have to be where He lived. Peace and beauty originated here.

After his few moments of reverence and appreciation for the perfectness surrounding him, Paul Johnson reached for his Orvis 3-weight carbon rod. *"Another bit of perfection"* he thought, as he gratefully caressed this thing of beauty. This was one of the few cases, he felt, when human inventions could be worthy of nature. In contrast with most other things humanity did that tarnished and despoiled the natural world, this fly rod belonged here; it did not detract from the place but rather was fully congruent with it. It was subtle and fragile, modest and unassuming; it blended in. Sighing deeply with satisfaction, he carefully strung his fly line through the guides and with a nail knot tied on a new, 7.5 foot tapered leader; he then used a surgeon's knot to finish off with three feet of a 7X tippet, the finest he had, with barely 2 lb. of tensile strength. The lightness of his rig perfectly matched the fine beauty of the watershed and its native inhabitants, the magnificent brook trout.

Paul fingered his way through his box of dry flies and quickly settled on an Ausable Wulff, his usual default fly. Floating high and proud, the Ausable Wulff—named for the fabled Ausable River of Michigan and even-more fabled fly-fishing legend Lee Wulff—was a wonderful attractor pattern. It did not imitate any particular insect per se, but rather seemed to attract trout as an all-round tasty bit. It was easy for Paul to follow it visually through rough and turbulent water, and was one of several patterns that he usually stuck with. Satisfied that all was well, he tied on the fly with an improved clinch knot, took a drink of water, slipped on his fly vest, zipped his keys and wallet into a safe pocket, and headed downslope for the water.

Reaching the bank after working his way over boulders and through ground vegetation of the cool hemlock grove, and quietly slipping down into the moving water, Paul felt the familiar wet chill penetrate his sneakers and nylon pants, reminding him of how cold and clear these fish needed the water to be. Paul did not own and never used waders, preferring instead to be immersed in the system in which he was a temporary guest. He chuckled at those folks who bought their fancy Simms $400 chest waders only to thrash around in shin-deep water in July with air temperatures of 85, when a good cooling was just what they needed. In contrast, he liked to "feel" the stream, understand it, and become a part of it as best he could. How could you do that behind a wall of neoprene? And so what if his feet numbed up after a bit? That's the price you paid for lightweight freedom in a wild trout stream. That was your guest entry ticket into a different world.

Before he began his fish quest, Paul always liked to pause in midstream and make a small offering of respect and gratitude for the abundance and glory of all that surrounded him. "For the fish, for the waters, for the forest, for the air and the sky, for all the Earth and all its inhabitants, I am deeply grateful." And he truly meant it. He never ceased to marvel at the mysteries that lay before him, not least of which was the fact that two simple gasses—hydrogen and oxygen—when combined in a 2:1 ratio, somehow morphed into the water that held his fish and made all life possible. If there was a greater and more-important miracle in the universe he'd sure like to know what it was.

Paul looked upstream and eyed a small backwater behind a large midstream boulder about 20 feet away; he judged it to be a good holding spot for a brook trout, who would be focused on the conveyor-belt of water coming around the left side, delivering food. The boulder provided a quiet and safe location from which fish could nab insects drifting by. Paul deftly made two false casts to lengthen his line, judged it to be the right distance, and on the third cast laid the fly three feet upstream of the boulder, right in the main line of flow. Like clockwork, as it drifted down past the boulder, a trout shot out and slapped at it, but did not hook up. Paul smiled at the results of his first cast of the season. This could be a really good day.

Paul waited a minute to let the trout relax, blew off his fly to dry it, and made a second cast to the same spot. *Bam!* This time they connected, and the water exploded in a mini frenzy as his quarry reacted to the hooked surprise that did not accompany the dozens of drifting insects that it consumed daily. It immediately went to the bottom, shaking its head to be rid of the shock in its lip, and then shot upstream 20 feet. Paul applied light pressure and turned the fish back downstream. The trout sped past him, this time two pools down as Paul carefully played him, retaining a tight line and following on foot, trying not to stumble and fall in this challenging and foreign habitat. After a few other darting movements the fish tired, and Paul was able to carefully reel him in to his feet. The fish gave a final splash and tried to take off when it saw legs and sneakers in the water, but Paul's even pressure enabled him to gently coax the fish into his hand and hold it upside down in the water, a move that often calmed them.

He then admired the stunning beauty of this species, never tiring of the sight. This 10-inch fish was brilliantly colored in a way that simply defied description. Rather than trying to describe it to non-fishing friends, Paul merely told them to look it up because nothing compared and you simply could not convey in words the stunning and brilliant beauty of *Salvelinus fontinalis*. He saw that the fly was a clean and classic hookup on the lower lip, and he gently backed the barbless hook out of the mouth. Returning the fish to an upright position, and keeping it in calm but moving water, he gently swished it forward and back to run oxygen-rich water across the gills of his tired friend. After 20 seconds the fish came to life and shot out to the shadows of the nearest boulder. Just like the fly-fishing visitors from New Jersey, Paul Simon and Bruce Bivens, Paul Johnson was a catch-and-release guy who had no interest in killing his take.

"It doesn't get any better than that!" Paul said to the rocks and trees as he stood up, looked around, and took in a deep and satisfied breath. He couldn't imagine a nicer day or anything he would prefer doing right now.

Paul continued working upstream, identifying the likely lies of feeding fish and working his Ausable Wulff to its fullest potential. It felt so damned *good* to be back out there since his last foray the previous October. *"I've got to make more time for this,"* thought Paul. *"Nobody on their death bed says 'I sure wish I had worked more.'"* No, regrets at the end of life were always that you didn't make more time to pursue your passions, and Paul reminded himself that there was more to this existence than making a living on the farm. He solemnly promised himself he would get out at least twice a month, more if he could, for the rest of the summer and fall.

Paul didn't have the consistent success that he did on his first casts, but he did pick up three more gorgeous little brookies, one a very respectable twelve-incher. He felt the anticipation build as he got closer to Peter's Falls and the big pool. He had high hopes for larger fish coming out of that hole and was getting near his target. But to sweeten the anticipation of fishing at the falls, and to appreciate the scene, Paul sat on a stream-side boulder for 10 minutes, sipped some water, and took it all in. No need to hurry; the pool and fish could wait.

And here he got philosophical, which always happened around the mesmerizing flow of water. He thought about a term he once heard in fly fishing, "the last 30 feet." This is where it all mattered, where success or failure was determined. To successfully ply this trade, you must understand that trout don't care a whit about you, your position in life, your possessions, your power, your prowess with a credit card. You can pay thousands of dollars to come to Vermont, hire a guide, buy expensive equipment, fancy clothes, but *you* are absolutely meaningless. If you don't respect the fish enough to abandon your own ego, if you haven't bothered to learn about them, to understand them, if you don't have the humility to leave your world behind and become part of theirs, you will fail, despite any riches or power you might think you have. All the fish care about is that fly you present—that last 30 feet—not how much your rod costs or what type of waders you wear or what you do for a living. If you could cast well with a broomstick and thread you would be just as effective as with thousands of dollars' worth of tackle.

Paul further lost himself in contemplation. To land a trout on a fly, he reasoned, to make gains in this other world, you must give up much of yourself—ego, pride, hubris. For here, being human, wealthy, feeing superior, has zero relevance, and in fact is a hindrance. You must transcend self and become a being more respectful, more humble, and more seamlessly integrated into the world to have success. You have to embrace the reality that the modern human world we have created has no currency whatsoever in these waters. Your credit card existence is rejected here as invalid. You need something much more real: you need to be raw and primitive. These fish thrived for millions of years; you, foolish human, are brand new on the scene.

Rousing himself from his reverie and straightening out his bones, Paul started upstream again and soon could hear the falls. Sure enough, he rounded a bend to the left, and there they were, 50 yards ahead, in all their massive glory. The water cascaded heavily yet gracefully down the three levels of rocks to swirl in the large pool at the bottom, before exiting through a powerful run defined by several boulders—no doubt deposited by a major flood at some point in time, and left untouched since then. Five years ago? Fifty? Five hundred? Who knew?

To Paul, those boulders represented the yin and yang of stability and change, and were the epitome of everything he loved about *hmmm. . . what the hell is that?* questioned Paul as his eye caught something strangely out of place upstream. Squinting to bring it into focus he thought, *that's a weird-looking log wedged there. Almost looks like a person, the way it's laid out.* He continued several steps closer and in an instant his blood ran cold, a chill enveloped his whole body, and his heart seemed to stop. "Holy shit!!" exclaimed Paul as he realized it was indeed a person, lying in the water, wedged between two boulders where the pool exited into its fast run.

"Jesus Christ!!" Paul emitted as he ran forward and tossed his Orvis rod into the bushes to his left. As he got closer he clearly saw a body oriented downstream, face-down, arms extended, long hair flowing in the current, and quickly recognized it, even from the back, as Billy Wilson. "*Billy*," shouted Paul as he approached. "Oh my God, oh my God. Billy, *Billy!*" Rushing to the inert body, he could see a small amount of blood oozing from behind Billy's right ear. He quickly turned him over and slapped the lifeless cheeks to no avail. He saw the lips were blue and the face ashen.

Paul grabbed Billy by the shoulders and dragged him to shore, no easy task as the kid had chest waders on and they had taken on much water. Paul turned him on his stomach, placed Billy's face to one side, and began to press on his back. By the third push he saw water exiting Billy's mouth, and continued until nothing more was produced, another four compressions. Quickly turning his patient onto his back, he began CPR—something he had learned in an evening session back at UVM. He pinched Billy's nose, covered his lips with his own, and expelled two strong breaths; he saw Billy's chest rise a bit. A sudden wave of nausea passed through Paul as Billy's icy cold lips and the smell and taste of the graveled stream bottom registered in his brain; he spat out a grain of sand that had been transferred from Billy's lips. The nausea passed quickly as Paul focused on 30 strong and rapid compressions to Billy's sternum, followed by another two breaths, followed by more compressions.

Paul continued this process for 15 agonizing minutes—though it seemed like an hour—periodically checking for spontaneous breathing or a pulse.

Breaths, 30 compressions; breaths, 30 compressions. Nothing. Finally, exhausted and sweating profusely, he stopped, admitted defeat, and accepted a bitter reality: Billy Wilson was dead, actually *dead*, and there was nothing he could do about it. Sitting back on his heels, and without warning, Paul Johnson began to sob. He hadn't known Billy well but that didn't matter right now. Another human being— one from his town who he had seen living his life like everyone else—had just died in front of him, and Paul was the only one to witness it. This individual had been born into the world, grew up, learned to walk and talk, went to school, matured, got a job, interacted with his community, did a thousand different things, had dreams and aspirations, lived for, what—21, 23 years?— and it all came down to this one place and moment and circumstance. Here. Now. Dead. Final. And here was Paul, the only witness to share in this profound event, this cessation of a unique life, this terribly sudden and unexpected end. Sobbing was all he could do for the moment, and he openly wept.

After calming his tears and gathering his thoughts, Paul stepped back and examined the scene. He quickly surmised that Billy had slipped on a rock and fallen backwards, hitting the back of his head on another rock, knocking himself unconscious. He was then grabbed by the current, which must have spun him face down and lodged him between two boulders, effectively writing his death sentence. Because blood was still oozing from Billy's skull, it couldn't have happened all that long ago.

Holy shit, thought Paul, *if I hadn't sat on my ass down there playing nature boy I might have been in time to save him.* After berating himself for delaying his arrival to the falls, once the logical part of his brain kicked back in he told himself that he had no idea how long Billy had been there and could not have known there was trouble ahead and it wasn't his fault. Still, if only he hadn't stopped for his little musings, maybe he could have helped.

Paul then noticed a fishing rod wedged between a couple of rocks upstream from where he'd found Billy. He realized this had to be the kid's rod, which was dropped during his fall. Paul walked out, unwedged it, and started to reel it in. As soon as the line tightened he felt life at the other end and the line moved across the pool. *Jeez,* thought Paul, *Billy had a fish on the line and was playing it when he fell.* Paul played the fish as well and soon realized it was a significant size. After several minutes of cat and mouse, he pulled in a gorgeous 16-inch brook trout, probably pushing two pounds—a near-trophy fish. Ironically, rather than killing the fish, the fish had killed Billy; the excitement of the battle must have caused the fall. Paul turned back to Billy's body. "Kid, you had a lunker on. I hope you realized how big it was."

Examining the flopping fish, Paul saw that it had swallowed the worm, and the hook was imbedded deeply in its gullet; small amounts of blood oozed from the wound, something that would rarely happen with a dry fly. Paul knew there was no way the fish would live, so he mercifully dispatched it with a quick and firm blow to the head with a rock; it shuddered twice and went still. The irony of a second killing today caused by a rock to the head did not escape Paul. He laid the fish in a large vest pocket. As he walked back to shore he noticed a metal stringer leading into the water. Hoisting it up, three good-sized and half-dead brook trout with metal clips through their mouths and gills weakly flopped around, expending the final energies of their life forces. He removed the large trout from his vest and added it to the body count on the stringer.

Paul knew his next move was to notify Carl Johnsgaard, the Oddertown Police Chief, about what had happened and to help him remove the body. But as there was no cell service up here on the stream, and precious little in Oddertown itself, he would have to drive back into town and look for Carl the old fashioned way, perhaps at a church service. He felt bad leaving Billy here all alone, but had no choice. He pulled his body a little further from the water and laid Billy's arms across his belly in a peaceful pose; he could do nothing else for him at this point.

As Paul walked back down the road to his truck he suddenly realized his hands were empty, other than the stringer of fish, and remembered that he had tossed his fly rod into the bushes when he saw Billy lying in the water. Somehow his $500 Orvis rod and reel no longer seemed all that important to him, and this beautiful day had lost its luster.

Chapter 11

Saturday, July 6, 2:00 PM

———

A LARGE AND SOMBER CROWD FILLED EVERY available nook and cranny of St. John's United Methodist Church of Oddertown. Whether they knew him or not, people from all walks of life and every social and economic stratum turned out to mourn and honor Billy Wilson, and help comfort his small and devastated family. His mother Pearl, younger brother Bobby, 17, and still younger sister Gail, 14, were seated in the front pew right of the center aisle, buffered at either end by his Uncle Bart and Aunt Louise, the full extent of the remaining Wilsons. They all donned stunned and vacant looks. Pearl held tightly the hands of her two remaining children, who simultaneously offered and sought strength from the physical connection with their mother.

Lou Quentin sat directly behind the Wilsons. Her red eyes and puffy, moist face betrayed the soft spot she had for Billy despite all previous outward appearances; not a hint of her usually tough demeanor was in evidence, vaporized by death's unexpected appearance. Lou's indescribably sad eyes darted around the church like a drowning person seeking a lifeline from anyone who might toss one. She could barely comprehend that Billy—with whom she had worked so closely for three and a half years and upon whom she had depended so heavily—would no longer be a part of her life and her business, and she felt the loss no less than if he was family.

Lou's buddy Raymond Pulan sat on her right side, with his mother Barbara to his right. Raymond tightly clutched hands with both of them and looked back and forth at the two people closest to him in the world, seeking comfort and reassurance, not knowing what to expect in the next hour.

The Odd Balls, Jim Watson, and Kate clustered together in the middle of the mass of humanity that was Oddertown. The Golightly family populated the last row and appeared serenely saddened; Charity seemed especially upset by Billy's death. Tony and Marie Delfasio stood against the right-side wall, near a seated Victor Kemper, Layla Liederman, and Dora Stephenson.

Every pew was filled and an overflow crowd stood along the sides and back of the church, and even spilled out the double wooden doors and onto the worn marble front steps. This was a community loss, and the whole of Oddertown would grieve together.

The miserably hot temperatures dictated that most formal wear—suits, sport coats, ties—be left at home in lieu of more-sensible short sleeves, dress trousers, and comfortable summer dresses. Nobody would question the mode of dress on this 90-degree, high-humidity afternoon. Many mourners brought fans to move the still air across their faces in a futile attempt to keep cool, and all windows and doors of the church were thrown wide open. Perspiration on faces and arms was the order of the day.

In the nave of the church—in front of the altar and to the immediate left of the family—sat a modest wooden casket on a rolling bier, shrouded by a simple but colorful pall. The large cloth featured a prominent cross in brown and green stitchery, positioned toward the forward end of the casket, above where Billy's head would be. Twelve white candles on stands, representing the twelve apostles, formed a U-shaped border at the left, foot, and right of the casket.

Paul Johnson, still shaken by his grisly discovery of Billy in the stream a week before, sat about two-thirds of the way back, on the left side, at the center aisle. His wife and children did not attend, choosing instead to pick up some of the slack at the farm during this extremely busy time; Paul had not gotten much work done during this upsetting week—he slept poorly and repeatedly wrestled with the awful memories of his encounter with sudden death—and consequently they were falling behind in their farm chores. It was just as well that his family stayed home, with the church being packed to overflowing.

As he sat there waiting for the service to begin— vaguely hearing the soft tones of the church organ playing a neutral and nondescript tune—Paul reflected back on the events since last Sunday, still trying to clear the cobwebs from the surreal experience in an attempt to make sense of everything. He couldn't get past the simple fact that, this time last week, Billy Wilson was alive and well and going about his business, and everything in Oddertown was normal. Nobody last Saturday could have imagined in their wildest dreams that young Billy had but one more day of life remaining. It was the devastating suddenness and preventable nature of the affair that perhaps were the hardest to reconcile. It was an absurd thought: slip on a rock and your life is over. Possibly a half century or more, wiped out by some algae and mud.

After retrieval of the body by Paul Johnson and Carl Johnsgaard—in the back of Oddertown's new but used Suburban police car that Billy only recently helped to find—a full police report was prepared in which Paul was the main source of information beyond the physical evidence. All details of his discovery and subsequent actions were recorded by Carl and forwarded to the county coroner. An autopsy performed on Wednesday in St. Johnsbury revealed that, just as Paul had surmised, Billy had slipped and hit the back of his head on a rock, behind the right ear. "Blunt force trauma," as per the official lingo, and his occipital bone had been fractured, indicating a hard blow. Billy had then, in an unconscious state, aspirated significant quantities of water into his lungs, and drowned within a few minutes. Time of death could only be estimated plus or minus an hour, but was perfectly centered on the time when Paul found him. Foul play was ruled out; in addition to no probable cause, tiny rock mineral fragments in his skull matched the rocks from the site of the accident. There was even a small smudge of algae and mud imbedded in the heel tread of Billy's right wading boot, showing the cause of the fall. Although everything made logical sense, and no fault was cast, Paul still felt a sense of guilt in not having reached the site sooner. The image of Billy's ashen face and blue lips would not soon leave his mind.

The organ finished its droning, interrupting Paul's thoughts, and the Reverend Eugene Hucks calmly walked out from the sacristy to the left. He stopped in front of the crowd, between the altar and the casket, and everyone stood. After recognizing the family with a bow of the head, he invited the congregation to join in singing the hymn "How Blest Are They Who Trust in Christ," whereupon the organ began playing and many voices joined in a beautiful, if not completely harmonic, rendition.

Pausing while the last organ note lingered in mid-air and then faded into a memory, Reverend Hucks invited the congregation to be seated, where-upon he addressed them. "Friends, we gather here today in this house of the Lord to praise God and to witness to our faith as we celebrate the life of Billy Wilson. Yes, we come together in grief, and acknowledge our great human loss. But we also come together in recognition and celebration of a life that touched all of us. May God grant us grace, that in pain we may find comfort, in sorrow hope, in death resurrection."

Yeah, right, thought Paul. *Where was your God when Billy was out there dying? God sure could have come in handy back there, Reverend.*

Hucks went on. "Jesus said, 'I am the resurrection and I am life. Those who believe in me, even though they die, yet shall they live, and whoever lives and believes in me shall never die.'" *Sorry, Padre, but Billy sure as hell died and I suspect he would rather have lived.* "'I am Alpha and Omega, the beginning and the end, the first and the last. I died, and behold I am alive for evermore, and I hold the keys of hell and death. Because I live, you shall live also.'" *Not in this case, God. Have a look in that box. I'm pretty sure he's dead as a lamp post.*

The Reverend continued with other words of support and comfort, and spoke directly to the family, declaring that their son, brother, and nephew was called home for other duties. They were assured that Billy was being accepted into a place of eternal glory and was loved and cherished. Any sins committed by the flesh would be cleansed by God, assisted by the prayers and unwavering faith demonstrated by those remaining behind in this life. Pearl Wilson felt comforted by these words; the belief that Billy did not die randomly, but according to God's plan, took some of the immediate pain from her. The thought of Billy residing in heaven with a loving God began to replace the abject and raw pain in her heart. In contrast, Paul scoffed at Hucks's words. His anger and personal witness to the tragedy only fanned his atheistic feelings, overwhelming any comfort anyone could offer, including the good Reverend's attempts.

Another hymn broke Paul's silent and dark thoughts, this time "A Mighty Fortress is Our God." He admitted to himself that the music was quite beautiful, but he was still angry and not won over by what he saw as empty platitudes. The rest of the congregants, by and large, not only were comforted by the words but seemed to further coalesce as a community; the Wilson's loss was Oddertown's loss and Oddertown would face this tragedy as one.

The Reverend then spoke again, to the family and to the congregation at large.

"I did not know Billy Wilson well, but I knew him well enough to be assured of these things. I know that he was a good and kind young man, dedicated to his family, to supporting them, to loving them. He loved and protected his younger sister Gail and brother Bobby, and he was a great comfort to Pearl, his dear mother, who adored her first born. Billy was always there for her, especially when family troubles struck and they found themselves alone."

Pearl broke down at this point and audibly cried for the whole congregation to hear. Her children both buried their heads in her arms, sobbing along with her.

Hucks waited patiently for the Wilsons to compose themselves before continuing.

"I know that Billy assumed the reins and responsibilities of head of family at an early age, and did all he could to assure his young siblings stayed in school and out of trouble, that they all had a roof over their heads, and food to nourish their bodies. I further know that Billy was a good and hard and honest worker. He loved cars and racing, second only to his love for his family, and he gave his heart over to a passion many of us are never fortunate enough to find. I also know that Billy loved God, and is loved by God. I believe Billy will find a good place in heaven, maybe even one with turbo-charged race cars and a big race track." His family smiled and nodded at the small bit of levity, which helped to break the tension in the room for a few seconds.

"And, my friends," said Reverend Hucks. "I know one more thing. I know that Billy's family will need the support of our entire community in the coming weeks, months, and years. Not only our neighborly comfort and moral support, which will be most welcome, but also our tangible, earthly gifts. As you know, Billy was the main bread winner of the Wilson family, and without him they will encounter many challenges ahead. But I also know, most of all, that the good and kind people of Oddertown will not let them want for long. I am confident you will look out for your neighbors, extend your hearts and your hearths to them. I know you will be there when they need it most. I would like to begin that loving support by taking up a collection for the family to address their immediate needs. Please, my dear friends, be as generous as you can as our baskets of loving kindness are passed among you now."

"But do not let your kindnesses end here. As today becomes but a distant memory and we all return to our normal lives, the Wilsons will continue to need your support. Check in on them, bring them a casserole, ask if they need help with a light bill. Their needs will continue far beyond today. In the name of Jesus, I ask your neighborly blessings, and I thank you."

As the baskets were passed through the pews, and the good townspeople opened their hearts and their wallets, the organ began the familiar hymn *I'll Fly Away* with most of the congregation joining in. The heat and humidity did little to enhance their harmonics, and sweat continued to glisten on every brow.

As the song ended, Reverend Hucks approached the head of the casket and placed his right hand

upon the cross of the pall. "My friends, please rise."
They all did as asked. Looking upward and raising
his left hand to the skies, palm open, he closed his
eyes and prayed with an especially intense confidence and solemnity, and with his strongest voice,
as if his words needed to rise through the high ceiling and clear up to heaven. "Into your hands, O
merciful Savior, we commend your servant Billy
Wilson. Acknowledge, we humbly beseech you, a
sheep of your own fold, a lamb of your own flock,
a sinner of your own redeeming. Receive Billy into
the arms of your mercy, into the blessed rest of
everlasting peace, and into the glorious company
of the saints of light. Amen"

"Amen," responded the congregation in unison,
as Pearl once more broke into uncontrolled weeping.

Again waiting for Pearl to collect herself, the
Reverend Hucks then ended the service with these
words, directed back at the congregation: "Dying,
Christ destroyed our death. Rising, Christ restored
our life. Christ will come again in glory. As in bap-
tism Billy Wilson put on Christ, so in Christ may
Billy Wilson be clothed with glory. Here and now,
dear friends, we are God's children."

The words nearly rubbed Paul raw. How could
anyone believe in a God that abandoned this kid
in his greatest time of need? Yet, these same words
that so inflamed Paul were a soothing salve on the
Wilson family's wound, on the entire town's loss.

"Internment will be by private ceremony tomorrow at the Oddertown Mapleview Cemetery," said
Revered Hucks. "Only family and closest friends
need attend. Now, the family invites all of you to
reconvene immediately at the Odderton Country
Store to partake of refreshments and continue the

celebration of the life of Billy Wilson. Go in peace, my friends, and with the eternal love of our Lord."

As the congregation stood and began to shuffle down the aisles toward the double doors and open air, they heard the strains of a lone bagpiper standing at respectful attention near the clock in Time Square playing *Amazing Grace*. Even the atheist Paul Johnson was moved to visible tears by the emotional depth of the scene. That song always had the capacity to wring out sentiment from even the most hardened skeptic.

When Paul emerged into the harsh sunlight to make his way over to Odd Country, he wiped his eyes dry and saw Jim Watson standing by himself under a box elder tree, enjoying the shade and listening to the bagpiper's final stanza. Paul joined him and they both smiled and nodded in mutual greeting.

"Beautiful song, eh?" inquired Paul.

"That it is," replied Jim. "Always gets to me, even if the religious message is lost on me. There's something very powerful in that song."

"Yeah, I know what you mean, Doc. Gets to me, too, even though I don't for a second buy into the religious stuff. You're pretty much an atheist too, right?"

"Well, close," replied Jim. "I consider myself an agnostic, Paul." They both smiled solemnly and nodded to the townspeople who walked by toward Odd Country. "As a scientist I know that I can no sooner *disprove* the existence of a God than anyone can *prove* it. It's a matter of belief and faith, which is exactly as it should be. Although I personally don't *believe* there is an all-knowing, all-powerful creator, I can't *prove* that. So to be fair, I go with agnostic.

And you know the real definition of an agnostic, right?" He paused… "Just a chicken-shit atheist!" They both chuckled. "We want to hedge our bets, just in case we're wrong!"

More chuckling. After a moment of reflection, Paul launched into what was really bugging him, finally feeling comfortable with a like-minded individual. "You know, Doc, I have a real problem with all that stuff about God loving and protecting and calling us home. What a line of crap. Billy wasn't called home anywhere, he stepped on a slick rock. Just a random accident. Some algae or diatoms growing on a hard surface killed him, pure and simple. Could have happened to anyone or no one. I want to scream when people say 'it was his time' or 'God called him home.' No, it *wasn't* his time, it was just a stupid accident! Billy was in the prime of his life, with most of it still ahead of him, dammit. He was robbed of probably 50 years of life and I'm pissed about it! Then they go making up bullshit stories about God loving him and wanting him at his side and other nonsense. Nothing of the sort; he made one little misstep and paid for it with his life."

Paul stopped for a minute to take a breath and gauge Doc's reaction before continuing. Doc merely gazed out at the crowd moving slowly past, digesting Paul's words. "It's not fair, Jim, but we know there's little in life that's fair, so get used to it. He got a shitty deal, that's all. If there really was a loving God, he would have made sure that Billy stepped one foot to the right or the left and protected him. Where was their loving God when Billy needed help? Why wasn't he there when Billy was vulnerable? I'll tell you why—because there *is* no such God. How can anyone believe there's a loving God ready and willing to take him home, but not a loving God to protect him when he needed it? I can't believe these people don't see that and have such a selective view."

After a pause to let thoughts settle, Jim replied. "Well, Paul, though I basically agree with you, these beliefs of theirs perform a really important function, especially now. Suppose they all felt as you do? What then? We'd have a grieving family and a whole town walking around angry at a senseless death that had no purpose. We'd have hundreds of people mad and scared and confused, finding no comfort for their loss. Just like you. But if they feel there is a larger plan, someone looking over them, some place they will go after death, something to give a senseless death some meaning, then they are calmed and comforted. Believing that God called Billy home gives the family reassurance, Paul. They will miss him but they believe that his death was more than random, that it was called for by a Supreme Being, that Billy is now in a better place. That's really important to everyone right now."

"Yeah, Doc, I know what you mean," sighed Paul, "but isn't truth and reality important? Isn't it better to face the facts and see life it for what it is? We're all just born, and eventually we die, some sooner, some later, doing the best we can in-between. Why hide behind these false curtains, making believe there is something more out there, something to look forward to after death? I think it just deludes us and distracts us from living a good life here and now."

"Well first of all, you don't have a market on truth," replied Jim. "This is *your* truth, Paul, but not something you can prove, any more than they can prove God exists. Second, maybe this is the *perfect* time for delusion, if that's what it is. What's the harm in providing comfort and meaning at this time? Sure, maybe you and I can accept what we see as the stark realities of life, but others think differently and need different beliefs. Especially now. His poor mother and sibs had something enormously important taken from them. They need to make some sense of this accident, and believing that Billy was taken for a reason by a loving God is a whole lot more comforting than thinking this was completely senseless and random and he was killed by algae. Let them have that, Paul, and let them find comfort in it. It doesn't matter that these aren't *your* beliefs. These are *their* beliefs and they will help get the Wilsons through a horrible time. That, and support from everyone here, including us agnostics and atheists."

Paul lowered his head and thought for a few seconds in silence. He then nodded in understanding. "I get your point, Doc. This isn't about me and my beliefs or needs. I guess it is bigger than that. I think I'm still so mad and shocked by the whole damned thing. I'm too close to the accident and not seeing the big picture, I suppose. But you're absolutely right; I need to at least respect their views right now. Well, I guess that's why you're The Wiz and I'm just a dirt farmer," Paul concluded with a sheepish smile.

With that, Jim put his arm around Paul's shoulder and said "C'mon buddy, let's go inside, have some refreshments, and help console the family in whatever way helps them the best. Who knows? It might even help you too."

Chapter 12

Monday, July 8, 6:45 AM

——————

AFTER THE SHOCKING DEATH AND SOBERING funeral of young Billy Wilson, the next order of business for Oddertown was to return to some semblance of normalcy, to find their old equilibrium after a seismic shock. Jolts to the community like this, though thankfully rare, upset the regular and comforting rhythms and flows of a town, and send folks yearning for the reassuring, if sometimes boring, repetition of everyday life.

The Odd Balls did their part in bringing the community back to regular form by faithfully gathering at Odd Country bright and early Monday morning. With everyone seated in their regular places, and breakfast just served up by Jodi, the men tucked into their fares; the familiar and comforting smells of breakfast helped suggest normalcy. Silas Miller led the way back to familiar and solid ground with his unwavering devotion to one waffle, a scoop of butter, and an ounce of maple syrup. Though initially more somber than usual, with no pinging and cutting remarks, the Odd Balls did their best to regain their stride and slowly loosened up the course of conversation. After some respectful reminiscences about Billy, and observations on the accident and the church service, they moved on to more-regular topics.

For the first time since the accident, Paul Johnson—who needed to find his equilibrium as much as anyone and hoped for direction from the Odd Balls—was able to reflect on the part of his fishing trip before his discovery of Billy. He regaled the boys with his recollections of stream conditions, the beauty of the morning, and his successes in landing several good fish before the awful discovery. The group was fascinated with his story of finding a 16-inch brookie on Billy's line, and speculated about Billy's last several seconds of living conscience and how excited he must have been trying to reel that one in. "At least he died doing something he loved," observed Jubal Keller, summing up the group's feelings and trying to put a positive spin on an otherwise tragic situation.

Willard Bennett then nauseated the boys with his vivid description of one of his sows giving difficult birth at 4:00 this morning to six piglets, made more graphic and realistic by the porcine odors accompanying the story and the fresh blood stains on Willard's shirt sleeves. Just when they looked around in desperation to change the subject, a welcome distraction manifested itself in the form of Charlie Harbrough walking in the front door.

Seizing the opportunity to talk about anything other than difficult piglet births—Carpe

Opportunum!—Only Owens quickly spoke up. "Now there goes a son of a bitch who nobody would sit around mourning if *he* died in Trout Brook," proclaimed Only. "I don't think too many tears would be shed if he disappeared from our radar." The boys nodded and quickly concurred with his observation.

"What's his problem, anyway?" added Phil Haderlie. "What the hell did we ever do to him to make him such a prick?"

"I don't think we did a damned thing to him," replied Silas Miller. "I think he came that way. That's just the way he is. He's been here, what, 30-some years? I don't recall a good word out of him the whole time."

Jubal Keller pitched in. "I heard that he used to live in the Midwest somewhere. Iowa or Ohio or some place. He was married back then, if you can believe it, and they think he killed his wife! Had to move to these parts to disappear from the law. He's probably still wanted out west."

"Now where'd you hear that, Jubal?" challenged Paul Johnson.

"Old Francois Lefitte told me years ago," he said. "Francois tried to be friendly with Charlie when he first moved here but he just got pushed away. But he did learn about the wife dying and said Charlie killed her. I thought everyone knew that."

"That old Canuck Francois barely spoke any English, Jubal!" countered Paul. "How could he know anything Charlie might have said? He probably misunderstood him."

"Well I n-never heard about a k-k-killing," observed Steve, "but I did hear that h-he was an alcoholic and a ch-child abuser and that's why he moved here. H-had to get away from little k-kids and disappear in the K-Kingdom."

They all watched Charlie suspiciously as he stood at the kitchen counter and ordered breakfast to go. He never stayed long at Odd Country, never ate there, and never engaged in any more talk than the minimum necessary to transact business and leave.

"There's definitely something mysterious about the guy," suggested Only. "Caleb told me one time that Charlie comes in to his flower shop every year in early May and has three bouquets of flowers wired to a cemetery or funeral home or some such place out in the Midwest, Ohio I think it was. Same time, every year, like clockwork."

"Really?" replied Silas. "I never heard that. I wonder if he did kill someone and now feels bad about it."

"I think you're a bunch of old-lady gossipers," observed Paul. "I think you're making up shit about old Charlie just because he sticks to himself and is a little different."

"A little different?" ejected Phil Haderlie. "He's a pain in the ass who hates everybody! He's never said a kind word to anyone and is just plain nasty, Paul."

"Well, have you ever said a kind word to *him*?" replied Paul. "Have you ever invited him to join us for breakfast?"

"I tried talking to him early on but he'd just grunt a few words and walk away," explained Phil. "You know, Paul, the street runs in both directions. I'm a live-and-let-live kind of guy, but the other guy has to give something back and show some decency. There're lots of strange types around here that

I might not agree with but we get along just fine because they try to get along back. But not him."

"Yeah, that's right," added Jubal Keller, with others nodding in agreement. "He's just nasty and doesn't want anything to do with us. I'm happy to leave him the hell alone if that's how he wants it."

"Me too," added Silas. "I was down to Doc Harrison's in Saint J a week ago for a checkup. Was sitting in the waiting room reading *Field and Stream* and out from the back comes Charlie, looking like his best dog just died. I said hi but he walked right past me like he hadn't heard me. Looked even more into himself than usual."

"I wonder if he has some kinda serious health problem?" asked Only, with a tinge of sympathy in his voice. "Maybe he got some bad news from the doc."

"Well I know for sure it's not his heart," replied Phil.

"How do you know that?" asked Jubal.

"Cause he doesn't have one!"

As the chuckling died down, Charlie wandered past the table to his old brass mailbox, nodding almost imperceptibly to the Odd Balls as he passed, pulled out a lone envelope that appeared to be a bill, and left Odd Country with his head down and without a further look in their direction. Paul Johnson chided the group again. "I think you guys need to give Charlie a break. We don't know anything about him. We don't know what he's been through or what might be eating at him. Yeah, he may be a nasty SOB, or maybe he's really hurting about something."

"You mean for 30 years?" asked Only. "C'mon, Paul, the guy's been a jerk ever since he moved here.

He hasn't changed a bit and isn't getting any better with time."

"I just think we need to lighten up on him, Own," chided Paul. "One thing my Dad taught me is that we don't know what the other fellow is going through or what kind of life he's had. Don't judge too harshly until you know what's going on in his life. The whole 'walk a mile in his moccasins' thing. So I'd like to think there's a good reason he's the way he is and cut him a break. I think you need to go easy on him, especially in light of Billy's death. I just think we need to appreciate the people around us while we still have them, that's all."

"Paul, I get what you're saying," admitted Only, "but it is damned hard to appreciate somebody like Charlie Horrible. He's rejected any kindness I ever extended toward him and there's only so much good will left in these old bones. It's not just his unfriendliness, which I could take. But you've seen him at Town Meetings and a few Select Board meetings. Cripes, he's opposed to anything and everything we try to do. I appreciate trying to keep taxes low, but he wants nothing done around here and wants to pay no taxes! He just doesn't care about anybody but himself. He'd be better off living as a hermit in a cave somewhere."

"And yet I think he h-has a lot of m-m-money," interjected Steve Benson. "I heard he has a big stash b-buried somewhere in his yard."

"Another report from Francois Lefitte, no doubt?" speculated Paul. "See, that's the sort of nonsense that puts people against people, these rumors that started three decades ago and then developed a life of their own. OK, so what if he has a pile of cash out back? That's his business and I don't care."

"Yeah, but you'd think he wouldn't be such a stingy bastard if that was the case," replied Willard.

"So maybe that's *not* the case then, Willard," replied Paul. "Maybe that means he *doesn't* have a stash and is living at the edge of his means. All the more reason to cut him a break because you don't in fact know that he has a pile of cash, or killed his wife, or fondles little kids. So lay off the guy is all I'm saying!"

"Ahhh, what's the fun in that?" asked Jubal Keller with his crooked grin in an attempt to lighten up the discussion. Which it did. "Yeah, I suppose you're right, Paul. We should just live and let live. If Charlie wants to stick to himself and be unfriendly, that's his business. I guess he has his reasons. Maybe he's got bad case of perpetual hemorrhoids or something."

"Well he's a hemorrhoid on this town, for sure, but yeah, that's his business," concluded Phil. "I guess I can let up on him too. There's more important things in life needing my attention, like a refill on my coffee, for example. Hey Jodi," shouted Phil across the room, pointing to his empty mug. "How about it?"

Thus, life in Oddertown, slowly but surely, piece by piece, had started to return to normal.

Chapter 13

Saturday, August 3, 11:35 AM

"MY FRIENDS, THE NEXT ITEM UP FOR BID is a 15-speed mountain bike," announced auctioneer Caleb Smith. "Get your thrills on our gorgeous hills with this beauty. This bike is solid and in ready-to-go condition, maybe could use some new inner tubes is all. Let's start the bidding at $50. Who'll give me fifty for a bike worth several hundred at least?"

The SOS auction had been in the planning for weeks now, and had been well-advertised through a good chunk of the Kingdom, as had the whole saga of the Odderton Country Store and its potential loss. The hope that people would turn out for the cause from other towns was well realized, and at least 175 potential buyers were stretched out on chairs and blankets throughout the length and breadth of Time Square on a warm and sticky day, with threats of afternoon thunderstorms being the only cause for concern. Caleb and the organizers were set up at the north end of the square under a large canopy, with microphone and speakers on loan from a local kid's garage band. Auction goods— donated by townsfolk and outsiders from far and wide—were stretched out well behind Caleb and his two assistants, Rusty Hinges and Jim Watson, who brought the items forward for bidding. Next to Caleb at a small table were George Mitchell and Kate, who kept careful track of all sales and collected money. At the far south end, Larry Carson was busy cooking up burgers, dogs, and Italian sausages, with two young assistants helping with sales and product flow. All proceeds would go to SOS.

The entire proceedings this morning began with a moment of silence in memory of Billy Wilson. Wendell "Gizmo" Lawson kept his promise to Billy and served as the collector of auction goods the previous day and was there to help load and even deliver goods to homes as needed. Gizmo also had just finished up his second week as Billy's replacement at Lou's garage, where he seemed to be fitting in well.

"OK, I have a couple of hands up at 50, do I hear 75? Can we get. . .OK, I have 75, let's see if we can get 100. Do I see 100?. . .100 anywhere? How about 90 then, can I. . .OK, I have 90, how about 100? Let's break 100 on this fine mountain bike. There we go, thank you sir, I have $100. Remember, this is all for a good cause, let's save this beautiful store over there and keep our community alive. One ten. Can I get 110 please?"

And so it went, through many dozens of items, ranging from kitchen and household goods to lawn mowers and chain saws, to more bikes and lots of furniture—tables and chairs, sofas, desks, bureaus—some, unfortunately, perhaps better suited for a trip to the county landfill. Art in the form of paintings, pottery, and woodworking was offered. Services were auctioned: four hours of house painting, two hours with a lawyer, a night's stay at a B & B in Newport, lawn mowing, car maintenance. A cord of firewood, cut, split, and delivered was donated by Rusty. One-hundred gallons of fuel oil from St. J. was bid upon. Gift cards from various businesses in the region—restaurants, a grocery store, hair dresser, garden center, hardware store—were auctioned off.

But the pièce de résistance, the oddest of all odd items in Oddertown this day was, perhaps predictably, donated by the eccentric artist Pernell Basington-Smythe. Pernell had generously donated a flamboyant original oil, in exaggerated colors, of Teddy Roosevelt in his Roughrider outfit with his arm around a buxom, fluorescent-pink-bikini-clad lass, his grin larger than life, with the scene labeled "Teddy's Big Stick." The framed painting resulted in more than a few raised eyebrows and hushed discussions among the town elders, while all the kids thought it was a hoot. It sold for $325—about one-fourth its real value, according to a disappointed Pernell—to an outsider passing through from Boston. Many in town were happy to see it leave the premises and disappear to Beantown.

Being lunch time, Larry Carson had his hands full at the grills, selling hot dogs, burgers, and sausages as quickly as he could grill them, along with drinks, chips, baked beans, and a selection of cookies and brownies. Throughout the proceedings, the team of Big Mac and Little Mac—the teachers

Lauren McCallum and Emily McIntyre—walked through the crowd selling 50:50 tickets: one ticket for a dollar, seven tickets for five, or 15 for ten, and you were entered into the drawing. The winning ticket would get to keep half of the take, the other half going to SOS.

Shortly after 2:00, and after most folks were fed, storm clouds began to seriously gather from the northwest, and the real threat of a thunderstorm loomed. Fortunately, by that time they had auctioned off most of the items and were scrambling to rid themselves of the last few, settling for low bids and quick sales. Finally, by 2:15 they were ready for the two final and greatly anticipated events. First, they would pick the winner of the 50:50. They had collected $780, a nice haul, meaning the winner would take home $390. Then they would draw for the canoe.

Caleb looked at the crowd and saw an eager face in the front row. "Raymond Pulan, please come up here and pick the winner of the raffle for us!" Raymond jumped up with a big smile, honored to have such an important role in the day's event, and marched forward, chest proudly puffed out, arms pumping front and back. "Go ahead, Raymond, stick your hand in the bucket, swirl the tickets around, and pick a winner." Raymond accepted his task with great solemnity, though he took much too long swirling the tickets before finally settling on one. He emerged with a single ticket and handed it to Caleb, just as distant thunder cracked on the horizon and rumbled through town.

"Woah, the thunder gods must have liked that one! Thank you, my friend, and good job. OK, everyone, take your ticket stubs out, because the winning number is 213. . ." He paused, knowing that everyone had the same first three numbers. "Anybody still with me?"

"Yes," they all cried out, holding their strings of blue tickets in front of them.

"OK," said Caleb. "Six. . ." a pause, with a few groans... "seven. . .who's still with me?" Several hands went up. "And finally... drum roll please... TWO! Two-one-three-six-seven-two. Do we have a winner?"

About two seconds elapsed before a young girl in the back cried out, jumping up and down, "That's me! I won!"

"Well come on up here, young lady, and collect your winnings!"

She looked up at her mom, who motioned her to go up front as asked. She took three steps forward, returned, and whispered something in her mom's ear; her mom replied with shrugged shoulders, a big smile, and a "that's up to you." The girl then wandered her way through the crowd and on up to Caleb, big grin on her face. He asked her name and then reported to the crowd that she was Anna, from Newport, and was 12 years old. Caleb handed over $390 and congratulated her. Anna beamed and showed off the wad of bills filling her hands, more than she had ever had in her life, as the crowd applauded politely. More thunder shook the air, obviously getting closer; the sky continued to darken and the wind picked up.

Then Anna motioned to Caleb, who bent over to listen to her. His eyes flew open and his mouth dropped in an expression of delighted surprise. He rose and addressed the crowd. "Ladies and gentlemen, 12-year-old Anna just asked me if she could keep $90 and donate $300 back to the SOS campaign. Can she ever! How generous and thoughtful. Yes, Anna, you certainly can, with our ever-lasting thanks. Now, friends, if that doesn't boost your confidence in our youth and our future, nothing will. Thank you, Anna, thank you so much." The crowd gave Anna a standing ovation as she returned to her mom, who was beaming with pride. Obviously somebody had raised that child properly.

"Well, friends, that puts the icing on my cake for today. Young Anna may have just put us over the top with that donation, what do you think?" Cheers and applause resounded again.

"OK, let's move this along. The final order of business before we get stormed on is to pick a winner for our canoe raffle. As you know, Jim Watson and his team have been selling raffle tickets for at least a month now. I'm told they sold 457 tickets, past their goal of 400, thus raising almost $2300 for SOS!" Applause followed.

"Jim, we thank you and your team and all those who bought tickets. And we especially thank Layla Liederman for the generous donation of her father's hand-made cedar-strip canoe. It is a beauty, as you can see here." Caleb caressed the gunnel of the canoe sitting on saw horses next to him. The varnish finish still shined smartly after many decades. Layla, standing nearby, smiled appreciatively, though with a hint of sadness at the canoe's imminent departure.

"Layla, I'd like to give you the honor of picking the winner. Come on forward please."

Layla approached the front and stuck her hand into the bucket filled with over 450 tickets, finally emerging with one and handing it to Caleb. Caleb looked at it and announced, "and the winner is.... you all ready for this?" More thunder rolling in. "Phil Haderlie!" Groans and applause went through the crowd, as folks saw they did not win but appreciated a local getting it.

Phil Haderlie sat up in his chair about half way back in the crowd, and after a brief hesitation addressed Caleb. "Caleb, I appreciate that but I have no use for a canoe. Hell, I can barely walk on solid ground anymore." The crowd all laughed. "Go ahead and pick another name. I'd like someone to get it who can use it."

"Well, isn't that the spirit now, folks! Thanks so much, Phil. Very generous." The crowd mumbled their appreciation and a few patted Phil on the back.

"OK, Layla, generosity is overflowing here today. Let's try this again, and get a winner. Better hurry, that storm's getting close." Layla did as she was asked and handed the new winning ticket to Caleb, who announced "Hope Golightly! Harmony, you just won a canoe. Is she here?"

"Yes I am," said a soft and lovely voice from the back. "How wonderful, thank you, Mr. Smith. I gratefully accept and would like to invite any member of the Oddertown community to use the canoe when they like. This should be a community possession and I would love to share it."

"Wonderful, Harmony! You hear that everyone? We sure have the spirit flowing through town today. See Harmony if you would like to use her canoe. And with that, I thank you all for your generosity, whether as a donor, a buyer, or an appreciative fan of Oddertown. I know you have helped move us closer to our goal of keeping the Odd Country in business. Please remember to shop and eat there as much as possible in the coming months and help Kate keep this thing going for another hundred years."

Kate stood and quickly grabbed the microphone from Caleb. "Everyone, I just want to say that I appreciate all your support more than you will ever know. This is such a fantastic community and you are all so dear and special that it makes it an honor for me to run this store. I hope I can continue to keep the doors open for many decades to come. Thank you all *so* much for your help and love."

"And thank you, Kate, and good luck!" responded Caleb. "OK, folks, time to skedaddle before we get soaked. Thanks, and bye for now. Drive safely in this rain coming."

A collective clatter and bustle built up as the crowd quickly dispersed, slamming their folding chairs shut and scrunching up their blankets, while Caleb and his crew hastily unplugged and stowed the speakers and amp in a nearby car just before the rain started to come down in widespread but large drops; Larry and his assistants got the two grills closed up and gathered the condiments and leftover food. They all ran across the road to Odd Country, shaking off the first rains that had just started to come down heavily.

"Woah, made it just under the wire!" exclaimed Jim. "We couldn't have timed it any closer. Got the whole thing in just before the skies opened up."

"Yes, someone must be looking out for us," chimed in Emily McIntosh. "That was a close call."

"Well, we managed to get the whole auction in, and that's what we needed," concluded Caleb. "I think we did pretty good, don't you?" They all concurred that the event had gone well.

While everyone settled inside and grabbed some drinks and snacks from the leftover food, and with rain now rattling the windows in heavy sheets, Kate and George slipped into a back corner and settled the accounts. Everyone was anxious to learn how much the auction had brought. They all chatted and reviewed the day's events—especially some of the weirder auction donations—while the number crunchers did their work. The storm was now right over them, with rain pelting the windows and thunder booming almost simultaneously with lightning strikes, nearly drowning out their conversations.

After about 15 minutes, and with the fury of the storm expended and the rain now down to a steady drizzle, Kate and George emerged from their cloister. "Well, you want to hear the numbers?" asked Kate. Everyone nodded eagerly and wanted some numbers.

"OK, the 50:50 netted $690, thanks to the generosity of that beautiful young lady Anna. I couldn't believe she did that. How encouraging!" They all acknowledged the extraordinary and touching generosity of this young outsider.

"And Larry grossed $1235 with his food sales. Way to go, Larry! We had approximately $375 in products, so he netted $860." Everyone applauded Larry's efforts.

"And now, what you've all been waiting for. The auction brought us....wait for it...wait for it...$8251!" Everyone cheered at the good haul.

George smiled shyly in the background. "Including the canoe raffle ticket sales of $2285," she continued. "SOS has raised $12,086. That's more than halfway to our goal!"

"Way to go, everyone!" complimented Jim. "We did great. Of course, we still have a ways to go, but we can see some light at the end of the tunnel. Now we need to think of ways to keep the effort going."

"Well maybe we can raffle off something else, if we can get another good donation," suggested Lauren McCallum. "Though I don't know what that might be."

"Tell you what, everybody," replied Kate. "You all did marvelous work on this and I think for now we should just relax, enjoy ourselves, and celebrate our success. Tomorrow's another day. Or maybe Monday."

"Good idea, Kate," said Doc. "I think everyone's a little exhausted right now and we can re-focus later on. Let's just enjoy this for now. Great job, gang!" Everyone applauded themselves. "Now let's help finish off these leftovers."

After a half hour, with the storm having moved on well to the east, the group slowly dispersed through heavy dripping from eaves and trees. Kate pulled Jim aside and took his hands in hers.

"Jim, I can't thank you enough for all you have done for me and the store. I no longer feel alone in this fight, and I like having you in my corner. Whether this all works or not, I will always be grateful for your help." She gave him a warm hug and kissed him on the cheek. Jim blushed a bit but did not mind at all.

Chapter 14

Friday, August 16, 7:45 AM

HAPPILY, THE STORE WAS ALREADY BUZZING with activity this Friday morning. Kate was busy in the kitchen filling breakfast orders while Jodi served tables and rang up customers at the register. The Odd Balls were in their usual place and nearly ready to push back their chairs, stretch, slap their full bellies, pay their bills, leave their tips on the table, and saunter out into the world to fill their time elsewhere. But first, another half cup of coffee and some final words of wisdom. For the road, as it were.

The front door chimed open and in walked Bobby Wilson, Billy's younger brother, and his buddy Andrew "Buck" Bailey, both 17. At the age of 12, young Andrew had bagged his first deer, a 227-pound buck that was the largest taken in this area for the previous three years. Ever since, Andrew had been known to everyone as "Buck," a title he wore with understandable pride.

The two boys were about to enter their senior year at North Country Union High, the same class as Jodi Simpson. Though average students in every way, with nothing special to show—academically, athletically, or artistically—for their scholastic careers to date, they were basically good kids who would eventually make solid and respectable citizens. Bobby might follow his brother Billy into auto repairs, and Andrew showed an interest in and aptitude for plumbing, his father's profession. He would likely, one day, be the next-generation owner of "Bailey's Plumbing and Heating." Today, however, those careers were but distant visions; the boys had other goals in mind. They looked nervous and agitated as they entered Odd Country and wandered back into the aisles and around the coolers.

A careful observer would note that Bobby and Buck could be heard talking and mumbling in low voices, their eyes periodically darting above the shelves and around the room. They seemed especially interested in locating Kate and following Jodi's movements. Finally, with Kate back in the kitchen, Bobby walked up to the counter while Buck stayed back to ponder the drink coolers.

Jodi came to the register where Bobby had a pack of gum to be paid for. "Hey, Jodi, uh, like how's work today?"

"You know, same thing as always. Pretty good I guess, like the tips are good, so that's kinda cool."

Amid these typical and awkward teenage greetings, Bobby fumbled around in his pockets looking for money to pay for the gum. When he dropped his pocket contents on the floor, with change scattering in all directions, Buck stealthily slipped past them toward the front door, though not as stealthily as he had hoped. Under his black hoodie sweatshirt that he was wearing on this warm August morning, Paul Johnson easily spotted the six-pack of Budweiser that Buck was attempting to relocate to other premises. As Buck walked through the front door and onto the porch, Paul got up, called to Kate, went out, and grabbed the boy by the hood, pulling him up short and ending his crime career on the spot.

"Hey man, what are you doing? What's with you, perv? Lemme go!"

Spinning Buck around, Paul asked "Did you pay for that beer? And are you twenty-one, Buck? I don't think so, on either count. C'mon, we need to go back inside."

Buck squirmed and made a sour and hateful "aww, gimme a break" face as they came back inside, where Kate had come out of the kitchen, wiping her hands on a towel, and met them at the door, the Budweiser clearly visible. Kate looked at Paul quizzically. "What's up?" she said.

"Kate, looks like we have ourselves a shoplifter here. Two, actually. Buck and Bobby were working as a team. Bobby distracted Jodi at the register while Buck helped himself to this six pack. I caught him as he walked out."

"Buck Bailey, I'm surprised at you! And Bobby Wilson, shame on you too!" lectured Kate. "You were both brought up better than this." The boys hung their heads, faces turning red and obviously embarrassed, though it was not clear whether the source of that embarrassment was stealing the beer or being caught in the act.

"I don't know what's worse," said Kate. "The fact that you are drinking underage or stealing from me. I've known you both since you were babies and I thought we were friends. I've always been nice to you and this is what I get in return? What have you got to say for yourselves?"

By this time the entire Odd Ball contingent had gotten up from the table and surrounded this criminal element like a pack of wolves encircling newborn calves ready for the kill. They would pounce at Kate's command if she only gave the word.

"I'm sorry, Ms. Kate," stammered Bobby, with tears beginning to well up in his eyes. "I never did this before, I swear."

"Me too, Ms. Kate. I'm sorry and I swear I'll never do this again. Like, really," added Buck.

"That's a start, but not enough," replied Kate, the pack of wolves snarling behind her and ready to pounce. All four of the boys' frightened eyes were now blurry with tears that threatened to overflow. "Explain yourselves."

"We had to do it," replied Bobby. "Some kids over in Johnsville dared us. They said we were pussies. . . oops, sorry, I mean, like, wimps and stuff, and said we couldn't get any beer, and we, like, said we sure too could get beer and, like, we would show them we weren't pus— wimps or nuthin."

"You *had* to do it, huh? You had no choice. They held guns to your heads I suppose? You had no chance to think for yourselves?" Kate did not need her pack of wolves; she was going in for the kill by herself, alpha female that she was.

The boys looked at each other through their tears and just shrugged their shoulders. They knew that they were dead meat, caught in the trap, and had no defense against this mob of predators.

"You want me to call Carl?" asked Paul. "I can get him right down here."

At the mention of police the two boys startled, looked up, eyes wide, true looks of fear now on their faces. "No, please, Ms. Kate, we'll do anything. We'll give this back and pay for it and, like, whatever you want," pleaded Buck. "We don't want to get in trouble with the cops. Please, please, Ms. Kate."

Kate pondered for a minute, staring the boys into complete submission. They fairly melted before her.

Finally she responded. "No, Paul, I don't think we need the police." Buck and Bobby immediately sighed with relief. "I think they've learned a lesson here," to which both vigorously shook their heads in quick and complete agreement. "But I haven't yet decided whether or not to tell their parents," to which both immediately returned to looks of dread. "I definitely will do that if these two so much as knock a blade of grass out of place the rest of the summer."

"We won't, we promise!" assured Buck. "Please don't tell our folks. My Dad will kick my ass—I mean butt—for a week. I swear, we'll be like good as angels. You won't hear a peep from us. I swear." Bobby likewise swore an oath of angelic goodness, wiping the tears from his eyes.

Kate paused again, took a deep breath, and stared at them, stretching out the fear factor. "OK, you two get out of here and keep straight. We'll *all* be watching you," as she motioned to her pack of wolves surrounding them. "And believe me, I'll remember this for a good long time."

"No worries, we'll be real good, Ms. Kate. Thank you, thank you, and we're sorry. Thank you."

The pack parted and the two young prey items escaped what had seemed like certain death; they darted back out into the wilderness with a new lease on life.

"You shoulda called Carl, Kate," offered Phil. "That's the only way to straighten these kids out."

"Nah, Phil, I think they're pretty scared. I just wanted to teach them a lesson and I think they got the message. And poor Bobby lost his brother just last month and must be way off balance. They're good kids and this is just a dumb teenage prank. We all did stupid things as kids, right? Even you, Phil?"

"Especially Phil!" responded Steve. "He w-was quite familiar to the c-cops as a kid, w-weren't you, Phil?"

"No need to go into that, Steve, thank you," replied Phil, the hint of a grin on his guilty face. "Point taken."

"Did you see the looks on their faces?" asked Jubal. "They about wet their pants," he laughed. "You actually had *me* scared, Kate!"

"Yeah, poor things, I came down pretty hard on them didn't I?" she said as they all had a good laugh. "Well, it's just tough love. I did it for their own good."

"Well, I'm gonna be sure to watch myself around you from now on, Kate," concluded Silas. "I don't ever want to get on your bad side." More laughs at the expense of two scared kids.

"The problem is, guys, these kids have nothing to do around town," observed Kate. "After school and all summer long, they have nothing. Not so

much as a ball field to run around on. And no jobs
here to speak of. They have way too much time on
their hands and no focus, so they just bum around.
They're bound to get into trouble."

"And they hang around Time Square, playing
music too loud, and looking for trouble," added
Silas. "Or if not that they're on their phones doing
God-knows-what. It's no wonder they try to lift a
six pack once in a while."

"Well, we're not going to solve the problem here
this morning," concluded Kate, "but I sure wish we
had a place for them to go and things to do. It's a
wonder we don't have more trouble from them. And
that's only because they're basically good kids, as I
said. We just have to help keep them on the right
path as long as we can." After nods of understanding all around, Kate concluded "Well, I've got to get
back to work."

"I'll put the beer back in the cooler," offered Paul.
"And I think you handled that well, Kate."

"Thanks Paul. I think it's what they call a 'teach-
able moment,' and I believe they learned their lesson well."

Because they were already up, the Odd Balls
continued out the front door and dispersed in their
many directions to carry on their day, still chuckling over the looks on those kids' faces. It was only
after most of them got home they realized that, in
all the excitement, they each forgot to pay for their
breakfasts and leave tips for Jodi. Perhaps the wrong
shoplifters were nabbed today!

Chapter 15

THE ODD BALLS HAD JUST FINISHED THEIR latest round of breakfast on a warm and sticky Kingdom morning, and their dirty dishes were pushed to the center of the table.

Paul Johnson got the group's attention and then pulled out a sheet of paper from his shirt pocket. "So check this out, gentlemen. I think you'll get a kick out of this," he said as he unfolded the paper.

"I hope this isn't another one of your liberal blah blahs," interjected Phil Haderlie right away. "I don't need to hear that kind of crap this morning. I'm hot enough already."

"No worries, Phil," said Paul. "I promise you'll love this. Funny stuff. Somebody posted this on their Facebook page and I copied it off."

"I still don't know what the hell a Facebook is," responded Phil. "Sounds like a damn mugshot book!"

"Hey, Phil, wake up, we're in the 21st Century," informed Jubal Keller. "Gotta get with it, my friend."

"The only thing I gotta *get* is to the bathroom more often!" countered Haderlie. "OK, so what's this great thing you got off your Faceshot page, Hippie Boy?"

"You guys know that comedian Jeff Foxworthy, right?" asked Paul. They all nodded that they did, and agreed that he was pretty funny. "Well he did this thing called 'You Know You Live in Vermont.' Lists all these things that, if you did or knew of, mean you must live here. I think you'll know some of these pretty well. So here we go, first one: *If you've worn shorts and a parka at the same time,*" read Paul, "*you know you live in Vermont.*" The group immediately laughed at a sight they had all seen.

"You know who used to do that?" asked Silas. "That kid Frisbee Phipps. Remember Frisbee? His name was Fred, I think, but they all called him Frisbee because he played it all the time. Damned kid would be wearing shorts in 20 degrees, with boots, a big heavy coat, and gloves. Darndest sight."

"I don't think that kid had the sense God gave him," concluded Phil. "That whole Phipps family was kinda wacko, remember? Course, I've seen plenty of other dopes here wear shorts in the winter, so the Phipps' never cornered the market on stupidity. I figure God made long pants for a reason."

"Alright, try this one. *If you know several people who've hit a deer more than once, you live in Vermont.*"

Willard Bennett jumped in. "My cousin Earl hit at least three deer last year. Ate all of them, too. I suspect he hits 'em on purpose."

"Hell, just about everyone around here hits a deer every year or two," added Jubal. "Yep, so that one's true."

Paul continued to the next one. "*If you have switched from heat to AC and back again in the same day, you live in Vermont.*"

"Well that can't be," exclaimed Silas. "I don't know anybody here who has air conditioning, do you? Maybe some of those flatlander second home-owners down around Woodstock might do that."

"I don't t-turn on any heat until November first at the s-soonest," chimed in Steve. "Shouldn't n-need any until then. And then it goes off April f-fifteenth. I figure it'll get warm again soon e-enough."

"OK, how about this one?" continued Paul. "*If you measure distance in hours rather than miles, you live in Vermont.*"

"Of course!" responded Jubal. "Miles don't make any sense here. A place could be eight miles away but it takes an hour to get there because it's all back roads and you have to clear a tree or two out of the way first. I always carry a chain saw with me, don't you?" The group acknowledged that they were ready for anything on these back roads.

"OK, I know you'll all know this one. *If you design your kids' Halloween costumes to fit over a snowsuit, then you live in Vermont!*"

They all howled at that one and began the reminiscences of years gone by when they did exactly that for their kids. It was common practice that you had to account for the possibility it could be well below freezing and maybe have a fair amount of snow on the ground in late October. "But you know," offered Paul, "that doesn't happen so much anymore. Halloween is usually pretty warm now. Sorry, Phil, but another sign that climate change has arrived."

Phil begrudgingly nodded and acknowledged that "Halloweens ain't what they used to be."

"So continuing with the weather theme," said Paul. *If driving is better in winter because the potholes are filled, you live in Vermont.*"

"You got that one right!" exclaimed Silas. "Winter's the only time the roads are any good around here. I hit so many potholes this spring I had to have my suspension re-built." They all chipped in with similar horror stories of bad roads eating up their vehicles.

"OK, a couple more," said Paul, trying to wrap it up. *If you think everyone else has a funny accent, you live in Vermont.*"

"Well they sure do," blurted Willard. "I can't hardly understand folks from New Jersey or New York City, and forget about anyone from down south!" The group concurred completely with Willard, one of the few times they could overlook his earthy demeanor and noxious smells and appreciate what he said.

At that point, the door chime interrupted their discussion and signaled another customer; in walked Jim Watson. Though he normally did not voluntarily sidle up to the Odd Balls, this morning he marched right on over, apparently a man on a mission.

"Good morning, boys," greeted Jim with a smile. They all returned his greeting in kind. "What're you up to?"

"Oh, I was just reading some of Jeff Foxworthy's

observations on living in Vermont," informed Paul. He proceeded to repeat the previous ones to Jim, who smiled and chuckled appropriately, having experienced many of them himself.

"OK, here's the rest of them, boys, real quick. *You live in Vermont if you've had a lengthy conversation with someone who dialed the wrong number; if you install security lights on your house and garage but leave both unlocked; if you know all 4 seasons—almost winter, winter, still winter, and road construction; if you have more miles on your snow blower than on your car; and, finally, if you find 10 degrees 'a little chilly.'*" Without detailed comment, but with the shaking of heads and some chuckles, they all identified with these "Vermonty" observations.

"So, Doctor Wiz, what brings you over to our table?" queried Phil Haderlie. "Looks like you got something on that smart mind of yours that you're just itching to get out."

"Well, as a matter of fact, Phil, I do," confirmed the Doc. "Fellas, I need your help. Actually, the whole town needs your help. You know we've been trying to raise money to help Kate save this store. We're doing well, and you all have helped, thanks very much, but we're coming up short. We need to do something more. We need to raise another nine or ten grand before February, or you may not be sitting here for breakfast after that."

"Phewwweee!" exclaimed Silas, "that's a pile of money. How you suggest we do that?"

"It is a lot, Silas, and we can't do it all at once, unless one of you has a stash we don't know about that you want to hand over. No, this has to be a group effort."

"So w-what do we do?" asked Steve.

"I thought we might try another raffle. The one with the canoe raised a couple grand and I think we could do that again if we have something good to raffle off. Leaf season is coming up and we'll have lots of visitors and I'd like to sell them a lot of tickets and get some out-of-state money coming in. But we need one or two good items to raffle. So that's where you come in. Anybody want to cough up something others will want? Remember, it's to save this spot where you spend most of your mornings."

The boys looked around at each other and they all wondered aloud.

"You know, everybody's trying to help," added Jim. "Even the grade school kids had a bake sale and they raised $110 for us."

"I know," declared Silas. "A good chunk of that $110 came from me."

"Me too!" chimed in Only, patting his expanding belly.

"Well, if the kids can do it, so can we. Any large item you might want to donate? A boat, a car, some machinery? Remember, it's tax deductible. And it's all so you can keep using this store for years to come."

After a silent pause, Phil Haderlie spoke up. "Well, you know, I'm not driving anymore and that '58 Chevy pickup's been sitting there. I start it to keep it running, so it's in good shape, but I don't need it and I can't drive it on roads. I could donate it, I suppose."

"Really, Phil?" asked Jim. "You would do that? You sure?"

"Yeah, why not?" said Phil thoughtfully. "It's just

sitting there. I don't think I could bring myself to sell it, but this is for a good cause. And if it'll keep me coming to breakfast, then why the hell not?"

The truck was an oldie but a goodie. It was functionally sound, but needed some work to get it back into good form. It was ripe for someone interested in restoration work and could make for a honey of a collector's item in the right hands.

The boys all agreed this was a great thing for Phil to do and thanked him. Jim shook his hand and said "You've got a deal!"

"Hey, Kate, c'mon over here!" shouted Jim to the kitchen. Kate soon appeared and Jim explained the latest fundraising project. She nearly jumped over the table to hug Phil and thank him for his gift. Slightly embarrassed, Phil sheepishly grinned and said it was no big deal. But it was a big deal to her, and once again raised her hopes that they would get through this thing and at least buy a couple of years to satisfy the full loan amount.

Next, Kate was to head over to Pernell Basington-Smythe to see if he would donate another piece of art for yet another raffle item. Jim indicated he would go ahead and print up raffle tickets and advertise the latest projects. They were determined that, one way or another, they would sell off enough of the town to keep this store going for a while longer. At the current rate, they just might have a chance of doing it.

Chapter 16

T HE HANDSOME AND WELL-DRESSED stranger stood out strikingly from the typical customer base that came through Odd Country. With neatly creased khakis, a checkered sport shirt with sleeves casually rolled up, and new and unscuffed Dockers leather boat shoes, he looked like an outsider trying his best to fit in to a place but perhaps just missing the mark. His wavy dark hair with touches of grey at the temples, his confident soft brown eyes, and a strong Roman nose, all contributed to a caricature of success that could not be hidden under a mantle of casual clothing. But there was also a friendly and approachable air about him that made him an enticing package.

The gentleman made two slow passes through the store, looking it over from floor to ceiling as if casing the joint for a future heist. When finished, he came over to the counter and ordered his lunch from Kate; as he did so he made sure to make her feel like she was the only person in the room and of intense interest to him. His piercing gaze and subtle smile were almost too intense, and they caused Kate to spend a bit more time looking down at the order she was writing than normal. After paying for his food he sat at the farthest table from the front counter, placed a manila folder on the table, and opened his newspaper, *The Newport Daily Express*. The other customers in the store—two Green Mountain Power employees on lunch break—stared at this customer, obviously "from away," with curious and raised eyebrows.

When Kate brought over his lunch order and sat it on the table in front of him he thanked her and then confidently said, "You're Kate Langford, yes?"

A startled Kate hesitated and, with raised eyebrows, replied "Uh, yeah, that's me. How do you know my name?"

"Fear not, Ms. Langford, I assure you I mean no harm. In fact quite the contrary. Please, you would do me a great favor if you would sit with me and chat for a few minutes while I enjoy my lunch— which looks wonderful, by the way. And I would be happy to order anything for you if you would allow me the honor."

"Uh, no thanks, I've eaten, but I'd still like to know how you know my name. And who are you anyway?"

"Ah, please forgive my poor manners, I'm so sorry. My name is Robert Malloy, but I go by Robb." He stood, extended his right arm, and they shook hands firmly, though Kate was hesitant and wary of his motives.

"Please," he said, sitting back down and motioning to a chair, "join me for a few minutes and I promise you won't regret it."

Kate looked back to the kitchen and saw that Larry was still there and well within calling distance, as were the two GMP workers. So she pulled out a chair and sat across from the mysterious gentleman.

After taking a bite of his grilled chicken breast sandwich on a Kaiser bun, Malloy wiped his mouth, confirmed that it was a wonderful sandwich, and then began their discussion in earnest.

"Kate—if I may take the liberty of using your first name—I am the CEO of Northeast Kingdom Development, Ltd, or NEK-DEL as we are informally known. Maybe you've heard of us?"

"No, I haven't actually," she admitted. "My worldly focus these days is pretty much limited to this store."

"Well, that's fine," he said. "There's no reason, really, for you to know us. We're a relatively new entity recently spawned from a larger development firm in downstate New York. We formed because we see great opportunities for high-quality, environmentally-friendly, and culturally-sensitive development in the Northeast Kingdom that would be a huge economic boost to the good people here. We are interested in bringing good-paying jobs to the region while we develop and enhance communities and resources that will greatly benefit folks in this beautiful region that, I'm sorry to say, has not yet enjoyed the growth and economic opportunities experienced by so many other parts of New England."

He paused to take another bite of his lunch, while Kate digested what he had just laid out. In watching him eat his sandwich she noticed no wedding ring on his left hand but a small band of untanned skin in its place. Either this guy was recently divorced or he had removed his wedding ring for some strategic purpose. Her guard went up.

"And. . .?" she replied. "Why are you telling me this?"

"Kate, we are looking for a foothold, a center of operations, a place from which we can begin our effort to help this region benefit from all it has to offer. With the unmatched recreational opportunities here—from skiing and other winter sports to biking and hiking and fishing and hunting and Lord knows all the other great outdoor features—we feel that NEK-DEL can bring prosperity and an improved quality of life to many people that make this area their home."

"That sounds very nice, but what does any of that have to do with me?" a still puzzled Kate inquired

"Ah yes, let's get straight to the matter at hand. Kate, I happen to know you are in a bit of a financial bind. I know that you owe a large amount on this store, that you might be having trouble paying it off, and that time is running short. I know you may lose the whole operation to the bank, and I'd like to help you. And here's the deal: I'd like to buy the building and land from you and pay off your entire bank debt, plain and simple. You would be free and clear of your troubles."

"You *what*?" expelled a shocked Kate. "Wh-wha... you just want to come in here and buy my store? For what purpose? And how do you know about my supposed financial problems anyway? That's very personal and private information!"

"OK, good questions both," he said. "Let me take those in order. As for my purpose, I'd like to use this as my headquarters. This central location could not be more perfect for our company, and the building would be an excellent facility for home offices for me, my architects, planners, and legal team. I haven't seen upstairs, obviously, but I trust there are several rooms up there, and this big main floor space could be nicely subdivided into office spaces. It is just what we need. It would be a beautiful and tasteful center for Kingdom improvements."

Kate briefly looked around, trying to picture the store partitioned into office cubicles.

"As for how I know of your financial problems, I'm sorry, but word does get around. Your problems with the store are well known in general, and in the business world the details are easily obtained. You'd be amazed what you can learn during a dinner and cocktails."

Kate now looked further shocked and didn't know whether to laugh, walk away, or slap the man across the face. She realized that this guy must be buddies with the bankers controlling her loan and they were less than discreet with her financial information. The bastards!

"Ms. Langford, Kate, look, I'm a good guy and I'm here to make a good deal for both of us. From every realistic indication it appears that you will lose this store. I know that hurts, I know it's been in your family for generations and I know you don't want to lose it but that is the grim reality of things. This place has had a good run and everything changes, nothing lasts forever. You can lose it to the bank and I can certainly come in and buy it from them at a discount and you'd have nothing. But that would take too long for my interests and I'd prefer to do the very decent thing and work with you, giving us both some certainty. Why not sell to me at a very good price for you, get free from the albatross around your neck, and move on with your life? You are young and beautiful, if I may say so. No doubt smart and talented, too. You have the opportunity to get away from here and start fresh on a new path. Why not take it?"

"Well, you've certainly swooped in here out of the blue," said Kate. "It was the last thing I expected today. To be honest, I'm flabbergasted. But just for the record, tell me what you had in mind. Please give me some details, Mr...?"

"Malloy, but please, call me Robb. And fair enough, I understand this is very sudden and I would want you to take your time, absolutely no pressure from me. But here's what I know. I've had an appraisal done on your place. It is a bit challenging, as there are no comparables to look at, but I think we have a pretty good idea of fair value. Without the debt, we think the building and land are worth $310,000. Add another $30,000 for contents—furniture, kitchen, coolers, and so forth, most of which we don't need but that's OK, I'd buy them from you as they're part of your equity. I can't count inventory in the value as it is not worth anything to me and you would want to just sell it off anyway. So we think valuation sits right at $340,000."

Kate kept a stone-like face, showing no emotional reaction, positive or negative, to his numbers.

"Of course, there is the debt hanging over you, approximately $110,000 at this time, if I have the numbers right, and I think I do. And I would pay that off so the title is clear. I could simply subtract that from the 340K and offer you $230,000. That's not a bad number at all, but I'm prepared to sweeten it a bit. I'd be willing to offer you a nice, round, $250,000, a quarter of a million. You take that to start your new life and I have a headquarters for my new operation. Win-win. How does that sound?"

"Mr. Mal. . . uh, Robb. . . when I got up this morning all I had on my mind and my agenda was how to get through another day and what to order for next week. I can't quite comprehend what you just laid in front of me, and my head is spinning just a bit. Selling the store is not something I have been considering and I would have a lot of contemplating to do before I could even *think* of giving you an answer. My initial reaction is to say no thank you and tell you on your way out to have a nice day, but in fairness to you—not that I owe you that, but still—I want some time to think over what this might mean for me. I can promise only that I'll think about it and will give you an answer in a reasonable amount of time, say a week or so."

"That sounds fine, Kate. I couldn't ask for more. Here is my card with all my contact information. And please take this folder; it has the offer I just verbalized laid out in writing. Call me any time that's convenient for you, day or night, and we'll talk further. I know I came in here out of the blue and you've been very kind to hear me out. Thank you. Let me just add that this is a golden opportunity for you that, fair to say, is unlikely to ever come along again. If you lose the store you'll have nothing; if you sell, you'll have quite a sweet pot of money to begin the next phase of your life. Either way, the store is gone. Please, do think it over carefully. And thank you for your time today and the delicious lunch."

With that he stood, placed a twenty dollar bill on the table for a tip, and confidently walked out the door, having left his *Newport Daily Express* on the table. Kate felt slightly dizzy and much bewildered as she grabbed the empty plate and money and headed toward the kitchen.

Chapter 17

Wednesday, August 28, 6:55 AM

"THERE'S SOME POSITIVE ASPECTS TO IT, IS all I'm saying," stated Only Owens. "It's not all gloom and doom. I hear she's gonna lose the store anyway so why not cash in? If she sells to this developer then at least she'll have something to show for it and there will be jobs and an economic boost to the area. Ya gotta admit that."

"Not necessarily, Own," responded Paul Johnson. "Sure, these developers always promise jobs when they dangle the carrot in front of you, but how many jobs actually go to locals? He'll probably bring in his own team of architects and lawyers and planners. How many of those types do we have sitting around Odd just waiting for a good-paying job to come along?"

"True enough, Hippie Boy," said Phil Haderlie. "But I'll bet there's construction jobs that'll come up and then folks around here will have a shot."

"Maybe, Phil, but those are also skilled jobs," replied Paul. "They probably have their own teams of builders ready to come in here. Again, we don't have a pile of skilled and experienced construction workers waiting around. Sure, maybe some unskilled folks from Odd might get low-level jobs as "go-fers" around construction sites, and maybe there'd be some summer jobs for high school kids, but I don't see anybody getting rich off this. NEK-DEL is not gonna suddenly employ a whole bunch of folks from town and transform us into a hotbed of wealth. That never happens with these deals, and money always floats to the top. I think it's a lot more promise than it will ever deliver."

"Well, how about the effects of g-general de-development in the area," asked Steve Benson. "I heard they'd r-really ramp up rec-recreation and that should bring m-money in."

"Steve, what would *we* see from that?" asked Silas Miller. "There's not much in Oddertown to attract recreationists. Yeah, they might want to eat breakfast or lunch here, but guess what? The store won't be here! What else is there in this little village for recreationists? They'd drive right on through, maybe buy some gas is all."

"Yeah, I s-suppose you're right," admitted Steve.

"These guys just want to exploit what we have in abundance," summed up Paul, "a beautiful landscape, clean air and water, great views, peace and solitude. All of which will disappear if they have their way, once they fill their bank accounts and then leave. They win, we lose."

"Well, I think we all agree that we'd rather keep the store just the way it is, even if there's a chance of jobs coming with this deal," summed up Jubal Keller. "None of us wants to see this place turned into a developer's headquarters."

"Ya got that right, Jube," added Willard Bennett. "Bastard thinks he can come in and make a few empty promises and fool the dumb-shit locals. Well he can march right on in here and kiss my sweet patoot, for starters!"

Though rather crudely put, everyone laughed and agreed that losing the store to a developer would be a huge blow to the town, and, jobs or no jobs, recreation or no recreation, would not be worth the risk. They didn't know what Kate was thinking—and she revealed little when they asked her, other than casting an angry look—but all hoped she agreed with them and would hang in there and fight for this store that was their home base.

Having gotten over the initial shock of yesterday's meeting with Malloy, Kate sat down last night and thought through all the possibilities and ramifications. This was largely a waste of time because it did not take long for her to reach a painfully obvious conclusion: she had no interest in selling to this outsider with his many promises. Yes, it would be a quick and easy way out of her personal predicament, but it would serve her town poorly and she would no doubt regret it for the rest of her life. In addition to permanently losing their center of community and all it provided, it really would not add much to the town. She quickly surmised, as had the Odd Balls this morning, that promised jobs and material wealth were unlikely to be realized by locals in any significant way, and it would wind up being a lose-lose situation; they would lose the store and lose control over their town and surroundings, and she would lose her life's focus and reason for getting up in the morning.

If there had been any doubts in her mind, they would have been settled by 6:30 this morning when she heard the Odd Balls discussing the offer she had received. Kate had told exactly nobody about what had transpired, not even Jim, as she did not want rumors—and all that comes with them—spreading. Yet they all knew all about it by the next morning. Her inquiry of the Odd Balls revealed that Malloy had started to spread the word among townsfolk right after leaving the store yesterday, making all manner of promises of wealth and abundance that his project would bring to Oddertown. The slick talker had quickly violated her confidence in what should have been a strictly private business matter, and he was out lobbying citizens to pressure her to sell. She could now see that he was not a person to be trusted. And to have the audacity to immediately call her by her first name! She could never deal with someone like that, even if she wanted to sell. And she didn't.

So right after the breakfast crowd cleared out and the kitchen was stowed away, Kate pulled out the Malloy business card and dialed his number.

"Hello, Mr. Malloy? Yes, this is Kate Langford."

. . .

"I'm fine thank you. I'll get right to the point. I've thought about your offer and I have decided to decline it.

. . .

"Yes, that was indeed fast and no, I don't need to take more time to think it over.

. . .

"No, another ten thousand dollars will not change my mind.

. . .

"No, not even twenty. I'm not trying to drive a hard bargain or playing hard to get, and I resent your insinuation. I do not wish to sell. Period.

. . .

"Not that I owe you an explanation, but I think I'm well on my way to meeting my debt obligations and I'm confident I will not need to sell. That's all I wish to say.

. . .

"Yes, I understand this offer won't last forever, and I assure you it doesn't need to. I won't be changing my mind. You will have to look elsewhere for your project. Please don't contact me again."

. . .

"OK, fine, and you have a nice day as well. Thank you. Goodbye."

As she hung up, Kate wished she was half as confident as she had tried to sound about meeting her debt obligations. In reality she still felt like she was in a deep hole and unable to crawl out, but she'd be damned if she'd let someone like Malloy come to her rescue and benefit from her misfortune. Outward appearances aside, there was something about him she had not trusted and they were confirmed by his lobbying actions yesterday. So she would slog through this to the bitter end, win or lose.

Chapter 18

◀━━━━━━━

"OK, MALLOY, YOU'RE UP NEXT. WHAT DO YOU have for us from that little Vermont backwater of yours?" asked H.J. Mattingly with his typical intense and imposing stare.

The regular weekly review meeting of the brain trust of Pan Eastern Development Corp. was proceeding as usual. Set in the walnut-paneled Board Room on the 27th floor of a 58-story high rise on Columbus Ave. between West 97th and West 100th Streets in Manhattan, the group of six upper managers and a dozen or so Project Leaders or Project Wannabees gathered around the 21-foot long, oblong mahogany conference table every Friday morning to review progress of the past week and lay out project plans for the following week. A large firm with multiple fingers in many pies, this was the time to coordinate, to keep top management in the loop on what was happening throughout the east coast, and to pitch projects that would make or break careers.

Though nearing retirement, the President and CEO, Hunter J. Mattingly III, still kept his finger on the pulse of every ongoing and planned project, fearing that his semi-idiot and unfocused playboy son, H.J. the Fourth, would royally screw things up if allowed control. Nothing at Pan Eastern moved forward without his approval, just as it had not with H.J. Mattingly Sr. or H.J.M Jr. for the last 68 years, who had each ruled the firm with an iron fist, readily squashing those who did not produce. The rules were overtly Darwinian and quite simple: the fittest survived and moved up; the losers disappeared into the oblivion of local suburban life in dead-end jobs.

His fitness not yet determined, over the last two months Project Manager Wannabee Robb Malloy had convinced the brass that there were real opportunities to gain a foothold in remote Vermont, some dopey place called the Northeastern Kingdom, where the economically depressed and sparsely populated area was ripe for development and profit. Robb had given several presentations to management on his plans for construction of well over 100 homes—mostly upscale McMansions for the wealthy second-home market—to be accompanied by numerous offices and businesses, development of both winter and summer recreation enterprises, and possibly even tapping into the clean rivers and aquifers for a bottled-water enterprise. He had heard that a stream called Trout Brook had especially clean water that would be perfect for bottling as "Pristine Vermont Waters." He believed he was looking at a $300 million development in the region over 10 years, and had persuaded the brass that the right approach would easily convince these simple hay-seeds that his ideas had their best interests at heart.

Robb had done extensive homework and believed he could win them over with a down-home sincerity and appropriate language that played to their sense of community and clean living. So he traded in his three-piece suit for khaki pants and checkered shirts, polished up his vocabulary with words and phrases like "environmentally friendly," "culturally sensitive," "sustainable," and "community-based," and then marched on up there to learn the lay of the land.

He had found his perfect foothold to begin the process: a general store in a little Podunk nothing of a village called Oddertown, filled with a strange collection of naïve goofballs. The store was on the brink of default and he could get it for a song. To impress his quarry during the hunt he prematurely donned the title of CEO of an equally premature enterprise, Northeast Kingdom Development Corporation, or NEK-DEL. Both entities would become realities once his plans materialized, and his personal income would immediately quadruple. He just needed to convince an inconveniently smart bitch named Kate Langford that selling to him was in her best interest. Robb was confident he would do that because he was smarter, and rather charm-ing. He had been staked a half million dollars by Pan Eastern to make that happen but was convinced he could do it for far less.

Robb sat up squarely in his chair to address Mattingly's query. "H.J., I think we're making good progress. I don't yet have it sealed, and this owner of the building I want to buy is being stubborn, but I'm confident I will win her over soon. She rejected my initial offer but she's in a bad way and would be a total fool not to take a sweetened pot. So I will give it a little time and then raise the ante. She's a pain in the ass, to be honest, but soon will be begging to sell to me.

Once that's done, we move in, take a month to reconstruct the place, and then are ready to get out and start buying up some farms. So many are either failing or on the brink that they'll have little choice but to sell and get out. Turns out the milk market has been way down, for whatever reason, and many of these yokels are hanging on to their 50 to 100 acre farms and a couple dozen cows by their fingernails. A really wet or droughty summer and they're history. Even without that, I think dangling a small sum in front of their hungry faces will do the trick. Most of them have no reason to want to stay. I mean, who in their right mind wants to milk cows and slop shit every day?" he chuckled. "Take some money and get the hell out!"

"What's your timeline Malloy?" barked H.J.

"I think I can have the purchase sewn up by October first," replied Malloy confidently, "and be settled into the reconstructed building by Thanksgiving if not sooner. We can start approaching farms during renovation. I hope to have at least two in the bag, maybe a couple hundred acres, by Christmas."

"Alright, keep on track. I don't want this dragging out," H.J. ordered. "Next up—Jackson. What's happening in the western Pennsylvania expansion?"

Chapter 19

Wednesday, September 25, 6:00 AM

B Y 6 AM KATE HAD BEEN UP FOR EXACTLY 3 hours and 13 minutes. She knew the time so precisely because at 2:47 AM all hell had broken loose and she would not soon forget it. The intervening three-plus hours had been perhaps the longest and loneliest of her life, but there was no point in calling anyone in the middle of the night to share her fear and misery; nothing could be done to change things. With flashlight in hand and rain jacket held over her head against the steady drizzle, she had long ago done her initial inspection in and outside of Odd Country and had a feel for the extent of the damage: the kitchen was gone; her car was gone; her hopes were, for now, gone. But she knew that, come six o'clock, there would be human company to share her grief and to comfort her, so she simply waited in the dark chill of the morning, seated in the dining area, blanket wrapped around her shoulders, shuddering and rocking in the gloom.

The rain had stopped by 5:30, and Jodi Simpson showed up punctually at 6:00 for her morning shift, as did Phil Haderlie and Jubal Keller for their breakfast and the regular Odd Ball convocation. Kate walked out front and met them as the newcomers stood with their mouths agape; even with minimal illumination from a nearby street light they could see that something horrible had befallen their store.

"What the hell happened, Kate?" asked Jubal in disbelief.

"Hi, boys," said Kate, trembling, still in a partial state of shock. "Well, I was sound asleep last night until 2:47 when I heard a crash that I can't begin to describe. It sounded like a bomb had gone off, and the whole building shook. It about threw me out of bed and my first thought was that the furnace had exploded. I threw on a few clothes, grabbed a flashlight, and ran down the stairs to find this. After looking around I saw that this huge limb of that old elm tree out back had crashed down on my kitchen. It's gone! Crushed! As is my car." The words choked in her throat and she just stood and shook her head, looking over the scene, shaking uncontrollably.

Jodi walked over and gave Kate a big hug. Jubal placed his hand on her shoulder and assured her that everything would be OK. Phil simply shook his head and muttered in wonder, "Holy hell."

As the darkness slowly gave way to hints of daylight, Kate walked the trio carefully around the right side of Odd Country and together they surveyed the scene that she already knew well. They could see that a major limb from the old elm tree behind the building—a good two feet in diameter at its base—had split off from the trunk and crashed down on

Kate's car, parked behind the store, and straight across the middle of the kitchen. It had rained on and off for several days, and last night brought strong gusts of wind as well. On closer examination with a flashlight they could see that the limb where it had attached to the trunk had been rotted to the core and finally gave out.

"Well, obviously no breakfast today, fellas," managed Kate as she held back tears. "I don't know when I can feed you again."

"Kate, that's the least of our worries," replied Jubal. "Let's focus on this mess right now. We're here to help you."

"I don't even know where to begin," admitted Kate, tears now flowing freely, shaking her head and staring at the mess. It seemed so surreal. The kitchen was destroyed! "I guess I need to call my insurance company once they open."

"That would be a good place to start," confirmed Phil. "Have you been inside the kitchen yet?"

"No, I didn't want to go in alone and in the dark," replied Kate. "I did peek in with my flashlight and it looks awful. It may not be safe to go in. But I would like to see the extent of the damage soon. From here it looks like a total loss."

"You were smart not to go in," acknowledged Jubal. "Let's wait for full light and then have a look."

At that point Only and Silas walked up and they received the same story of what happened, this time from Jubal and Phil. And they repeated it all again when Steve and Willard wandered into the scene. By now it was getting brighter by the minute and the awful specter began to reveal itself in plain and honest light. It looked simply horrible.

The group decided to go in through the front door of the store and get a closer peek at the damage. Everyone was relieved to see that the store itself was untouched other than a broken front window and some gouged outside trim and shingles; all the significant damage was, fortunately, confined to the kitchen. The kitchen had been added to the main structure back in the 1970s by Kate's parents when they decided to start serving food. It was housed in a one-story, simple shed-roof structure added to the right side of the building, about 14 feet wide and 28 feet long, and that is what took all of the damage from the limb. The group quickly acknowledged that it could have been much worse. First, nobody had been hurt, and second, only the kitchen area was damaged. Had the whole tree come down, it is possible that the main structure—and Kate along with it—could have been lost. As bad as things were, they were thankful it happened the way it did.

By now it was approaching 7:00 and full daylight. Kate went to her phone and dialed Jim Watson. Apologizing for calling so early, she explained what had happened, and of course Jim was shocked and immediately asked if she was OK. She assured him she was unhurt and then asked if he could come down, for moral support if nothing else; he replied that he had just gotten dressed and would be there in five minutes. In the meantime, the morning crowd began to populate the store, and word was starting to spread through town about what had happened. The same shock and surprise cloaked everyone as they heard the news.

As promised, Jim Watson was there within five minutes. He parked along Time Square, jumped out, ran across the street and into the store, and immediately hugged Kate, assuring her that things would be OK and the whole town would be there for her. She immediately felt comforted by the confidence of her friend, and knew he would help her figure out what to do next. As wonderful as all the other folks were, she trusted Jim Watson more than anyone, and turned to him for guidance. He was, after all, the Wizard of Odd; she felt she would need his wizardly advice now more than ever.

After their greeting, Jim looked through the serving counter and into the kitchen and gave a "whew" after he grasped the extent of the damage. The place was crushed and likely a complete loss. Thank goodness this happened during the night and not while the kitchen was in heavy use during the day, or several people could have been killed, starting with Kate and Larry. They all agreed that if the limb had to go, the middle of the night was good timing indeed. The thought of the limb coming down four hours later was too much to even contemplate. At minimum, Kate almost certainly would have been seriously injured, if not killed.

"Kate, have you called your insurance company yet?" inquired Jim.

"No, I thought I would wait until 8:00. I figure they're not open until at least then."

"OK, that makes sense. Before we do anything else I think we need some pictures of the damage," suggested Jim. "I brought my camera and can try and get good documentation before anyone touches anything."

"Oh, great idea, Jim. Thanks," acknowledged Kate.

Jim returned to his car, grabbed his camera, and took several pictures of the interior of the kitchen through the serving counter before walking around outside, snapping more, trying to show the scene and details from every angle. About a dozen pictures, including several of her car, seemed to fully capture the necessary visual information.

Returning inside, he conferred with Kate and, with her agreement, announced to the small crowd that the store would be closed at least for today and they should all please clear out and let them take care of things. He also asked that nobody touch anything inside or out. The crowd understood and filed out. Kate next called Chief Johnsgaard and asked him to come by to at least know what was happening, and maybe write up a police report if that would help with the insurance. Then she went upstairs to look for her insurance folder.

At 8:00 AM sharp Kate called her insurance company and got a recording that their normal business hours were 8:30–5:00. So she and Jim waited a half hour before calling again, during which time Carl Johnsgaard came by, examined the damage, and strongly suggested that nobody should attempt to go inside the kitchen. Much of the ceiling was hanging down and electric wiring could be exposed. Kate explained that there was several hundred dollars' worth of refrigerated and frozen food in there and she would at least like to salvage it if the appliances were not running. They then realized that the propane line to the stove should be shut off. That was easy, as the tanks were outside at the back of the house and the line, fortunately, had not ruptured. Carl simply turned off the valve at the tanks.

While Kate dialed her insurance company again, Carl looked for safe access to the refrigerator and freezer, which were positioned along the outside wall toward the rear of the kitchen. He found possible access through a damaged entry door on the outer wall and determined that it should be safe enough to get in and ferry out any perishable food. While doing that, Kate connected with her insurance company at 8:30 but was informed that her agent was tied up and would have to call her back. While waiting, Carl began to write up his preliminary observations for the police report, and took some of his own pictures with his cell phone.

Finally, at 9:05 she received the call and reported what had happened. The agent was quite sympathetic and reassuring, but indicated that they had had several other calls already this morning due to wind damage from the storm and an adjustor would not be able to get out there until tomorrow, mid-morning. The agent asked her not to touch anything at the scene, though she did get permission to remove refrigerated and frozen items if it was safe to do so. Kate had no choice but to wait a whole day before she'd have any idea of what her immediate future might hold. Frustration and fear competed for her dominant emotion at this point, with each one momentarily taking the lead.

Then Kate remembered Larry Carson. She called him and told him what had happened, and indicated that he was out of his kitchen job until further notice, maybe a month or two. He would still be needed to help with general duties, but his hours would be drastically cut back. Larry understood and graciously offered to help in any way he could, but Kate still felt bad that he would be under-employed for a while.

By this time nearly two dozen townspeople had gathered in front of Odd Country, looking over the damage, shaking their heads, expressing their concerns, and speculating on the near future. Several, including Phil and Willard, offered to get their chain saws and begin removing the tree. Kate thanked them but said the insurance company instructed her not to touch or change anything until the adjustor inspected the damage.

Because they could do nothing else until tomorrow, Kate, Jim, and Carl decided to go ahead and remove the refrigerated and frozen items. Jim ran home to get two coolers to unload the frozen items into, and Kate found some cardboard boxes to hold refrigerated goods for transport. She determined that she had lots of space in her personal refrigerator upstairs, and Jim volunteered to hold any overflow items at his place as well. She went to the electric panel in the basement and turned off the main breaker to the kitchen, ensuring that electrocution, at least, was one hazard eliminated.

Carl and Jim wanted to go in alone but Kate insisted on getting in there as well to help rescue her food, as she knew where everything was; she also wanted to get a closer look at the damage. They carefully entered the kitchen through the outside door that was now hanging open. After determining that the tree limb seemed stable and well supported—partly by Kate's appliances—they crawled under, over, and through various large and small branches and over a soggy floor to get to the freezer and refrigerator. Though both were damaged and helped support the limb, their doors opened and granted full access after some branches had been moved aside. They started with the freezer and loaded up one and a half coolers' worth of goods, mostly meats. Then they filled three cardboard boxes with items from the large, commercial refrigerator before maneuvering the goods back through the tangle of limbs and branches and out of the opening.

Then, one-by-one, the team trundled the coolers and boxes around back and up the outside stairs to Kate's apartment on the second floor. They loaded what they could of the frozen and refrigerated items into her refrigerator, but had half a cooler of frozen goods and a box and a half of refrigerated items left over. They would have to take these to Jim's house soon, before the items defrosted or spoiled.

On the way back out they looked over Kate's old Subaru and concluded that, in addition to not being able to open any of the doors, there was little there to rescue anyway, so they let it be. After establishing that everything was as secure as it could be and there was little more they could do, Carl wrapped yellow caution tape around the damaged area and left to begin his regular duties, with abundant thanks from Kate. Then she and Jim went inside the store, looked everything over, and decided there was nothing more to be done there. Fortunately, electricity within the store was untouched and the coolers there were running fine.

"Kate, I need to run this stuff over to my place," said Jim. "Why don't you come back with me and spend the day there? There's nothing more you can do here until the insurance adjustor comes tomorrow and we can think this over and figure out a plan on what we need to do next."

"Jim, I suppose you're right," admitted Kate, looking around yet again as though further examination would somehow change the scene. "I want to stay and do something to fix it, but honestly there's nothing I can think of to do. So yeah, I'll take you up on that. Thank you *so* much!"

They quickly wrote up a sign that said "Closed Until Further Notice; Maybe Tomorrow?" and hung it in the broken front window. Then they locked up the store. After loading the remaining cold goods into Jim's car they headed up Center Street to his house and a near-term future that was completely uncertain, other than looking rather bleak. Jim knew that one job today would be to keep Kate's spirits up, no easy task.

Chapter 20

Wednesday, September 25, 10:35 AM

———

ARWIN GREETED JIM AND KATE LIKE LONG-lost cousins she had not seen in years. You would never guess by the dog's enthusiasm that Jim had only been gone a few hours. Darwin barked and whimpered and ran in circles, beside herself that her friend was back. Her wagging tail knocked a knick-knack off an end table and it took a good two minutes of greeting and reassuring to calm her down. Jim then let the crazy dog outside to run off some steam and keep out of their way.

After unloading the remaining goods into Jim's refrigerator and freezer for safekeeping, Jim and Kate realized they had not eaten anything yet today, and both were ravenous. They pulled some of Kate's bacon and eggs out of the fridge and made a full breakfast, complete with her orange juice, toast, and coffee. The rich and comforting smell of the bacon cooking especially got their juices flowing and it was all they could do to wait for everything to be finished before they tore into their fare.

Soon the breakfast was laid out on his modest dining room table adjacent to the kitchen and they eagerly indulged themselves. A full stomach helped to calm them both down and allowed them to take a few deep breaths, step back, and assess the situation while they waited for the insurance adjustor to come tomorrow and give them an idea of what Kate would be facing. Kate commented on how Robb Malloy had contacted her again, about 10 days ago, with a sweeter offer for the store, now up to $285,000. "Had I known this was going to happen I might have been tempted to take it," she concluded, but they both knew she didn't mean it.

After they cleared out the breakfast dishes and loaded the dishwasher, Kate turned to Jim and suggested he could now take her back home; she didn't want to impose on him and take up his whole day. "Kate," Jim responded, "I had absolutely nothing planned for the day, so you are not imposing. In fact, I'd enjoy the company. And I don't think you should be alone right now. You've had a significant shock and a loss, and you need somebody with you. I hope you don't mind if it's me."

"To be honest, there's nobody I'd prefer to hang with right now, so thank you, and yes, I'd love to stay. You are my sounding board and I know I can rely on you for comfort and good advice. I appreciate it all."

"OK, good, that's settled, then," concluded Jim. "Maybe we can spend some time figuring things out."

"I guess the question is, where do we go from here?" said Kate. "Assuming insurance covers my losses, what should we be doing in the near term?

You know, at minimum, this will set back our fund-raising efforts quite a bit."

"That it will, probably, but let's not think about that right away, Kate. Let's focus on the store and your business. So as far as we know the store itself is intact, and that's good. You can continue Odd Country even while the kitchen is down. You think you can open tomorrow?"

"I don't see why not. I'll tape some plastic sheeting or a tarp over the serving counter to block off the kitchen, and cover the broken front window, but other than that I don't see that any other changes are needed. But I also don't need to open at six. All my early business is breakfast." Then something clicked. "Dang, what will the Odd Balls do? They really thrive on their morning breakfasts and I'd hate to let them down. Plus, they were a good solid bit of sales right up front. I could count on $40-$60 three mornings a week like clockwork from those boys. Not to mention other breakfast customers. Sometimes we'd get twenty or more in a morning, and that could be a couple hundred dollars. Oh no, then there's Jodi! She'd pull in around 20 dollars each morning and put it toward her college fund. This will really hurt her." Kate was visibly getting herself worked up over the rippling effects of the event.

"OK, let's take it one step at a time," replied Jim, placing a hand on her shoulder. "Let's not get overwhelmed."

"Yeah, sorry, you're right. Seems like so many things are affected by this. OK. . . ." She took a deep breath and paused. "I'm good."

Darwin appeared at the back door, barking incessantly, demanding to be let in. Jim opened the door and they went through a miniature version of the intense reunion experienced when they first arrived home. Darwin—thoroughly lovable though she was—definitely had separation issues.

"God, she's crazy," concluded Jim, petting Darwin to reassure her that he was not going anywhere. "Alright, back to it. I have some plastic sheeting in the basement and some masking tape. We can tape over the window and kitchen opening first chance. No problem. Consider it done. Next, what time you want to open?"

Kate thought about it for a moment, then said, "Maybe 8:00 would work. And close at 6:00, just like normal."

"That sounds reasonable," said Jim. "So we'll find some cardboard or something to write up a sign with new hours and stick it in the front window. Problem solved."

"You make this sound easy, Jim. Thanks." Darwin was now at her feet, pressing against her legs and begging for attention, which Kate was all too happy to give. Running her hands through the thick and rich blond-brown fur gave her a comforting feeling. The dog even smelled good, receiving regular baths from Jim, and consequently her coat was lush and clean.

"Well, just take 'em one at a time," said Jim. "Nothing secret there. OK. Next. Odd Balls. They count on you and you count on them. Do you think you could open up early just for them and cook their breakfast upstairs? This would feed them, bring you some income, and keep Jodi working a bit."

"What a great idea, Doc! I couldn't offer them a full menu, but could make eggs, bacon, and sausage at least. Poor Silas won't get his waffles but I think he'll understand, and maybe even survive. Isn't that right, Darwin?" Kate purred to the dog's muzzle, her hands cupping the endearing and thoughtful face. Darwin's eyes were puddles of joy, and her ears perked up at any human voice, with the whole face tilting and becoming quizzical and expectant.

"So can you open breakfast for everyone or just them?"

"Let's start with the boys and see how it goes. It'll be difficult enough as is, and we can see how well it works. I should be able to handle five or six breakfasts from the upstairs kitchen. Oh wait, I can't do that!"

"Why not?"

"I don't have a permit from the health department to serve food from up there. It has to come from an inspected and approved kitchen. I'd be breaking the law big time, selling food from upstairs." Kate frowned at this latest issue.

"Hmmm," thought Doc. After a long pause, "What about this? What if you don't *sell* them food? You could invite them as your guests for breakfast. If they should happen to make a donation to you personally when they are finished, then they are not buying breakfast. And if they should happen to want to tip Jodi for her service, then so be it."

"Oooh, I like the way you think, Jim. No wonder they call you the Wiz. Oops, sorry, I wasn't supposed to call you that."

"That's OK, Kate. I know it is a compliment coming from you."

Kate covered a large yawn; she was starting to feel the effects of the last eight hours.

"So lemme think," she said. "If I'm opening the store at 8:00, maybe I could invite them for breakfast at 6:30. No menu, they can just tell me what kind of eggs and side meat they want. They know what I charge for things, so if they leave money on the table for my gift of food, then who am I to refuse? Great plan." Turning to the dog, she added, in a child-like voice, "Darwin, isn't your daddy so smart?" The dog's expectant face and wildly wagging tail seemed to agree with anything Kate said.

"How about I talk with them and suggest the plan? That way, you're not directly involved and asking for a 'donation'," said Jim, his fingers making quote marks in the air. "I'll make it clear that they are expected to pay the full amount, and maybe then some for the privilege of eating there."

"Sounds good, but let's not start this week. Give me a couple days to get back in the store and then we'll start her up next week. We'll continue with Monday, Wednesday, and Fridays." Kate then yawned for the third time in the last five minutes. She was starting to crash.

"OK, we've got a plan for the near term, Kate. We've done enough for the time being. How's about you go and take a nap? You only had a few hours of sleep last night, and after the adrenaline surge your body will be crashing."

"I can't argue with you there, Jim. I feel like I'm really flaming out and nap would be nice. Thank you," as she yawned yet again.

"C'mon back here with me." Jim walked her down the hall to the first door on the right. "Here's my guest bedroom, with its own bathroom. Make yourself at home. Sleep as long as you'd like. I'll be here whenever you wake up."

Kate hugged Jim warmly and kissed him on the cheek. She held his face in her hands and thanked him again. "I don't know what I'd do without you, Dr. Watson. You are a dear."

"Awww, pish posh," replied Jim. "Just go rest up. You're needed later."

After drawing the curtains shut, Kate laid herself down on the comfortable bed in the snug little guest room and was sound asleep within two minutes.

Chapter 21

Wednesday, September 25, 4:25 PM

J IM MANAGED TO KEEP DARWIN QUIET AND KATE
slept heavily due to a combination of only three
and a half hours sleep the night before, and
the physiological crash that followed a morning
of intense adrenaline- and cortisol-induced stress.
Upon waking in Jim's guest bed late afternoon,
she didn't know where she was at first, but then
the events of the last half day rushed back in and
informed her. Stretching and yawning, she slowly
turned herself out of the bed and trudged into the
bathroom. After peeing and splashing water on her
face, she began to feel refreshed and re-focused.

"Ahh, *there's* sleeping beauty," observed Jim as
Kate emerged from the hall into his living room,
with Darwin rushing over to assure her she was
still well loved. She greeted the dog by cupping
the dog's face in her hands, and touching her forehead to Darwin's, which brought that endearing
quizzical look from the dog. Jim put down his
book—ironically enough, Chris Bohjalian's *The*

Sleepwalker—and rose from the far end of the sofa to greet her. "How are you feeling? Did you sleep?"

"Oh boy, did I! Like the dead. I feel much better now and really needed that. Thanks so much Jim," replied a rejuvenated Kate. "I feel like I'm alive again. But this morning seems like three days ago already, and totally unreal. Did that really happen or was that just a bad dream?"

"I'm afraid it was real, my friend. But a mere bump in the road, I assure you," he added with a false and unconvincing sense of optimism. "We'll get through this. Can I get you something to drink?"

"Just some water right now. I think I'm dehydrated."

"You got it." Jim poured and handed her a tall glass of cool water, which she immediately sampled with large gulps. Sliding down her throat, it had a restorative and healing effect. She was starting to feel human again.

"And what have you been up to while I slept so blissfully?" inquired Kate as she settled into the near end of the big, overstuffed, brown leather sofa, which crinkled and sighed comfortably as she settled in. She took another big swallow of the water.

"Mostly caught up on some reading, though I did nod off a bit too," he admitted. "I hate that—I try to get some reading done and three pages into it I'm dozing off. I think I'm a reading narcoleptic! But I did make some headway and it was nice to escape into a good piece of fiction for a while."

"I sure could use a good, fictional story right now. Maybe one where my store is intact and the loan is paid off and life is easy. Suppose you could write that one for me?" she asked, finishing her glass of water.

"Hah, yeah, we're trying to write that story but I guess like any good novel it sure hasn't been easy or quick, has it? I still think we'll get there. Somehow."

"I wish we could write faster. I'd like to know how the story ends!"

"Soon enough, my friend, don't rush it. Hey, you ready for a cocktail? It's well past four o'clock and I think we've earned it today."

"I think I'm re-hydrated so it sounds good to me. What are you offering?"

"I was thinking of having a margarita, but I also have wine, beer, bourbon, gin, and so on."

"A margarita sounds great, Jim. No salt please."

"You got it," said Jim as he headed into the kitchen. "I make my own mix with real limes and real sugar. None of that high-fructose corn syrup crap they sell pre-made."

"I like the sound of that."

Jim soon returned with two margaritas on the rocks and they clinked glasses. "To being whole again," toasted Jim.

"To being whole!" echoed Kate. Taking her first sip, she added "Ooh, that really is good. Hits the spot." She inhaled a long, deep breath, held it for two seconds. . .and then slowly, easily, let it flow out and away; she felt a comfortable sense of relaxation settle through her body. After all the stress of recent times, and especially last night, she felt like she'd earned some respite, however brief.

Kate walked to the large bay window that domi-nated the front of Jim's living room and scanned the view. "You know, Jim, I just realized, I've *never* been in your house!"

"Really? Well, don't take it personally. I almost

never entertain. I live a pretty quiet life at home. It's only in town that I'm a wild and crazy guy," he joked. Kate chuckled at the absurdity of Jim being wild and crazy; his stability and sense of self control were very appealing features to her.

Turning back to the window she took in the expansive view, which was so picturesque it almost looked fabricated. Jim's house stood near the site of Francis Odderton's original homestead that started the town. Set on a small rise that continued back into a heavily wooded ridge, the house commanded a stunning panorama. The front looked down into the Odder Creek valley, with the stream off to the left, its slight meanders cutting through forests and a few pastures. Oddertown sat about a half mile down the valley, but Kate could see little evidence of it, other than the spire of the Methodist Church, due to the heavy tree cover. To the far left and right, the valley was embraced by densely wooded hillsides that rose about 400 feet above the valley floor. Like so much of Vermont, most of the area was second-growth forest, 125-150 years old since it was originally logged, stripped bare, and abandoned, causing massive and damaging erosion to the region at the time. Now stabilized, and with hard lessons learned, the area was again on solid footing and calendar-picturesque.

Sipping her margarita, Kate suddenly realized that the trees had started to take on their autumn colors, and was shocked that she hadn't noticed this before. She stared at the yellows, oranges, browns, and reds that were steadily replacing the intense chlorophyll green that had blanketed the area for the last four-plus months. "Doc, I can't believe how oblivious I've been," she said, scanning left and right. "I didn't even realize the trees were changing color! How could I miss that? What else have I missed? I mean, look at this scene, it's bloody gorgeous!" she exclaimed, hand sweeping outward to emphasize her point.

Coming up to stand next to her, Jim concurred that this was indeed brilliant. "My favorite time of year, Kate. I love the crispness in the air and of course the colors. But my favorite part is the smell, believe it or not. I like that rich and earthy and moist smell of decomposition as leaves are starting to recycle back into soil. Funny. Though it's death and decomposition it smells so alive to me, so rich and abundant. It smells like life. It holds promises for an abundant future."

Side by side, they sipped their drinks and quietly took in the scene, in no hurry to move on. Life's pause button, pushed for just a minute.

Kate finally broke out of her reverie and scanned the rest of the living room. The sofa sat in the middle of the room facing the bay window, and was bordered by two maple end tables, with a maple coffee table in front, covered with several books and magazines. A large braided rug of faded merlot color added warmth and tied it all together. Behind the sofa was open walkway space bordered by a full wall of bookshelves, filled top to bottom and left to right with hundreds of books, neatly arranged by topic: science, history, philosophy, contemporary culture, fiction, classics, nature, and so on. Obviously Jim's interests were broad and encompassing. In the front, right-hand corner of the room, almost as an afterthought, sat a recliner facing a modest-sized television. A few pieces of art, mostly depicting Vermont landscapes and nature scenes, decorated the walls. Some bits of nature—bones, feathers, large seed pods, pieces of granite and gneiss—accented the bookshelves, emphasizing Jim's connections and commitment to the natural world. The whole setting was comfortable, welcoming, organic, and tidy.

Kate walked over to the bookshelves and pointed to the books. "Do you mind?"

"Help yourself," replied Jim, happy to have someone else peruse his library.

After scanning several rows of books and pulling a few down to examine, Kate came across a compelling triptych—three small photos arranged in three attached frames. She picked them up and carefully examined them all. They each contained the same woman, with Jim also appearing in the center picture.

"So this is Maggie, huh? I've not seen her before; she was an attractive woman. Her face in all these pictures has a look of total serenity. She looks like she's at peace with life."

"You just summed her up, Kate. She was the happiest, most balanced and serene person I've ever known. Even when she was sick, she seemed to have a deep understanding of life well beyond anything I could ever hope for. That's maybe what I miss most about her, her ability to be centered and accepting and somehow know what the big picture was all about. I really miss that. She was my compass and my gyroscope." Jim teared up a bit and looked away. "She made me better than I am."

Kate put her arm across Jim's shoulder and held him for a moment, side-by-side. After an appropriate pause, she said softly, "Tell me about these pictures, if you don't mind."

"These are my three favorite pictures of her because they capture the range of who she was." Pointing to the left picture he said "This one is her working at a soup kitchen, helping to feed the homeless. She always tried to help those less fortunate and worked there once a week. She loved it and always felt she received much more than she gave. So it constantly made her go back next time and try to give even more."

Jim paused to take a sip and drew in a deep breath to steady himself. "This one on the right is her last day of teaching before retirement. The entire school gave her a surprise party because she was loved by all, even the kids not in her class. Mrs. Watson was a favorite and she helped so many kids, counseling them on her own time, even buying them supplies when they couldn't afford it and feeding some when they would have gone hungry. They made her a giant red paper heart that day and they all signed it." He had to pause again for composure, a tear emerging from one eye. "So many kids wrote that they loved her and would miss her," he was barely able to get out. He sniffled, the words lodging in his tight throat. Kate hugged him again from the side. "I still have that heart upstairs with all the love and well wishes written on it."

"And then finally, hah, this one," he said, smiling and pointing to the middle photo. "We hiked up to the top of Mt. Abe one Saturday. It's a challenging hike but not horrible. Just long and you have to keep at it, a real endurance test, some pretty good rock hopping. We were so proud of ourselves when we finally got to the top and felt so virtuous, but totally beat. So we're sitting there enjoying the incredible view that we felt we had earned with such hard work when up to the summit comes an old Asian couple. I swear, Kate, they were in their mid-80s if they were a day, and they weren't even breathing hard. I don't think they broke a sweat! Just waltzed up there like it was nothing."

Kate laughed at the imagery.

"We looked at each other, saying what the...? Finally we went over and talked with them. Turns out they were from Nepal and walked the Himalayas their whole lives. Been doing that since they were kids. Mt. Abe was nothing to them but a little warm-up hill! That made us feel a little better. Now *that* was a good day." After a momentary and thoughtful pause, he continued, "I wish you could know at the time how significant different events in your life would be, how they would stand out later as page markers in that novel of where you've been. You might appreciate them more at the time."

"I know what you mean, Doc. Sometimes it takes hindsight to focus our lives and we miss things when they first come around. I guess we should all be paying more attention and not wait until later to realize what we had. I'm afraid some important things are lost to us that way."

Kate put the photos back on the shelf and finished her margarita. "You ready for another?" inquired Jim.

"Sure, why not? Twist my arm. I've got nothing else to do today. May as well get looped," as she handed over her empty glass.

When Jim returned with the refilled glasses, he saw that Kate had picked up another photograph in its own frame, this one of Maggie obviously sick and in the hospital, hooked up to various tubes and medical monitors, and smiling despite the pain and resignation on her face.

"And this one, if you don't mind my asking?" she inquired hesitantly.

"Oh yeah, that one," Jim replied with a slight grimace, and then a thoughtful pause. "I keep that out to remind myself of the worst and most-selfish decision of my entire life. Maggie did not want to go through chemotherapy. The doctors said it might extend her life a couple of months, but could also just make her ending more difficult. She wanted to just use her remaining time as best she could but I pleaded and begged and finally pretty much insisted that she do chemo. I wanted to leave no stone unturned and wanted to try anything to keep her going as long as possible."

Jim paused, took in and let out a deep breath, and shook his head slowly, obviously in deep emotional pain, while staring at the floor. Kate waited silently and respectfully.

"Well, the chemo didn't work," he finally continued, "and it made her so sick and in fact probably robbed a good month or so from us. She had a miserable and painful death as a result of me being so goddamned selfish. I just did not want to let her go and was thinking of *my* needs, not hers. It was an awful, terrible thing I did to her and I'll never forgive myself."

"Jim, you obviously had the best of intentions for both of you and surely she knew that."

"Yeah, she did, and insisted she didn't regret trying, but she just said that to protect me. So I look
at that picture every day to remind myself that I'm
not as smart as I sometimes think I am. I don't want
to forget that, Kate. I don't ever want to do something so selfish like that again to anyone. I failed her
when she most needed me. The people you most
love deserve better than that."

Putting back the photo, patting Jim on the arm,
and settling back onto the sofa, Kate asked him to
tell her more about Maggie and their life together,
if she wasn't prying too much. Jim said she was not
and he would be glad to.

"Kate, not to sound too much like a cliché, but
we truly were two halves of a whole. You hear about
soul mates and all that, and I always thought it was
total bullshit, to be honest. I never thought it was
possible that two people could be so made for each
other, or that they would actually find each other. I
mean, what are the odds? It is something like one
chance in a billion that *those two particular people*
who are so-called soul mates would actually find
each other. But then Maggie and I did and we were
the poster children for the soul mate concept. Just
remarkable. We felt comfortable with each other
and in sync, I swear, from about 30 seconds after
we met. It was absolutely effortless with us. I will
never, ever, take for granted what we had. It was
really miraculous."

After a pause of reflection, Kate encouraged Jim
to go on.

"I'm not sure what more to tell other than we
were so damned happy together. We respected each
other, we supported each other, and we celebrated

each other. We lived for each other. Sure, we had our occasional disagreements like everybody does, but they were always short lived and never amounted to anything. I think we—well, Maggie mostly—always managed to keep the larger picture in focus; she always said we had this one life and it wasn't a dress rehearsal and we'd better get it right the first time because there were no second takes. Because of her we were happy most of the time. She embraced life and all it gave—good or bad—every day. It was like every day was a new gift with great possibilities, or no possibilities at all, and that was OK too. Every day just *was*, and that was enough for her."

Jim looked over and saw that Kate was fully engaged and smiling at his recollections.

"And the weird thing is, as much as I miss her—which is a helluva lot—I think her lessons sank in enough that, even though the pain is still there, I am managing to enjoy life better than I might have thought remotely possible at this point. She's still my compass and gyroscope, still guiding and helping me along, every day."

"Jim, you are so fortunate to have found such a special person," responded an appreciative Kate. "And she to have found you. Sounds like you had an extraordinary thing going there. I'm happy for you, though sad that she's gone. But you are honoring her life so well by the life you are living here. You've had such a positive impact on our community in such a short time. She would be very proud of you."

"Thanks, Kate. I think she would be too, and I want to continue to make her proud of me. That's the way I try to lead my life. That's what motivates me. I want to be a better person for *her*."

Some sips and quiet reflection followed their exchange, and they gazed out the window at the bright and colorful scene. No traces of the previous night's storm remained, and the sky was now deeply blue and the air clean and crisp. They both felt comfortable in their momentary silence.

"So what about you, Kate?" asked Jim, finally breaking their silence. "What happened in your marriage if I might be so nosy?"

"Hah, not nearly the pretty picture you paint. Kind of ugly, actually."

"Well, I'm listening if you want to spill your guts."

After a brief thought, Kate started her story. "I think my marriage is best summed up by the word 'superficial.' We were both taken by outward appearances and forgot to check under the hood to see what kind of engine was inside. I was eye candy for him, and he was the same for me. Jason Langford is a good-looking guy, rugged and athletic. Women are drawn to him and I was one of them. I was taken in by his looks and machismo, but it turns out that he was too, and he used them to his full advantage."

Kate stood up, walked to the bay window, and spoke to the changing tree colors. Behind her on the sofa, Jim simply listened. Darwin looked up from her curled position on the braided rug and seemed anxious to hear the rest of the story.

"He grew up in Boston and was kind of 'big-city arrogant,' conceited about his looks and sophistication and worldliness. Of course I didn't see that until after we were married. I only saw the surface and his confidence. Coming from this little backwater speck of a town I was so impressed and taken with him and didn't look deep enough. He was narcissistic, thought he was God's gift to the world. But none of that was apparent to me until it was too late. I was so foolish. Or I guess naïve."

She turned around and now spoke directly to Jim. Darwin sat up at full attention, ready to hear more.

"In our fifth year of marriage I caught him cheating. It was on a business trip and he swore it was a one-time mistake; as far as I knew it was. He promised it would never happen again and begged for a second chance and I gave it to him. We were fine for a while, even really good, but two years later I caught him again. Turns out he had been having an affair with someone from his office for a year and a half. It had started only six months after his promise to be faithful to me!"

"What a dope!" concluded Jim. "Obviously he didn't know how good he had it."

"You're damn right, Doc!" replied Kate in a voice louder and sharper than she might have liked. "And I realized that too late. I should have been out of there a lot sooner. Anyway, I headed for the divorce lawyer and just wanted out. Which I got. I'm so glad we put off having kids until our careers were more settled. Poor things would have been caught in the middle of some real ugliness."

Kate turned back to stare out the bay window. "In retrospect I needed someone with greater depth, with solid character. Even without the cheating, I can see now it would not have worked in the long run. He just didn't have enough substance for me. All glitter and no filling. I sure wish I could have had a little bit of what you and Maggie had."

"Is there anyone special in your life right now?" inquired Jim.

"No. I've been too focused on the store. And besides, the pickings around here are pretty slim, as you may have noticed. I mean, c'mon, what does Oddertown have to offer? Willard Bennett for goodness sake?" She grimaced and shuddered at the thought of that image. "Right now I have enough challenges in my life. Of course, if *you're* available…" said Kate with a mischievous grin, and obviously joking. Mostly, anyway.

"Yeah, right, old fart like me. Quite the catch," laughed Jim. "Well, I'm at least a whole step above Willard, right?"

"I actually think you have a lot to give, Doc. Don't close yourself off to life just yet. There may be someone out there who you need and who needs you. She wouldn't be Maggie, but you can't use her as a measuring stick. That was a once-in-a-lifetime deal. But maybe someone else could still bring some joy into your life and you into hers. Just don't close the door is all I'm saying. Don't cheat yourself."

"I guess that's good advice, but I don't see getting involved with anyone any time soon. Again, it's not like the pickings are abundant for me either. My God, though, Layla Liederman makes me nervous. She's tried a couple of times to hit on me, asking me over to dinner and such. There's no way I'm going near that old broad!"

They both laughed and clinked their glasses in mutual understanding and agreement.

After a brief pause, Kate said "Tell ya what. I need to impose on you to take me home anyway, so why don't we head on down there now and I can cook us up some dinner from some of that food sitting in my fridge? May as well eat as much as we can before it goes bad."

"Well, that sounds like a capital idea! Yeah, let's do that."

"You OK to drive a half mile or so Doc? Wouldn't want Carl throwing you in the slammer on a DUI!"

"I think I can handle the big trip after two margaritas," smiled Jim. "Traffic shouldn't be too bad. I'm thinking the Oddertown rush hour should be coming to a close about now."

As they were getting into his car, Kate turned to Jim. "I really do appreciate all you did for me today. This would have been so much worse without you. I can't thank you enough Jim. And spending the day up here got me out of my head for a while. I really feel refreshed after stepping back from the place. Thank you so much for everything."

"No problem, Kate. Glad to do it and I thoroughly enjoyed the company."

But when they pulled up in front of the store, Kate's stomach tensed as she saw the damage once again. The reality of it all came flooding back and she immediately returned to her feelings of dread and depression. After a good afternoon away and some badly needed distraction, she was thrust back into the real world and reminded that she had lost a kitchen and a car, and had no idea how this would play out. She nearly felt sick to her stomach as they walked up the front steps into a damaged Odd Country and worked their way back to the old stairs that led up to her home. This was going to be a long and difficult haul, with no happy ending in sight.

Chapter 22

Thursday, September 26, 10:17 AM

———

THE MORNING IN ODD COUNTRY OPENED like no other in recent memory. With the kitchen destroyed, Kate didn't quite know what to do. At 8:00 she turned the "Closed" sign to "Open" and simply sat back and waited for customers. No breakfast to cook, no dishes to clean up, no Jodi to chat with. So she sat and stared at the plastic sheeting covering the opening that led to the former culinary center of her life, contemplating what the next few months might hold. The image was unclear at best, and likely not pretty.

Customers soon arrived in larger-than-normal numbers, mostly to commiserate, see the damage, give her a hug, and maybe buy something they didn't really need but which might help bring some cash into the shop. She appreciated all of them, and felt a bit more positive with each one.

At mid-morning, Kate's stomach sank when the door chimed and in walked, of all people, Robb Malloy, once again dressed in his faux country casual outfit, standing him out like a wannabe good 'ole boy. *What the hell does* he *want?* she thought to herself. *Goddamn parasite.*

"Hello, Kate," he said as he approached her from across the room. "I heard what happened, and I'm so sorry. I really am. Are you OK? Nobody hurt?"

"No, nobody was hurt, fortunately," she forced herself to say. "And I'm fine, thank you. What can I do for you?"

"Well, let me ask, do you have insurance that will cover this? I do hope so."

"Yes I do, thank you. Why are you here?"

"Kate, I wanted…"

"It's Ms. Langford, by the way. I never gave you permission to use my first name."

"Sorry, somewhat presumptuous on my part. I had hoped that by now we would have business to conduct and would be partners, of sorts."

"Well we don't and we aren't, Mr. Malloy," Kate replied coldly.

Malloy frowned a bit, contorted his mouth, and hesitated slightly before he took a breath and continued.

"Ms. Langford, I dropped by this morning to propose my same generous offer. I thought that perhaps with your sudden change in circumstance you might want to re-consider what we discussed earlier. Even with the kitchen and all its equipment gone, I am prepared to offer you the same $285,000 for the building and land. And you can keep the insurance settlement as well. I doubt you will be able to recover from this setback, and you would make out quite nicely with my deal. I'm here to help you out of a bind."

And to help yourself to the bones, thought Kate. She took a deep breath, looked off to the side, and tried to keep her emotions—especially her temper—under control.

"Mr. Malloy, let me be clear. I am not now, nor will I ever be, interested in your offer. Yes, this is a setback for me but I will deal with it. I do not need you to swoop in and save the poor damsel in distress." Malloy began to protest his innocence but Kate firmly held up her hand, stopping him in mid-sentence. "I plan to stay here," she said, "keep the store, and run it for a good long time to come. I do not wish to be rude but please, please, accept my decision, go away, and do not come around again. My answer will not change."

"Ka-, uh, Ms. Langford, I know this is a difficult time for you, and I appreciate that you think you don't want to sell. But I'd like to leave my offer on the table for one month. Once the reality of your situation sinks in, you *might* want to reconsider, and I will be amenable to discussing it with you at that time. I'll leave you be now, but I want you to know that I remain an option for you. Again, I'm very sorry for your troubles. Truly, I am. Thank you, and sorry to upset you; that certainly was not my intention."

With no further word—and with Kate slightly aghast at his persistence, his predatory behavior in immediately sensing a weakness in his prey, and his unwillingness to accept her answer—he smoothly and calmly walked to the front door and slipped back into his world. She shook her head, slapped a wall, and re-grouped for the coming challenges.

Chapter 23

T HE INSURANCE SETTLEMENT WAS DISAPPOINTING, to say the least. The adjustor, a nice young fellow who grew up in and worked out of Newport, was as sympathetic as he could be, and tried to put Kate's fears at ease and assure her that all would be taken care of. But his naïve young hands were tied by the rules, procedures, charts, and algorithms of the insurance industry and his company. When the dust settled she received only $1250 for her 16-year-old Subaru—a figure that did not surprise her—and $31,620 for the kitchen, including re-construction plus all the appliances, food-storage units, prep surfaces, and cabinets—a figure that very much surprised her. The contents alone would run at least $19,000 to replace, possibly more. That left less than $13,000 for building reconstruction.

Kate contacted Paul Simon, the fly-fishing lawyer from New Jersey, once she found his card among her scattered business papers. After offering his sympathies and help, Paul encouraged her to appeal the kitchen settlement, and wrote a lawyerly letter—pro bono—to the insurance company, but to no avail. It turns out that her grandfather's insurance policy on the store had full replacement coverage for the building, but only coverage for the *current* value— not replacement value—of the contents, a fatal flaw. The policy also carried a $1000 deductible. Once again, she would pay for Grampa Simon's unintended but very real mismanagement.

To make matters worse, her policy carried no rider for reimbursement of lost business. So in addition to a low settlement, she would lose more than half of her regular income each day that the kitchen was not open. She received a settlement check within a week, for $32,870, all of which would be applied to the kitchen. Any car replacement would only be wishful thinking at this point; she was grounded in Oddertown for the foreseeable future.

Fortunately, two Oddertown carpenters—the brothers Tim and Jim Kittleson—and their apprentice helper Mason Monroe offered to re-build the structure at their cost for materials and with some of their labor donated. A project that normally would have cost upwards of $24,000 they would do for an estimated $16,000. Kate appreciated this more than she could say, and it was a huge help, but it would still put her in the hole for over $2100, plus she now had no car, and half the regular income from the store. She would need to dip into any remaining savings, money that was intended for the bank repayment. And if construction and appliances came in any higher than estimated—a distinct possibility for these sorts of things—Kate would have to dip into the public funds raised so far for the loan, something she was loathe to do, but could be forced into. Goddamn tree!

The Odd Balls happily signed onto her plan of coming for breakfast as her guests, and they dutifully made donations when they left, along with tips for Jodi. And they always rounded up the prices, so that an order that normally would be, say, $6.50 would now bring $7.00. Many townsfolk came by periodically and made donations, leaving fives, tens, and even an occasional twenty in a jar at the checkout for the rebuilding fund. Many also dropped the change for their purchases into that jar. As deeply kind and moving as these actions were, in a practical sense they would not do a great deal to ease the debt; they were pennies against the dollar.

Construction of the kitchen behind the plastic sheeting over the serving area was going well. It had taken three days to clear and haul the debris, and then framing of the new structure began immediately over the existing slab foundation. The replacement kitchen was now framed out and the plywood on the roof was being installed today. The repeated and rapid 'kathunks' of nails being driven by compressed air, though distracting to the breakfasters, was a welcome sound, and each one brought Kate a little closer to re-opening the kitchen. Things were progressing at a good pace—even better than hoped—and Kate was thankful.

Jodi was not able to waitress this morning, as she had an early-morning practice for a play at school. She had won the role of Irene Molloy in her school's production of *Hello, Dolly!* and would occasionally be unavailable to Kate, who was forced to double as the server as well as chief cook and bottle washer in her absence. The few extra dollars in tips she pocketed would not be enough to offset the extra running up and down the stairs she had to incur, but such were the cards she was dealt, and she played them out as best as she could. Besides, she told herself, the extra exercise would help keep her in good physical shape.

Kate had already made several trips up to and back from her kitchen this morning, getting all of the Odd Balls' orders filled, when Willard reminded her that he had asked for an extra side of bacon to go with his sausages. Phil also needed his rye toast, which she had forgotten. So back up to the kitchen she trudged to keep her boys satisfied. It was getting old but she was happy that she at least had some breakfast business and did not complain about the extra work, even to herself. She grabbed the two items from her kitchen, set them on her serving tray, and made yet another trip down the old and creaky stairs.

The sudden crash startled the Odd Balls, who all involuntarily jumped, and then Kate's moans of pain bolted them out of their seats and over to the bottom of the stairs. "Kate, Holy Christ, are you OK?" asked a startled Silas Miller, the first arrival, with the rest close on his heels. Kate was rolling on the floor in obvious pain, holding one arm and curled into a fetal position; a serving tray, broken plates, bacon, and toast were scattered around her.

"Oh crap, I'm hurt!" she cried.

"Where are you hurt?" asked Paul Johnson, pushing past the others. "Talk to me."

"I think it's my wrist, and my ankle. Owwww, it really hurts. Oh shit, I don't need this now, goddammit!"

Paul knelt down next to her and gently tried to calm her and stop her from rolling back and forth. The others gathered round in deep concern.

"OK, Kate, listen to me. Shhh, listen. Look at me. Kate, please, look at me." She managed to focus on Paul. "Is your head OK? Did you hit your head?"

"No, I don't think so."

"Can you see OK? Do you have clear vision?"

"Yeah, I think so," she said through blurry tears.

"OK, now tell me where you're hurting," ordered Paul.

"My left wrist, I came down hard on it. I think I broke it. My ankle too, left ankle. Owwww, dammit."

"OK, anything else, Kate? Kate, look at me. Focus on me."

She looked at Paul and said "I think that's it." The Odd Balls mostly stood and stared, hands on their knees, not knowing how to help.

"Alright, now, can you sit up at all? Can I help you sit?"

"Yeah, I'll try."

Paul gently grabbed Kate from behind, under both armpits, and helped her to a sitting position; she emitted another scream of pain along the way. He then looked at and felt the back of her head and neck, and everything seemed normal. "Slowly turn your head to the left and right," he said. She did, with no problems or pain. "Now up and down." That checked out as well. A visual of her wrist by Paul revealed no obvious fracture, though the area already seemed like it might be swelling.

"OK, good. Now, Kate, can you move your left hand at all? Gently. Give it a try."

She tried to flex her wrist and cried out in pain. "OK, no more of that. Now what about your ankle? Let me have a look."

Her socks and rubber moc boots prevented a

good look at the ankle so he asked if she could move it at all. Kate tried and again cried out in pain.

"OK, tell you what. Let's get some ice on these spots and then we need to get you to the hospital. Guys, one of you run upstairs and put some ice cubes in a couple of plastic bags. Kate, do you have bags up there?"

"Yeah, uh. . .center drawer of the island."

Steve Benson took off up the stairs to get the ice.

"Alright, who can run Kate down to St. J.?"

Before anyone could answer Kate interjected "I'd like to see if Jim Watson can do it. Can somebody call him?"

"Sure, Kate. Jubal, give Jim a call and explain—" but Jubal Keller was already on his way to the phone.

"How you doing, Kate? You hanging in there?" asked Paul.

"Oh I'm just fine and dandy, Paul. Never better," she replied, with an unconvincing attempt at a smile. "I gotta tell you, it really hurts."

"I know, and we're gonna take care of that. You'll be fine, I promise. It will all heal, and you'll be good as new. What happened, anyway?"

"I think I just missed the last step—owww! I must have thought I was on the bottom but I wasn't. I felt my ankle twist and then—owwwww—shit, I landed on my wrist." She was rocking forward and back, left arm supported against her chest by her right hand.

Steve returned with two ice-filled zip-lock bags and Paul gingerly applied the first one to her ankle. She again screamed in pain, despite his attempts to be gentle about it. He laid the ice pack as best as he could on top of the ankle and then got her to apply ice to the wrist that she was holding. Kate was able to do that reasonably well, keeping her arm against her body.

Jubal then returned and announced that Jim was on his way. While they waited, Paul at least managed to get Kate up into a chair—a painful process for her. She could put no weight on her left ankle, and they feared it was broken. Her mind cleared and focused enough to instruct the group that the store could not open today, and they promised they would take care of things, no worries. *Just great; another day with no income*, thought Kate.

Paul considered giving her a couple of ibuprofen for the swelling but then thought better of it in case the hospital wanted to give her other, more-powerful drugs that might not interact well, or if she needed surgery. So they waited.

Jim arrived in a few minutes and that brought a new spate of tears from Kate as he said, "I hear you had a little spill."

"Oh, Jim, I've really done it now. As if we didn't have enough shit to deal with…"

"It's OK, we'll deal with this too. You ready to go to the E.R. and have them take a look at you?"

"Sure, I've got nothing better to do today."

Jim carefully got his shoulder under Kate's left arm, taking her weight off her left ankle. Paul steadied her from the right side and they lifted her out of the chair. The three ambled out the front door to Jim's waiting car, loaded her up with more cries of pain, and headed down to Northeastern Vermont Regional Hospital in St. Johnsbury, 25 minutes away. "Helluva way to start your day, Kate," observed Jim as they drove south past Time Square and the few remaining fall colors on its old maple trees.

Chapter 24

THE STAFF AT NORTHEASTERN REGIONAL DID A good job with Kate, though why everything in a hospital emergency room takes so long remained a complete mystery; they were there for over five hours. This gave Kate ample time to sit and think about her latest predicament, and she could not help lapsing into despair in-between the E.R. doctor's examination, X-rays, and waiting for results. Everything seemed to be crashing down around her. Short of the building burning down, she wasn't sure how this could get much worse. With Jim waiting in the lobby and unable to temper her thoughts while she laid on a gurney, and while coming under the influence of pain killers, Kate sank to such a low point that she actually wondered whether her next call should be to Robb Malloy to just sell him the damned place and get the hell out! But before she could travel too far down that dark tunnel, Dr. Brad Beasley came back with her results.

X-rays provided both good news and bad. The good news was that her ankle was not broken, just a bad sprain that would swell, turn several interesting colors over the coming days, and then slowly heal. No surgery, no real treatment needed. They wrapped it and she was to ice it for a day or two, stay off it completely for two weeks, and then use it only sparingly for another couple of weeks. The bad news was that the wrist was indeed broken; the ulna was cracked right above the hand, and the small pisiform bone where it meets the ulna was chipped. But the good news was that surgery would not be required; a soft cast and eight weeks immobilized should make her 95% whole. She would probably have some minor limitations of movement and lingering discomfort, but would otherwise be OK. But the bad news, again, was that, even with health insurance, her little hospital visit would cost over $450 out of pocket for deductibles and co-payments, money she surely could not spare.

On the drive back north, Jim convinced Kate that she should stay at his place at least for tonight and possibly longer. She was in no condition to go up and down stairs, and needed some TLC early on. They also needed to discuss, yet again, what to do about Odd Country in the near term. It was not obvious how she could work at the store until she was able to at least get back on her ankle. Kate reluctantly agreed. "Jim, I can't believe how I'm imposing on you yet again. You are a Godsend, and a saint, and I'd be totally lost without you, but I feel so bad that I'm putting you through yet another trial with me."

"Not to worry, Kate. As they say, this is what friends are for. You would do it for me, right?"

"In a New York second I would! But still, I will owe you even bigger now."

"Let's just get you healed up and back on your feet. Really, Kate, I don't want you all worried about putting me out. I'm retired, I live alone, I have no pressing obligations, and this will give me something to focus on. Honestly, it's nice to feel needed again after being alone for five years."

"Well then, I'm so happy I can serve you in that way," replied Kate, exhibiting the first hint of a smile since her fall that morning. Some oxycodone had taken the edge off her pain and she was finally relaxing, though she did not like the dopey feeling brought on by the drug. She had always been repelled by the many so-called "side effects" of drugs so easily dimissed by the pharmaceutical industry. They were *real effects*, dammit, don't marginalize them to the side! Dopiness and horrible constipation and dizziness were just as much a result of oxycodone use as pain relief, so just admit to it.

Finally at home, Jim left her in the car while he went inside and put Darwin in the back yard until Kate was in and settled; he did not want the dog's uncontrolled enthusiasm to knock her over again. It was not easy getting Kate into the house, but they managed, and it was certainly better than trying to get her upstairs into her own home. The hospital gave her crutches but they were useless at this point. Though she could easily tuck one under her left armpit, she could not grasp it with her broken left wrist. They would need to figure out a better way for her to move. For now, Jim got her settled into his recliner, and raised the leg support to help control swelling. He then got an ice pack and laid it on her ankle and set a glass of water on the table next to her. Finally they were both able to take a deep breath, relax, and settle in from the trauma of the day. Jim let Darwin back into the house and it took her a good two minutes to complete her over-enthusiastic greetings and settle down.

"So Kate, realistically I don't see how you can go home until you can at least walk a bit on that ankle. You can't go up and down stairs, and you can't even walk around your house to get meals or use the bathroom. I do believe you are a captive here for at least two weeks."

"Oh, Jim, I can't impose on you like that. There's gotta be—"

"Stop right there," he interrupted, holding up his hand. "This is not an imposition, I am happy to do it, and it is settled. Case closed. No further discussion. You're staying here. The guest room is ready to go."

Kate thought for a minute, smiled meekly, sighed deeply, and concluded "I really can't argue with that. I do need help and I will have to swallow my pride and take it. Doc, you are too sweet. Thank you, my dear friend."

"OK, good, that's settled. You will have your own room and bathroom, and are pretty much at my mercy for everything else."

"I believe you are full of mercy, and I place myself in your capable hands, Sir," concluded Kate with a nice smile.

"Tonight I'll run down to your place and get whatever you need. Changes of clothes, toiletries, books, whatever. You can make a list and tell me where things are and I'll get them. And you can't be squeamish about personal items. Yes, I'll need to get into your underwear drawer. We're both adults here, it'll be OK."

Kate smiled. "I don't mind at all if you get into my underwear, Doc. . . . Wait, that didn't sound quite right," she giggled, as did Jim. "You know what I mean."

A little laugh was good medicine right about now.

"OK, so are you ready to discuss the store?"

"Well, I'm a little whacked out from this pain killer, but I'm actually feeling kinda good so I think I can focus. Yeah, let's talk." Jim sensed that the oxycodone was starting to make her a bit euphoric, one of the dangerous side effects that could lead to addiction. He would need to keep an eye on her and get her off the stuff as quickly as possible.

"I don't see how you can run the store for at least a couple of weeks," began Jim. "I mean, we could plop you down there but all you could do is sit and watch. So I think we need to come up with a Plan B. I'm sure you don't want to close it for two weeks or more. Right?"

"Oh no, I couldn't close it! That would cut off all cash flow when I most need it. And what would customers do for their needs? It *has* to stay open, but how?"

"Do you know of anyone else who can run it? Do you have any backups?"

"Not really. Larry Carson comes the closest. He knows how to run the register and he stocks shelves. Jodi can do some too, but she's in school during much of the day."

"Well then, maybe a call to Larry would be in order to see if he can try running the store. I'd have a go myself but until we get a routine sorted out here I don't want to leave you alone for hours on end."

"OK, let me call him."

Jim handed his cordless phone to Kate and she dialed Larry's number from memory, which was still working despite the oxycodone. Larry's mother answered and indicated he was not home but should be back by four or so. She would have him return her call.

Larry called back at 4:30 and Kate gave him the full story, with which, of course, he was sympathetic. Because he had largely been laid off when the kitchen was destroyed, he had taken on some temporary construction work with a friend who gave him what hours he could and had just returned from that job. But Larry said he could beg out of that and go full-time at the store. He would need some training on opening and closing, reconciling the cash register at the end of the day, and ordering and receiving; he already knew all about keeping the shelves stocked. He promised to meet Kate and Jim at the store at 7 PM and try to cover all the bases so Odd Country could open again the next morning and limp along until she healed. Until then, she just needed to relax and let the healing begin. And not get too used to that narcotic.

Chapter 25

Thursday, October 10, 5:10 PM

"So how's your pain level, Kate?" inquired Jim as they sat in the living room, he on the sofa, she in his recliner, rotated around toward him and away from the TV, with her legs elevated.

"Not too bad, all things considered," she replied. "Kind of dull aches at this point. The oxy-whatever seems to be doing the job, though I want to get off it soon. I can feel that I'm kind of liking it so that tells me I've gotta get off before I develop a craving. I think I'll take only one more tonight to help me sleep, and then tomorrow I'd like to just try ibuprofen and see if that does it."

"Sounds like a good plan. So can I get you anything right now? More juice, a snack? Dinner won't be ready until 6 or so."

"No, I'm good, Jim, thanks. You go ahead with something if you want."

"I'll just stick with this glass of juice for now," he said, "in full solidarity with you and your alcohol abstinence while on drugs." She smiled at that, and raised her glass of orange-mango juice.

"How's the ice pack? Does it need refreshing yet?"

"No, I think it's plenty cold, thanks. I have to be careful not to freeze my ankle. That's all I'd need!" she sighed. "I still can't believe this happened. I mean, I was *just* starting to get the kitchen situation a little under control. I was just getting used to the low insurance numbers and trying to figure out a way ahead. I might have had a little glimmer of hope—not much, mind you, but a tiny glimmer—and then this! Shit, Doc, I'm beginning to wonder if the universe is trying to tell me something."

"Nah, Kate, just a random event, that's all. There's no hidden message here, just really bad luck."

"What's that saying?" she inquired. "If I didn't have bad luck I'd have no luck at all? Seems fitting right about now."

"Well, I've got to admit, I didn't think it would be this difficult. I thought you'd be at or close to your 22K goal by now, but you're actually further away than a month ago. It is a bit discouraging, for sure."

"Jim, I can't believe I'm saying this, but, I'm even starting to wonder if I should take the deal from that slimy bastard Malloy. I mean, I hate the thought of him and his pirates inhabiting my store. It makes my skin crawl! But on the other hand I could clear out all my problems at once and be done with it. And have a nice little nest egg to start over with something new. And maybe they *would* bring an economic boost to the area. But as it stands, I could lose the store, get nothing for it, and he can buy it from the bank at a discount and get it anyway, with me the sorry loser. Am I cutting off my nose to spite my face? I don't know if it's the drugs talking right now, but that deal is starting to look a bit tempting. What do you think? Should I even consider it?"

After a long pause, during which Kate began to wonder if Jim had heard her, he finally cleared his throat and spoke. "Kate, I can't advise you what to do. To be honest, after my horrible decision to convince Maggie to have chemotherapy, I have little confidence in advising anyone about big, life-altering decisions. I guess I'm gun shy and just can't do it. I really don't know the right answer, and would be hesitant to tell you if I thought I did. I really question anymore if my decisions are best for the other person or just me being selfish."

In a mere few seconds while talking with Kate, Jim reflected back to that awful time when he convinced, nay begged, Maggie to take chemo. It still pained him to remember those final weeks and the unbearable things she went through. And he knew that most of the misery was his fault, a result of his wanting to do anything to hang on to his love for as long as possible, and in the process utterly failing to realize what was important to and best for her. *I will not do that again,* he reminded himself. *Either decision here can be a really bad one, and I'm not going to push her in one direction or another. If it goes badly, I don't want to feel responsible yet again. I'm not going there.*

"I understand, Jim, and I know this has to be my decision, but I just wanted to bounce it off you as a sounding board and see what you thought. But I get what you're saying." Although she was disappointed, she did understand where he was coming from and at any rate knew that this would need to be her decision, one that she alone would have to own and accept.

"You're really between a rock and a hard place," offered Jim. "If you hang in there and lose the store, you'll have nothing, but at least you'll know you've given it your all and might feel good about yourself. If you sell the store to this guy, you'll have the money but no store and might regret it for the rest of your life. And you would always question yourself about whether you might have pulled it off. I really can't advise you one way or the other and I honest to God don't know how I would go if it was me."

"Yeah, tell me about it," she replied, taking another sip of juice.

"But I will strongly advise one thing: don't make any decisions until you are off those drugs for at least a couple of days. Lord knows what they're doing to you."

"Oh, I got you there. I'm OK overall, but I do feel kind of dulled out at times, like I'm sitting under a hazy cloud, then I get a burst of extreme happiness. I realize I'm not at my sharpest right now, and I'm just kind of thinking out loud. And I can't believe I'm even considering the possibility of selling, but I guess that means I've hit a low point. Maybe I'm starting to panic a little. I really can't see a way out, and the future looks pretty bleak right now." Her mouth tightened as she stared down at Darwin, faithfully lying by her side on the braided rug.

"Well, you're not going to solve anything today, so give yourself a break. And it's only been a day since you were injured, so be patient. Hey, I better go check on the chicken in the oven. That's a much more immediate decision that I know I can handle," concluded Jim.

Jim pulled the glass baking dish with the chicken halves on a bed of rice out from of the oven and set it on the stove top. As he probed the thighs and breasts with his insta-read thermometer to test for doneness, the phone rang. He walked back in the living room and answered it.

"Hello, this is Jim."

Raising his eyebrows and looking at Kate, he replied, "Uh, yeah, she is here as a matter of fact. Who's calling please?"

Putting the mouthpiece to his chest he whispered to Kate, "I don't believe this, and speak of the Devil himself. It's Robb Malloy. Do you want to speak with him?"

Chapter 26

Monday, October 14, 9:05 AM

⬤━━━

A
FTER A BREAKFAST OF HOT OATMEAL WITH
cinnamon, sugar, and sliced bananas on this
crisp and chilly morning, Jim cleared away
the dishes and got Kate settled back into the recliner.
They had stopped icing her injuries by Saturday evening and she had been on only ibuprofen for three days now. At this point it was just a matter of letting the tincture of time work its magic and heal her wounds.

At Kate's urging, Jim planned a short hike for later this morning to experience the remaining fall colors and smells that he so enjoyed. He would of course take Darwin along and let the dog run herself crazy and chase chipmunks through the woods and over rock walls. Kate was trying to have minimal impact on his life and had convinced him he needed to get on with things and not just fuss about her. They needed to establish routines that did not include him hovering over her; she could hobble back and forth to the bathroom and otherwise start to fend for herself.

"So when are you two heading out?" inquired Kate.

"Oh, I thought I'd wait until about 10 or so," he said. "Let the sun get a little higher to warm our bones."

"So what are you up to right now?" she further inquired.

"Nothing, really. Just hanging around. What's up?"

"Well, I wondered if we could talk for just a minute. I've reached a decision. I know you don't want to be involved, but I'd like to tell you before I call Malloy, if you don't mind."

"Yeah, for sure, please tell me what you're thinking," a curious Jim replied, somewhat nervous about the outcome. Despite his unwillingness to advise her, he secretly and selfishly hoped that she would not sell.

"Well, I've thought about little else the last few days after my head cleared. I've tried to analyze every angle, every possibility, every aspect of a deal or no deal. I've thought about the up and down sides of either decision, ways to hang in there and raise more money, effects on the town if I sell or don't sell, even what I would do and where I would go if I suddenly had the $300,000 of his latest offer—he must really want this place, by the way, if he went that high."

"That's for sure. It must be the perfect location for him," observed Jim.

"That and it's also ready to go. He wants something now so he can move in by the end of the year. He's itching to get going and I take it he's not having much luck finding alternate sites in the area; I guess he's willing to do whatever it takes to get my store."

"So what have you decided?"

"Jim, it turns out none of that stuff I analyzed so carefully actually guided my final decision. Instead, I thought back to my family. And I had one of those *Waves of Clarity* wash over me that I occasionally get, and it reminded me where and who I am. I'm the sixth generation owner of this place now. Those five previous generations all had challenges, and nothing came easy to any one of them. My great, great, great, great grandfather Peter fought at Gettysburg, saved Joshua Chamberlain in the process, and then came back and built this store from the ground up, literally. My grandfather Simon fought at Normandy and sustained war wounds, and kept the store going. My parents died just up the road while running the store and then Simon came out of retirement to keep it and an 11-year-old girl going. Some of the others broke the law by bootlegging to keep Odd Country solvent. They *all* went through their own version of Hell, every single generation. They each had their challenges and they all survived them."

"And I so distinctly remember what my grandfather told me the day before he died. It's so burned into my psyche that I can recite it almost word-for-word. He said 'Remember, it's the people, Kate! When all is said and done, that's all you have, these good people here. Know the people and listen to them and give them what they need. And sometimes all they need is a little bit of you, so be generous, Kate. Always be generous, and you'll be amply rewarded.'"

"Jim, how can I sell this place and walk away with a pile of cash with that dying advice hanging over me? How can I sell when my ancestors did everything in their power to make a go of it here and to make this little village what it is today? I wasn't raised to quit and I'm not going to let down a whole lineage of good people just because the going is tough. They didn't give up. And dammit, neither will I! I don't care if he offers me a half-a-million dollars; I couldn't look myself in the mirror the next day. So when it comes right down to it, right or wrong, I'm here until the bitter end and I'll figure a way through this—with your continued help, I hope. I'll be damned if I'll give in at this point, and they'll have to drag me out of here kicking and screaming. I may be crazy, but I'm determined. And that's my final answer."

"Would you like the phone and Robb Malloy's number?" is all that Jim said, with a satisfied smile.

"You bet I do. Let me at that SOB once and for all!"

Chapter 27

——————

"HEY, LOOK WHO'S HERE!" EXCLAIMED LARRY Carson with a big grin as Kate hobbled in the front door on crutches, with Jim close behind. Larry and several customers—including Layla Liederman and Lou Quentin, who were in for a mid-morning coffee and some good gossip—applauded, and Kate broke into a broad smile. "Thanks, everybody. It's so good to be back in the store. And look, it's still standing," she teased, scanning the interior.

Larry had done a fine job keeping the store going over the last two weeks and a grateful Kate was ready to ease back to work on a limited basis. Though still quite sore and sporting a rainbow of interesting colors, her ankle now supported a little weight. They had worked out a system by which she could use the crutches, even with her broken wrist, making them useable for limited walking. She tucked the left crutch up under her armpit and then wrapped her left forearm to the crutch handle with an old necktie of Jim's. That way, there was no weight on her wrist, but by swinging her arm forward and back she could reasonably move the crutch and slowly get around.

Once word had spread that Kate was injured and Larry was largely on his own running the store—which could get a little overwhelming at times for one person—several townspeople pitched in to help on a voluntary basis. This was especially important during this busy leaf-peeping season, which had brought a welcome upsurge of visitors through Oddertown. Rusty Hinges's wife Marie put in some volunteer hours, as did Dora Stevenson from Duke's, and Lauren McCallum, who helped late afternoons after teaching. A few high school seniors who had looked up to Larry when he was a football star even volunteered their time after school and on weekends to help stock shelves or clean up. This included Bobby Wilson and Buck Bailey, who still felt bad about the attempted Great Oddertown Beer Heist and wanted to regain Kate's good graces. She appreciated their efforts and now felt the slate was clean and trust was restored.

But it was the young Golightly women who stepped up in a major way and were the biggest help. Faith, Hope, and Charity—sorry, Feather, Harmony, and Chastity; no, make that Charity—took turns coming in to assist Larry in whatever way they could, which usually involved working the register. They neither wanted nor expected anything in return.

Local customers understood the challenges and tolerated any glitches, and once the situation with the store was explained to visitors they quickly caught the spirit; many were happy to drop spare change or even larger donations into the SOS fundraising jar on the counter. And amongst all this busyness, work on the kitchen rebuild continued apace. In short, the community at large rallied round and made sure that their store withstood this latest test with nary a hiccup to show for it.

Larry and company aggressively sold raffle tickets for Phil Haderlie's old Chevy truck and Pernell Basington-Smythe's art to anybody who came in. This time Pernell offered a local Vermont landscape painting done just for this project, with no hints of Teddy Roosevelt, bikinied ladies, or any other exotica. This was rather dull for poor Pernell, who was motivated to dress only as a boring hiker for the project, but much more acceptable to the average raffle ticket buyer, and sales were decent.

"Kate, it's so good to see you up and around," said Larry. "How're the ankle and wrist?"

"Well, better, but I still have a ways to go," reported Kate. "Don't expect me to do a whole lot of walking around just yet. And I'll have to put off left-handed arm wrestling for a while longer."

"Looks like you've had things here under control, Lar," observed Jim.

"Yeah, I think we've done OK, all things considered. I've had some great outside help. Those Golightly gals have been wonderful. They take turns volunteering, and one or another of them has been here most of the time. Harmony is here right now, checking in a new shipment in the back. They've kind of taken this up as a cause. You know how they can be when they believe in something."

"I'll have to find a nice way to thank them," replied Kate. "Now let me see what's happening with the kitchen construction. Jim reported back to me a couple of times and took some pictures, but I'm anxious to see it for myself." Kate hobbled on her crutches over to the serving counter and peered in. "Wow, look at that! It's beautiful!" The shell was now complete, and an electrician was installing outlets and light fixtures, working around two fellows painting the drywall. The new setup was bright and cheery and seemed solid, and Kate's spirits were immediately lifted as she saw the potential for her revived space.

"This is looking great, isn't it, Doc?"

"It sure is, and this is a whole lot better than the old kitchen, don't you think?" replied Jim. "Maybe in the long run this will be a good thing."

"I sure hope so." Turning back to Larry she asked "When are those new appliances we ordered coming?"

"I just checked yesterday and it should be early next week, right around Halloween. I think we can be up and running by early November. We'll need to inventory the frozen foods soon and see what's still good. Then get resupplied on the refrigerated and non-perishable items, which I can do in a run to Saint J. I think we're getting close, Kate!"

"This is actually ahead of schedule. We had estimated mid-November. For once, we have a *good* surprise! Maybe that's a sign of things to come," concluded Kate. "But right now I need to sit down; my ankle is not happy." Jim helped her over to a chair at one of the tables, where she carefully sat down and uncoupled her arm from the crutch. "Please, guys, sit down for a minute with me."

"Larry, Jim and I were scheming and think maybe we could do some sort of grand reopening. Really try to boost the kitchen sales up front. You think you can handle breakfast as well as lunch?"

Larry thought for a few seconds and then concluded "Why not? We'd really need to do some good prep work and make sure we had lots of supplies on hand, but I think I could do that. I don't think I could do your cinnamon rolls, though. Maybe keep it simple at first?"

"Absolutely!" replied Kate. "Just the basics. Let people know we are back and try to get some volume through here. Maybe a limited menu at first, cut out some of the pain-in-the-butt items."

"OK, sure, I'm in."

"But we'll need to get you some help. We need something of a sous chef to help prep things, and also someone to wait tables for lunch, and maybe even help Jodi at breakfast. Jim has volunteered to be your assistant in the kitchen, if you think that might work."

"Really? Dr. Watson will be working for me? That seems kind of... strange," Larry indicated, quizzical face looking over at Jim.

"Why?" asked Jim. "Just 'cause I could be your grandfather? Look, don't worry, Lar. You will be in full command of the kitchen and I'll be glad to take orders from you. I may be an old fart, but I can handle a knife and a whisk, believe it or not. I promise to be a good student and behave myself." He gave Larry a big smile and patted him on the forearm.

"Well, yeah, sure," said Larry. "If that's what you all want to do."

"And maybe we can get the Golightly girls to wait tables," inquired Kate. "They can even keep their tips. You think they could handle that?"

"I don't see why not. I'll talk with them today."

At that moment, as if on cue, out from the back came Harmony Golightly. "Well speak of the devil!" greeted Kate.

"Hello, Kate. How nice to see you. I didn't know you were coming in yet," replied a smiling Harmony.

"Sorry I can't get up, Harmony. Come over here and give me a big hug." After the affectionate squeeze, Kate added, "I can't thank you and your sisters enough for all you have done for me the last few weeks. I understand you've been a big help to Larry."

"Well, we are honored and happy to do anything that helps this community. Anything to keep the harmonic balance in order and the positive energies aligned."

"I understand that, and I have another huge favor to ask, if I may," said Kate, while Harmony's positive energies were aligned or whatever they were doing. "We hope to open for breakfast and lunch in a week or so and I won't be able to do much right away. Larry and Jim will handle the kitchen. I wonder if you and your sisters can wait tables during breakfast and lunch and also work the register all day? I can't pay much right now, but you would at least be able to keep all your tips."

"I think I can speak for Feather and Charity when I say we would be delighted to help in any way that we can. But I must insist on one change to your plan."

"And that is?"

"We cannot keep the tips, as that would upset the special harmonic balance of our intention. We will simply put tips in the donation jar, and store that positive energy there."

Kate smiled. "Anything that works for you, Harmony, is fine by me. Who am I to threaten the balance? Thank you so much for your beautiful kindness."

Harmony simply smiled gently, bowed away from the table, and floated off to other energy flows elsewhere in the store.

"Well," said Kate quietly to Jim and Larry. "I'm never quite sure what to think after my interactions with the Golightlys, but thank goodness—or Gaia, or the universe, or whatever—that they are here!"

Jim and Larry knowingly shook their heads, with wry smiles. The Golightlys were, if nothing else, splendidly unique.

"OK, great, that's settled. And Larry, I'm going to try moving back in upstairs in a day or two, if I can handle the stairs. Poor Doc has been taking such good care of me, but its time he got his house and life back. I'm sure he'd love to be able to keep the toilet seat up once in a while!" she smiled his way. "By the time we re-open the kitchen in a week or so I may even be of some use, maybe washing dishes if nothing else, or possibly working the register. Doc will come in early and help you prep. He says he can be in by six, but I'll believe that when I see it." She smiled, an affectionate twinkle in her eye.

"Hey, whaddya mean?" replied an indignant Jim Watson. "You'll see it just fine, and I'll even be chipper and cheerful. Oh ye of little faith will eat thy words, Kate Langford."

Kate smiled and took both of their hands in hers. "You know, we might just get through this thing yet. But win, lose, or draw, I'm so happy to be going through it with friends like you. Even with all this bad stuff, I feel really blessed. Words seem so inadequate, but *thank you*."

Chapter 28

———

"CAN I HAVE EVERYBODY'S ATTENTION FOR A minute?" called Kate above the din. "Just for a minute please, and then we can all get back to the festivities." She waited a few seconds for conversations to end and attention to be re-directed to her at the front register, where she held her glass of rum-laced egg nog.

"Thank you. I hate to interrupt your dedicated drinking and eating—well, mostly drinking—but I wanted to say a few words while you are all still semi-coherent," she said with a smile, answered by knowing chuckles and raised glasses. "As you all know, this has been a difficult year, both for me personally and for the store. We've had more than our fair share of challenges and pain and setbacks, and we don't yet know how this will end. But I do know that I couldn't have come this far without each and every one of you wonderful people, and I couldn't have felt this loved and cared for anywhere else. I am so deeply and eternally grateful for all you've. . ." Kate paused, welling up.

The small crowd—the Save Our Store group, the Odd Balls, the Golightlys, the various and sundry volunteers, the Kittlesons who reconstructed the kitchen, and everyone else who helped the last year—collectively felt her emotions and lightly applauded her. "We love you, Kate!" offered Charity, the feeling reinforced by several "yeahs" and "you betchas" from the gathered throng.

They had all been invited for a Christmas Eve potluck as a thank you from Kate for all the work they did this year on behalf of her and the store. An 8-foot-tall fir tree, harvested by Rusty Hinges, sat in the corner by the brass mailboxes. Kate had adorned it festively with strings of small white lights and a collection of her family's treasured Christmas decorations from four generations. Her favorite—a delicate, oblong, clear-glass ornament that belonged to her grandmother—hung in a prominent place front and center. The store's interior was likewise decorated with bright and cheery hangings of the season that concealed the underlying stress and strain that defined life in Odd Country these last many months. Papering over reality helped to boost morale, but did not change the fundamental fact that they could very well lose their store in about five weeks.

Kate's ankle and wrist had healed on schedule and now were largely functional; she retained only the slightest of limps at this point. The wrist was operative with only minor pain, although strength in her left hand was significantly reduced and would take some more time to recover. The grand re-opening of the kitchen had been a success, socially if not economically. Larry, Jim, and the Golightly women all performed admirably for several weeks until Kate returned, and, despite a few early glitches and bumps, the new kitchen worked beautifully. The initial burst of activity and return to normal cash flow righted the ship in the short term, but did nothing to cut into the debt.

Final costs of the kitchen rebuild exceeded the insurance settlement by nearly $4000, and the lack of restaurant income for nearly six weeks, along with her unexpected medical bills, deepened the hole even further. Kate's savings were now exhausted and she had to dip into the SOS funds to the tune of $2800, which took them down to about $9000. The two raffles brought in a total of only $1950, well short of the hoped-for $3000. When the dust settled and pennies were counted, the SOS fund now had just under $11,000, less than half of the $22,000 needed to extend the loan another three years, when the remaining $88,000 of the original loan would then be due, plus interest.

After recomposing herself, Kate continued. "I just needed you all to know how much I appreciate everything you have done for me. It is overwhelming and I will never forget it. You are all so special to me. So I thought it would be nice to spend Christmas Eve together, as a family. You are all my family, crazy though you may be, and I can't think of anyone I'd rather spend my holiday with. So thank you, thank you, *thank* you!" she concluded, applauding them. "Now enough of my blabbering and let's dig into all these wonderful dishes you concocted."

"Not so fast!" interrupted Jim Watson, stepping forward from the crowd and setting down his drink next to the cash register. "You have thanked us so much but we need to thank *you* as well."

"Me? I haven't done anything but gotten injured," protested Kate.

"Are you kidding? This is a nasty predicament and through it all you've hung in there and remained positive. You could have just sold the place to that developer and walked away with a nice nest egg to start over somewhere else. But you didn't, Kate. And why?" asked Jim, scanning the crowd of friends, who were all smiling back at him. "Because you understand two things. First, you understand the historical importance of this store and your place in it. You know your role in the lineage of Oddertown and Odd Country and you accept it. Whether a burden or a blessing, you vowed to continue on when you didn't have to, come hell or high water. You are honoring your ancestors all the way back to 1882, Kate, and we are so proud of you for that." Kate looked simultaneously appreciative but embarrassed with the accolades being placed upon her. She smiled and looked at the beautiful stamped tin ceiling, her long Christmas earrings dangling with her movement.

"And second," continued Jim, now speaking more quietly and solemnly, "you understand the importance of this place to our town and its people now, today. You know that community comes alive here and that these people," he stated, pointing to the gathered crowd, "your friends and neighbors, *count* on you. You haven't walked away from that responsibility. So, Kate, you really are the hero in this story, like it or not. You're the force and the vision here; we're just your helpers. Here's to Kate everybody!"

The crowd of 40-something people erupted into serious and sustained applause while Kate erupted into tears and hugged Jim more tightly than ever, whispering her thanks into his ear. Letting go and wiping away grateful tears yet again, she composed herself sufficiently to say "OK, enough of this nonsense, let's eat, drink, and be merry already. It's Christmas Eve!"

The crowd of friends enjoyed the food, drinks, Christmas music, and each other's company for several hours. With so many people gathered and everybody bringing something, the food choices were nearly unlimited. Ham, turkey, and a pork roast provided by Odd Country took center stage, complimented by various side dishes including Layla's famous deviled eggs, Tim Kittleson's smoked trout, Steve's venison stew, and the Golightly's vegan pork and beans (don't ask). Egg nog, wines, beer, and spiked punch helped to lubricate the social scene, though nobody needed lubrication to feel comfortable with the others; if the group was not close-knit before the trials of this year, it certainly was now. It did indeed seem like a big, whacky, happy family. Even the Golightly's got along well with Phil Haderlie, joking and laughing in as unlikely a mix as you could imagine. Political leanings and divergent life philosophies were absolutely meaningless tonight. Community took priority, and any differences shrunk and faded into the distance.

Most revelers dispersed into the clear, cold night by 10:00, and after Kate, Jim, Larry, and his parents cleaned up the final mess, it was just Jim and Kate remaining at 10:40, the store now eerily quiet after the lively party. Once they sat down at a table with their remaining glasses of wine in front of them, they realized how tired they were and how much energy had been put into this party. And they agreed that every bit was well worth it. It was a good end to a difficult year and the perfect way to recognize and thank everyone.

"So, Kate," said Jim, looking across the table at her.

"So, Jim," replied a smiling Kate.

"I think it's time for a serious discussion."

"I agree," replied a still slightly-looped Kate, who thought that Jim wanted to talk about their growing friendship and the togetherness and forced intimacy that nursing care always brings. She was feeling closer to Jim all the time and had wondered if he had felt the same, and perhaps expected it to move to another level at some point. She thought it would be a good idea to finally bring it out into the open and discuss it.

"I've been doing a lot of thinking about the elephant in the room."

"The elephant?" Kate inquired innocently enough. "What elephant might that be, Jim?"

"The February loan deadline," began Jim, surprising and disappointing Kate that this was to be a business rather than a personal discussion. "And I've made a decision."

"Yeesss....?" said an edgy and now-deflated Kate

"Now I'm going to say something and I don't want any arguments from you. Got that?"

"I can't promise anything, Doc," answered a stilted Kate to an oblivious Watson. "You know how I like to argue."

"Well, not this time, please, so hear me out. I don't see how you'll come up with the $22,000 any time soon. You'll be a good ten- to twelve-thousand short. I don't want to see this store lost for that amount. So here's my Plan B—or is it C or D by now? Anyway, I have an IRA worth about $15,000 and I'm going to cash it in. . ."

"Oh no you're not!" interrupted a now-animated and angry Kate, jumping up from the table with newfound energy. "I'm not going to see you dip into your retirement for me. You've done way too much already and I'd sooner lose this store and my home than have you bailing me out. No way, José!" It was debatable how much of her over-reaction stemmed from not wanting his money or her disappointment that he was seemingly oblivious to her personal feelings toward him.

"Now, Kate, stop it and sit down! You know this makes sense," replied Jim in an unusually firm and raised voice. Kate had a stone face on now, arms firmly folded in front of her as she blatantly refused his command to sit. Between her disappointment that this was not a discussion about their relationship, and the shock of Jim offering big money, she was uncharacteristically hostile toward him.

After a quiet moment Kate finally sat back down, and Jim continued.

"Consider this as a selfish move for me," he said. "I want the store saved for *me*! I love this town and the store and I rely on it. Everybody here does. I'm not gonna let a stinking ten or twelve thousand dollars ruin all that. Can you just imagine, a year from now, looking back—Lord knows where you'd even be by then—and saying 'If only I had gone a little further. If only I had accepted that money from Jim, I'd still have a store and a home. Now it's all gone and I'll *never* get it back.' Do you really want to be in that situation? After six generations and 137 years of ownership? And for what? Pride?"

Kate looked at him with confusion and conflict written across her face. She began to stammer a response but Jim cut her off.

"And there's another thing I need you to hear. I'm not sure you can fully appreciate it at your age because you haven't yet built up the crust that time eventually forms on a person. But as I've gotten older I've gotten more reflective. I think that's natural and everyone does it. By this time in life a person has had their career and their family, they've done a lot of things they want to do, and they see fewer years ahead of them; they begin to think about what it all really means. They start thinking legacies, and what their time here will have meant, what will be left once they are gone. Kate, if I can help you save the store but don't, I could never forgive myself. It would be a huge disappointment and it would haunt me. It would mean I failed, badly. But if you would allow me to do this, it would mean so much to me. It would mean I did something important for this town and for you, something that would far outlive me. It would allow me to leave a mark, and that's important to me at this stage of life. It would be a legacy for me. Please, Kate, don't deny me that meaning and pleasure."

Kate rubbed her forehead with both hands and took a deep breath. After a long and thoughtful pause she looked up. "Jim, I'm confused and exhausted. I can't even think straight any more. How can I take your money? And then, how can I *not* take your money? My brain says you're right, but my heart says no. I'm already so indebted to you for all your help. And even if we did this I would still have the huge debt and I don't know if I can pay that off even in three years, so I might be back in the same spot then. I just wanna. . .go hide in a hole somewhere."

"Kate, you've come a long way and it would be a shame to quit now when you're so close. Please, let me do this for you. And for me. I said it was selfish, and I really mean that. It's not just losing the store I'm afraid of. It's losing you, too. We've become close friends these last several months, haven't we?"

Kate perked up at this new revelation from Jim. "We have, and that means so much to me, Jim."

"Alright, why take a chance on losing that too? I really want you sticking around a long time." Kate smiled at that sentiment. "Let me make up any balance due when February first rolls around. I promise I won't cash in my IRA until the last minute; maybe a miracle will happen in the meantime. But if we come down to the wire and there's no other choice, I'll cash it in, you pay the debt, and we can move on to the next steps. You can pay me back whenever, although I'd be just as happy if this was a gift. Or give me free sandwiches and beer for the rest of my life, I don't care. But believe me, this won't cut too deeply into my retirement savings. I've got other IRAs and retirement income, I'm certainly not going to starve. I really want to do this, and I hope you'll let me. Please, Kate. For you. For me."

After yet another pause and apparent soul searching, during which Jim had no idea if his arguments had won the day, Kate finally responded. She stood up, stepped over to Jim, leaned down, took his face in her hands, and kissed him warmly on the lips.

"Thank you, Jim," she managed, tears now rolling freely down her cheeks. "I don't deserve you, but I love you and I accept your kind gift." She stood and hugged his head against her belly, rocking back and forth, stroking his unruly hair, both silently immersed in the moment.

After a half minute she sat back down, took his hands in hers, smiled, and asked rhetorically, "Dr. Watson, what am I gonna do with you?" shaking her head. "I just don't know what else to say."

"How about 'Merry Christmas, my friend'?"

"Okay, that sounds good. 'Merry Christmas, my dear, dear, friend.'"

Chapter 29

———

TOWNSFOLK FORMED A STEADY STREAM UP the icy front steps—carefully sprinkled with sand for traction—and into the warm embrace of Odd Country, thoughtfully stomping their boots on the porch to clear off snow from the recent 14-inch dump before they crossed the threshold. They removed their jackets, hats, and gloves, and dropped them on the serving counter. The pile grew so high and unstable that it threatened to succumb to gravity and tumble over as some 75 people made their way inside and grabbed seats or unfolded their own summer lawn chairs—seemingly out of place on this freezing January night—all chatting and anticipating what was to unfold.

Odd Country was packed to capacity, and friends and neighbors lined up cheek by jowl to take in the evening's program. The only person with any real breathing room was Willard Bennett, who enjoyed his usual three-foot clearance. Four more people could fit into the room were it not for Willard; he never seemed to notice.

All of the Odd Balls were there, though somewhat irked that their usual table was already taken up by interlopers; did nobody understand the principles of territorial property rights earned through regular use? Raymond Pulan, smiling and excited, came in with his mother and Lou and sat toward the front, while Rusty Hinges and his wife settled their lawn chairs along the back wall. Even the unsociable Charlie Horrible made his way in and found a spot in a far corner, nodding his head once or twice along the way but speaking to no one. And on it went, with all the usual suspects finding a nook or cranny to settle into for the next hour or so. A buzz of excitement filled the air.

They had all gathered because Jim Watson was about to give his third of what was by default becoming an annual lecture to the good people of Oddertown. Two years before, the Select Board was looking for some intellectual activity to punch up the dead of winter and kick start folks' brains after all the food and frolics of the Christmas holiday, and came up with this idea. Their local Wizard would give a presentation for the layperson on some scientific topic within his range of expertise. The only two rules were that it was to be scientifically sound and should be understandable to anyone with a 10th-grade education. The first year he spoke about animal adaptations for winter survival in this area, and last year talked of the importance of habitat connectivity to long-term sustainability of wildlife populations. Both topics were well received and discussed around town for weeks afterward, keeping brains active in the dead of winter. The crowd was in great anticipation for this years' talk, the topic of which was a mystery. They only knew the title, *The Time of Your Life*, which gave them absolutely no clue what in the heck he was going to talk about. Jim intended it that way.

At 7:05, Select Board Chair Caleb Smith called the unruly crowd to order. It took a minute or so for everyone to settle down and wrap up their conversations with their neighbors, some of whom they had not seen much since autumn.

"OK, folks, time to quiet down and focus forward, please. Settle in as best you can. I know it's crowded. Behave yourselves now. As you know, we are fortunate to have living among us an authority on scientific topics that most of us know little to nothing about. Dr. Jim Watson has once again kindly agreed to regale us with his knowledge and insights from his experiences as a professor at Green Mountain College.

But before we get to that, I have a new wrinkle to add this year. As you know all too well, the Odderton Country Store is in a major financial bind and we're in real danger of losing it very soon. We are down to a few weeks, in fact. There is a real possibility that, come Groundhog Day, we not only won't be looking at six more weeks of the store, but the doors will be locked permanently." Groans went up from the audience. "Kate and a group of good folks have been working hard since last summer to raise funds to keep it going. They've done a fine job, as have all of you who have donated money, bought raffle tickets, donated to the auction, or otherwise worked hard to keep the store going, and I think the whole Save Our Store effort deserves a big round of applause."

Everyone responded accordingly, clapping enthusiastically and nodding their heads in agreement. "Of course we were making pretty good progress," Caleb continued, "until that damned storm stopped all our momentum a couple months ago. And then Kate got hurt. But the kitchen has been rebuilt, everything's back to working order better than before, and Kate is whole again, thank goodness, but precious time and income were lost.

So tonight I'd like to suggest something different, something wicked big. I hope you'll go along with it. Kate will put out drinks and snacks that we'll enjoy after the talk, as she always generously does. But this year I'd like to suggest you consider making a donation when you take that drink or cookie. And I'd like you to consider making it the most expensive damned drink or cookie you've ever had in your life!" They all chuckled. "Imagine paying ten bucks for a piece of cake or $20 for a glass of wine. I dare you to do that! Hell, I double dog *dare* you to do it!!" More chuckles.

"I hereby challenge Oddertonians to pay an outrageous and ridiculous amount for that drink and snack, but especially for the store that we all love and use. We are coming down to the wire—this is it folks, this is the whole ball game—and we need to step up big and do some crazy things if we are to have a store this time next year. And to put my own money where my big mouth is, I am priming the pump with $50 for my refreshments!"

The crowd ooohed and aaahed and spontaneously applauded as Caleb pulled out a small wad of bills, unfolded them to verify the amount, and placed his cash in a large plastic mayonnaise jar with a slit in the lid.

"Now I know we are not a wealthy bunch and not everybody can do that," he continued. "Nobody will be judged by what they give or don't give. No accounting will be made. I simply ask that you look into your hearts and dig into your pockets and give what you feel comfortable with to help this store. *Your* store that has been here over 137 years! I'd like it to be here for 137 more, so please, please give until it hurts. OK, enough of the sermon, and thank you."

"I now turn the floor over to Doc Watson, who has once again agreed to share his knowledge and insights, this time on 'The Time of Your Life,' whatever that means. Take it away, Doc."

Polite applause rolled through the store as Jim made his way to the front. He was happy that nobody else in town knew of his offer to bail out the store's debt if it came to that. For one, he did not want to thwart any further fundraising or philanthropy. For another, he did not want personal accolades. In fact, he made Kate swear that, if it came down to Jim cashing in, she would say she discovered a life insurance policy on her grandfather last minute and cashed it in.

"Well, I hate going after Caleb" grinned Jim. "He's always a tough act to follow. Thank you, my friend. You actually managed to put my talk—'The Time of Your Life'—into perspective. You gave larger meaning and context to our gathering tonight so that it's more than me blathering on about some esoteric subject. So thank you, Caleb, for reminding us what is really important here."

"Folks, tonight I want to do something a little different. Well, a lot different, actually. Rather than talk about a specific scientific topic, I want to use science to put humanity into a proper time scale, into something that people can relate to. I want to spend tonight thinking about our place on the planet, and put our lives into a perspective that few people can truly appreciate. I want to talk about deep time, and our place in that time."

The crowd stirred, not quite sure what this was all about. Faces got serious and a few frowns appeared as people focused on Jim's words.

"I want to invite you on a journey through time and space with me, and challenge your minds. I think it's an exciting ride and you may want to buckle your seat belts!" Jim paused for effect, turned on an old slide carousel machine, and clicked into place the first slide, a picture of a wooden ruler.

"To start the journey, please consider a one-foot ruler. You all have one and yours may be wood, or clear or colored plastic, but the material doesn't matter."

"The material sure does matter" interrupted Phil Haderlie. "My first grade teacher had a metal one and she used it on my knuckles all the time!" The room chuckled at the reminiscence.

"Well, Phil, you probably deserved it, and I suspect maybe you still do," responded Jim, who didn't mind some audience participation and joking to keep the mood light. "But the important thing for us is that they all have a common size—12 inches. A universal measure you can all appreciate, even you, Phil." Phil acknowledged with a smile.

"Now imagine that your ruler represents one year

of time, and each inch is one month. January goes from zero to one inch, February from one to two inches, and so on. Now please ponder for a second what one month or one year feels like. A month—just one inch on your ruler—can feel like a long time if you are working at a boring job or you are in pain or recovering from a surgery. For a child, the month of December can seem an eternity, waiting for Santa to come. In short, a month or a year is a lot of time in which a lot can happen, both good and bad."

"Now back to that ruler. Stare at it please, and imagine it as a year of your life. It doesn't matter which year—it can be your tenth, your most recent, or any year in between. But think what that distance means, and try to identify with it in terms of time. Really friends, please, I'd like you to stop, close your eyes, and picture it for a minute; one year, one foot." Jim waited about twenty seconds and watched his audience, many of whom did close their eyes to ponder.

"OK, thanks. Now, here's a picture of a football field, 100 yards long. This happens to be Gillette Stadium, where our Patriots play their home games. Go Pats!"

"But I'm a Giants fan!" yelled Only Oswalt, to a resounding chorus of boos from most of the room.

"That doesn't matter, Own. Works with any team. OK, now, think about how old you are. Twenty four? Forty six? Eighty one? Whatever your age, please mentally place that number of rulers on Gillette Stadium, starting at the goal line—the present year—and stretching out onto the field of play, back in time for the number of your years. We now see a bunch of rulers laid end-to-end on that field, the number corresponding to your age."

Jim put up a new slide with three sets of rulers superimposed on the field. "If you are 24, your line of rulers would get out to the 8 yard line. If 46, you would land just past the 15 yard line. If 81—congratulations!—you would get all the way to the 27 yard line. The oldest humans who ever lived might make it to the 40-yard-line; nobody has ever reached the 50."

"I think some of these old farts I hang out with around here go out beyond the 50 yard line," offered Jubal Keller with a grin. "At least they look like it." Folks nodded knowingly, and Jim gave an approving smile.

"Using this view of time, and placing it on a familiar playing surface, you begin to get a feel for your own life relative to longer time spans. If we view that football field as looking backward in time, with the present being our own goal line, then the entire field goes back 300 years, to the early 1700s, well before the United States was a country. World War II started at about our own 25 yard line, the Civil War was near midfield, and the American Revolution occurred around 80 yards out, or the distant 20 yard line. The Industrial Revolution began and developed somewhere between 65 and 80 yards away. We can quickly see that a *lot* has happened in those 100 yards, including the birth of our nation, the widespread use of fossil fuels, all modern inventions beyond the horse and buggy, virtually everything we identify with in our lives, are all contained within those 100 yards."

The crowd murmured a bit as the scope of this time metaphor began to sink in.

"OK, now let's ponder this a little deeper. The whole field, as I said, goes back to around 1719. A football field is not a huge distance and we can all picture it. Most of us could run one in under a minute; some people can do it in under 10 seconds."

"It would take Phil about two hours, Jim!" advised Silas, with laughs all around.

"And these are supposed to be my friends," replied Phil, though he did not disagree with the assessment.

After everyone settled down again, Jim continued. "If you put your life in context of that whole field, your lifespan starts to look pretty small. Ten yards? Twenty? Thirty? Not far, yet it seems like a long life." He looked around at the many eyes focused on him.

"Everybody with me?" Nods and "yeps" assured Jim that the crowd was engaged. "Now, if you could go to that far end of the field and travel back correspondingly in time you would enter a world where we were still British subjects and you would be carrying black powder and musket balls to defend yourself or find your dinner. The fastest that any human being had ever traveled up to that time was on the back of a horse. The highest anyone ever got above the ground was in a building or climbing up a tree; the thought of airplanes or even hot-air balloons would have been beyond the ability of most people to even comprehend. All this in just 100 yards."

As he clicked to the next slide, which showed two football fields end-to-end, Jim continued. "Now let's add another football field on to the end of this one and we get to the early 14-hundreds. Christopher Columbus' birth was still nearly 12 yards in the future and there was no thought by most European powers of sailing very far into the Atlantic Ocean. We were pinned to the shores of Europe and Africa, science was not yet born and we believed that the sun and stars revolved around the earth. Remember, just two football fields back."

"You mean the sun doesn't revolve around the earth?" exclaimed the wisecracking Layla Liederman.

"No, Layla, I've heard it actually doesn't," replied a smiling Jim, before moving on. Her flirtatious return smile and intense eye contact were unnerving.

"Anybody ready for some real time travel now? OK, let's take off in some bigger leaps, this time to the development of agriculture, when humans first realized they did not have to hunt and gather all their food but could plant and cultivate some of it. This started around 12,000 years ago, or *40 football fields away*. It is hard to picture 40 fields, so let's convert it to something we know: two and a quarter miles. That's about the distance from Odd Country up to Fosters' Corner." Jim clicked to the next slide, showing a map with the route he just spoke of.

"That doesn't seem long until you remember that one foot is one year and your life is somewhere between, maybe, 5 and 30 yards long. So lay out twenty or thirty yards to represent your entire life and then put that against the distance to Fosters' Corner and you begin to see a huge stretch of time, an immense period. Basically, my friends, *everything* that made modern humanity occurred in this 2-plus miles. Agriculture, tool use beyond stones and rough metals, living in cities, development of government, domestication of animals, the concept of money and trade, boat building and long-distance travel, cultural exchange, food preparation and preservation, medical knowledge, development of organized religions, writing and language diversification, science, technology, Ben and Jerry's, cheddar cheese, Big Macs, all occurred in these two-plus miles." Jim paused to let this sink in.

"If we stopped there you should be impressed; your lifespan on this planet is merely the last few yards of two and a quarter miles. A little spit of a distance, really nothing. But let's continue the journey further. Around 40,000 years ago, our species—*Homo sapiens*—was at the end of a long coexistence with another, larger, human-like species which we now know we interbred with: Neanderthal man." Clicking to the next slide, Jim revealed a color rendition of a more-primitive humanoid. "Yeah, that's right folks, we interbred with them and you all have Neanderthals to thank for about 2-3% of your genetic makeup," said Jim as he pointed around the crowded room.

"What? That's nonsense!" expelled Charlie, his first words since he arrived. "I'm a human, not a Neanderthal!"

"Sorry, Charlie, but it's true. Unless you are pure African-American, your European ancestors were interbreeding with Neanderthals, and we have the genes to prove it. Maybe that explains things for a few folks around here," finished Jim with a big smile. The crowd laughed and clapped approvingly, while Charlie maintained his regular scowl.

"So interbreeding with our Neanderthal cousins takes us back to about 7.6 *miles* on our time scale." Another click brought up another local map with 7.6 miles drawn on it. "Remember that your lifespan is 30 yards or less. Lay your 10 or 20 or 30 yard lifespan down on the ground and now walk past it for 7.6 *miles* and say hello to Neanderthal man. If your mind isn't starting to boggle just a bit, I'll have Dr. Delfasio check for a pulse." Tony smiled at the reference.

"But why stop here while we're on a roll? The first humans—*Homo sapiens*—the likes of you and me—appeared about 200,000 years ago. On our time/distance scale that is nearly 38 miles." Another click, another map. "So that means if you walked 38 miles—a good 10 to 12 hours straight at a reasonable pace—you would cover the entire span of the human species on this earth. Only the last 30 steps would cover the span of a living 90-year-old. Thirty steps out of 38 miles. Think about that for a minute!"

After an appropriate pause, he continued. "I could go on with dinosaurs and all life on earth, but I don't want to lose you. Suffice it to say dinosaurs went extinct about 12,310 miles ago on our scale, or roughly half the distance around the earth at the equator. Life started on earth about 682,000 miles ago, which is a trip from here to the moon, and back, and most of the way there again. An average human lifespan is about 25 yards of that. Twenty-five yards." Watson paused again for effect, and to let the numbers sink in. The crowd mumbled among themselves for a few seconds.

"So, my friends, what's the point of all this craziness?"

"Yeah, what's the point?" came a voice from the back, laughing.

"I'm glad you asked! Well, first, time scales of

life on earth are immense and nearly unimaginable. I've tried to give you a scale where we can start to visualize and appreciate the extraordinary amount of time that led us here, and the tiny proportion of that amount that we inhabit with our individual lives. In putting our lives in context we all tend to focus on recent history—decades or a century or two, maybe a few generations, 137 years for this store, but we need a more-accurate calibration of our place in the world. Feeling important? Put your life in context of life on earth, or just humans since agriculture began. We have an extremely limited capacity to understand time, deep history, where we came from, and what that means to us today." Some of the crowd visibly stirred.

"Second, if we can recognize the reality of our context we can start to see that the impacts of humanity on this planet are very large and *extremely* recent. If we take the development of agriculture as the point at which we began to really change things, we can see that this is merely the last couple of miles on a journey of life on earth that is well over 600,000 miles long, or more than 27 trips around the earth at the equator! Think about that for a minute: walk and swim around the earth 27 times. If you managed 40 miles a day it would take you 15,000 years! And only the last 2-plus miles—the last half hour of your journey—are even affected by humans. If we instead consider the industrial revolution to be the start of a really significant impact on the world, then that is just the last *65 yards* of our 27 equatorial journeys, or a half minute of walking." The crowd visibly connected with Jim's analogy and seemed somewhat dazzled and a bit overwhelmed.

"What do these mind-boggling numbers mean to us in a practical sense, to our lives here? Well, several things, and this is really the point of my talk. First, they mean that *all* of humanity's impacts and changes to the planet are a very recent experiment with no precedence to even speculate on an outcome. We are in uncharted waters, friends, and largely have no idea of the long-term magnitude of humanity's impacts on the earth. Second, species and ecosystems that existed for *thousands of miles* on our scale have been disrupted, for the most part, only in the last few tens of yards. We don't have a clue what this means for us. But we do know, for example, that species that existed over thousands, hundreds of thousands, or even millions of generations are quickly going extinct in the last couple of yards of our journey, due to us. We have no idea what the consequences of that might be for us, other than certainly not good."

Jim paused again to let the facts settle in. Everyone looked serious and their collective body language told him they were uncomfortable with his observations and conclusions.

"Third, climate disruptions—call it global warming, climate change, whatever you will—are being seen, again, in the last 10 to 20 *yards*, though their origins go deeper, and again, it is due to us. Climates have shifted significantly over time but never this quickly and never due to one species, or any species at all, for that matter. Any climate change deniers have no historical record to lean on." Even Phil Haderlie seemed to take note of this.

"And finally, we have developed amazingly advanced technologies in, again, a few tens of yards in our journey, yet intellectually we are really no different from our ancestors from 100 yards or even 5 miles distant. Our brains are exactly the same as those who chased mastodons for their dinner or fought with swords and axes." Jim clicked onto a slide of early hunters with spears surrounding a mastodon.

"We have the exact same brains as those folks. Are we equipped and able to handle technologies such as nuclear power or atomic weaponry or genetic engineering when we are still, mentally, hunters and gatherers or early gardeners?" He brought up the classic picture of the nuclear mushroom cloud.

"So I suggest to you, my dear friends, that perhaps this time perspective should demand humility on the part of our species, not recklessness, as caretakers of the Earth. We are really a very young species, still an evolutionary experiment. By comparison, dinosaurs as a group lasted for about 166 million years or over 31,000 *miles* on our scale; we have been around for 200,000 years or 38 miles, just over one-tenth of 1% of the reign of dinosaurs. We're totally the new kids on the block!" Again, Jim paused for effect.

"We have so completely taken over the world that many scientists now recognize that we are in a new geological epoch, created by humans. It is called the Anthropocene. The Pleistocene, or the ice ages, started over 2.5 million years ago and lasted until the Holocene, which started at the end of the latest ice age, nearly 12,000 years ago. But we have now moved into this Anthropocene, defined not by ice ages or geological change, but by complete human domination of the planet, as much as any asteroid or ice age ever did. It is really quite extraordinary if you stop to think about it. Our complete takeover of the planet is madness when placed in the true context of time. And of course it is self-destructive to us and destructive to virtually all other life on the planet, life that has existed for hundreds of thousands of miles on our time scale without our presence." Jim turned off the slide projector.

"So, my friends, that's my cheery message on this cold January night in this tiny speck of a town on a large planet that is rapidly changing in an instant. If nothing else, I hope this puts all our lives into perspective in the long march of life, without making any of you feel too insignificant. Because I can tell you, you are all extremely significant to me. Thanks for taking this trip with me. I'll be happy to answer questions and then we can dig into those goodies that Kate has provided."

After the applause and a series of good and probing questions, and socializing with snacks that went on for another hour, the crowd finally dispersed shortly after 8:45. Jim, Caleb, and Kate stayed behind to clean up and discuss the evening, which they all felt went well. When everything was ship shape they finally opened up the donation jar and dumped out piles of cash, and a few written IOUs from folks who didn't have much on them. Their careful count revealed that the 78 attendees had paid for their drinks and eats with donations totaling $1418, an average of over $18 per person. For something that normally was free. In a tiny town with little wealth, by people struggling to get along. Kate was all smiles, between her tears of gratitude. She sincerely hugged Caleb for his efforts, and then Doc, thanking him for all he had done. Her hugs were getting longer and more intimate all the time. But he wasn't complaining.

Chapter 30

———

"HI, JIM. C'MON IN. THANK YOU FOR coming by."

"No problem, Charlie, glad to do it. Though it's kind of a mystery why I'm here."

Charlie Harbrough had called Jim Watson that afternoon and asked him to come by that evening if he had some time. He wanted to talk to him about something; that's all Jim knew. An invitation to talk from Charlie Horrible was about as frequent as Halley's Comet, and as likely as a blizzard in July, so Jim was quite intrigued.

"Well, the mystery will soon be revealed. Can I get you a bourbon? I was about to pour myself one."

"Sure, on the rocks would be good." As Charlie disappeared into the kitchen Jim looked around at the dated and sparsely decorated living room. He had never been in Charlie's house, and wasn't sure anyone from town had ever set foot where he was standing. The place was like walking through a time

295

warp back to the 1980s. The sofa looked old but unworn. In contrast, the recliner was threadbare, with deep depressions where elbows would rest, and was obviously where Charlie spent much of his time. The few other pieces of blocky and unremarkable country-style furniture appeared sparsely used as well. The television was a heavy, deep, box-like relic that more resembled an antique than anything used today. An end table past the sofa displayed old and fading pictures of a woman and two kids, a girl and a boy. Faded and yellowed curtains hung from two windows. The whole place smelled musty and closed up and unloved.

"Here you go," said Charlie, returning from the kitchen, arm extended with a glass of bourbon on ice. "Have a seat."

Jim sat on the sofa, while Charlie settled into his recliner, wincing slightly in the process, and rotated it to face Jim. He took a big sip of his bourbon, neat, set the glass on the small adjacent and worn table, and then spoke.

"I really liked your talk last week, Jim. To be honest, I'm surprised I did. But it got through to me in a way. It forced me to think about things and it put my life into perspective. Big perspective, actually, and made me realize what it all means for me at this time and place. It took me out of myself and made me think through my life, and where I'm headed next. It even helped me make some important decisions. It was more valuable to me than I can say, and I thank you for that."

"Well, I'm glad it meant something to you, Charlie. We get caught up in the details of everyday life and it's easy to forget our place in the bigger picture. I like to think about these things periodically just so I don't take myself or my problems too seriously."

"I see what you mean, Jim. Now if you don't mind I'll skip the rest of the small talk," said Charlie abruptly, "and get right to why I asked you here."

When did he not *skip the small talk?* Jim wondered.

"Jim, I know what people around here think of me. I've heard the talk, and the gossip, and the stories. I see them whisper as I go by; I hear them at meetings whenever I speak up. I know they don't like me."

"Now that's not entirely true," interjected Jim, trying to be more polite than accurate.

"Now don't bullshit me, Jim, and let me have my say," replied Charlie, left hand raised, eyes tightly focused, cutting him off. "I need to say this. They don't like me and I don't blame them a bit. Fact is, *I* don't like me. I've been a jerk for over 30 years now, and I've come to realize I wasted my time here. I wasted my life. But there's a reason, and I want you to know it. And eventually, I want the townsfolk to know it. Not that it's an excuse for being an asshole, but it's at least a reason. I'm telling you because I believe you are a good and honorable man and will tell my story properly, at the appropriate time. Eventually, I'd like the townsfolk to know what I'm about to tell you. I at least owe them that."

"OK, Charlie, I'm listening." Jim felt uncomfortable with, but deeply intrigued by, Charlie's brutal honesty. He took another sip of his bourbon.

"Jim, I used to be a nice guy, a decent fellow. Never anything special, no education beyond high school, but I was a respectable person and a good community member. People liked me and I liked people. I grew up and lived in Akron, Ohio, and was a long-distance trucker. Used to drive those big 18-wheeler rigs all over the country. It wasn't a glamorous living, but it was a good one, solid and dependable. I enjoyed the road and I supported my family well. Yeah, I was married, believe it or not. Suzanne was her name. My high school sweetheart. Got married three months after graduation. Her folks and mine said we were too young but we thought we knew better, and turns out we were right, too. I loved that gal something fierce, and couldn't wait to tie the knot."

Charlie paused at this point and stared at the floor, borderline emotional and obviously thinking back to his younger days. Jim waited patiently until Charlie took a deep breath, looked up, and resumed. "Well, I tell you, we were happy, Jim, and life was great. We had fun together, and when I wasn't on the road we spent every possible minute together. After several years we decided to start a family. It didn't happen right away but we eventually had a little girl, Sarah. God, she was the cutest thing you ever saw! Curly blond hair, little button nose. Daddy's little girl," Charlie said with a slight smile, the first one Jim had ever seen on him.

Charlie paused again in thought and remembrance, and Jim remained silent. He hadn't heard this many words out of Charlie in the entire four years he'd lived here.

"Three years later, along come a son, Benjamin. Ben. Handsome young man, smart as a whip, too. I'd never been so happy. I had everything I wanted. A beautiful wife, two beautiful kids, a nice home, a good job. What more can a man want, or expect?"

"Not much, Charlie," offered Jim. "That's about all we need."

"That's them over there in those pictures, by the way. You can see for yourself what I had."

Jim scooted over to the end table and examined the faded pictures. They were indeed a fine-looking group. The boy appeared to be about four or five, and the girl seven or eight. Suzanne was beautiful, as Charlie had said, and had a face that projected excitement and joy in life. One photo included a man with the group, and after a few seconds Jim recognized a much-younger Charlie, who was smiling and looked quite happy. It seemed so incongruous. And then Jim knew this story was not going to end well.

"So there we were, Jim. We had it all, the American Dream. Happiest family you ever saw. Until May 10, 1985. I had been down to Atlanta on a three-day run. Delivered a big pile of tires down there and returned with a load of appliances. It was a Friday and I was due back home by four o'clock. Promised to take the family out to dinner once I got home and showered up. We would catch up on the week and figure out what we wanted to do for the weekend. I was coming up I-77 and making good time. No problems at all, listening to music, singing along, happy to be getting home. And then I made the biggest mistake of my life. I missed my damned exit. I couldn't believe it! I was so relaxed and happy, I just missed it. It didn't seem so bad at the time, I would just take the next one, only three miles ahead, turn back, and come in 15 minutes later."

Charlie paused for a sip of his bourbon and again stared at the floor for several long seconds. Jim waited patiently.

"Except, a quarter mile down off the next exit was the site of a horrible accident. A big cattle car had jackknifed on a curve, flipped, and took four cars with it. There were dead and wounded cattle all over the place, and some unhurt ones running around in a panic among the traffic. One car was smashed pretty flat. The whole thing snarled up traffic completely. Stopped us cold. They had to extricate some of the people with the jaws of life. It was grisly. Turns out three people died along with a bunch of cattle. Cops had to shoot the wounded ones."

Jim grimaced at the thought of that scene. Another pause for another sip.

"So I sat there, waiting, pissed off that I got myself into this situation by not paying attention and missing my exit. Never should have been there. I should have been home already and heading out to dinner with the family. By 5:00 we were still sitting there, everything shut down. So I radioed the home office and asked them to call my wife and tell her what was happening. I wasn't moving any time soon and they should go to dinner without me. We had promised the kids, and they were looking forward to it. So that's what they did."

"Eventually we got unsnarled and I made it back to the dock and delivered my load. By now it was after seven-thirty and I just wanted to get home and cleaned up after a long week away. I was anxious to make up for lost time with the family."

Charlie paused and stared off again into the distance, at nothing in particular. Jim felt awkward while nothing happened for seconds on end, and he began to wonder if Charlie had fallen into a trance.

Then, after another sip and a large deep breath, Charlie continued. "I drove down my street and as I approached my house I saw a police cruiser out front. I knew this couldn't be good news. I got out and the two cops asked who I was and then said they needed to speak with me. There had been an accident. Not the one I saw, but another. My family was returning from dinner. Three blocks from home a drunk driver ran a stop sign and T-boned them. Going about 50, they figure. Killed them all, Jim. Sarah was 9, Ben 6. Suzanne 32."

Saying the names of his family out loud brought tears to Charlie's eyes, and he outwardly sobbed. After more than three decades, the wounds obviously were still fresh. Jim expressed his condolences as best he could, and felt a lump in his throat. After regaining his composure, Charlie continued.

"Jim, I died that day too. My body continued on, but my spirit died. Everything I had of importance was taken from me, just like that. I wished I had been in that car."

More tears, more sips of bourbon. A handkerchief.

"I had no idea what to do. I buried them, of course, but the pain was so intense I didn't know where to turn. I couldn't hardly even go into my house. They were everywhere I looked."

Jim knew that feeling only too well, and the thought only enlarged the lump in his throat.

"I would sit for hours, hugging their clothes, smelling them, crying like a damn baby. I never knew a person could have so much pain. I didn't think it was possible."

A further pause to recollect, a further connection by Jim with this familiar agony.

"The sonofabitch who killed my family had two previous DUIs, yet there he was, out driving. I went to his trial and testified about my family and my loss. I don't know how I got through it, to be honest. He got an eight-year sentence and was released from prison after six for model behavior. He took my whole family away for life, and he only lost six years!" Charlie got louder and more agitated as he recalled the injustice of it all. "Seven months after his release he was driving drunk again and ran over and killed a 10-year-old boy in Cuyahoga Falls. They finally put the SOB away for 30 years. Killed four innocent people and he still gets to live, goddammit!" Charlie was nearly shouting at this point.

"That doesn't seem fair," acknowledged Jim.

"Sure as hell isn't!" shouted Charlie. After a moment, more calmly, "Anyway, after the trial, I was lost. Stopped going to work, just wandered around in a daze, spent half my time crying at the cemetery. Finally one day, I didn't know what else to do, I was desperate. I thought of killing myself but instead I got in the car and started driving, just to get away from there. Had no plan, just drove. Could just as easily have gone west or south, but happened to go east. Wound up in these parts, Maine, New Hampshire, Vermont. Stumbled through here and saw this house for sale. Was tired of driving and just bought it on the spot, for no particular reason other than I needed to be anywhere but back home and this seemed pretty far away. I just couldn't go back. Too painful. Figured I would try and start over here." The story sounded eerily familiar to Jim.

Charlie asked Jim if he wanted another bourbon, which he agreed to—a break in the proceedings to release some tension seemed in order. Standing up while visibly wincing, Charlie took both glasses and disappeared to the kitchen. Jim again examined the pictures on the end table; really sweet family. He could see, even in the faded photos, how devastating their loss would be.

Charlie returned with their two drinks, ice clinking loudly in the quiet house, the only other sound the ticking of a clock sitting on the TV.

"I sold my house in Ohio and got a settlement from the insurance. Wrongful deaths and all that. Even after the bastard lawyers took 40% I had more than enough to live on comfortably, if that's what you call this existence. Thought I would start over but it was still empty here. I never have been able to get over that loss. And I've never lost my bitterness and hatred."

"I can see how you would hate the guy that took your family, Charlie. Totally understandable," offered Jim, sympathetically.

"That's only part of my hatred Jim. Most of my hatred is reserved for myself. I have hated myself for over 30 years for missing my exit. Had I been paying attention, had I done what I was supposed to do, had I just done that one simple goddamn thing of getting off at my exit, *none* of this would have happened!" Charlie's voice was loud again and he was deeply agitated. "I'd still have a complete family, probably grandkids by now. *I* took their lives, Jim! *I'm* just as much to blame as that asshole that hit them. And I've never forgiven myself!"

"Come on, Charlie, don't you think you're being too hard on yourself? People make mistakes all the time. That's part of life. We're human."

"Yeah, but most mistakes don't result in losing your whole family, Jim!" shouted Charlie in return.

"The three people that I truly loved in this world died because of *me*. That drunk may have hit them, but I put them there to be hit. And I have always hated myself for it."

They sat in silence for a minute. Jim didn't have a clue of what to say, and this seemed to be a time when the less said, the better. Obviously Charlie needed to let this out and Jim was willing to hear his burden.

Finally, Charlie spoke again, in a quieter and more-controlled manner. "So the reason I'm telling you all this is that, when the time is right, I want the good people of this town to know why I was Charlie Horrible, as they call me. There was never anything wrong with any of the people here. They are good and decent people, Jim. But how could I like anyone else when I didn't like myself? How could I reward myself with the friendship of others when I hated myself? I did not deserve friendship, and I made damn sure I didn't get any. I've been punishing myself all these years, whether intentionally or not. That drunk got his prison term, but I went free. So I built my own prison for myself—person by person—and have served my life sentence within it, no chance of parole. These folks in Oddertown deserved a better neighbor than me. I realize that now and I apologize. I need them to know it wasn't them at all, it was me. Not an excuse, but an explanation. And an apology."

Again, a silent moment as it all sank in, only the clock ticking. Ice clinked as Jim took on more bourbon to fill the void.

"So why now, Charlie? Why are you telling me this now?"

"Well," chuckled Charlie in an ironic way, "there's the kicker. Hah, I guess this is poetic justice, or whatever. Jim, last spring I was diagnosed with prostate cancer. Turns out it was an aggressive kind. They implanted one of those little radioactive plugs, but it didn't help. The cancer has spread to my bones and bladder. Doctor says I have maybe 4-6 months left. So I figure now is the time to get all my accounts settled."

"Oh, Charlie," sighed Jim, while shaking his head. "I'm really sorry to hear that. I wish we had known sooner, we could have helped you with things. What about chemotherapy? Can't they do anything else for you?"

"I don't want to do that. Might give me a couple more months is all, and at what price? No, I'm ready to get this over with soon enough. I screwed up my life and there's no use prolonging it."

"Is there anything I can do, Charlie?"

"Well, you just did it by listening. As I said, it's important to me at this point that people know the truth about me. It's too late for me to change, but at least folks can know why I was the way I was. They can go on thinking the worst of me if that pleases them, but at least they will know. As I said, when the time comes, not before. You'll know when that is."

"Of course I'll speak for you, Charlie. Happy to set the record straight."

"Thanks, Jim. I figured I could count on someone like you. I do appreciate it, and I feel confident you'll do the job well. Now, there's one other thing I'd like you to do for me if you could."

"And what's that?"

"I'd like you to come by again tomorrow morning, about 11 AM, and help me with something. I'm not as strong as I used to be and can use a hand. I'm beat tonight and need to hit the sack now. Can you come by tomorrow?"

"Sure, no problem. Be glad to."

"Thank you, Jim," replied Charlie, clinking glasses to seal the compact. "I don't deserve this good treatment, but I am glad to have it. I will be in your debt. Now, can I refill your drink?"

"No thanks, Charlie. I should probably shove along home before *I* drive drunk and get in trouble."

"OK then, and again, thank you, Jim," stated Charlie in a somber manner as he stood, locked eyes, and sincerely shook Jim's hand. "I truly appreciate your help. See you tomorrow around 11."

"See you tomorrow, Charlie."

"Oh, hey, meant to ask," as they walked to the front door, "how's the effort to save that gal and her store? You folks got the money together yet?"

"Well, it's not looking too good right now, Charlie. We were doing OK but that storm and the tree falling really set us back. I don't know yet if we'll make it."

"You have some sort of deadline to pay up I hear?"

"Yeah, February 1, coming up pretty soon. Our best hope is that the bank takes pity on her and extends further. Fingers crossed." He didn't want to mention, even to Charlie, that he would, if needed, bail out Kate at the last minute, at least for this more-immediate deadline.

"Looks like I shoulda bought a couple more raffle

tickets, I suppose. Well, I hope something breaks. She's a good gal and that store is needed here."

"Yeah, she is, and it is. Something's gotta give. OK, see you tomorrow, Charlie."

"See ya, Jim. And thanks again."

As Jim got into his car and started it up, he wondered what he would be helping Charlie with tomorrow. As he drove north through Oddertown he had no clue, and would just have to be patient.

Chapter 31

———

THE FRESH, FOUR-INCH BLANKET OF SNOW deposited overnight caused no problems or worries for Jim Watson as he dutifully drove his Subaru down his unpaved driveway and onto his unpaved side street—Francis Lane, the location of the original farmstead of Francis S. Odderton—that would join up with Center Street, the main drag through Oddertown. Charlie had called Jim at 8:00 to verify that he would still be able to come by at 11:00. He sounded a bit nervous and tense, but Jim assured him he would be there, snow or no snow.

Jim slowly drove south through town and admired the beauty of the new-fallen snow on this crisp, sunny morning. He loved it when a storm moved through quickly, dropped its peaceful blanket, and then cleared off to expose impossibly blue skies and a brand new landscape. He wore sunglasses against the bright glare of the sun off the virgin-white snow that gave the town that classic, calendar-worthy beauty inherent in so many New England settings.

He reminded himself how fortunate he had been to have spent all his life in such delightful and welcoming places. It was a good day to be alive.

The light snowfall did nothing to affect the normal business of a normal day, which continued apace in town the same as on any clear and warm spring morning. Lou's Garage had two cars under repair and Gizmo Lawson was happily busy. Duke's Tavern was receiving several beer kegs through the front door, the Odds 'n Ends had a customer or two browsing through the used goods, and Odd Country had its typical flow of traffic in and out, ready to accommodate a lunch crowd. Reverend Hucks came out of the Methodist Church headed to his car and gave Jim a smile and friendly wave, which was warmly returned.

Two hundred yards past the southern end of Time Square, Jim turned left onto Odder Drive and then made an immediate right into Charlie Harbrough's driveway. He drove past several stately old maple trees and on up to the house, a low, rather undistinguished ranch design that could use some TLC. Though the house was fundamentally sound, the outside, like the living room that Jim experienced last night, could benefit from some attention and updating. He looked over the Spartan and ragged landscape and the dulled out and peeling paint, and concluded that the place simply had no character; a person could drive by and never take a second look. An undistinguished single-car garage sat detached about 50 feet to the left of the house, and a small, ugly metal shed was plunked down between the house and garage, apparently with little thought given to position or appearance. The place looked entirely unloved, which, in fact, it was.

The whole uninspired Harbrough estate—using that term loosely—sat at the edge of about a three-acre lawn out back that provided nothing of benefit but required Charlie to mow it on a regular basis. Jim had long wondered why Charlie didn't either plant a garden and some fruit trees, or simply let it go back to forest. He never understood maintaining a large lawn just to. . .maintain a large lawn. Mowing such an expanse that was otherwise useless made no sense to him. Maybe now that a line of communication had been established, he could broach the subject with Charlie of letting natural succession do its job to eventually return the lawn to forest. He understood that Charlie owned some 28 acres of the woods that bordered the open expanse and blanketed the lovely hills to the east. Maybe he could convince Charlie to increase his forest holdings and wildlife habitat for the future by letting the woods take over, and in the process decrease his workload in his few remaining months by not having to mow a useless lawn.

Jim turned off the engine, got out, and enjoyed the scrunching of the crisp, powdery snow under his boots as he walked around the front of the car to the side entrance door. Jim felt invigorated by the morning snow and cold, and well up to whatever task lay ahead. As he was about to knock on the storm door, he saw an envelope taped to the inside of the glass, with "Dr. Jim Watson" written across the front. He opened the door and peeled the envelope from the glass.

Jim took off one glove, felt the nippy, 20-degree air on his right hand, and opened the sealed envelope to remove its contents. He quickly saw there were two sheets of single-spaced, neatly typed material, along with a hand-written note on top of them. He began to read the note, which started out "Dear Jim." After two sentences he felt an icy chill grip his entire body. "Oh no, Charlie." He looked over toward the garage. "Christ, what have you done?"

He started toward the garage and then thought better of it. Returning to his car, he decided he would need to find Police Chief Johnsgaard. This beautiful day had quickly turned ugly.

Chapter 32

——

BEFUDDLED AND CONFUSED TOWNSFOLK HAD been streaming into Odd Country out of the unusually warm January day for the last 15 minutes. Over the last couple of days Kate got out word—through email, signs in the store, and word of mouth—that everyone was invited to the store on Saturday at 5 PM for an important announcement that would affect the town for years to come. Food would be provided. That's all that anyone knew, but everyone had drawn the same unthinkable but unavoidable conclusion: the store would close down next week and she was feeding them for the last time and unloading her stores of food rather than see them go to waste. Perhaps there would also be a "fire sale" of all the shelf goods. The only real question was whether the store was going to the bank or had been bought by that developer Malloy. Everyone to a person was in a sad and somber mood. They felt like they were gathering for the funeral of a good friend; the only thing missing was the death announcement, which they were about to receive. Bad news is best delivered in person.

Odd Country was packed end to end, as concerned residents filled the eating area as well as all the aisles and every available space. Even Willard Bennett had no extra room around him as folks crowded in like sardines. There was no place for coats and hats, so they merely held them at their sides as they waited for the bad news to be delivered. A subdued din filled up whatever airspaces were not packed with bodies as Oddertonians speculated on what their town would be like without their beloved store. Nobody in six generations had experienced Odd without it; the mere thought of no Odd Country was surreal.

Jim Watson stood on a chair and called for everyone's attention. When his initial plea to the unruly crowd failed, he banged on a cooking pot with a knife and the sharp sound did the trick. Everyone's eyes were suddenly riveted on him.

"Hello, everyone, and thank you for coming. I see we've had a great turnout and you're packed in here pretty tight so we'll try to keep this as brief as we can. I really appreciate everyone coming out for this. I hope you can all breathe in this tight space." They could, though the several closest to Willard were visibly stressed.

"So just tell us, Jim, when is the store closing?" came a concerned voice from the back. "Give it to us straight." Several others echoed their desire to get to the bottom line. The crowd's fear was palpable, their sadness visible.

"Not so fast now, folks," replied Jim. "You're jumping to conclusions and I think you've gone down the wrong path. So let me correct that for you." The crowd continued its gloomy murmuring, now even more confused.

"You all heard that Charlie Harbrough took his own life about ten days ago. He sat in his old truck in his closed garage with the engine running and died of carbon monoxide poisoning."

"No loss and good riddance," came a cruel but honest voice from the back that summed up the feelings of much of the town.

"Well, hold on there. I think you'll feel differently when you hear what Kate has to say. Kate?"

Rather than stand on the chair and risk more broken body parts, Kate used a step stool to sit up on the serving counter shelf, which raised her up above the crowd just enough to be seen.

"Let me first add my thanks to you all for coming tonight. I know how much this store means to you and how hard you have worked and fought to help keep it. That work ends tonight."

A slight moan went through the crowd at the thought that this was it.

"I want to read you something. Several days before Charlie Harbrough took his own life, he met with his lawyer to settle his affairs. He verbally dictated a legally binding document to his lawyer and I'd like to read that to you now. This is dated Friday, January 10 of this year, and these are Charlie's words, verbatim:"

"This statement serves as my last will and testament, and an explanation of things to the people of Oddertown. I lost my family in 1985 under tragic circumstances; Dr. Watson can explain the details if anybody wants to hear them. This town has been my only family since then and all I ever really had. I never was nice to the people here and for that I'm sorry. My personal loss and pain took over my life and robbed the best years from me. I know that I was a total ass, to be honest, and I wish things had been different. But they weren't and it's too late to change."

The assembled mass was quiet and confused, and hung on every word as Kate paused and then continued.

"But at least I can make up for things now; it's time for payback. I owe this town a big debt for putting up with me and this is my way of saying 'thank you and I'm sorry.' I know how important the Odd Country Store is to everyone. It is the center of things here and we all use it in a lot of ways; it's important and I'd hate to see you lose it. So I hereby will to Kate Langford, upon my death, all my cash and investment holdings, which should be more than enough to get her out of this financial mess she's in and keep the store going. Anything left over can go toward store improvements or whatever else she wants to do with it. To Oddertown itself I give all my physical property, including my house, land, truck, and all possessions in the house. Sorry if it's a mess in there but I've been sick. You can do what you want with it: sell it all and use the money to help pay taxes, keep the house for something, maybe a bigger town office and hall, whatever. It's yours now. With these actions I hope my account is now paid in full and hope maybe you can remember me as a little more than a crabby and hateful SOB, which I am, I admit it. But we are who we are, and as I leave this place for the last time I tip my hat to you all and thank you for putting up with me all those years. I just wish I could have been a better friend and neighbor to everyone, but it is way too late for that. I failed in this life and have to accept that. I hope you can find it in your hearts to somehow forgive me."

The room was silent and stunned as Kate put down the sheet of paper and looked around. Then an "I'll be damned" was heard in one of the aisles, soon answered with a "holy cow" of bewilderment.

"So what does this mean, Kate?" asked Lou Quentin.

"It means that Charlie Harbrough has saved this store and maybe this town, Lou. I'm saying that he has paid the debt and Odd Country will keep going as long as people care to come in here. I'm saying we are saved. It's over!"

The crowd applauded, but was still too stunned to react much and seemed unable to fully grasp the extent of the announcement.

"But I don't get it, Kate. Did Charlie Harbrough kill himself for us?" asked an incredulous Jubal Keller.

"Jim, you better take over," suggested Kate. "Tell them the rest of the story."

Jim got back up on the chair. "Folks, the night before he took his own life, Charlie asked me to come over to talk to him. We had a couple of bourbons while he told me some things about his past."

Jim proceeded to relay the tragic story of the Harbrough family being killed and how Charlie never forgave himself for their deaths, how he had punished himself for the rest of his life and never again could be happy. Jim explained that Charlie pushed everyone away because he hated himself for what he did and felt he did not deserve any happiness in his life. Charlie believed that he, in effect, killed his wife and two children.

"So you see, when he was so gruff and nasty with everyone, it wasn't *you* he was nasty to, it was *himself*. He lived in a mental prison and gave himself a life sentence. At the end, he wanted you all to know that, and he wanted to apologize for his behavior. A very sad case, if you ask me."

The assembled crowd murmured as this new information sank in.

"I wish we had known," said Silas Miller. "We could have helped him. Or at least we would have understood. Now I feel really bad about how we treated him."

"Yeah, we didn't do so good by him," muttered Phil Haderlie. "But hell, how could we know? We just thought he was a jerk!"

"Poor Charlie," offered Lauren McCallum. "He could have used some real understanding when we all just scorned him. I usually tried to avoid him, to be honest, just because he made me so uncomfortable."

"Folks, you couldn't have known what was going on with him," countered Kate. "This was his doing and his choice and we all handled him the best way we could. We all reacted to him pretty much the same. You shouldn't feel guilty."

"So why did he kill himself now?" asked Paul Johnson. "Do you have any idea Jim? Was it to give Kate his money?"

"Ahh, now *there's* the interesting question, Paul," replied Jim. "It turns out he had metastatic prostate cancer for most of this last year, but he didn't tell anyone. He was treated for it but the treatment failed. Recently his doctor gave him four to six months to live. But that means he had until spring or summer. So why did he end it now?"

Jim paused to let the assembled ponder for a few seconds.

"There's two reasons I can think of. Well, maybe three. First, maybe he was in physical pain and wanted to end the suffering. Possibly, and I did see a little evidence of pain the night I sat with him. He mostly seemed fine and comfortable and he enjoyed his bourbons, as far as I could tell, but he winced a couple of times when he sat or got up. But if he hadn't told me about the cancer I wouldn't have thought much about it, maybe just old bones getting stiff. So I think he was in some pain but I couldn't say how much."

"Second, maybe the mental pain of his life got to be too much. But then why wait 30-plus years and end it right now? Unless maybe the cancer on top of his guilt put him over the top. I suppose that could be, but I tend to doubt it.

"Third, and this is what I think happened, he may have ended his life at this time to save this store and this town. The timing is too coincidental to dismiss. He knew he was going to die soon anyway, so why not get something positive out of it? He knew of the bank deadline coming up and made the decision a few days before ending it that his money would go to Kate. The last thing he did that night we talked—as I was about to leave—was to casually ask me about the store and how we were doing on fundraising. I think he wanted to double check and make sure we still needed the help. I think he wanted his money to go to saving the store but he knew that if he didn't die for several months yet, it would be too late and the store would be gone by then, and probably owned by a developer. I believe that's when he decided to go ahead with his suicide. I think in the end he wanted his life to mean something, and this is how he could do it. He wanted this store to be his legacy."

Pausing to look around, Jim concluded "Good people, we will never know for sure, but I do think that Charlie Harbrough chose to shorten his life to help all of us, and to save Odd Country. I believe that was his final apology, and thank you, and farewell to us."

"Well, I'll be damned," uttered Willard Bennett, pretty much summing up the reaction of the crowd. "Never would have guessed it."

Others tossed out similar thoughts as the people of Oddertown collectively digested the news and re-thought their opinions of one 'Charlie Horrible.'

"People," shouted Kate above the growing din. "There's more. Can I have your attention again please? Just a few more minutes, I promise."

The crowd quieted down and re-focused their attention to the serving counter.

"I'd like to take a minute to tell you what Charlie's generosity and sacrifice means to this town. First, as of yesterday afternoon, the entire debt of the Odderton Country store has been paid in full and retired. The store stays here for as long as you can stand it!"

Spontaneous applause broke out, and the somber feelings were finally replaced by honest joy and relief. You could see the tension disappear from people's faces as they smiled, hugged, and patted each other on the back. When the noise died down, Kate continued.

"Second, after paying off the debt there was plenty of money left over, and I don't feel right keeping it. Well, maybe just a little," she said with a smile. "I'll replace my poor old crushed car for sure. Anybody have a used Subaru for sale?" Some laughter rippled through.

"Mostly, I'd like to see it go into the community, where it belongs. I will use some to really upgrade the store, both outside and in. Expect some nice changes in the coming months. First thing I'm doing is bringing in a Creemee machine! Chocolate, vanilla, maple!" Several folks endorsed that idea with their applause.

"But more importantly, I have decided to invest in the town's future by establishing the Charles Harbrough College Scholarship Fund with an endowment of one-hundred-thousand dollars!" Some 'whoahs' emerged from the crowd, along with applause. "This will enable us to award a scholarship to one graduating Oddertown Senior each year. He or she will receive one-thousand dollars for tuition at any accredited college or university for their Freshman year. Every year they maintain at least a B average, they will receive one thousand dollars for the next year, for up to four years total."

Applause again broke out, with people smiling, nodding, and a few hugging each other.

"Thank you, Kate!" shouted Jodi Simpson, who would graduate this spring and was immediately hopeful for a scholarship.

"Don't thank me, Jodi, thank Charlie. It's his generosity that did this. I will be forming a review committee soon and we will draw up the requirements and review procedures. Awards will be made on both merit and need, though I can't think of too many people in Oddertown who wouldn't be in need. So stand by, Seniors!" A few hoots of joy came from several of the younger folks in the crowd.

"Finally, Charlie left his house and property to the town. As a Select Board member I have put discussion of that property on the agenda for our next meeting. I will recommend that we turn it into a community recreation center, for both kids and adults. The rooms can be renovated into various recreation areas for games, reading, maybe after-school tutoring or study centers. Maybe have a space for movies or dances. That big field out back is perfect for a sports field for football, soccer, baseball, whatever. And if the Select Board decides to go this route—with your input of course—it will cost money to create the center. I will gladly fund the renovation with up to seventy-five thousand dollars from Charlie's bequest."

Shouts and applause erupted again, with "go Kate" and "thank you" emitted here and there from the aisles.

When it finally settled, Kate spoke again, this time more solemnly. "My friends, none of this would have happened without the sacrifice made by Charlie Harbrough. I know what we all thought of him, and I know how he treated us, but we now understand the tragic circumstances that created the Charlie we knew. He was ultimately a good and decent man who suffered heartbreaking loss that most of us can't even begin to fathom. It turns out Charlie wasn't horrible at all; a horrible thing happened to him that destroyed the man and his life. I think we can appreciate that now."

Many heads were hung and throats were tight as people stared at the floor or blinked at their neighbors, nodding in silent understanding.

"With that in mind, I would like us to please have a moment of silence to remember the Charlie Harbrough that we knew, and to honor the man we now know he really was, deep down. Let's try to honor the good and decent and terribly wounded Charlie Harbrough and thank him, in our own ways, for his life among us and his contributions to this town, which will live on for generations."

Thirty seconds of dead silence were broken only by numerous sniffles and wiping of noses from the more than 100 bowed heads.

"Thank you all, and thank you, Charlie," concluded Kate, looking upward. Dozens of "thank you Charlies" echoed softly and earnestly through Odd Country.

"And a final announcement. Looks like my contacts with other general stores and deeply rooted families throughout the Northeast Kingdom paid another great dividend. Nobody—and I mean *nobody*—in the region was willing to deal with or sell property to that slimeball developer Robb Malloy. He is gone, closed out of development in this area. He clearly had only his interests in mind and I think he would have been disastrous for this region. So good bye, Robb!"

The crowd cheered one more time at this additional bit of good news. What Kate did not know, and could not know, was that Project Manager Wannabe Robb Malloy, recently of Pan Eastern Development Corp. and presumptive new CEO of NEK-DEL, had just started his new career as an aluminum siding salesman in Paramus, New Jersey; he would work largely on commission and had experienced an immediate 70% pay cut. Ellen, his wife of 13 years, did not go with him to New Jersey and has filed for divorce.

"Now, my friends," said Kate. "It's time to celebrate. Thanks once again to the generosity of one Charles Harbrough and the culinary talents of Larry Carson, who has been slaving away all day, we have prepared a feast for you in our beautiful new kitchen. Yay Larry! We have barbequed chicken, pulled pork, and a whole bunch of side dishes. And there's wine and beer and cider and soft drinks aplenty. Our only challenge will be space. So we'll please form a line into the kitchen, you can fill your plates, grab a drink and settle where you can. Use the stairs, the floor, the front porch, wherever you can find a spot. As a community and as an extended family let's now celebrate Charlie Harbrough and the bright future of Oddertown thanks to him!"

As the crowd again cheered and started to file toward the kitchen, Kate added, "Oh, I almost forgot—Odd Country will be closed tomorrow, Sunday, all day. I need the rest and I'm sleeping in!"

What Kate did not tell the crowd was that she would spend much of Sunday afternoon writing thank-you notes and stuffing envelopes with generous checks to Larry Carson, Marie Hinges, the builders Tim and Jim Kittleson, the Golightly sisters (even though they likely would return or donate the money), and everyone else who stepped forward and volunteered during the time of crisis. Good people jumped in during an emergency and gave of themselves without hesitation and with no thought whatsoever of compensation; she could not let good behavior like that go unrecognized and unrewarded. Kate would make sure that they all received what would have been their regular wages, and then some. This would be the fun part!

Chapter 33

THE LAST OF THE TOWNSFOLK HAD CLEARED out and Jim, Kate, Larry, and a few others had cleaned up everything; all was now ship-shape and stowed away, ready for Monday morning's 6 AM opening when Jubal and Phil would amble up the front steps, personalized coffee mugs in hand, and Kate's cinnamon and walnut buns would be fresh out of the oven. The new kitchen performed marvelously, and would be much better moving forward than the old one ever could have been. Perhaps things do happen for a reason. There was even some talk about hiring a full-time chef—perhaps Kate would send Larry to culinary school—and opening for dinner, but that was for future consideration.

Now, well into the evening, it was just Kate Odderton Langford and James Daniel Watson left, seated at a table, like the last two remaining and bloody survivors of a long and deadly battle. Or at least that's how it seemed. The last six months they had to meet one challenge after another and they were both exhausted. But they were also pleased with how they had met adversity head on and how they had always been there for one another.

"So we did it, Doc," said Kate across the table. "Admittedly not 'we' so much as Charlie, but we fought to the end, damn the torpedoes. And it almost was the end, too. This was way too close a call for my taste! Thank God for Charlie, bless his heart."

"I have to admit, Kate, I don't know where we would be without him. Sure, I could have bailed us out of the immediate problem, but that way bigger problem would still be hanging over us for three years. There's only so many raffles and auctions this little town can take. I really didn't know how or where we would have come up with that kind of money. I guess this was the miracle we were hoping for. And from such an unlikely source."

"So, Jim, I've noticed more and more that you've been referring to 'us' and 'our problem' and talked about what 'we' would do," said Kate, using air quotes around the appropriate words, finally addressing *her* elephant in the room. "Have you and I become a 'we' these days?"

"Well, uh, it's, you know…" Jim stammered. "I mean… yeah, I guess I… uh… sort of adopted the problem with you. I mean… I just wanted to help and… yeah, of course it's *your* store and I didn't mean to overstep my bounds." Beads of perspiration were beginning to show up on his forehead.

"Relax there, Mouse Man," assured Kate, patting his hands. "I don't see you overstepping any bounds. Your stepping is very welcome. If anything

I think we need to take down some more boundaries between us." She watched the perspiration on
Jim's forehead increase and could see his face getting
red. "You know what I mean?" she asked, bending
forward and looking up deeply into his eyes.

When there was no response except nervous and
darting looks around the room, Kate continued.
"Tell ya what," she said as she stood up, pulling Jim
up with her. "How about we grab us a couple of bot-
tles of 19 Crimes off the rack and go upstairs to my
place and discuss these boundaries a little further?"

As she pulled him toward the wine rack, Jim
naively replied "Oh no, I can't drink all that much
wine and then drive home."

"Who said anything about driving home
tonight?" countered Kate as she handed him one
bottle and cradled the other in her right arm. "Did I
say you were driving home tonight? I've stayed with
you often enough, Doctor Watson; it's time for me
to return the favor." With her left hand she cradled
Jim's right elbow and led him up the creaky wooden
stairs to her private quarters.

"But you don't have a guest room, right? I mean,
where am I..." Out of the corner of his eye Jim
caught her playful and knowing smile and his voice
trailed off, the sudden realization hitting him. "Oh,
um..."

"You know, Doc, for the Wizard of Odd, sometimes you can be really slow on the uptake."

Chapter 34

———

K ATE HAD CLOSED FOR THE DAY AND HAD just finished reconciling the cash drawer. It was such a luxury to not be thinking about cash flow constantly, counting every nickel, emptying the donation jar, and worrying about debts. She could now run the store the way she wanted to and think about and plan for more interesting things in the future, like expanding into new areas. Maybe a pizza oven? How about a craft microbrewery out back with a growler service? Perhaps a cheese-making business in partnership with a local cow or sheep farmer? She now had the resources and stability, and it was fun to fantasize and speculate.

As she headed toward the stairs and up to her house, a soft knock at the front door turned Kate around. She walked back and saw that it was Pearl Wilson, Billy's mother.

"Hi, Pearl," greeted Kate as she opened the door. "Sorry, but we're closed for the day."

"Oh I know that, Kate, but I wonder if I could talk to you for a minute. I promise I won't be long."

"Sure, c'mon in," motioned Kate, closing the door behind them against the winter air. "What's up?"

"Well, I had the strangest thing happen today. I received a certified letter this afternoon from my mortgage company indicating that my entire mortgage has been paid off, over $6000! And my property tax has been paid for the whole year as well."

"Really?" replied Kate. "That's wonderful! How did you manage that?"

"Well that's just the thing, I didn't! Apparently some good soul paid these off for me, anonymously. After I thought for a bit about who could have done this, I realized that *you* are my chief suspect. Kate, did you do this?"

"Me? Why, I'm sure I don't know what you're talking about," responded Kate, innocent eyes wide open.

"C'mon, Kate, who else around here has that kind of money? I can't imagine anyone else who could do that."

"I can't either," replied Kate, with a deeply thoughtful look on her face. "Maybe you have a secret admirer somewhere!"

"Kate, seriously. I know you inherited that money from Charlie and have been so generous with it toward the town. I really think you must have done this."

"Well, you won't hear *me* taking the credit," replied a coy Kate, smiling innocently. "I guess you'll just have to keep looking around for the guilty party."

Pearl stared Kate in the eye for several seconds but could not crack her façade or spot a tell. She finally grabbed Kate and hugged her tightly. "Well, I need to thank somebody and I think you're a good liar and a wonderful friend, so thank you, Kate, thank you. You're a blessing for this town. I can't believe this has happened to me, and you have no idea what a relief it is. I feel like I can breathe again. So thank you, if it *was* you."

Kate hugged her back and merely said, "I'm very happy for you Pearl. I hope this gift from whoever it was really helps your family."

Pearl bid her goodbye with another thanks as she headed out the front door. Kate turned back and felt light as a feather as she bounded upstairs, taking steps two at once for the first time since her ankle injury. She could not keep a broad smile from creasing her face, or a satisfied laugh bubbling up from her soul. Life was so good.

Chapter 35

Friday, May 1, 6:40 AM

"So I WENT DOWN TO THE HARBROUGH Recreation Center yesterday," reported Phil Haderlie as Jodi was delivering their breakfasts. "It's done now and a pretty nice place. Anybody seen it yet? They did a nice job on it."

"Yeah, I was out there the other day," replied Jubal Keller. "I agree. I think we'll have some good times down there. Maybe get some card games going, eh? I hear they're putting in ball fields and a basketball court out back in the next week or two. Be nice for kids to have somewhere to hang out and play. Keep 'em out of our hair, anyway. Someone said they might try to start a baseball league with other little towns around here and use that as the field."

"And did you know that Bobby Wilson and Buck Bailey volunteered for some of the reconstruction work?" asked Only Owens. "I think they're still trying to get back in Kate's good graces. Hah, she put the fear of God into them that day!"

"Not only that," added Silas, "but I heard the town is hiring them as councilors for the summer to keep the younger kids in line, and maybe keep *them* out of trouble in the process. Sounds like a good deal all around."

"The best p-part is, not a p-penny of tax dollars went into it," observed Steve Benson. "Thanks to ol' Ch-Charlie.

"Yeah, Charlie did well by us, the old fart," concluded Silas Miller. "You know, I kind of miss him in an odd sort of way, tell you the truth."

"Yeah, me too," added Willard Bennett. "I feel bad we didn't pull him into the Odd Balls. He'd have made a good one. Bloody hell, he was the oddest ball among us!"

"That's for sure," agreed Phil. "I guess deep down somewhere inside I really kinda liked Charlie. Just didn't know it at the time. He was a pretty good guy underneath it all. Never really hurt anybody to speak of, you know? Just grumpy and sour all the time is all."

"You know, he *was* a decent guy, wasn't he?" replied Silas. "A pretty good guy, that Charlie."

"Yeah, Charlie was OK," added Jubal. "Should have been part of us all along."

"Huh?" asked an incredulous Paul Johnson. "Seriously? Do you hear yourselves? For years you had nothing but bad things to say about Charlie. He was 'Charlie Horrible,' remember?"

"Ah, Paul, don't always focus on the negative. He was alright," replied Phil. "Sure, maybe he wasn't exactly one of us but I always thought he was a pretty decent guy underneath."

"Yeah, that's right, Charlie was a good guy," added Jubal. "I liked him."

"Yeah, Paul, don't be so hard on Charlie," chided Silas. "He really did well by this town."

Paul sat dumfounded and slack jawed as he surveyed the Odd Balls. He had just witnessed a spontaneous revision of local history, and did not know what to make of it. Charlie went from horrible to a saint, in one swift, uninterrupted motion!

As conversation continued around the table and moved on to other topics, it dawned on Paul that sometimes, just maybe, a revision is not a bad thing if it improves life and heals old wounds. Like religion, having unquestioned faith in someone might be the best way to reconcile and move forward. So yeah, Charlie Harbrough was alright. A good guy. A *really* good guy, as a matter of fact. Don't let anyone tell you otherwise!

Epilogue

⬤——————

IN A LOCAL AWARDS CEREMONY HELD FOR THE six graduating Oddertown Seniors, preliminary to the much larger official graduation ceremony at North Country Union High at 3:00, Kate Langford announced the winner of the first annual Charles Harbrough College Scholarship. She couldn't have been more pleased as she called Jodi Simpson up to the gazebo in Time Square to receive her award. Jodi's face fairly exploded with joy and tears as she hugged Kate and thanked her and the committee for their selection. Kate hastened to make it clear to the audience of mostly parents, relatives, and friends that, given her close relationship to Jodi, she recused herself from the selection process, and that the rest of the committee—Jim Watson, Paul Johnson, and Lauren McCallum—made the selection.

Jodi will matriculate at the University of Vermont in the fall, majoring in Environmental Studies, which surprised her parents and teachers, who all were sure she would go into something more artsy. But apparently Jim Watson, unknowingly and unintentionally, had a strong influence on Jodi as she listened to his conversations these last few years in the restaurant and attended his mid-winter community lectures. In particular, Jodi is deeply troubled by climate change and the future of the planet, and wants to see if she can do something to solve that problem. Who knows, she just might! Odder things have happened.

Acknowledgments

———

No man is an island, and certainly no writer. So first, and most broadly, I thank the great little state of Vermont for being who and what it is. I have never lived in, or even visited, a state with so much going for it in such a small area; let's not screw it up. The strong sense of community, intense self-reliance, willingness to help a neighbor, appreciation of all things local, resistance of corporate ugliness, protection of its environment, and general funkiness are all lessons that other states could well learn from. Life here is so special and very sweet, and I hope I have done it some small justice in these pages.

Second, and closer to home, Brandon Vermont welcomed us with open arms some 12 years ago and has done everything it could to make us feel that we were brilliant to have moved here. Through good times and difficult trials, the people of Brandon have always proven themselves worthy of admiration and respect, and they always seem to find a way to make life here work just a little bit better. Thank you Brandon!

Third, and very close to home, I cannot adequately thank several people who took enough interest in my work to devote their time, energy, and skills to make the final product much better than it otherwise would have been. Phoebe Chesna, Margaret Flagg, Molly Kennedy, Nancy Meffe, and Jean Somerset read all or parts of the book and offered very constructive criticisms and suggestions, and Margaret Flagg provided the original artwork line drawing at the start of the book. I thank author William Noble for a lengthy and enlightening lunchtime discussion of books and writing, and for initial feedback on *Odd*, and Chip Williams for a discussion on insurance. Green Writers Press Editor par excellance Rose Alendandre-Leach dug deep, challenged me, pushed, pulled, and cajoled. The result was something far better than I ever could have envisioned at the outset. She brought this book to new heights and made me a much better writer, and I thank her for that. Publisher Dede Cummings saw something here and trusted and believed, and was a pleasure to work with.

And of course, Nancy Meffe, the dearest person in the world, knew when to encourage, when to kick butt, when to sympathize, and when to challenge; most importantly, she tolerated—without mercy—no lazy writing on my part. She is always there for me, unfailingly, without question, and with love and enthusiasm, and she makes me continue to wonder how in the world I could possibly have been so fortunate in this life.

To all, my eternal gratitude.

And finally, though I am always inspired by and observe life around me, and am of course influenced by life experiences, any resemblances of fictional characters in this book to any real persons, living or dead, are probably figments of the reader's imagination and should be enjoyed and then dismissed. With the one exception of the use, with his permission, of the name and persona of my young friend Carson Leary, this whole thing was just plain made up. But despite that, to me, Oddertown really does exist, and I wish it every good fortune, as some wonderful people live there.

Cast of Characters in Order of Appearance*

———

Simon Odderton: The 90-something fourth generation owner of the Odderton Country Store, and grandfather of Kate Langford.

Kate Langford: The 39 year-old divorced owner of the Odderton Country Store (also known as "Odd Country"). She recently inherited the store, along with a large debt, from her grandfather, Simon Odderton.

Jodi Simpson: A 17-year-old high school student who works the early breakfast shift at the Odderton Country store before school.

The Odd Balls: A group of older, mostly retired Oddertown men who gather regularly for breakfast at Odd Country. The group consists of:

Willard Bennett: a pig farmer who usually reeks of his stock;

Steven S. Benson: an unfortunate stutterer who suffered from constantly fighting parents;

*The list of characters does not include very minor characters who appear in passing, or deceased individuals mentioned in discussion.

339

Phil Haderlie: a conservative, anti-government veteran of the Korean War;

Paul Johnson: a younger, 40-something organic farmer, known by the others as "Hippie Boy";

Jubal Keller: a friendly, politically moderate retired gentleman and Korea Veteran, with a ready smile;

Silas Miller: a retired banker with failing eyesight and an addiction to waffles for breakfast;

Only Oswalt: another Korea veteran with a strange and unfortunate first name.

Larry Carson: A former football star at North Country Union High who works for Kate as the lunch cook at Odd Country.

Victor S. Kemper: An elderly barber in Oddertown with a penchant for drinking cheap bourbon.

Dr. Anthony Delfasio: A large-animal Veterinarian who cares for all the farm animals in the region.

Dr. James D. Watson: A 68 year-old retired and widowed Professor of Ecology, who moved to Oddertown four years earlier. Known locally and affectionately as "The Wizard of Odd."

Lauren MacCallum: A widowed, early-50s teacher at the Oddertown elementary school.

Darwin: The 4-year old golden retriever belonging to Jim Watson with an undying desire to recycle aluminum cans.

Paul Simon and Bruce Boven: Two fly fishermen from New Jersey who visit Odd Country for lunch.

Charlie Harbrough: An unfriendly, curmudgeonly old Oddertown resident who folks call "Charlie Horrible."

Louanne (Lou) Quentin: The short, tough, gender-vague owner of Lou's Garage, with a love for comic books and a soft spot for Raymond Pulan.

Billy Wilson: A young mechanic who works for Lou and loves cars and NASCAR.

Raymond Pulan: A 25-year-old man with Down Syndrome, and good friend of Lou Quenton.

Caleb Smith: The much-loved Oddertown Postmaster and Select Board Chair, with a small flower business on the side.

Gregory Mitchell: A quiet, boring, but highly dependable elementary school teacher who also serves on the Oddertown Select Board.

Carl Johnsgaard: The Oddertown Chief of Police and its only police officer.

Emily McIntyre: A new, young and enthusiastic teacher at the Oddertown Elementary School.

Marie Delfasio: The wife of Dr. Tony Delfasio.

Malcolm "Rusty" Hinges: A massive but gentle and kind-hearted logger who looks and sounds rusty.

Dora Stevenson: A middle-aged waitress at Duke's bar.

Layla Liederman: The wild, outgoing, colorful, and thrice-divorced owner of Odds 'n Ends 2nd hand store and junk shop.

The Golightly Family, Faith, Hope, and Charity, and assorted ancestors: A back-to-the land family who are stuck in the peace, love, and flower generation of early 1970s communes.

Pernell Basington-Smythe: An eccentric artist and author who dresses up like the characters he is currently painting or writing about.

Pearl Wilson: Mother of Billy Wilson, the mechanic at Lou's garage.

Reverend Eugene Hucks: The Pastor of St. John's United Methodist Church of Oddertown.

Bobby Wilson: Billy Wilson's younger brother, age 17.

Gail Wilson: Billy Wilson's younger sister, age 14.

Andrew "Buck" Bailey: Friend of Bobby Wilson, also 17.

Rob Malloy: An out-of-state developer who wishes to buy Odd Country from Kate as his headquarters in the Northeast Kingdom.

Tim and Jim Kittleson: Brothers from Oddertown who are building contractors and carpenters.